HOT TARGETS

"Arm 'em all, Snake Eyes, and let's go huntin'!"

Colonel McKenna raised the flap, selected the pylons and armed all missiles. At the bottom of the HUD, fifteen small green lights indicated the active weapons.

"Delta Blue, active," he came back.

Easing back the throttle, McKenna tapped his hand controller forward and the nose of the stealth MakoShark fighter tilted down twenty-five degrees. The screen jumped to radar display and the target indicator came up.

"Hot damn, there he is!" the weapons officer said.

"Lock on and execute."

"Heat-seeker committed and . . . gone!"

The Wasp II's cut through the sky at about 1,700 miles per hour.

"Impact, seventy-three seconds."

The air tanker began to dive. Too late.

Two blinding explosions ignited the black sky as hot splinters from the destroyed engine ripped into the plane's fuel tanks.

DELTA BLUE

WILLIAM H. LOVEJOY

ZEBRA BOOKS
KENSINGTON PUBLISHING CORP.

As always,
for Jane, Jodi, and David,

and for Miss Ethel Turpin,
stern high school English teacher
who taught the first, most difficult
rule of writing: Apply butt to chair.

ZEBRA BOOKS

are published by

Kensington Publishing Corp.
475 Park Avenue South
New York, NY 10016

First printing: October, 1991

Printed in the United States of America

One

Above the canopy was utter blackness.

There was no moon, and the skies were overcast. Not even starshine for orientation.

A perfect night.

Below, on McKenna's far left, was a smattering of lights. Bernburg, probably, but he wasn't paying much attention to the peripheral towns. The lights of a few boats sketched the course of the Saale River.

Directly ahead of him, the red digital numerals of the Heads Up Display floated in space and registered in his mind. Altitude, 1,150 feet. Heading, 012 degrees. Speed, 650 knots. The tailpipe and skin temperatures were low. The bird was coasting.

The instrument panel below provided readouts in blue digital numerals and letters, many of them duplicates of what appeared on the HUD. Centered in the panel was the eight-inch cathode ray tube that repeated the imaging mode selected by the WSO, the weapons system operator in the back seat of the tandem cockpit. The screen had direct visual, map overlay, radar, infrared, and night-vision capability and currently was displaying the pale green images picked up by the night-sight lens mounted in the nose. The lens multiplied ambient light 40,000 times and provided them with a view of the ground that was almost as good as daylight.

At that altitude and speed, however, McKenna couldn't see much more on the screen than a set of dark and light green, irregular checkerboard squares. The yard lights of farmhouses were bright dots flashing past. Thick mottled green forests were splashed about. The terrain features, less than 500 feet below, disappeared from the camera's sight almost as soon as they appeared. Occasionally, forested hills seemed to close in on him, but he didn't do anything about it.

The WSO was in control.

McKenna had flipped up the visor of his helmet and was enjoying every breath he took. The tangy taste of the oxygen/nitrogen mix of the life-support system got old after a while.

Tony Munoz's voice came over the open intercom. "Got a one-five-hundred hill on your right, Snake Eyes. You wanna take her left a couple points or splash it?"

"Gotcha, Tiger."

McKenna saw the hilltop coming up fast on the screen, and he nudged the hand controller to the left as he toed in some corresponding left rudder. When the heading on his HUD went to 010, he leveled out.

"Right on," Munoz said.

The pilot's seat in the MakoShark was a semireclining lounge with four-way adjustable armrests on which his forearms rested. Near his left hand were the short throttle levers, and above them, the switch panels related to engine, radio, and environmental control. On his right were the armaments, electronics, trim, flaps, and landing-gear control panels. Aft of the panels on both sides of the cockpit, more awkward to reach, were the less frequently used control panels and circuit breakers. Aircraft attitude was directed from the stubby, ergonometrically designed handle that fit smoothly into the palm of his hand. If he released it, it stayed in the position in which he left it. To the right of the hand controller was a slanted keypad for entering numeric commands into the on-board computers. One of those commands was McKenna's personal code adjusting the resistance and movement of the controller to his own taste. Learning to fly with the hand controller had taken McKenna a few months. He had not liked giving up the stick control of F-15s, F-104s, and the other supersonics he flew.

Not at first. Now, he couldn't imagine going back to primitive methods.

The rearview screen—a four-inch CRT to the left of the

main screen—came to life at Munoz's command, showing a green landscape receding rapidly into verdant nothingness. The MakoShark's configuration didn't provide the pilot and backseater with much vision to the rear, and a camera lens with direct visual, infrared, and night-vision capability was mounted in the tail.

"IP in thirty seconds, Snake Eyes."

"IP in thirty."

The Initial Point was the landmark on which the bomb run was calculated.

"Arm 'em, *amigo*."

McKenna raised his hand to the armaments panel, dialed in "BOMB LOAD" on the selector, raised the protective plastic flap, and flipped the switch up.

"Armed, Tiger. Your choice on number."

"Roger. I need four-zero-zero airspeed and nine-five-zero altitude."

"Roger, four-zero-zero and nine-five-zero."

McKenna gripped the two in-board throttle levers for the turbo/ram jet engines and began to ease them back, watching the HUD readout. He deployed 20 percent speed brakes and tipped the nose downward. When he had Munoz's speed and altitude, he pulled in the speed brakes.

The ground images accelerated their own speed on the screen as the MakoShark dropped to 400 feet above the earth.

"IP comin' up."

The IP was a small town called Kothen, a couple miles south of the Elbe River. At three in the morning in Germany, there were only a half-dozen lights showing as they shot overhead. Throttled back, the MakoShark's noise level was minimal, and the inhabitants of the village probably would not even hear them.

Any villager standing outside his house, testing the weather, might hear a windy *whoosh!*, but he certainly wouldn't see them.

"IP . . . mark!" Munoz chanted.

Five seconds later, the backseater said, "Bomb bay doors, Snake Eyes."

Anticipating the instruction, McKenna had the flap raised and his thumb poised. He flipped the toggle and had a green LED a half-second later.

"Doors clear," McKenna said.

"Come to zero-one-nine."

McKenna rolled into the new heading.

He watched the CRT. A transparent orange bomb sight circle with a vertical cross in it had appeared at the top of the screen. Its movement on the screen was directed by either Munoz's hand controller or the movement of his helmet, whichever mode he selected. In necessary situations, the weapons targeting could also be accomplished by the pilot in a similar fashion.

"Five seconds to target," Munoz said.

Munoz increased the telephoto range of the camera lens and the river immediately came into view. The banks were heavily forested.

"Son of a bitch!" Munoz said. "Pearson was right."

"She usually is," McKenna told him.

Four long convoys of barges and towboats were moving northward on the Elbe, with no running lights showing.

The bomb circle on the screen jumped around until Munoz centered it on a copse of woods lining the southern bank. Orange letters suddenly appeared in the upper-right screen: "LOCK ON."

Munoz had turned the control over to the computer, then committed the drop. No matter what McKenna did with the craft now, the computer would instantly recalculate the bomb release point.

The release came four seconds later.

McKenna did not feel much of a change in the MakoShark as the two canisters dropped out of the bay. He flicked his eyes to the rearview screen and saw the parachutes popping open before they disappeared from the screen. Each of the canisters appeared to be a thick juniper bush and would disappear nicely into the foliage. They would float toward the earth until, at 100 feet above the ground, small explosive bolts released the vaporous parachute and allowed them to drift downwind.

"Hard left, Snake Eyes. Come to three-four-five."

"Roger."

As they sailed over the river, and the darkened strings of barges, the MakoShark turned to follow the river, drifting over the northern bank. Against the lighter surface of the river, McKenna saw the dark shadows of men moving aboard the tugboats, but not one of them appeared to notice the MakoShark as it passed overhead.

The bomb sight picked out a cluster of trees on the far bank, the computer locked on, and seconds later, two more sensors ejected from the payload bay. Two of the ultrasensitive electronic listening posts were utilized at each site, just in case one malfunctioned. Pearson's computers would accept the incoming signals, identify the sending sensor, define the direction of travel on the river, and compile a log of traffic. Additionally, the frequencies and resonances involved helped the computer to determine the approximate size of the watercraft.

"Can I have my airplane back, Tiger?"

"This hummer's all yours, *jefe.*"

Feeling pretty good about himself, McKenna clicked his visor into place, automatically turning on the oxy/nitro feed. He retracted the bomb bay doors, then shoved the jet throttles forward to their stops and raised the nose with the hand controller. Ahead was about twenty miles of nearly deserted area, with few people to hear any increased output from the MakoShark's twin turbo jets. The MakoShark responded with her typical agility. He took her up to 7,000 feet before she cracked the sound barrier. The sonic boom would echo through the forests and perhaps frighten a few folks out of their sleep.

Tough shit.

The HUD velocity readout had changed to Mach numbers and was displaying Mach 2.5 when they crossed the northern coast in clear skies at 50,000 feet over Rostock. The lights of shipping in the Baltic Sea winked merrily. Far to the east, the pale light of dawn was creeping toward them.

"Want to go north, Tiger?"

"Until we go south."

"I'm switching over."

"Do it to it."

McKenna activated the rocket control panel and checked the readouts. The two rocket motors operated on solid-fuel propellent and were considerably safer than liquid-fueled engines. The drawback to solid-fuel rocket motors had always been the lack of control. Typically, the solid fuel was encased in a cylinder, and once ignited, burned at a steady rate, raising pressures and exhausting through a nozzle, until the fuel was expended. For the MakoShark, the designers had developed a pelletized solid fuel which was stored internally in wing-mounted tanks. Under the pressure of compressed carbon dioxide, the pellets were forced into the combustion chambers at a rate determined by the opening of nonblow back valves. The valves were actually the throttle control, and McKenna could vary the thrust output from 55 to 100 percent, from 68,000 to 125,000 pounds of thrust on each of the two rocket motors.

Munoz double-checked him, following the checklist the WSO had put up on the rearview screens.

"Fuel supply?"

"Nine-point-five thousand pounds," McKenna said. "Almost full up, and showing two-one time."

"CO-two reserve?"

"Twelve thousand pounds PSI."

"Igniter test?"

"Testing. Got one, got two . . . now three and four."

"Activate igniters one and two."

McKenna flipped the toggles for the primary igniters in each of the rocket motors. Three and four were backup systems.

"Igniters are live, Tiger."

"Open CO-two valves."

McKenna opened the valves, pressurizing the solid-fuel pellet tanks.

"Done."

"Activate throttles, Snake Eyes."

"Active."

"Throttles at standby position."

He pushed the outboard throttle levers to their first detents. Pulling them farther back killed the motors.

"Throttles in standby," McKenna reported.

"Comp Control?"

"Punching in six-five percent." McKenna touched the pad in the top row of buttons that read "RKT THRST," keyed in the six and the five, stored the data, then tapped the "STDBY" pad.

"Go for it."

Pushing the throttles to the next detent, McKenna started the fuel flow.

The response was immediate, and he felt himself pushed back in his seat. Green flashes on the HUD showed both motors had come to life.

"I have ignition," McKenna said.

"Copy. Let's cruise."

McKenna keyed in the final command for the computer, hitting "RKT THRST" a second time, then watched as the throttles moved forward on their own. He could always override the computer manually, but the computer had the ability to keep the rocket motors generating the same amount of thrust, preventing the craft from slewing to one side or another. Moments later, the thrust readout showed 81,200 pounds on each motor, the velocity readout was climbing to Mach 4, and the altimeter was spinning upward through the numbers. Sixty thousand feet, 70,000 feet, 80,000.

McKenna was forced back into his seat as the gravitational force rose to 3.8.

He killed the turbo-ram jet engines at 110,000 feet. In either turbo or ram mode, the atmosphere was too thin for engine operation.

At 150,000 feet, McKenna leveled out and commanded the computer to reduce thrust to 60 percent. The MakoShark was cruising along at Mach 5.5. Almost 4,000 miles per hour.

The G-forces began to drop off.

Four minutes into the burn, he pulled the rocket throttles all the way back to kill the motors. The rockets used fuel at a prodigious rate, consuming the entire five-ton fuel load in twenty-four minutes at 90 percent thrust. When operating for long distances in suborbital altitudes, from 100,000 to 300,000 feet, the rocket motors were used intermittently. Since he had not used full thrust for this burn, the time available indicator for the rocket motors now read 17.4 minutes.

The sun was fully up at their altitude, but McKenna could see the line of darkness on his right. The curvature of the earth was discernible in the east. Above and on his left, the sky was a dark purple. At higher altitudes it would go black, a perfect carpet for the sharply lit starscape. Where there was no cloud cover in place, the lights of cities blinked like earthbound stars.

There was no sound, one of the delights McKenna found in high altitude, multisonic flight. He felt suspended.

"I don't know about you, *Kapitän,* but I think my day's already been made. I'm gonna sleep for the rest of it."

"And miss the rest of the trip?"

"It's a short one, anyway. Wake me when it's over."

McKenna had no doubt that Tony the Tiger would be in a coma within two minutes. He could sleep anywhere.

McKenna keyed in the coordinates for Peterson Air Force Base and let the computer work out the navigation, allowing for the parabolic downward curve of their glide. The navigational computer was in continual contact with three or more of the eighteen NavStar Global Positioning Satellites in orbit which triangulated the MakoShark's location. The GPS helped the computer to establish their latitude, longitude, altitude above mean sea level, velocity, and ground speed. The accuracy level was correct to within a few feet of position and a half mile of speed.

In a direct line of flight over the top of the world — actually passing 800 miles south of the north pole, over Greenland, their target in Germany was located slightly over 5,000 miles from their destination in the middle of Colorado. With two rocket boosts en route and an average speed of Mach 5, the computer estimated that Peterson was now ninety-one minutes away. The computer made pretty accurate guesses.

Dialing one of the backup radios into a satellite relay channel, McKenna found an oldies rock station and "Sleepwalk" filled the earphones built into his helmet.

The Artic ice pack was eerily beautiful, not totally white, but streaked with blue-shadowed crevices. From this altitude, it looked inviting, smooth and receptive. Deceptive, too, McKenna knew.

They crossed the U.S. border a few miles east of Grand Forks, North Dakota, at 80,000 feet.

Unchallenged.

The North American Aerospace Defense command, headquartered deep in Cheyenne Mountain outside of Colorado Springs, allowed them to slip unnoticed in and out of the country simply because the Mako and MakoShark craft of McKenna's 1st Aerospace Squadron belonged to NORAD.

Besides which, unless Kevin McKenna activated his modified IFF—Identify Friend or Foe—transponder, the radar sites lining the American borders never saw him.

The MakoShark utilized every facet of stealth technology in her construction. Internal ribs were cast of honeycombed carbon-impregnated fiberglass that reflected radar probes at odd angles, and not back to the radar transmitter. The skin of the craft was also carbon-impregnated plastic and coated in a midnight-blue paint containing microscopic iron balls which conducted electricity and deterred radar reflection. Radar signals slithered around on the surface of the MakoShark, instead of bouncing back. The radar cross-section (RCS) was so slim that the craft had to be within five miles of a powerful conventional radar before she returned a signal, and that signal was weak enough to go unnoticed.

When the lights of Pierre, South Dakota, appeared below his nose, McKenna prepared to start his jet engines. The Pratt and Whitney J-101s were an advanced design of the JT11D engines used in the retired SR-71 Blackbird. Normally turbofan engines with 39,000 pounds of thrust each, flexible cones in the air intakes enabled the engines to operate in a ram-jet mode. The elongated, triangular cones were segmented for expansion and contraction, and when pulsing, they controlled the air flow into the intakes, ramming compressed air into the engines. The ram-jets, which almost doubled the output thrust, were used at high altitude, up to around 110,000 feet.

Airstarts were not possible in the ram-jet mode, and McKenna had learned that the denser air at 45,000 feet was best for restarting the turbofans.

Sunset was streaking orange on his western horizon when he went through 45,000 feet at a negative twenty degree angle of attack. The speed was down to Mach 1.2. He opened the turbojet throttles far enough to contract the engine intake cones for normal air flow, then stabbed the ignition switches with a forefinger.

The HUD indicators immediately showed power on both engines, and the RPMs came up quickly.

"Shit, Snake Eyes. You woke me up early."

"Won't hurt you a bit, Tiger. You're the only guy I know who sleeps twenty hours a day."

"Preparin' myself for those days when I can't sleep at all."

"When did that happen last?" McKenna asked.

"'Eighty-three or 'Eighty-four. One or the other."

Kevin McKenna and Anthony Munoz had been flying the MakoShark together for over three years, but before that, they had flown together in USAF F4-D Panthers and other aircraft. They were well aware of each other's habits and idiosyncracies. Without McKenna's asking for it, Munoz put the GPS signal on the CRT, then overlaid it with a local map.

On his screen, McKenna saw the borders of Wyoming, Nebraska, and Colorado as well as a piece of northwest Kansas. Major highways and cities were shown, as were the prominent peaks to the southwest. The blinking orange dot in the middle of the screen was the MakoShark, and the map scrolled downward as they followed the computer's imposed heading of 189 degrees.

By the time they passed over the Nebraska panhandle, McKenna had the speed subsonic at 600 knots to erase their shock wave, and Peterson Air Force Base was an orange dot at the top of the screen. A fair amount of conditioning was required in order to become accustomed to the map overlays. North was not always at the top of the screen. Rather, the top was always their direction of travel. Map "North," in this instance, was 189 degrees, just to the right of true south.

It was after eight o'clock in the Mountain Daylight Time zone. As dusk settled over Denver, the lights in her downtown high rises and the sprawling suburbs flickered into life. McKenna keyed a few changes into the computer, to give Denver and the new international airport in Adams County a wide berth.

Sixty miles out of Colorado Springs at 30,000 feet, McKenna punched in the frequency numbers on the UHF for Peterson Air Control, then keyed the transmit mode with the finger button on the hand controller.

"Peterson Control, Delta Blue."

"Go, Delta Blue."

"ETA in nine."

"Geez, Delta Blue. How about giving me a little warning someday? Squawk me."

McKenna initiated his IFF transponder, creating an artificial, and identified, blip on Peterson radar screens.

"Delta Blue, Peterson Air Control. We've got you. Wind two knots, out of zero-zero-nine. Temperature four-six degrees. If you care about it, and if it were light out, the visibility would be great."

"I don't care about it."

"I thought not. Okay, you're cleared straight-in on Nine."

"Copy straight-in on Nine. Delta Blue, gone."

Despite its stealth on radar, the MakoShark was visible to the naked eye, of course. And while there had been pictures of it published in newspapers and *Aviation Week,* the Defense Department preferred to keep the craft an arm's length away from the media and the casual observer. Consequently, takeoffs and landings during daylight hours were rare occurrences. Night landings of the MakoShark were now second nature to McKenna. MakoShark arrivals and departures took precedence over other aircraft.

McKenna heard the air controller suspending other operations.

Far to the west, the main east-west runway went dark.

In the darkness, and despite the lights of nearby Colorado

Springs and the Air Force Academy, McKenna could not see it. The skies were clear, not even a cloud bank to blot out the stars. The mountain peaks to the west were dead spots, barely discernible against the stars. He backed off the throttles, deployed the speed brakes, and lost altitude to 12,000 feet as he circled in from the east.

Five minutes out, Munoz asked, "You ready, Snake Eyes?"

"Go over."

The screen changed to infrared imaging, and McKenna switched his attention to it. At the top edge of the screen, the hot lights surrounding the base provided a red-orange, splayed signal, otherwise there was nothing.

Two minutes later, he had the landing strip. It was lit along both sides with infrared lights, and on the screen, was as visible as Dulles International. Had he looked through his windscreen, he would have seen only darkness.

The long parallel row of lights got longer as the craft descended. McKenna deployed full flaps and landing gear, pulled the throttles full back, and felt the MakoShark sag a trifle. It wasn't very adept at slow speeds.

Above the instrument panel screen, the graphic readouts for the Instrument Landing System showed his angle-of-descent right on the money, but he was slightly below the glide path. That was a result of coming in heavy, with a greater than normal solid fuel load.

He advanced the throttles a fraction and watched the blip rise up into the glide path tolerance.

On the screen, the infrared lights started to spread.

A glance at the airspeed readout showed 285 miles per hour.

"Right on, *amigo.*"

The tires squeaked when they touched down.

McKenna used his left hand to pull both throttle levers inboard and back, neutralizing the turbine blades, then easing them into reverse thrust.

The nose dipped as the powerful engines revved up, attempting to slow the craft, which with its fuel loads, weighed close to 180,000 pounds.

The turbofans screamed on either side of him, overcoming

the insulation and sound-deadening foam lining the cockpit. McKenna loved that scream.

Halfway down the strip, he began to toe in brakes, and the MakoShark slowed to a creep a hundred yards short of the end of the concrete. McKenna idled the engines as Munoz cut off the infrared cameras and the screen went blank.

Activating the nose wheel steering and connecting it to the hand controller, McKenna turned the craft to the right and saw a shaded blue flashlight blinking at him. He eased the controller back to center to follow it.

Releasing the catch, he flipped his helmet visor up, which automatically closed off the oxygen/nitrogen supply.

With his left hand, he found the switch to depressurize the cockpit, then raised the canopy. He heard the hydraulic *whoosh!* as Munoz raised his own canopy. The cool air rushed in, coated with the aroma of pine and JP-4 jet fuel. It smelled good to him after so many hours in artificial environments.

Ahead, the flashlight blinked again, and McKenna guided the MakoShark directly into her hangar.

Two

For a man approaching sixty, Gen. Marvin Brackman was fit, if a trifle overweight. He was five-feet, eleven-inches tall, and he weighed 180 pounds, almost all of the excess wrapped around his waist. Bordering on portly, some would say, though not directly to him. His hair was exceptionally thin and fully gray, topping an elongated face with sad brown eyes, a thin, aristocratic nose, and a straight, wide mouth that surprised people when it smiled as often as it did.

Brackman was commander, United States Air Force Space Command, which included the North American Aerospace Defense Command. His headquarters was located deep inside Cheyenne Mountain southwest of Colorado Springs, and the nearly five acres of space hollowed out of solid granite contained a maze of passages and facilities resting on a sea of steel springs. The springs were supposed to reduce the shock effects of a nuclear attack.

NORAD was one of the "C-cubed" systems—command, control, and communications—operated by the Department of Defense. Like the National Military Command Center in the Pentagon and the Alternate NMCC at Fort Richie, Maryland, NORAD handled normal crisis situations with ease, but would probably remain utilitarian only during the first stages of a nuclear war. All of the command centers were prime targets, and after they were obliterated, command and control would shift to airborne command posts, Boeing E-4Bs known as National Emergency Airborne Command Posts, or NEACPs, or "Kneecaps."

Brackman had learned to live with his potential fate, but many visitors to the NORAD headquarters appeared to him to be overly nervous.

The heavily fortified antenna compound on the exterior of the mountain gathered signals from all over the world. The Ballistic Missile Early Warning System (BMEWS), with its over-the-horizon radars, the Defense Early Warning System (DEWLine), Teal Ruby and KH-8 and K-11 satellites in space, and submarines and ships at sea fed their intelligence pickings to NORAD. The results were filtered, combined, and stored in the computers, ready for instant display on one of the plotting screens. At any particular moment, NORAD and her sister command centers could pinpoint the location of most ballistic missiles, aircraft, and naval ships in the world.

The massive operations center controlled the flow of trillions of bits of information, the operators manning rows of complex consoles on the main floor. Brig. Gen. David Thorpe was in charge of the operations center, and he oversaw it, along with the shift duty officers, from an enclosed and windowed platform raised above the center floor. Through the windows, they had an unobstructed view of the massive screen mounted on the far wall of the center.

Brackman opened the door and entered Thorpe's aerie. None of the three men and two women at the command consoles leaped to attention for the commander, and he didn't expect it. Brackman didn't believe in diverting attention from the task at hand.

Thorpe, a natty and meticulous man, checked his watch, climbed out of his upholstered chair, and met Brackman by the door.

"I hope you're not running a search-and-destroy mission for me, Marv. I lost track of time."

"No. I'm running late myself, David. I've been putting out congressional fires."

"Bonfire?"

"More like an overheated toaster."

The two generals slipped out into the corridor and headed for the conference room.

"Any anomalies?" Brackman asked.

"None. Red Banner Fleet is running a war game in the Baltic, but we were notified of that last month. The Persian Gulf is quiet."

"Almost boring, huh?"

The intelligence officer laughed. "Damned boring."

"I hope you're not going to put me to sleep," Brackman said.

" 'Fraid so."

The half-dozen officers waiting for them in the conference room came to attention as they entered, and Brackman told them, "As you were."

He took a seat at the table and let Thorpe proceed with the meeting. The weekly Intelligence Briefing stayed on Brackman's schedule whether or not there were noteworthy developments in the previous week. He needed to maintain a consistent overview at all times, just in case—like today—some senator called with a question.

David Thorpe went to the head of the room and stood at a lectern next to the wall-mounted screen. One by one, he introduced the series of intelligence professionals who reported on the status of hostile, or potentially hostile, armed forces in the world. Numbers, numbers, numbers. ICBMs, SAMs, strategic bombers, naval fleets and task forces, reconnaissance satellite tracks altered, the logistics of supply.

Thorpe was right. It was boring as hell.

Finally, the brigadier introduced the single woman in the room.

Brackman had met her on several occasions, but mostly knew her through her personnel file. Amelia Pearson was a tiny woman, four inches above the five-foot mark, and gave the impression of a small package of frenetic dynamite, instantly ready to detonate. She had dark red hair cut delightfully longer than air force expectations and pale green eyes. Even in a summer uniform, her figure invited exploration, but General Brackman had given up exploration at Pamela Brackman's command thirty years before. At thirty-three, Pearson was unmarried and intensely devoted to her career. She held a doctorate in international affairs from the University of California at Los Angeles and had also read at Trinity College.

She also wore the silver oak leaves of a lieutenant colonel in the United States Air Force.

"Gentlemen," Thorpe said, "Lieutenant Colonel Pearson, intelligence officer of the First Aerospace Squadron."

Pearson got up and moved to the lectern. She moved with confidence and grace, Brackman thought, and maybe a trace of overconfidence. Her eyes surveyed her audience with unflinching calm.

Tapping a few keys on the lectern's control panel, Pearson changed the screen from the last briefer's view of Kuwait to an almost bare map. The eastern coast of Greenland was shown, along with the Greenland Sea, the island of Svalbard, which was Norwegian, and part of the Barents Sea. North to south, the map ran from the North Pole to the Arctic Circle.

As soon as the map was in place, Pearson entered another code, and twenty-four yellow dots appeared on the map. Nine of them were sprinkled in a rough line along the southern edge of the Arctic ice pack, and fifteen of them dotted the northern Greenland Sea.

"General Brackman, gentlemen, in yellow, you see the empire of the Bremerhaven Petroleum Corporation."

Brackman looked over at Thorpe, but the intelligence chief was studying Pearson. Thorpe had told him last week, when Pearson requested a chance to present her case, that it might be a little off-the-wall, but was worth hearing.

"Bremerhaven Petroleum Corporation was formed in unified Germany three years ago, and the company went into operation almost immediately. The charter states that its primary business is the exploration for new oil sources and the transportation of that oil to the German mainland by way of subsea pipelines.

"The area of operations is approximately fifteen hundred miles north of discoveries in the North Sea, and the venture was scoffed at by many prominent geologists. And yet, while there has been no public acclaim, the company has apparently met with some success. There are twenty-four sites currently. Each site consists of a geodesic dome housing the operational equipment and living quarters, apparent storage tanks, and a helicopter landing pad."

The screen changed to show a recon photo, probably taken from a Keyhole satellite. The well shown was ocean-based, the oversized dome supported on a three-legged platform. Brackman didn't know the distance of the photo, which was fairly great, but the platform appeared to him to be larger than normal.

"The rate of expansion has been considerable," Pearson went on. "Five platforms were moved into position in the first year, nine in the second year, and the balance, including the sites on the ice, within the last year. Support ships for the pipe-laying operation have been at work for the entire three years."

The screen again reverted to the map, but this time, dotted lines indicated the paths of pipelines interconnecting all of the wells.

"Any questions about the physical layout, gentlemen?"

Brackman studied the map, then asked, "Is every drilling rig still in the same place in which it was first situated, Colonel?"

"Yes sir, it is. That is the first point that prompted my curiosity. I would have expected that some wells would have come in dry and the drilling equipment moved to another site."

"So would I," Brackman admitted. "But you have a second point to make?"

"Yes, sir, I do."

A series of photographs came up on the screen, each one held for viewing for about three seconds. There were flights of Panavia Tornados, Dornier 228s, and Eurofighters, usually in pairs. There were several patrol boats, a couple of missile frigates, two missile cruisers. All of them wore the markings of the reunified German air force and German navy.

Brackman wasn't surprised at the photos. After the reunification of East and West Germany, there had ensued a long period of economic chaos. In an effort to create jobs and increase the standard of living for her citizens, the new Germany had opened dozens of industrial plants and shipyards in the east. Many of them produced military aircraft, ships, and other materiel under license from other manufacturers. The military men in countries belonging to a downsized NATO had voiced some alarm, but the politicians were certain that everything was under tight control. Germany needed an economic boost that didn't require foreign aid from Britain, France, the Soviet Union, or the United States.

Germany was merely rebuilding her defensive capability to counteract the loss of NATO forces stationed within her borders. She still suffered some paranoia from a history of conflict with the Soviet Union.

And Brackman suffered, too, when he thought of Rhein Main, Wiesbaden, New Amsterdam, Hahn, Bitburg, Spangdahlem, Ramstein, Sembach, and Zweibrucken air bases, all built with American dollars. The German flag flew over them now, and the German Luftwaffe controlled their skies.

"These aircraft and ships," Pearson said, "are patrolling the pipelines and wells of the Bremerhaven Petroleum Corporation."

"No shit?" blurted General Thorpe.

"No lie, sir."

"What's the frequency?" Brackman asked.

Pearson didn't even refer to notes. "So far, sir, we have tentative identification of eleven naval ships of three thousand tons displacement, or greater, continually on station. We don't know the exact ships."

A tap of the console brought eleven more dots to the screen, these in blue. Brackman noted that the ships were well positioned on the perimeter of the well-drilling operations.

"The ships are relieved about once a month," Pearson said. "In the air, patrol flights originating primarily from New Amsterdam make a circuit four times a day, but the flights are staggered. There is no set routine."

"How many nations patrol their oil fields, Colonel?" Thorpe asked.

"There are some, General Thorpe. Saudi Arabia, Iran,

23

Iraq, for instance. British naval units pass frequently through the North Sea oil fields. However, most of these examples involve oil fields that are nationalized. Very few private oil companies rate security from their governments. And none receive security coverage at this volume or frequency."

"That's all that bothers you, Colonel Pearson?" Brackman asked.

She frowned. "I think it's worth a closer look, sir."

"Who should do the looking?"

Pearson smiled. "I think the First Aerospace can handle it, General."

"Go for it, then, but let's keep it damned quiet, Colonel."

When Amy Pearson left Trinity College, she had been prepared to take on the world and make a name for herself.

She had come to realize that there were many ironies in her life. "Taking on the world" had become a reality, rather than an exaggeration. And she was not allowed to make a name for herself. She knew that her name would never achieve household recognition.

And the greatest irony of all: she didn't care.

Not anymore.

Taking a direct commission in air force intelligence had been impulsive, but she had had good assignments, and she had mastered the technological requirements quickly. Better, her commanders had recognized her qualities, and she had advanced through the ranks faster than her contemporaries.

She was damned good at what she did, and the results were visible. That was the important part. Amy Pearson made things happen. Just look at the meeting with the commander-in-chief of the Space Command.

After the meeting with General Brackman, David Thorpe had taken her to dinner at the officers' club, then summoned an air force sedan for her. The sergeant driving breezed his way through the southern environs of Colorado Springs, taking Lake Avenue, then the Hancock Freeway, out to Academy Boulevard. Still, by the time he turned

24

onto Fountain Boulevard, it was almost nine o'clock.

She hated wasting time, and she was eager to get started on her new assignment.

After passing through the base's main gate, the sergeant headed for the sequestered hangars that housed one of the ground-support groups for the 1st Aerospace Squadron. She got out of the car with her briefcase, thanked the driver, then approached the security control in the fence surrounding the hangars.

The air policeman on duty knew her by sight, but he still examined her identification with a critical eye and ran her briefcase through the X-ray machine before opening the gate.

Before she reached the small door set into the back of the hangar, it opened to reveal Maj. Calvin Orison. Known as High Cal because of his rotundity, Orison was the commander of the support detachment.

"Hi, there, Amy."

"Cal. How are you?"

"Lonely."

She grinned at him as she stepped over the threshold and into the hangar.

One MakoShark and two Bell JetRangers were parked inside. As soon as she saw that the Learjet assigned to the detachment was missing, she knew.

"Where's McKenna?"

"Well, now, Amy . . ."

"Damn it! He's supposed to be here."

"You ever known Kevin to be where he's supposed to be?" Orison asked.

"That son of a bitch! I want a phone, right now."

"Take it easy, Amy. Now and then, you got to give the man a little . . ."

"Now, Cal."

Amy Pearson wasn't much good at letting other people finish their sentences.

The summer season in Aspen was the best season by far,

Kevin McKenna thought. He preferred warm to cool, hot to frigid. He didn't mind loafing around a swimming pool, and he absolutely hated loafing around the base of a mountain, trying to splice broken skis or legs together.

The only drawback to summer in Aspen was the lack of snow bunnies.

McKenna and Munoz had checked into separate rooms at the Aspen Inn at seven in the morning. McKenna slept until noon, and Munoz slept until three.

Then they idled around the swimming pool, absorbing the sun's rays, watching the vacationing teachers, and drinking Bloody Marys. After two drinks, they switched to Bloody Marys that contained only the stalks of celery. In younger days, that weren't too far behind him, McKenna had never counted his glasses or cans. Now, with unpredictable flying schedules, and especially with the MakoShark, he had fallen into a habit of moderation.

When they went out on the town like this, Maj. Tony Munoz stuck close to Col. Kevin McKenna because he didn't have the same will power over Bloody Marys, Margaritas, and Johnny Walker.

Munoz was sitting in a canvas-webbed chair at a right angle to McKenna. The Arizonian was a tawny brown, with hard-ridged muscles lining his arms, legs, chest, and stomach. He had dark brown hair that matched his eyes and a smooth, almost round face that suggested that he did not have a care in the world. He didn't.

The two of them had met when Capt. Anthony Munoz had been assigned for a year as a weapons system trainee in McKenna's squadron. McKenna was a major then and had taken the WSO into the backseat of his F-4D. By the end of the year, the two of them took second place in their class in the Red Flag combat exercises out of Nellis Air Force Base in Nevada. With a little finagling, they managed to get Munoz's temporary duty converted to a permanent assignment.

"It is dark. You realize that, *jefe?*"

The sun had indeed dropped beyond the western peaks, leaving a nice blush of orange and red on the horizon, and the quick cooling of the mountains was raising goosebumps on McKenna's chest. A few yellow lamps were lit around the pool, and the surface of the pool itself was lit from below with a soft, bluish tint that wavered from the action of a couple becoming amorous.

McKenna had become so accustomed to rapid changes in temperature that he hadn't paid attention to the night falling. He only watched for the important things, like unaccompanied vacationing female teachers and secretaries harboring some thought of adventure.

Usually, he was able to attract one or two. At thirty-eight, he was in excellent shape, the stomach flat and hard, the 175 pounds just right for his six-foot frame and heavy bones, the black hair full, a trifle long, and slightly unkempt. His eyes were listed as green on his driver's license, but actually slipped over into a light shade of gray. His eyes were extremely sharp, not missing much, especially hostile aircraft in otherwise empty-appearing skies. It was one of the reasons he had picked up the nickname, "Snake Eyes." Another reason was his willingness to take a gamble, now and then. McKenna was an Air Force Academy engineering graduate who had planned on becoming a general. One star, at least. That ambition had eroded slightly after he learned to fly and found out that he was pretty good at it. Not many generals were allowed to fly as much as they would have liked. McKenna had had one tour with the Thunderbirds demonstration team, had flown as a test pilot out of Edwards Air Force Base, and had served as an instructor/liaison pilot in F-15 Eagles and F-16 Fighting Falcons for the Saudi and Israeli air forces, in addition to standard assignments with USAF wings. A lot of it was boring, and a lot of it was exciting. It got more exciting on the morning, five years before, when Gen. Marvin Brackman called him at the Bachelor Officer Quarters at Edwards.

"McKenna, a couple people I know said you could fly anything with wings."

"Even if it's only got half a wing left, General."

"Would you rather make full colonel or fly?"

"I'll fly," McKenna had said.

"Maybe you'll do both. By the time you get down to the

27

flight line, I'll have an F-15 cleared for you. I want you at Peterson by ten o'clock."

It had been a short interview, and McKenna had not returned to Edwards.

"Hey, Kev. I mention it was gettin' dark?"

"Yeah, Tony. You did."

"We gonna sit here all goddamned night, lookin' for what ain't gonna appear?"

"I saw a couple possibles," McKenna said.

"So did I. Holdin' hands with friendly types."

"Reluctantly, I'll say today was a bust."

"Me, I saw one of those, too. Coveted by her husband."

"That leaves dinner, I suppose."

"I've been known to eat," Munoz said.

"Almost anything," McKenna agreed.

They went up to their rooms to change into sport shirts and jeans, and then met in the lobby. Paring down the list of restaurants by flipping quarters, they ended up with a yuppie place called the Eager Angus, and took a cab out to it. The place was hanging ferns and brass and used brick and cozy nooks, but they got a window booth with a view of Buttermilk Mountain — when it could be seen — and someone had said the prime rib was "really, really" prime.

It was. An inch thick, and juicily rare, and covering an oversized platter. The baked potato melted when McKenna looked at it.

Munoz dribbled black pepper over everything — beef, salad, and potato.

"You think that's good for you?"

"Hey, *amigo*. It's the only damned thing the surgeon general hasn't banned."

Halfway through the meal, two young ladies were escorted to a table across the room, on the other side of an unlit, round fireplace full of orange trees.

"Oh shit, oh dear," Munoz said. "I'm in love."

McKenna turned to look. "With the blonde or the brunette?"

"Doesn't matter. You get your quarter out, we flip."

"Don't gulp your food, Tony."

Just before McKenna was ready to call his dinner complete, a waiter showed up at his elbow.

He looked up.

"You wouldn't happen to be Colonel McKenna?"

"If I said no?"

"I'll tell the caller to try somewhere else."

"Ah, hell. I'd better not."

McKenna got up and followed the waiter into the foyer and picked up the phone.

"McKenna."

"Damn you, McKenna. I've been calling all over Aspen. I've made nineteen calls. You're always, always supposed to leave word."

"I'm having dinner. It's very good."

"We have to take off in an hour."

"Not good," he told her. "We're just about to meet two lovely young ladies. Or perhaps you'd like to join us, Amy? Could be fun."

"We're leaving in an hour," she insisted.

"No hurry. I figure about three A.M."

"We have an assignment."

"Oh. Well, that's different."

The MakoShark was absolutely the most beautiful thing Maj. Wilbur Conover had ever seen. Its heritage was SR-71 Blackbird, but the air force's design team—from Lockheed, Martin Marietta, Boeing, Hughes, and Rockwell—had gone far beyond a design that was twenty-years' advanced for 1964, when the Blackbird first flew.

Like the Blackbird, the MakoShark was delta-winged, with a long, long fuselage, and flattened. Chines along the side of the narrowing forward fuselage gave it a visual pancake appearance.

The resemblance stopped there. She did not have rudders. Rather, the wing tips canted upward at seventy-degree angles, leaning outward, to serve as rudders. She did not have the cylindrical nacelles protecting her propulsion systems. The housings were elongated rectangles with rounded edges, and the wing appeared to pass through them. Forward, at the bottom of the wing, the nacelle curved upward to its opening. Jutting out of the opening was the ramjet cone which was not actually a cone as on the SR-71s, but a very wide and flexible triangular piece now blocking the entire mouth of the nacelle. The turbofan engines were not in alignment with the intake, but raised above it, sucking their air supply from an upward-curving tunnel. The reason for that configuration was that spinning turbine blades were excellent radar reflectors. With the blades not directly behind the intake, the possibility for radar contact was reduced.

Similarly, with the jet engines mounted well forward in the long nacelle, their exhaust was channeled slightly downward in another curving tunnel that was wrapped with tubing carrying freon gas. The refrigerant cooled the exhaust considerably, so that by the time it exited the tail pipe, its infrared signature was practically nonexistent at 70 percent throttle settings. Infrared tracking sensors just might pick up a small signal at 90 percent throttle, and would at 100 percent.

But they wouldn't know what they had. An infrared signal with no radar return?

To further diminish the radar cross-section, the turbofan blades were not made of metal. They were plastic, combined with carbon fiber for strength. While some designers had experimented with engines made of ceramics—not detectable on radar, the MakoShark's designers had elected to stay with the more reliable and higher output metal-encased engines, using plastic and carbon and polymer for weight-reduction and RCS-control wherever they could get away with it. The engines were, however, enclosed in a honeycombed structure that diffused and absorbed radar probes.

The rocket motors were mounted inboard of the jet engines, in the same nacelles, and were also protected from radar by the honeycomb layer. There was just enough metal in the MakoShark to give it a radar return about the size of a bald eagle when it was within five miles of the transmitter.

Because every ounce of thrust from the rocket motors was necessary for its mission, there was no way to disguise the infrared signature when the craft was flying on rocket power.

Usually, however, the burns did not last for more than four minutes. Nine minutes was the max. Shooting stars, way out in the stratosphere. Meteors burning up. Nothing to be concerned about.

The trailing edge of the delta wing was curved, again for antiradar purposes, and contained the oversized flaps, elevators, ailerons, and trim tabs. Every surface was ultrasmooth, finished in the deep midnight-blue paint that made the MakoShark disappear into the night a hundred yards from an observer. Placed in appropriate locations were the tiny exhaust nozzles of the thruster system. Where the air was rarified and the craft's attitude unaffected by the movement of control surfaces, the thrusters were utilized. There were no rivets to be exposed; every joint was bonded. There were also no telltale insignia, no aircraft numbers.

The cockpit was located just behind the needle nose, behind the forward avionics bay. The canopies were flush with the lines of the fuselage. Directly aft of the cockpit was the technician-accessible compartment containing more avionics and the computers. Behind that compartment was the payload bay — twenty-two feet long by ten feet wide, and behind that, in the tapering fuselage, were the primary fuel tanks feeding the JP-7 aviation fuel to the jet engines.

The payload bay was multipurpose, accepting a variety of modules. A bomb rack module, a cargo module, and up to two passenger modules could all be jacked into place. The passenger modules weren't very comfortable. Each of them was nine feet long, containing four airline-type seats, environmental control, and a large TV screen on the forward bulkhead. Passengers didn't like to feel trapped in a windowless, plastic cocoon; they had to be given a view of something. Almost anything would do.

Additionally, four pylons could be fitted to the wing, just inside the engine nacelles. The pylons accepted external fuel tanks, cargo pods, electronics modules, and a variety of lethal weaponry.

Very beautiful in its sleekness and its functional utility, Wilbur Conover thought. And this was his very own. His Delta Yellow.

Capt. Jack Abrams entered the windowless hangar and walked up behind him, his shoes clicking loudly on the concrete floor. "How long are you going to moon over her, Con Man?"

Conover turned to grin at his WSO. "Hell, I don't know. Couple more hours."

Abrams shook his head, which reflected the fluorescent lights mounted high in the ceiling. He had gone bald long before he reached forty, and he compensated with a bushy mustache. His pate was smooth, but his face was heavily lined, mirroring a mind that worried about lots of things—equipment breakdowns and the health of his pilot among them.

Conover was three inches taller than Abrams's five-ten, blond and blue-eyed, and his demeanor was almost the exact opposite of his WSOs. He laughed a lot, got hung up in a romance whenever he could, devised pranks and practical jokes for many victims, and used the company's computers to design elaborate scams. Fortunately, he had never attempted to put one of his cons into operation. Since little, unexpected glitches frequently occurred in his practical jokes, he might well have ended up in jail.

Conover had been born in Albany, then reared by an uncle and aunt in New York City when his parents were killed in a boating accident. He had blazed his way through Columbia University, then joined the air force.

Conversely, Jack Abrams had been born, raised, and schooled in New York, then immigrated to Sacramento with his parents. He attended the University of California at Berkeley before entering the air force.

The two of them had not met until they were recruited by Kevin McKenna, but since that time, two years before, had been almost inseparable.

"C'mon, Will. It's eleven o'clock in the morning. She's fueled and ready to go. Let's you and me find a San Miguel."

The fueling crews had topped off Delta Yellow's liquid and solid fuels half an hour before. The cargo module was loaded. There was nothing to do now but wait.

"Okay, couple beers." Conover headed for the door, and Abrams fell in beside him.

"I'll take you on at Ping-Pong."

"Why do you put yourself through this, Do-Wop? I whip you every time."

"I've been practicing."

Conover took one last look at his MakoShark before stepping out into the oppressive heat.

The hangar was two stories tall, with administrative offices and storage space on the second floor. Abrams described the hangar as "humongous." At the moment, it contained three C-123s, two business jets, a T-37 jet trainer, two Bell JetRangers, and a single Mako—the unarmed and unstealthy version of the MakoShark, in addition to the MakoShark.

The two men mushed their way toward the residential areas under a very hot sun. The humidity was similar to a wet dishrag pressed against Conover's face. He didn't much care for layovers at Wet Country, the nickname for Merlin Air Force Base.

The base was one of three dedicated to support of the 1st Aerospace Squadron, and it was the largest by far. Most of its operations were overt, though flights of the MakoShark were generally accomplished at night.

Located on the island of Borneo, on the coast north of Sangkulirang, the complex contained three massive hangars, dormitories, warehouses, a long finger-pier that accepted deep-draft freighters and tankers, a two-mile-long runway, and a launch complex. The local governments and the government of the Indonesian Archipelago didn't interfere with their operations in the least. Conover assumed that the right palms were well greased.

The coastline, a mile away, was freckled with palm trees. Around the complex, the rain forest had been cut back, but seemed to close back in on them daily, as if it were reluctant to give up territory rightfully its own. Orangutans and gibbons screamed at each other, or at the intruders, and occasionally, a leopard appeared at the jungle's edge, sniffing the wind.

Abrams had to take quick steps to keep up with Conover's long strides.

33

"What's the damned hurry?" the WSO asked.

"I thought you were thirsty."

"I am."

"Well, I just want to find an air conditioner."

The recreation center was a single-storied frame building centered among the four dormitories. Behind it was the dining hall. The sign above the double-doored entrance identified it as the "Recreation Center," but the residents called it "Heaven on Earth, or more simply, "Heaven."

There wasn't much else to do at Wet Country, except go down to the beach and swim with the sharks.

Inside was a movie theater, a lounge, several television rooms able to pick up the world's programming, a snack shop, and a large room full of pool tables, Ping-Pong tables, card tables, and electronic games. It was blessedly cool.

Conover and Abrams bought four bottles of San Miguel at the bar and carried them into the rec room. At midday, there were only a half-dozen men and women with free time, and they didn't have to wait for a Ping-Pong table.

"You sure you want to do this, Jack?"

"Damn right. I got me a system now."

"Never happen."

"You wait." Abrams took a pair of glasses from the pocket of his flight suit and donned them.

They had big clear lenses, with orange gunsights imprinted on them.

He won the first six points because Conover couldn't stop laughing.

Gen. Felix Eisenach, a resident of Berlin for most of his life, was in his midfifties, a bit pompous, and a bit broad. His hair was pure white, and the eyes in his beefy face were a strange silver/green, quite penetrating, he thought. Once, the hair had been blond and the figure much leaner, more closely resembling the photographs of his male Prussian forebears. Like Baron Otto von Eisenach, his aging father, he was accustomed to command.

His command had been a long time coming, however, as had his promotion to his current rank. Eisenach's advancement had been suppressed at the recommendation of various NATO advisors from British, French, and American services. He had been required to cool his heels in ineffective staff positions: supply, logistics, intelligence, military advisor to the *Bundestag*—the lower legislative house of the republic—for twenty-five years. Every promotion had come late, at the top end of his seniority on the promotion list.

Just when his frustration had achieved its upper limits, his world shook itself like a wet hound, and everything changed. NATO forces—and his oppressors—withdrew from the fatherland, and the German military resurrected itself. And then his assignments baby-sitting legislators and bureaucrats paid off. He had gained powerful and influential friends.

The hierarchy of the military—air force, navy, and army—was rapidly juggled. Those who had toadied to the occupation forces were summarily retired, and the professional soldiers—like Eisenach—were promoted to deserving ranks and assigned to appropriate commands. Eisenach's expertise in logistics had gained him the *VORMUND PROJEKT*.

The seat of government for the new Germany remained in Bonn, but Eisenach's program was located at Templehof Air Force Base in Berlin. He could not have been happier.

The GUARDIAN PROJECT was a unified command. Eisenach had air force, army, and navy units assigned to him. The units were deployed all over the country, and when he had first taken over, his headquarters had been composed of two offices at Templehof. In four years, however, he had successfully expanded the headquarters to include three office buildings, two hangars, several barracks buildings, and a number of other facilities. In microcosm, it represented similar expansions made throughout the German military.

Eisenach's driver picked him up at his home on *Tiergartenstrasse*. Overlooking the manicured and sprawling grounds of the massive *Tiergarten*, the three-story town house had been in his family for 200 years, the urban residence of a succession of barons. Now, the eighty-five-year-old Baron Frederick Otto von Eisenach was tended by a nurse on the third floor, and *General und Frau* Eisenach entertained on the first two floors.

As his black Mercedes 500 SEL weaved its way through heavy traffic along *Tempelhofer Damm,* Eisenach sat in the back and studied the parks and shops and office buildings. He was immensely pleased with the progress taking place. The remnants of the Wall — several miles behind him — were all but gone. Berlin was returning to its former grandeur, as was the entire fatherland.

And best of all, he would live to see it. He had once despaired of that goal.

The sedan passed through the gates of Templehof, took two turns and approached his headquarters. It was a red brick, two-story building surrounded by well-kept green grass. The white sign with black letters in front read:

16th Logistics Command
F. Felix Eisenach, General
Commanding

Eisenach spoke to his driver, "We will go on to the Personnel Division."

"Yes, sir."

A block farther down the street, the driver pulled the Mercedes to the curb and leaped out to open Eisenach's door for him. He got out and strode up the walk toward an *oberleutnant* who stepped outside to hold the front door. He returned the officer's salute, entered the building, and headed directly for the conference room.

General Eisenach was a conscientious commander. He felt it imperative that he be aware of each of the 7,000 men in his command, and once a month, without fail, he and his adjutant, *Oberst* Maximillian Oberlin, met with personnel officers to go over the records of the men assigned to him.

Oberlin and the *major* in charge of personnel were waiting for him. Eisenach returned the salutes, and all of them settled into chairs at the table. A stack of records folders was centered on the table.

"Well, Max, what have we today?"

"The noncommissioned officers of the 232nd Engineering Company, General."

They were now reviewing the *unteroffiziers* of each company. The review of officers had come first, naturally, and had been completed two years before.

"Very well. Let us get started."

Major Adler began with the first folder. Opening it, he read the name and the pertinent facts, then passed the folder to the general so he could look at the picture stapled inside. Many were quickly scanned, and the folders restacked at the end of the table.

On the fifth, Eisenach noted that the picture was that of a black man. A *feldwebel.*

"Where is this man from?"

Adler leaned over to read from the file. "Johannesburg, South Africa, General. The sergeant has been in the army for seven years, and with the 232nd for eighteen months. He has expertise in mining operations."

Eisenach mused, studying the file, then said, "I believe that a man with this background would be more beneficial to the republic with one of the civilian mining companies. Why don't we see to his discharge from the service? With a letter of recommendation to, say, the Federal Geologic Company."

Oberlin made the note. "Of course, General."

Bundesgeologisch Gesellschaft, of course, would not be interested in the man. Perhaps he would return to South Africa.

The eleventh record was also of interest.

"Sergeant Alexander Dubowski?"

"From Gdansk originally, General."

And Jewish.

"His specialty?"

"Rotary-bit maintenance," Adler said.

"Do we not have an oversupply in that military occupational specialty?"

"We do, General."

"We should reduce the number of personnel in over-supplied MOSs, so as to free up slots in specialties where we have need," Eisenach noted.

"As you wish, General," Adler said, "however . . ."

"Yes?"

"Dubowski has almost nineteen years of service. Another

year and he could retire with a pension."

"Major, our concerns must lie with the fatherland, and not with individuals."

"Yes, of course, General. That is so."

The tractor towed them out of the hangar, disconnected the tow bar from the nose wheel, and scurried out of sight. The blue flashlight signaled McKenna that it was safe to start his engines.

Munoz called the checklist, and the turbofans were turning over within four minutes. McKenna let them warm for a minute.

"How you doing down there, Amy?" he asked over the intercom.

"I'm fine. Let's get this over with."

"How about a movie, Amy?" Munoz asked. "I can give you *Rio Bravo* or *Terms of Endearment.*"

"I'll give you terms of endearment, Tony." Her voice was icy, McKenna thought. Still in a snit because he wasn't where she wanted him to be when she wanted him to be there. She acted as if their ranks were reversed.

"This is your captain speaking," McKenna said. "Close your visors and hold on to your valuables."

He lined up on the runway, guided by the infrared lights on the screen, then slapped the throttles forward. The rocket control panel was active, ready for instant use if he detected any faltering from the turbofans. When the MakoShark was fully laden, as it was now with the passenger module, a cargo module, four loaded pylons, and maximum fuel, the craft weighed almost 100 tons. Any hesitation from the jet engines meant meeting the arroyo-ridden, washboarded landscape east of Colorado Springs intimately. The rocket motors were kept on standby, just in case he needed a boost.

The takeoff was uneventful, and by the time he passed over the Black Squirrel River, he had retracted the gear, trimmed out the controls, killed the rocket panel, and was holding 600 knots on 75 percent power. He went into a climbing turn to the right, headed for the Oklahoma panhandle.

Over North Texas, Munoz gave him a heading of 175 degrees, and McKenna boosted on the rocket motors for three minutes, closing down the ramjets, and achieving Mach 6 at 130,000 feet.

"Let's cool it for a while, *jefe.*"

"*Problema,* Tiger?"

"Somebody saw the burn. My threat receiver is showin' radar scans lookin' for us. Probably an AWACS airborne outta Guantanamo, but I like to give those navy guys fits."

"Can you give me something to look at?" Pearson asked.

"Comin' up."

McKenna's screen switched to direct visual, the image changing as Munoz depressed the lens and raised the magnification seven times. On the curved horizon to their left, daylight was breaking, lighting up cerulean oceans topped with fluffy white clouds.

"How's that, darlin'?"

"Better."

"What's our window, Tiger?"

"I need two-one-point-five minutes, Snake Eyes."

For this leg of the flight, they had to match up with an access window that occurred only once every 3.6 hours. The computer, which kept the data in memory, was now busily calculating the NavStar position data and plotting the course.

When his velocity dropped off to Mach 5.5, McKenna initiated another burst of two minutes which raised the speed to Mach 7 and took them up to 250,000 feet of altitude. The sky became blacker.

Sixteen minutes later, Munoz said, "Comin' up on the boost point."

"Lay back and enjoy it, Amy."

"Go to hell, McKenna."

McKenna tapped the commands into his keyboard, turning full control of the MakoShark over to the mass of silicon in the avionics compartment.

Immediately, the computer activated the Orbital Maneuvering System, firing thrusters to shift the attitude of the craft. The nose tilted upward, the left wing dipped.

Munoz aimed the camera head-on. The screen gave Pearson a picture of black velvet, with stars so sharp they looked like diamonds fresh out of twinkle.

McKenna could not hear the burn when it began. There wasn't enough atmosphere to carry the sound. He could feel the vibration shivering the structure.

The HUD display gave him the numbers. He knew that Munoz was monitoring all systems on his CRT. It was the speed that always amazed him. He felt himself shoved back into his couch.

The Mach readout flickered quickly: 9.5, 11.0, 14.6, 17.0.

There was no ground controller to intone: "Passing through sixty miles altitude. Velocity now twelve thousand miles per hour."

Mach 18.2.

Almost abruptly, the MakoShark rolled onto its back, the Earth directly above them. Blue of the seas prominent Ecru and gray land masses. Mother Earth glowed. Two hundred miles up. The nose of the craft pulled slightly downward— relative to McKenna—seeking a new path. The G-forces lessened considerably as the momentum of his body caught up with that of the vehicle.

Mach 20.3.

Mach 22.9.

Eight minutes, forty-seven seconds into the burn, the rocket motors shut down.

Mach 24.3.

Mach 26.1.

Over 18,000 miles per hour.

Escape velocity.

"Closin' at two hundred feet per second," Munoz said.

"There's home," Pearson said. There was some awe in her voice, McKenna thought. It never went away. Not for her.

It never went away for him, either.

Home was still forty miles away, but on the magnified screen it seemed much closer.

Floating there, with Mother Earth a multihued mass above it.

40

Raggedy-looking.

A huge hub sporting sixteen variable-length spokes, each with an odd-shaped, odd-sized fist on the outer end.

Home.

Themis.

Three

The Cessna Citation assigned to the commander, USAF Space Command, landed at Andrews Air Force Base in Washington a few minutes before ten o'clock in the morning.

Marvin Brackman ducked for the low doorway and descended to the tarmac. Returning the salute of the driver holding the rear door for him, he tossed his briefcase into the rear seat, then followed it.

The Chevy sedan took the Capital Beltway and the Woodrow Wilson Bridge across the Potomac, then turned north on Route 1. Maryland and Virginia both were in full dress, the foliage and the grass lush and damply green from an early morning shower. Brackman hadn't checked the weather, but he assumed that by noon, the heat would be typically Washington, hot and wet.

The driver let him out at the River Entrance to the Pentagon, and Brackman crossed the wide expanse of concrete to the doors. Inside, the concourse was packed with tourists and, Brackman figured, about half the 25,000 employees on a coffee break. The stars on his shoulders and the scowl on his face cleared a path for him, and he reached the second floor, E-ring office of the chairman of the Joint Chiefs of Staff at 1035 hours.

He was ushered directly into the office overlooking the river by Marilyn Ackerman, the admiral's longtime secretary.

Adm. Hannibal Cross had been chairman for just over three years, and he was good in the job. A recruiting poster figure—lean and crisp, with a deep-water tan and weather wrinkles at his eyes, Cross also possessed the eagerness to attack politics with the same deftness he had utilized aboard carriers off Vietnam.

Also present was Gen. Harvey Mays, the air force chief of staff. Mays was a veteran of Vietnam, also, where he had flown F-4 Phantoms. The shrapnel and burn scar on the left side of his face kept him off posters, but he was an adroit and capable commander.

"Sorry I'm late," Brackman said. "We had head winds."

"Or excess baggage," Mays said, looking at Brackman's waistline.

"Jesus, Harv. You know how many calories I'm on, already? I lost two pounds."

"In the last month?" Mays laughed.

The three flag officers shook hands and settled into the conversational grouping of couch and chairs in one corner of Cross's office. Brackman opened his briefcase and placed it on the low oak cocktail table in front of him while Marilyn filled coffee cups and passed them around.

After exchanging several routine updates, Cross said, "Okay, let's get to it. You said something about Germany, Marvin."

"Yes, I did. My gal Pearson, who's the intel officer aboard *Themis*, came up with it."

Brackman passed out printed copies of the maps Pearson had displayed at Cheyenne Mountain, then photos of the well, the aircraft, and the ships. He completed his briefing in less than five minutes.

"This the only shot you have of the well?" Mays asked.

"At the moment, yes. I don't have a satellite in position for a better view, and won't have for another nine days. If we change the orbit on a KH-11, we might well alert some people we don't want alerted. However, I'll have a close-up for you as soon as McKenna makes a run over the area."

"It's difficult to judge the scale," Cross said, "but this dome gives the impression of being larger than necessary."

"Yes, it does, in comparison with the size of the helo pad. And yet, given the weather conditions, it may be mostly in-

43

sulation."

"Maybe," Cross said.

"We're hoping to get a snapshot that includes a chopper on the deck or a man outside the dome, so we can do some measuring."

"You said this has been going on for three years?" Mays asked.

"Correct."

"And we never cared before?"

"Everybody drills for oil," Brackman pointed out.

"All right," Cross said. "McKenna's going to shoot some pictures. What else should we be doing? I'm not going to the National Security Council or the President with what you've got here."

"No, I don't want to jump the gun," Brackman said. "I would like a CIA assessment of current German energy sources and uses. Let's find out if these wells are on-line and pumping oil to the mainland."

"Let me talk to Krandall over at Langley," Mays said. "I can get something quietly."

"Good," Cross agreed. "And I might put in a call to General Sheremetevo. We've been pretty open with each other lately, and perhaps his people have some ideas."

Vitaly Sheremetevo was a deputy commander in chief of the Soviet air forces, in charge of the PVO, (Protivovozdushnaya oborona Strany) the largest air defense force in the world.

"We don't want to raise any alarms," Harvey Mays said. "Those people over on the Hill come unglued anytime we bitch about a possible military buildup in Germany."

Brackman agreed with Mays. Some people in seats of power were too willing to believe the best about the intentions of adversaries, past, present, and future.

"Still," the admiral said, his eyes fixed in thought, "our position is worse if we spring surprises on the politicos. Now that I've had my second thought, I believe I will speak to the President. It might be a good idea to have State query the Germans about, say, the success of their venture in the Greenland Sea. That way, we're on record as having pursued

44

a diplomatic channel."

Brackman wasn't sure he would do it that way, but then he wasn't the boss, either.

"Hey, Cancha?"

Maj. Frank Dimatta spoke into his helmet mike. "Got something, Nitro?"

"Two somethings. Bearing oh-four-three, we've got a solid return. It must be the Air France 747 Josie keeps nagging me about."

Capt. George "Nitro Fizz" Williams called Delta Green's on-board computer "Josie." For no reason that Dimatta had ever figured out. Before they departed *Themis,* Williams had programmed Josie with the scheduled commercial flights in their area of operations. It wouldn't do to latch onto the wrong bird.

"And the other?"

"Could be our boy. He's at our bearing three-four-nine, ninety miles. And his heading is in the general direction of Cape Town."

"You want a visual pass, first?" Dimatta asked.

"Nah. If it's the wrong one, I just won't let go of the Wasp."

They were lightly armed this trip, just two Wasp II missiles on each of two pylons. The Wasp was a multipurpose missile developed strictly for the MakoShark. While the ordnance pylons could take the modified Phoenix and Sidewinder missiles, as well as pods housing twenty millimeter rotary machine guns, the Wasp II had proved versatile. It had a range of seventy-five miles compared to the Phoenix's 125 miles or the Sidewinder's eleven miles. It covered the range at Mach 2.5. The Wasp had retractable fins and a variable exhaust nozzle, useful in low- or no-atmosphere conditions. Targeting was by independent radar-seeker or by visual control, guided by the video camera in the missile's nose. The WSO could watch the target on his panel CRT and guide the missile toward it by shifting his helmet.

The warhead was composed of twenty-one pounds of high explosive inside a cone of machined metal containing depleted uranium. It could pierce armored plate, and when it detonated, the cone, scored on the inside surface like a jigsaw puzzle, became shrapnel that ripped and tore at anything in its path.

"I'm not going to arm the warhead, Cancha."

"Fine by me," Dimatta said. He was an Italian-American from New Jersey who had served as an advisor with NATO forces, in addition to his six years as an air force test pilot. He was dark, easygoing, and a lover of exotic foods. The only thing that really got his adrenaline going was downing hostile aircraft.

"Seventy miles, and I put him at two-eight-thousand," Nitro told him. "Let's take her down."

They had been coasting along at 70,000 feet above the dark side of the dark continent after their recon run over Afghanistan and Iran. The outboard pylon on the starboard wing carried a photo reconnaissance pod. It contained high-resolution cameras shooting 2402-type and infrared films.

Far to the northeast, night would be falling on Mali and Ghana. Below, and to his left behind him, Dimatta could see the lights of Kananga, Zaire. The lights of other small towns and villages were visible, too, but they were infrequent and spread wide apart. Africa was mostly dark.

At 30,000 feet, Dimatta started bringing the speed back until he dropped below the sonic threshold. He saw a flash of cream lightning against the earth. The moon reflecting off a piece of the Sankuru River.

"All right, good," Williams said. "He's making two-two-oh knots. That's about right."

Their target was an elderly Beechcraft Super-18, a reliable twin-engined light cargo or passenger plane forty years past its prime. Pearson's information had this one headed toward a rowdy tribe in South Africa with a load of AK-47s, RPGs, a few flamethrowers, and a million rounds of ammunition.

The screen in front of Dimatta showed the target clearly, about forty miles away. The Air France jetliner was to the east now, a hundred miles away.

"You think Pierre's going to see this, Nitro?"

"Nah. Not a Wasp trail at this distance. Hey, this guy's going down in rain forest so thick, they'll never find the pieces."

"ELS?"

"Emergency Locator Signal? On an old C-fifty-four? You got to be kidding, Cancha. Even if that plane went down, the owners wouldn't want it found."

"Yeah. Okay. Cancha give me a heading?" Frank Dimatta had picked up his nickname in the air force as a result of his frequent use of the crunched words, "can cha." Since then, he had consciously tried to avoid it, but it slipped out once in a while.

"Let me have four points to port . . . yeah, that'll do it. I've got thirty miles, and I'm going to video. Give me number one."

The screen in front of Dimatta abruptly shifted to a night-vision enhanced image, but it was from the point of view of the Wasp II on the outboard side of the port pylon. The rain forest was a rippling green blanket. Williams zoomed the lens, searched left, right, then down, and found the tiny black speck moving across the blanket. The speck got larger, took on the shape of an airplane.

Dimatta dialed in "Pylon 2," on one selector, then "1," on the next selector, raised the flap, and armed the missile's propulsion system. The WSO controlled the arming of the warhead.

"Missile's hot." He thought he felt his blood pumping faster.

"Got it. No warhead. Targeted."

The orange target symbol appeared on the screen, lapped over the large black speck.

"Launching."

The picture on the screen jiggled as the missile leaped from its launch rail. Williams was guiding the Wasp with his helmet, shifting minutely if the target symbol drifted off the Beechcraft. As the supersonic missile closed, Williams reduced the zoom power of the lens.

In a second, Dimatta saw a real airplane.

A second later, he knew it was a Beech Super-18.

The focus was on the left wing . . . the wing grew large in the screen . . . the fuselage disappeared . . . huge engine

47

nacelle . . . .

The engine whipped past, then the view was of green forest, then blackness as the missile crashed into the jungle.

The WSO immediately shifted to the MakoShark's video system and found the Beechcraft.

It was in an abrupt left turn, diving for a few thousand feet, then straightening out.

"Right on," Nitro said. "That son of a bitch is going to be wondering what it was for the next ten years. He knows he was one meter away from eternity, but he doesn't know how or why."

"That going to be enough? Want another one?" Dimatta's vision felt super-keen. Everything was so clear. He loved it.

"Nah, not yet. Let's watch awhile."

The MakoShark was ten miles from the Beech now, and Dimatta retarded the throttles some more. The HUD registered 400 knots. He nosed over and began to lose altitude at a thousand feet a minute.

Williams let Josie guide the video camera, having locked it onto the target.

The Beech seemed to be staggering. The pilot couldn't keep it level or flying straight for a few seconds. Finally, he got his nerve back and began to climb.

"Someday, we're going to fuck up and actually hit one of these bastards," Dimatta said. "Pearson might even stop giving us practice targets."

Pearson didn't know they actually fired missiles at live people. Whenever her intelligence net found some bad guys transporting contraband, she passed it on to Dimatta and Williams, strictly, she said, for the purpose of practicing night interceptions.

"Someday, if we're lucky," Nitro said, "the President's going to turn us loose on drugs and gunrunners."

"Cross your fingers and anything else you can cross."

"Let's go find a hot one and a cold one," Williams said.

"Can . . . give me a heading."

Eighteen minutes later, Dimatta found the infrared landing lights and put the MakoShark down smoothly at Jack Andrews Air Force Base in the middle of Chad in Northeast

Africa. Most of them called it "Hot Country," because it was.

During daylight hours, it was forbidding territory. Located on the southern edge of what was known as the Bodelo Depression, the nearest village, Koro Toro, was over a hundred miles away. It was rough and rugged desert composed of clay and sand sediment without one redeeming feature. The temperatures could reach 124 degrees and often did.

At night, it wasn't much less forbidding. A good moon gave the terrain surrounding the base the appearance of a lunarscape. Pale, wind-sculpted rock and sand formations. It looked dead; nothing moved. The air was clear, though, and the stars shown with exceptional brilliance.

Like Wet Country, Merlin Air Force Base, the base in Chad was semicovert. The MakoSharks could operate in the barren reaches rather freely during daylight hours, but when they were in residence, they were parked and serviced inside Hangar One, just in case the airbase was being observed by satellite or Foxbat reconnaissance craft. There were three more hangars and a single massive three-story residential building that contained dormitory rooms, apartments, recreation rooms, and dining facilities.

Also like Wet Country, Hot Country served as a launch and recovery base for the HoneyBee resupply rockets. The launch complex was located to the west of the main base, linked to it by a twin set of railroad tracks.

The HoneyBee vehicle was state-of-the-art in rocketry. It was forty-six feet long and nine feet in diameter, segmented into four compartments—nose cone, which contained the electronics; payload bay; fuel compartment; and propulsion system. For launch, there was an additional booster engine that was jettisoned at 300,000 feet and was not recovered.

The reentry shroud over the nose cone, cast in ceramic, was good for six or seven return trips into the atmosphere and was then replaced.

In a typical mission out of either Chad or Borneo, supplies brought in by C-123, C-13O, and C-141 cargo transports were stored in Hangar Four and packed into cargo modules. In Hangar Three, recovered rockets were refurbished, then moved to Hangar Two for final calibration, fueling with the solid-fuel pellets, and insertion of the cargo modules. From there, the HoneyBee was moved to one of the three launch pads on cradled flatcars and craned into position.

The launches had become so routine that they were now less than spectacular to the people involved with them. Depending on time and relative position, a HoneyBee generally achieved rendezvous with *Themis* in about three hours. In nine years, only four HoneyBees had been lost on launch and seven had malfunctioned in space, but been recovered. Six had been destroyed upon reentry or recovery.

Recovery was also routine. The vehicle descended by parachute and was netted by specially fitted C-130 Hercules aircraft. The C-130 attempted its first pass at about 30,000 feet, so that if it missed, it would have time for a couple more passes. As it flew above the top of the parachute, a loop of cable trailing from the aircraft snared the parachute shrouds, then the rocket was winched aboard, sliding into a rollered cradle in the plane's cargo bay. It was the same system occasionally employed to rescue downed pilots.

Occasionally, the Hercules missed its quarry, and the HoneyBee splashed down in the sea or crunched down in the desert. Then, the Chinook helicopters took over.

It was important to complete recovery for the HoneyBees frequently came back with cargo aboard. Pharmaceutical concoctions formulated in the almost pure vacuum and zero-gravity of space, electronic components assembled in the same conditions, biological experiments, and ultraclear telescopic photographs were a few of the services performed by the air force for contract customers. The air force was highly paid for these services, and for transporting client employees—biologists, chemists, engineers—to *Themis* for short stints of duty.

Transportation of client personnel was accomplished aboard the Mako, and there were six of them based at the three support airbases. It was McKenna's idea. They were an unarmed and unstealthy version of the MakoShark, finished in flat white, and they served an additional purpose. The Mako was a platform for McKenna's training of flight crews before he made final evaluations of the crew and introduced them to the MakoShark. Dimatta and Williams had spent four months in a Mako.

The HoneyBee and the Mako aerospace vehicles were the overt side of the operations. Though the MakoShark was known to exist by friendly and unfriendly governments, its capabilities were still a tightly kept secret.

Dimatta and Williams stayed with Delta Green until it was parked in Hangar One, then performed their post-flight checklist. A second MakoShark, tentatively coded Delta Orange, was parked next to them, but it was a month or more away from completion. When they were finished, they walked over to the nearly deserted dining room, which was always open, and sat at a table by the window. The view was of flat expanses of sand, a few clumps of brush, and far off, the flat gray runway.

The menu was limited outside of the normal three meal times, and DiMatta was forced to settle for reheated sauerbraten.

George Williams ordered a salad heaped with tomatoes and cucumbers and red onions and sprouts, oil-and-vinegar dressing on the side. No nighttime chef was going to overdo the dressing for him. Williams was a fitness freak. At six-two and 160 pounds, he appeared five or six years younger than his thirty-three. The bright red hair and green eyes added to his youth.

When their plates were delivered, Williams said, "You know what they put in that stuff, Cancha?"

"Yes. And I wholeheartedly approve." Dimatta forked a chunk of the beef into his mouth and closed his eyes, savoring the flavor.

"It's going to clog up your whole system."

"I'll die a happy man. Your problem, Nitro Fizz, is you don't know how to enjoy life."

"You're going to die before your time."

"We may all die before our time," Dimatta said. "But you'll have ulcers, worrying like you do. Me, I'll be fat and satisfied. And if we had any unattached women around here, I'd be more satisfied."

51

The hub was gigantic, a cylinder of 300 feet of diameter by 200 feet of width. One half of it was constructed like a honeycomb, containing twenty-eight cells, eight of them large enough to accept a Mako or MakoShark behind closed doors. The smaller cells were used to port resupply rockets or for the containment of fuel and other stores.

On the interior end, each of the hangar cells had a window and control station overlooking the hangar. From there, the docking operator could suck the oxygen/nitrogen atmosphere out of the hangar, open the outer doors, guide the Mako or the MakoShark inside, and then close the doors and recharge the atmosphere. The MakoSharks were kept out of the view of satellite eyes and earthbound telescopes. Additionally, it was much easier to service the craft inside the mother ship. Bobbing around in clumsy spacesuits outside the space station encouraged accidents.

McKenna spent part of the morning — *Themis*'s artificial day was keyed to Eastern Standard Time — supervising the servicing of Delta Blue. The interior, vaultlike door to the hangar was open, and technicians moved freely into and out of the hangar, propelling themselves through the zero gravity with accustomed ease. Grab bars were spaced throughout the hub for the purpose of initiating or arresting movement.

Delta Blue floated in the middle of the hangar, secured only by a half-dozen bungee straps. With her momentum matched to that of *Themis*, the straps were necessary only to prevent rotation or fore-and-aft movement if a technician pushed off her skin too hard. The dark-blue finish seemed to absorb light from the fixtures mounted all around the gray-painted bay.

The cockpit canopies and the payload bay doors were open as a service technician scurried about with a vacuum hose, seeking any trace of dirt or dust. Minute, foreign objects floating in the station's atmosphere were taboo. The passenger module had been removed and lashed to one side of the cell, along with another passenger module and several cargo modules. One of the nice things about a weightless environment was that almost any heavy task could be accomplished by one person.

Fuel hoses from the feeder outlets of the hub were attached to the craft, tended by another technician. A flashing red strobe light mounted in one corner indicated that fuel was being transferred. To further emphasize the danger of that operation, a low-toned chime kept repeating itself.

Inside the pressurized hangar, environmental suits were not necessary, and everyone, McKenna included, wore the light blue jumpsuits that had evolved as the clothing of choice aboard *Themis*. They were comfortable, allowed freedom of movement, and were easily maintained. The soft-soled boots were incorporated as part of the jumpsuit.

When the tech with the vacuum was finished with the forward cockpit, McKenna pushed off the wall, shot across thirty feet of space, and grabbed the windscreen. Twisting around, he pulled himself down into the seat and locked his toes under the rudder pedals to hold himself in place.

Powering up the computer, McKenna called up the MakoShark's maintenance log. The computer automatically kept a record of the hours used on all of the critical subsystems. Upcoming maintenance requirements were flagged. McKenna scrolled the log up the screen, but did not see anything imminent. A couple more flights, and the doppler radar was due for calibration. The turbo-ram jets would go for another 1500 hours before requiring overhaul.

The chime went silent and the red strobe quit blinking as the fuel technician detached his special fittings and began to retract the hoses into their receptacles.

McKenna didn't have his helmet, with its microphone, so he reached into the crevice between the seat and the side of the cockpit and found the alternate microphone. Tapping in the frequency for *Themis*'s maintenance office on the radio pad, he said, "Beta One, Delta Blue."

A few seconds passed before someone got to the console. "Beta here."

McKenna recognized the voice of Lt. Col. Brad Mitchell, who was the chief vehicle maintenance officer.

"I'm ready to dump data."

"Okay, hold a minute. Delta Blue. Go."

McKenna keyed the command into the computer pad, and all of the updated maintenance data files from the MakoShark were transferred into Beta One's computer files. Beta One maintained current files on all vehicles operating outside of the atmosphere.

"Okay, got it. Anything pressing, Snake Eyes?"

"I don't think so, Brad."

"Is Shalbot out there?"

McKenna looked around and saw T.Sgt. Benny Shalbot, the head avionics technician, hanging onto the hangar door frame. "He's here, just thinking about it."

"Well, tell him to get his ass in gear, then get over to Hangar Four. Delta Red's got a nav radio problem."

Delta Red was a reserve craft.

"Got it, Brad. Blue out."

McKenna released his toehold, tapped the seat sides with his fingers, and rose out of the cockpit.

"Hey, Benny, your boss is looking for you."

Shalbot, a gnome of a man with curly white hair, a bulbous nose, and an infectious grin, said, "And if I'm not careful, Colonel, he's going to find me."

Shalbot shoved off the door frame, towing a large black box behind him, did a somersault in midflight, and landed with practiced ease on the nose of Delta Blue.

"He said something about a navigation radio problem on Delta Red," McKenna said.

"Fuck. Second time in two trials. I'm going to have to change it out. You got any glitches, Snake Eyes?"

"None that Tony or I picked up on."

"Good."

Positioning the black box—one by three by two feet in size—in midair above the windscreen, Shalbot opened its lid and withdrew a long umbilical cord. Diving head first into the cockpit, he plugged the multiple-pin connector into a receptacle at floor level on the left side of the cockpit. He rose feet first out of the cockpit, tucked his legs, and rolled upright.

"You need me for anything, Benny?"

"Nope. Go sleep or something. Hey, Snake Eyes, you get a chance to do something this trip?"

"No. Got close, but got called off at the last second."

"Shit. That's what this goddamned job does for you."

Not his job and not McKenna's job. This job. It was all one effort, every task melded into the singular task, and most of the forty-nine people who were aboard *Themis* regularly felt like they were part of a team, as Shalbot did. And like anyone in any large organization McKenna had ever known, Shalbot was instantly prepared to complain about the job. He would also be instantly ready to defend it. He was part of an elite team.

Shalbot activated his PDU—Portable Diagnostics Unit—and began the sequence that would test every electronic circuit aboard the MakoShark for operation within specified tolerances. One malfunctioning integrated circuit board, or one diode overheated too many times, could turn success into catastrophe, and the MakoSharks' electronics were tested each time they arrived on *Themis*.

McKenna launched himself off Delta Blue and sailed through the doorway to grab a handhold and deflect his flight downward along a wide corridor. All "up" aboard the satellite was toward the center of the hub, and all "down" was away from it.

The side of the hub opposite the hangar/storage half was a maze of corridors, offices, and more storage spaces. Technicians darted along the corridors with purpose, appearing from and disappearing into labs and maintenance areas. He passed the maintenance office, waving at Mitchell as he went by, then slowed to peek into the exercise room. Technically, it was Compartment A-47, but outside of the station commander and the maintenance officer, McKenna didn't know anyone who called it that.

It was a large space, fitted on all walls—there was no true ceiling or floor—with specialized equipment for maintaining muscle tone. In the center of the wall opposite the door was a small centrifugal weight machine. All of those aboard *Themis* who did not regularly return to the earth's surface were provided with an exercise regimen by the station's doctor. And everyone spent ten or fifteen minutes a day spinning in the artificial gravity of the centrifugal weight machine.

At the end of the corridor bisecting the hub, McKenna came to the curved hallway that went clear around the outer diameter of the hub. Gripping a grab bar for an instant, he deflected his direction and pushed off again.

At irregular intervals along this corridor were self-sealing round doors that led into the spokes. Currently, there were sixteen spokes, though the corridor also had an additional eight doors, locked and painted red, to accommodate the addition of eight more spokes. On opposite sides of the hub, there were also airlocks allowing passage outside the satellite for repair and maintenance.

Four of the modules at the end of their spokes were residential, containing sixteen individual sleeping quarters, recreation/dining spaces, kitchens, and personal hygiene stations. The personnel complement was divided into separate dormitory areas primarily for safety, rather than for social or organizational reasons. If there was an accidental blowout in one of the residential modules, three-fourths of the personnel complement would still be intact. Explaining that cut-and-dried safety consideration to temporary residents like a physicist or biologist brought an ashy shade to their faces.

Other spokes led to the nuclear power plant, the laboratories, the production plants, and the command section. Primary electronics, ventilation, and power were located in the hub, feeding the spokes, so that the loss of any spoke would not cripple the ship. The exception to that rule was the nuclear plant, but backup batteries and solar power sources would still be available for a limited time. The "hot" side of the hub, exposed to the sun, mounted a massive solar array.

McKenna arrived at Spoke One and tapped the large green button mounted on the bulkhead. The automatic door wheezed, rotated two inches to free itself from the locking tangs, then swung open on its massive hinge. The hinge was mounted solidly to the bulkhead, and two bars from the top and bottom of the hinge met in a "V" at the center of the round door, allowing the door to pivot around an axle at the point of the "V." Decompression in any compartment automatically closed every door on the station.

Once he had clearance, McKenna pushed himself through the opening, pressing the red button on the other side. The door closed behind him, and he pulled himself along the spoke. It was twelve feet in diameter and double walled. Between the walls ran the ventilation ducting, electrical conduits, heating and cooling coils, and thick insulation. Since the satellite did not rotate, there was a hot side and a cold—night—side. The variation in temperature from one side to the other was several hundred degrees, and one computer alone was kept busy cooling and heating the satellite's skin in order to keep the interior livable.

Access panels were irregularly spaced along the spoke's forty-foot length. Spoke One was the longest of the spokes. The design of the station allowed for unexpected expansion, as well as for oversized modules at the end of a spoke. Including the largest modules and the spokes, *Themis* currently had a 470-foot diameter, the equivalent of more than one-and-a-half football fields. To those approaching the station from space, it was a speck in a vast emptiness. To first-time visitors aboard, it was an amazingly complex and huge city.

The interior of Spoke One was lit with three flush-mounted lamps, and there were no windows.

Windows were in short supply on *Themis*. There was one large round port in each of the four dining rooms and two in the command module. None of the portholes in the dining rooms could observe the hangar side of the hub. If visiting scientists from Air Force-client companies were aboard, they would never see any of the MakoShark arrivals or departures.

On the outer end of the spoke, McKenna negotiated an automatic door in order to reach the command spaces.

The module was forty feet in diameter and sixty feet long, divided into a number of compartments. As commander of the 1st Aerospace Squadron, McKenna rated an office here, if it could be called an office. It was a four-by-four-by-seven-foot cubicle in which he could strap himself to one padded wall and operate his "desk." The desk was a computer and communications console with three cathode ray tubes recessed into the desk top. It allowed him visual access to three documents simultaneously, or if he split the screens, to six documents. Additionally, he could tap into any of the radar or video monitoring systems.

Except for the console, the cubicle's arrangement wasn't much different from his sleeping quarters, and McKenna frequently slept there.

The commander of *Themis,* Brig. Gen. James Overton, the deputy commander, Col. Milt Avery, and Amy Pearson had similar cubicles. A much larger compartment was utilized by one of the three communications/radar operators on board. Other compartments were designed for storage or contained computer and electronic gear, safety equipment, and emergency environmental suits.

McKenna pushed himself down the short corridor past the smaller cubicles and into the main control room. On the outboard end of the module, the command center was twenty feet deep by almost the full diameter of forty feet. The dominant feature was the centered four-foot, round port providing a view of the earth. At the moment, the focus was on the Mediterranean Sea. The earth seemed to glow, radiating her greens, blues, and tans. The cloud cover was particularly white this morning. It had a rose tint to it.

The command center was a functional place, without much thought given to aesthetics. Conduit and ducting was flattened against the bulkheads, snaking around consoles and black boxes. There weren't any seats available, though there were a number of Velcro tethers spotted around to keep people operating consoles from floating away from the job.

Avery, the deputy commander, was earthside, on a week's leave, and Overton was the man in charge. The commander of *Themis* was forty-four years old and carried the image of that fatherly airliner captain. He had dark hair graying nicely at the temples and steady gray eyes. At six-four, he was tall but solidly built.

He looked around from his station near the porthole as McKenna floated into the center.

"Your birds all sound, Kevin?"

58

"We may have to change a radio on Red, but otherwise, we're in great shape, Jim."

"Good. I think Colonel Pearson is going to want you to wring them out a little."

McKenna grinned. "How come she always gets what she wants?"

Pearson stuck her head out of her cubicle, then pushed her way out of it. "Because I know what I'm doing, McKenna."

The light blue jumpsuit did nice things for her.

And for McKenna.

She also wore a matching headband to hold all that gorgeous red hair in place since gravity wouldn't do it for her.

"Of course you do, Amy. I trust you."

"That's a one-way street," she told him.

McKenna sighed and thought, one of these days. . . .

At eight in the morning, the sun was already high on Zeigman's right shoulder. It was not as high as it would have been if he were flying at a normal altitude.

The sea was sixty feet below, the white caps visible, the spray glinting as a twenty-knot wind whipped the waves. On his left oblique, dark storm clouds were brewing, their tops roiling, but they were a couple hundred miles away. He would be long gone before the squalls hit.

He had picked up the crosswind half an hour before and had had to alter his course a little. The airplane was skittish at this altitude if he got his left wing too low.

Skittish airplanes never bothered Mac Zeigman. He had been flying since he was fifteen, taught by an uncle from Hannover in an old Aeronica. By the age of eighteen, he had commercial and instrument ratings, as well as some experience flying helicopters and jet aircraft. For six years, he had roamed the world, flying whatever presented itself, for whatever the client would pay.

Zeigman's given names were actually Gustav Matthew, but an Australian he had met in Pakistan had decided on, "Hey, Mac," and he had adopted it. He had never considered

59

himself a Gustav or a Matthew, anyway.

Wherever he was in the world, Zeigman lived his life to the full, and it had aged him quickly. At thirty-two, his life was mapped in the small burst veins of his nose and upper cheeks. His face had a red glow resulting from rich food, Kentucky bourbon, Japanese wine, and good German beer. What had once been a relatively handsome face sagged a little now. There were bags under his washed brown eyes from late party nights and early flight mornings. His hair was thick and dark and widow-peaked. The body was still hard and lean, with only a bit of a paunch. He burned off calories with steady work and frequent high-adrenaline escapades. His work was what he loved.

And for the past five years, his work had been steady. Zeigman had been recruited by *Oberst* Albert Weismann to a direct commission as a *hauptmann* in the German air force, and a year later, promoted to *major*. Since he was already a squadron commander, he expected to be an *oberstleutnant* very soon.

Weismann commanded the *Zwanzigste Speziell Aeronautisch Gruppe* (20.S.A.G.), comprised of Zeigman's *Erst Schwadron*, Metzenbaum's *Zweite Schwadron*, a transport squadron, and a helicopter unit. The air group supported the GUARDIAN PROJECT and was based at New Amsterdam Air Force Base near Bremerhaven. The seaport offered Zeigman nearly any form of revelry he could have hoped for.

The Luftwaffe offered him the kind of flying he required.

Zeigman's squadron was equipped with twelve Panavia Tornados. A multination, multicompany — Aeritalia, British Aerospace, and Messerschmitt-Bolkow-Blohm — design and production effort, the Tornado met several combat roles. It was equally capable of battlefield interdiction, counter-air strike, close air support and air superiority functions. In the ADV (Air Defense Variant) model, originally built for the Royal Air Force, it took on the additional tasks of air defense and interception. The 1st Squadron of the 20th Special Air Group had ADV models.

It was a dual-seat fighter with variable-swept wings, adjustable from 25 to 67 degrees of sweep. A key characteristic was the exceptionally tall vertical stabilizer, also steeply swept back. With Texas Instrument's forward-looking and ground-mapping radar, Foxhunter Doppler navigation radar, and a GEC Avionics terrain-following radar, the Tornado could go almost anywhere its pilot wanted it to go, and in the worst of weather conditions.

And when it got there, it could use its IWKA-Mauser 27 millimeter cannon or any of up to 9,000 kilograms of free-fall, retarded and guided bombs or a variety of air-to-air and air-to-surface missiles. The 1st Squadron's Tornados were generally armed with air defense weaponry such as the AIM-9 Sidewinder missiles.

And the Tornado got wherever it was going at 2300 kilometers per hour. *Major* Zeigman loved it.

Frequently, like this morning, Zeigman performed his patrol without his backseater. He preferred solitude when he was flying, and when the visibility was good, he didn't need the radar or weapons control.

At sea level, Zeigman was using fuel rapidly, though he was holding the fighter at 600 knots, well below its top speed. He did not care. Somewhere, 9,000 meters above him, was his tanker.

When he saw the tip of Svalbard Island rise on the horizon, Zeigman turned to a heading of 340 degrees. Three minutes later, a ship appeared in his windscreen. He adjusted his heading once again, and headed directly for it.

Two miles out, he identified the silhouette as that of the missile cruiser *Hamburg*, the flagship of *der Admiral* Gerhard Schmidt. Grinning to himself, he lost yet more altitude, to less than twenty feet above the wave tops.

Obviously, since he had not been challenged, the cruiser's radar had missed him, lost him in the clutter of radar return off the waves.

Dialing his radio to the frequency assigned to the marine division of the *VORMUND PROJEKT,* Zeigman thumbed the transmit button on the stick and yelled into his helmet microphone, "BANG!"

He pulled up abruptly, rolled inverted, and passed over the ship, in front of the bridge, fifty feet above the foredeck.

There was consternation on the decks, seamen running wildly about. White faces pressed against the bridge's windshield, heads swiveling to follow him.

Zeigman gave them the finger, a gesture he had learned from American mercenaries in Zaire and Angola.

Rolling upright, he continued his patrol, and when the radio began to squawk with indignant German naval demands, he switched frequencies again.

Within five minutes, he reached the first of the platforms, *Bahnsteig Sechs*. Passing within a mile of it, he did not devote much of his attention to activity aboard the platform. He had seen them before, and they all looked alike.

Instead, he scanned the skies and the seas for intruders. That was the job, and the job, as always, was boring. Once in a while, he would see a few fishing boats out of Greenland, but unless they approached within a couple miles of a platform, they were left alone.

Only military vessels and aircraft of any nation were to be challenged, and though Zeigman often hoped for such a confrontation, none had yet materialized.

The routine route around the sea-based rigs was accomplished in twelve minutes. He saw two whales sounding in the slate-gray seas, moving toward the south. He called *Bahnsteig Drei* with the information that a large iceberg was drifting in their direction. From March through September, the ice pack spawned large and small chunks of ice, and three huge seagoing tugboats were stationed in the area to nudge them away from a platform if necessary.

The platforms on the ice were in a ragged row that stretched over seventy kilometers in distance from east to west and were about twelve kilometers from the edge of the ice shelf. They were visible from a few miles away because of the slight mist that seemed to hang over them, frequently pluming up and away with the wind. Zeiman assumed that heat converters within the domes created the mist.

The ice pack was not smooth. Pressure ridges jutted from it, in long, jagged replicas of lightning. Some reached an altitude of several hundred feet. Crevasses that could swallow whole airplanes, much less a *schneekatze*, a snow cat, belonging to one of the rigs, appeared abruptly and unexpectedly. Pollutants from the atmosphere grayed the surface and took the edge off the whiteness, but the sun's reflection was still dazzling, and Zeigman kept his tinted visor lowered.

He followed the row eastward, away from the storm brewing in the west. If there was much wind in that storm, to fling the snow crystals about, the ice-bound wells would be whited out. A helicopter from one of the resupply ships was landing at *Bahnsteig Neunzehn*. The men at *Bahnsteig Vierundzwanzig* were engaged in a volleyball game outside the dome, on the helicopter pad, and he waggled his wings at them as he shot overhead. He would not report the frivolity. Zeigman did not give a damn what they did on the rigs. Oil was oil, and only when it was refined into JP-4 to feed his engine did he pay attention to it.

As the last well passed under him, Zeigman advanced his throttle and pulled the nose up. Dialing the Nav/Com radio into the air group's net, he triggered the transmit button. "Pelican One, this is Tiger Leader."

"Go ahead, Tiger Leader," the tanker pilot told him.

"Pelican One, in four minutes, my fuel state will be critical. Where are you?"

The pilot gave him the coordinates. "You are always near critical, Tiger Leader. You should plan better."

"Ah, but it is more fun being on the edge," Zeigman told him. And it was.

Four

McKenna was asleep in his office when a none-too-gentle slap on the shoulder awakened him. He rocked against the restraint encircling his waist.

Looking to his left, he saw Pearson's face in the gap between the curtains that closed off his office cell.

"I've got the map ready, McKenna."

Since the time McKenna had made a playful pass at her two years before, Pearson had come to regard the differences in their military ranks as insignificant. McKenna cared less about military titles and military courtesy, except where it was absolutely necessary, but he wished that she would call him something besides "McKenna." It was always said in a flat, neutral tone.

He brought his left hand to shoulder level, cocked it at the wrist, and waved at her. "Hi, Red."

She liked that nickname a little less than he liked "McKenna," from her. Wrinkling her nose at him, she said, "Wake up and come on out here."

Sighing, he pulled the Velcro straps loose, pushed out of the cubicle, and followed her graceful arc into the command center. Overton was waiting beside the console under the viewing port. A blowsily white view of Antarctica was showing.

The other side of the world was displayed on the main

console screen, one of seven screens available to the command center. Three technicians hovered, monitoring the consoles.

Pearson's map of the Greenland Sea now had green circles representing each of the wells, and inside each circle was a number.

"We don't know," she said, "how the German's are identifying the drilling platforms, but I've given each a number, according to when it went into operation."

There didn't seem to be a pattern, McKenna noticed. The rigs on the ice had been emplaced last. Their numbers ran from sixteen to twenty-four, but not in order. Sixteen was in the middle of the line, twenty-three on the east end, and twenty-four on the west end. So much for the vaunted German sense of organization.

The offshore wells were just as muddled, with number one in the center of the irregular cluster.

"Couldn't you have renumbered a little, just to make it easier?" he asked.

"Your logical mind can't handle this, Colonel Mc-Kenna?"

In front of the general, McKenna got a title.

"We'll do it your way," he said.

"Thank you."

Overton told him, "One of the problems we have, Kevin, is that our standard satellite coverage is naturally more concerned with Europe, Asia, and the Barents and North seas. Only sporadically do we get a pass over the Greenland and Arctic seas, and even then, we haven't been particularly watchful. The data we have on hand is limited."

"You're certain these wells are being overprotected, Amy?" McKenna asked. He still wasn't sure that her suspicions were well-founded.

"From the information I've gathered, *I* am. And NORAD is similarly intrigued."

"Okay, point made. What do you want?"

With a clear-polished nail, she traced a route over the screen of the monitor. "We want close-up shots of at least three of the platforms, and we want infrared and low-light film of all of them. There are also naval ships in the area, and you should get as many of them as you can."

"We have any ideas on the shipping?"

"The long-distance photos we have suggest a few armed vessels and some supply ships. The missile cruiser was identified by its deck and funnel layout as the *Hamburg*. I'm going to check on her assignments through the covert channels."

"And the patrol aircraft?"

Overton answered. "After we backtracked through the old photos, we suspect they originate out of New Amsterdam Air Force Base. They're Panavia Tornados and, occasionally, a pair of Eurofighters or Dornier 228s. Amsterdam has four air wings assigned to it, Kevin, all of them equipped with similar aircraft, so we can't pinpoint the squadron or group. If you happen to run into a plane, get its tail number, would you?"

"Sure thing, Jim."

"Anything else, Amy? Want me to bring back a pizza and a six-pack?"

Her pale green eyes studied him, perhaps with a trace of amusement in them, but it didn't transfer to her mouth. "Just the photos, Colonel."

"I'll go get my Brownie. Oh, Jim? Conover and Dimatta are due back in a few hours. Would you tell Will to stand down and Frank to prepare for a second run on the wells? We'll get some backup on whatever I find."

"Will do, Kevin," the general said.

After the hatch spun and locked behind McKenna, Pearson tapped the keyboard and cleared the screen.

She could feel General Overton studying her. Pearson knew he was a competent judge of people, and he was constantly on the lookout for signs of abrasiveness between members of his crew. In the confines of *Themis*, teamwork was essential. Arguments between station personnel did not contribute to the mission, and if the warring factions got out of hand, Overton would ship the least necessary person earth side immediately. He had done it before.

She was absolutely certain that the general considered McKenna more necessary than he did her. Though she liked the commander, and she thought he liked her, Overton wouldn't allow anything to interfere with the command assigned to him.

Pearson knew he was waiting—had been waiting for months—for her to say something about her dislike for McKenna. And then, boom, she would be on the next Mako flight to Peterson.

She wasn't going to give Overton the chance, or McKenna the satisfaction, of getting rid of her. In every position she had ever held, she had had to stand her ground, fight for her rights, and she wasn't giving up, now.

She had analyzed her reaction to the squadron commander before. It wasn't that McKenna was unattractive. The lines in his face, the pilot's squint of his eyes, gave him the appearance of maturity and made him rather ruggedly handsome. His dark hair, though too long, seemed to always stay in place, even in the zero-gravity environment. And yet, there were other things that bothered her. His playful attitude in serious situations jangled her nerves and contradicted the maturity she expected him to display. She knew he was a highly competent pilot, and that competence was sometimes reflected in the deadly slate gray of his eyes. There was a subtle arrogance to the man, as if he knew too well his own capability. He *expected* things to happen as he planned, just because *he* was in control.

And the men in his squadron thought he was god. They would do anything, legal or illegal, for him. That was what irritated her most, his loyal following. She was also expected to be a fan. Besides herself, no one else seemed to recognize that he was just a man.

A man who was supposed to be a professional, just as she was a professional. Recognizing her contribution. Staying at arm's length, maintaining the professional distance. Not patting her on the fanny when he felt like it.

"Are you all right, Amy?"

She looked up from the blank screen. "I'm fine, General. Just getting organized."

Pearson smiled at him, then pushed off from the console, floated across the center, and entered the communications compartment, the "Radio Shack."

T. Sgt. Donna Amber, one of the three women on board, had the shift, and she was anchored before the primary console, monitoring the circuits in use aboard the station. Amber was a mousy woman—brown hair clipped short, brown eyes, tiny. She was also amazingly proficient at the complex radio, video, radar, and computer console.

From one speaker issued the sounds of some hard rock group.

"Do you want to kill that, Donna?"

"Sure thing, Colonel." She depressed a keypad, and the high-pitched guitar was silenced. "We have work to do?"

"Yes. First, we want to tap into NATO."

"Comm net, or data base?"

"The data base," Pearson told her.

Amber checked the readout mounted on the wall that gave her the station's celestial coordinates. "Okay, I can get there through a Rhyolite II channel."

Themis had access to a wide variety of communications networks and computer data bases, utilizing microwave, VHF, and UHF relays in several satellite systems. Commonly, they used the Air Force Satellite Communications System (AFSATCOM) or the Critical Communications Net (CRITICOM), but frequently, because of their orbit characteristics, they could lose contact with those systems. Then, the station linked up through other satellites, such as the Rhyolite. This particular link, though Pearson no longer thought about the details, went through the Rhyolite at 22,300 miles above the earth, to an American DSCS III at 500 miles, to a NATO IIIB, then to the microwave antenna complex outside Brussels, Belgium.

Although *Themis*—1st Aerospace Wing, and its 1st Aerospace Squadron operated under the Space Command of the U.S. Air Force, the role of *Themis* was multipurpose, responding to the needs of many agencies, and the station had access to NATO, CIA, National Security Agency, Defense Intelligence Agency, FBI, Treasury, and State data bases. Almost everyone aboard the station had cryptographic security clearances of the highest order.

While the sergeant set up the communication links, Pearson pulled herself into position in front of a secondary computer screen.

When the screen told her she was connected to the North Atlantic Treaty Organization Military Data Base, she entered an access code that brought up a menu:

1) GENERAL INFORMATION
2) PERSONNEL INFORMATION (RESTRICTED ACCESS)
3) MILITARY INFORMATION (RESTRICTED ACCESS)

She tapped "3."

1) PUBLIC RELATIONS OFFICE
2) NATO INFORMATION (RESTRICTED ACCESS)
3) WARSAW PACT INFORMATION (RESTRICTED ACCESS)
4) COMMUNICATIONS CONTROL (RESTRICTED ACCESS)
5) NUCLEAR CONTROL (RESTRICTED ACCESS)
6) AIR CONTROL (RESTRICTED ACCESS)
7) NAVAL FORCES (RESTRICTED ACCESS)
8) GROUND FORCES (RESTRICTED ACCESS)
9) INTELLIGENCE OFFICE (RESTRICTED ACCESS)

She keyed the number "2." Pearson was still somewhat

amazed at the fact that unified Germany was still a member of NATO, but knew that it was primarily because of the German distrust of the Soviet Union. And though NATO had been dramatically downsized in forces, influence, and role, it still operated an extensive intelligence collection function.

And here she was, snooping in the confidential data of a supposed ally.

She entered two more seven-digit codes, allowing her access to all but the most highly classified data files. Using the *Hamburg* as her key, she called up all of the available data on the ship, its current assignment, and its primary officers. When she saw that it had been designated as the flagship of Adm. Gerhard Schmidt, she called up his file, also.

She stored the information in the *Themis* mainframe computer, cleared the screen, and went searching for data on New Amsterdam Air Force Base. She called up the files concerning the base's air units, commanders, and role and mission, then stored that in her own machine.

Pearson checked for a file on Bremerhaven Petroleum Corporation, but there was nothing there.

"All right, Donna, let's go to the CIA, then the DIA."

"Coming up, Colonel."

From both agencies, Pearson extracted similar information, though again, nothing on Bremerhaven. She supposed that General Brackman was requesting an investigation. Later, she would run a comparison program against all of her files, eliminate duplicate information, and come up with comprehensive files. After she culled those, she would print out a short, but complete briefing report.

"Is that it, Colonel?"

Pearson thought for a moment. "Do you suppose, Donna, that you could get into the German Defense Command's computer?"

"I doubt it," Amber said, "but it'd sure be fun to try."

Pearson wondered why everything had to be fun.

* * *

70

Felix Eisenach's helicopter landed at the Bremerhaven naval facility at four o'clock, half an hour past its scheduled arrival time. The Messerschmitt-Bolkow-Blohm B0105 was olive drab, marked only with the blue, red, and yellow German flag and, below it, the yellow flag with two stars denoting a *general-major.* The slate-gray MBB B0105 parked next to it carried the single-starred flag of a navy admiral.

Bremerhaven was a lively, buzzing port, swarming with civilian shipping. Panamanian, Norwegian, Kuwaiti, British, and Soviet freighters and tankers lined the docks and crept slowly in and out of the mouth of the Weser River. A Japanese ship disgorged multihued little cars at one of the large piers.

In the naval yards, thirty-four ships were moored out or made fast to the quays, side by side, four and five deep. Launches and supply tenders poked among them like hungry water beetles. Shore-based cranes waddled back and forth on their rails, trundling cargo nets filled to capacity with crates and boxes. Sailors and civilian workers scurried about on important errands. Eisenach noted with some satisfaction that many of the ships displayed fresh gray paint, sharp edges, the newest radar antennas. In some report he had read, the German High Command had boasted of a 30 percent increase in naval units over the past five years. Most of the new vessels fell into medium-displacement ranges—assault transports, helicopter ships, destroyers, and small missile frigates. There were two new missile cruisers, the *Hamburg* and the *Stuttgart,* and two new submarines. The cruisers and the submarines were powered by nuclear reactors.

As the rotors slowed, Eisenach pushed open the door and stepped down from the small helicopter. He ducked his head, held his peaked cap in place, and walked toward the waiting sedan.

Kapitän Werner Niels, Schmidt's aide, climbed out of the car and saluted.

71

Returning the salute, Eisenach raised an eyebrow.

"The admiral arrived earlier, General Eisenach, and went on to the officers' club. He awaits you there."

"Very well, *Kapitän*. Let us join him." Eisenach slipped into the rear seat, and Niels went around to get in on the other side.

Admiral Schmidt was frequently too independent for Eisenach's tastes. The man could have waited a half hour for his commander to arrive. But no, Schmidt had been in command of ships for a long time, and he was as accustomed to making his own decisions as he was impatient. And Eisenach suspected that Schmidt felt some aversion to reporting to an air force general officer.

Perhaps, also, Schmidt was somewhat frustrated. He had wanted command of the 1st Fleet, but had been cajoled and threatened into accepting command of the *Dritte Marinekraft*. Though he commanded eighteen major vessels, Schmidt did not consider the task force's mission as vital as Eisenach did.

The driver pulled away from the helicopter pad located on the quay and found his way through the labyrinth of warehouses and fabrication plants that crowded upon the docks. Sailors came to attention and saluted as they went by. Toward the back of the base, they passed parade grounds, large brick barracks, and administrative buildings. Elm and oak trees lined the streets, and the grass plots around structures were closely clipped.

The officer's club was solidly built of red brick and was new. Eisenach and Niels got out and walked up the pristine sidewalk to the double glass doors, the *kapitän* holding one of them for him.

Schmidt was waiting for him in one of the private meeting rooms, a stein of lager in front of him. The admiral often boasted that he drank only beer. He was a large, florid-faced man in his early sixties. His steel gray hair was shorn to almost nonexistence, and his blue eyes were unwavering. The skin of his face was firm, but his ears jutted outward from his skull like semaphores.

"Well, Felix, you have finally arrived."

Eisenach was not going to apologize to a subordinate for being late. "And Gerhard, you have started without me."

Schmidt smiled. "I have been at sea for twelve days. I was thirsty. I am also hungry. Are you ready for dinner?"

Eisenach looked at his watch. "It is early, but yes, we can eat."

Schmidt nodded to Niels, and the aide left the room, closing the door behind him.

The general took one of the castered and upholstered chairs opposite Schmidt. He fished in his pocket for a package of American Marlboros and lit one. Schmidt shoved an ashtray across the table toward him.

"All right, Gerhard. You asked for this meeting."

"Right to the point?" Schmidt said. "No chattering over the sauerbraten?"

"I must return to Berlin immediately after dinner."

"All right." Schmidt sat up in his chair and leaned his elbows on the table. His eyes became more serious than normal, and they were normally serious. "I am going to request a transfer to First Fleet."

"You'll end up in a staff job, Gerhard."

"Perhaps, but only for a while."

The door opened and Niels came in with another stein for Schmidt and a Scotch and water for Eisenach. Werner Niels's memory was very good, Eisenach thought. He tasted it and guessed that it was his preferred Glenlivet.

After the aide left again, Eisenach asked, "What brings this on, Gerhard?"

"Nothing brings it on. My disenchantment has always been there. The navy does not work well under an air force command that cannot distinguish the pointed end of a ship from the ass-end. For God's sakes, Felix, all we do is sail back and forth like an endless clothesline. My tactical and strategic training exercises are farces. Morale is slipping badly."

"I should think your men would be extremely happy," Eisenach said. "Of your sixteen surface vessels, four are ro-

73

tated into port for two weeks at a time. That is a lot of shore leave."

"Leisure time that deteriorates the level of readiness," the admiral said. "I am a realistic man, Felix. I do not embellish my reports to my superiors. The Third Naval Force is not a crackerjack unit. It is falling apart, and your planning group in Berlin does not allow me to do anything about it. They think they have airplanes to boss around. The mission of standing sentinel to a bunch of oil wells is not awe-inspiring to my ship commanders or their personnel."

"That accounts for this morning's incident?" Eisenach asked.

Schmidt snickered. "The idiot in the Tornado? Yes, he caught us by surprise. And do you know why?"

"You will tell me."

"That is damned correct. Your planning staff has absolutely no concept of naval operations. They keep us strung out in single file, like that clothesline I mentioned, when I should have my ships clustered in battle groups. Jesus Christ! You can't have a cruiser like the *Hamburg* exposed like it was today. I should have had destroyers on the flanks."

Eisenach nodded, but reluctantly.

"It would have served you right if that Tornado pilot had punched us with a Kormoran antiship missile."

"What do you suggest, Gerhard?"

"I suggest I go back to the real navy."

Eisenach studied the navy man for a long moment before speaking. "Gerhard, you and I are not friends. Perhaps that is impossible. However, I respect you as a military man, and I do not want to lose you. If I were to remove the planning group from the chain of command—you would report directly to me—would that change your mind?"

Schmidt leaned back in his chair, studying Eisenach's face. He took a long drag from his stein.

"I want to change the makeup of the force."

"In what way?"

"I want the *Stuttgart* and another missile frigate. I'll keep

74

eight destroyers and release the rest. I'll keep the subs, but I'll put one at a time toward more fruitful training."

"To what end, Gerhard?"

"I would create four three-ship surface battle groups. We will not often be in port, for my detached groups will be sent off on training sessions. I must broaden their thinking, and their horizons, Felix."

"And that will keep you on the job?"

"It's either that, General, or I tell my ship captains that they're not really oil wells."

With several short blasts of the nose thrusters, McKenna drifted Delta Blue backward out of its hangar and watched as the doors folded to the closed position like the petals of a tired rose.

The red warning strobes mounted on the spokes and at four points around the hub blinked clearly at him. They were only activated during departures and arrivals.

The earth looked inviting, rosily lit along a line from Leningrad westward. The dark side melted into the blackness of space, defined primarily by the stars it blotted out. The moon was an eerie white disk far down on his right.

When the aerospace craft had cleared the space station by several hundred yards, Munoz said, "Okay, Snake Eyes, flip her ass over."

McKenna chuckled. "Roger, Tiger. Flipping."

Using the hand controller, now connected to the thrusters, McKenna gave the MakoShark a nose-down command. Spurts of nitrogen gas spiked the vacuum, and the craft slowly turned over until the tail was pointing in the direction of travel. The cockpit was head-down to the earth.

He pulled back gently on the controller, igniting the thrusters, to stop the roll.

"Lookin' good, *amigo*. I'm gonna hook into the brain now."

McKenna checked the HUD. The readings looked good, though the cockpit temperature was lower than it should be. He nudged the slide switch to raise it. The velocity showed him Mach 26.2. Flat moving out, he thought, though the only sense of movement came from watching the growing gap between the MakoShark and *Themis*, which was now on the bottom edge of the rearview screen.

The primary screen displayed the randomly appearing numbers that Munoz was programming into the computer. The computer did, in fact, remember typically used coordinates for returns to Peterson, Jack Andrews, or Merlin air bases, updating them automatically for the position of the earth at the time of departure.

"Got any idea at all where you'd like to end up, Snake Eyes?"

"I think it'd be nice if we hit a hundred thousand feet somewhere in the vicinity of the Barents Sea. Maybe even the middle of it.

"You want to make the first run over the ice?"

"To the west, yeah."

"That's not what Amy-baby had in mind."

"Amy-baby's not flying it."

"Good goddamned point, *jefe*. The Barents Sea, it is."

The screen flickered with more numbers as Munoz plotted the reentry path and entered the variable weight data—pilots, cargo, pylon loads. The computer insisted on knowing, within certain tolerances, the center of gravity and the total weight of the MakoShark before it finalized the numbers. Since none of the variety of components interchanged on a MakoShark had weight aboard the space station, every object placed on board had to be checked against the master weight file on the station's computer. The mass of a cargo or munitions pod, a camera, a film pack was double-checked against the file, then fed to the MakoShark's on-board computer.

When his data was entered, Munoz ran the test program, which compared all of the new numbers with what the computer knew was possible. The machine accepted the new information congenially by flashing green letters: "ACCEPTED."

"Start up procedure."

"Ready, Tiger."

They went through the rocket start checklist, up to the point of ignition, then McKenna turned it over to computer control.

In the upper-left corner of his CRT, new blue lettering appeared:

REENTRY PATH ACCEPTED
REENTRY SEQUENCE INITIATED
TIME TO RETRO FIRE: 0.12.43

"Shit," McKenna said. "Twelve minutes."

"Hey, *compadre,* that ain't bad. We've had to wait over an hour before."

In calculating the duration of retro-rocket bursts, the angle of attack into the atmosphere, and the trajectory to the desired point on earth, the computer also had to determine at what time the reentry program was to begin. The MakoSharks, however, had a distinct advantage over the Space Shuttles, in that they had power available after returning to the atmosphere. It allowed them a great deal more flexibility in reentry scheduling. They had many more windows of opportunity open to them.

McKenna punched the communications button for *Themis.* "Delta Blue to Alpha. We've got retro burn in one-two-point-four-one."

"Alpha copies," General Overton said. "Have a nice night, Delta Blue."

"Colonel Pearson there?"

"I'm here, Delta Blue."

"Get this, Amy. Twenty-four, twenty-two, twenty-one, seventeen, sixteen, eighteen, nineteen, twenty, twenty-two, fifteen, twelve, ten, nine, thirteen, six, fourteen, eight, seven, two, five, three, four, eleven, one."

"Very good, Colonel. You memorized the order."

"Told you I could do it."

"Hey, wait a minute," Pearson said, "That's backward."

"Delta Blue out."

Pearson called several times in the next five minutes, then gave up.

Overton called, too. "Alpha to Delta Blue."

"Go Alpha."

"You've changed the op?"

"Fuel savings," McKenna professed.

"Roger, confirm fuel conservation."

On the intercom, Munoz said, "Snake Eyes, we ain't savin' shit."

"I know, Tiger, but it irritates the IO."

"That ain't the way to get into her jumpsuit, *gringo.*"

"I don't want to get into her jumpsuit," McKenna lied.

Actually, he had decided to fly the ice first for a particular reason. Despite her stealth characteristics, the MakoShark was vulnerable to the naked eye when seen against a light background, like blue sky or white ice. A storm had passed through the target area around noon, but conditions were now clear, and in the summer, the northern regions did not become fully dark. If, by some chance, a German patrol plane was up by the time Delta Blue made its low-level run, there was a possibility of detection. McKenna wanted the higher-risk portion of the flight out of the way, first.

At thirty seconds to burn, McKenna tightened his straps and double-checked the oxy/nitro fittings. He snuggled his helmet down and rotated his shoulders against the gray-blue environmental suit. The suits they wore were considerably advanced over the EVA suit in which Armstrong sauntered on the moon's surface. The fabric was a combination of Kevlar, silicon, and plastic, very tear-resistant and very flexible. When inflated, there was less than an inch of space between the fabric and the skin in most places. It depended for some people on the amount of food intake. Frank Dimatta had been refitted for new environmental suits twice, and McKenna had warned him to watch his weight. In the pressurized cockpits, the suits were not inflated, but they would automatically fill if the cockpit seals failed. The helmet-to-suit fitting was comprised of a pair of collars with a series of meshed grooves, allowing almost full freedom in head rotation.

"Four, three, two, one," Munoz intoned.

The CRT countdown readout went to zero.

McKenna knew the rocket motors were firing from the vibration in the craft's frame and from the thrust indicators on the HUD. The thrust on each motor climbed rapidly to 100 percent.

Themis slid off the rearview screen as white fire encroached from each side of the screen.

The Mach numbers started to dribble off.

The burn lasted for two-and-a-quarter minutes.

At Mach 20, the computer flipped the MakoShark over once again so they were facing forward, but the angle of attack into the atmosphere would not be nose down. Like the Space Shuttle Orbiters, the MakoSharks pancaked into the heavier soup of the atmosphere. The HUD reported the correct angle of attack, 40 degrees.

The leading edges of the wings, the nose, the pylons when they were mounted, and the nose cones of exterior ordnance or pods were composed of a second skin combining reinforced carbon-carbon, Nomex felt, and a ceramic alloy that resisted temperatures that rose to 2700 degrees Fahrenheit on the leading edges of the wings. Additionally, the nose cone and the wing leading edges contained an arterial network of cooling tubes through which supercooled fluids were pumped. The system had had very few failures, and none of those fatal, and McKenna thought it considerably superior to the Space Shuttle's individual tiles.

Half an hour later, at ninety miles of altitude, McKenna felt the first dragging fingers of atmosphere pulling at the MakoShark. Two red lights in the lower-left corner of the HUD indicated that the computer had begun pumping coolant through the heat shields, as well as initiating cockpit air conditioning.

He watched as the exterior temperature sensors began reporting the effects of aerodynamic heating. The skin temperature on the top side climbed to 450 degrees Fahrenheit. Leading edges were already near 700 degrees.

Munoz transmitted the message to *Themis*. "Alpha, Delta Blue. We're goin' black."

"Copy, Delta Blue."

When the heat-shield temperatures exceeded 2300 degrees, the surrounding atmosphere was ionized, resulting in a blackout of communications.

In the cockpit, McKenna felt the heat, but it wasn't entirely uncomfortable. Kind of like hanging around the pool on a summer day in Aspen. More disconcerting was the red-orange film that enveloped the cockpit canopy. He lost all visual contact with his black world.

Four minutes later, as the windscreen began to clear, working down through the colors from burnt orange to amber to yellow, Munoz called *Themis*. "Alpha, Delta Blue. Altitude two-four-zero thousand feet, velocity Mach twelve-point-six, fourteen minutes to objective."

"Copy, Delta Blue."

McKenna had lost track of the number of times he had made the reentry—well over 350 times—but passing through the blackout still made the blood pump and the adrenaline flow. It took several moments to come down from the high.

Coming out of the blackout, the computer put the nose down a trifle, to 32 degrees.

When the speed was down to Mach 6 and the altitude to 125,000 feet, McKenna said, "I'm going to take it back, Tiger."

"You damned barnstormers are all alike. Seat-of-the-pants bullshit."

That was true to a great extent. McKenna started flying because he liked to fly. Though he had come to trust the computers most of the time, going along for the ride still wasn't the same.

He said a silent thank-you to the computer, then canceled its control.

Dropping the nose to maintain his speed and glide,

McKenna began a wide, wide turn from his heading of 84 degrees to due north.

"That's Moscow off the port wing," Munoz said.

"Good night, Moscow."

The march of night had crossed the British Isles and most of Greenland now, and the lights of Moscow were orderly at eleven-thirty. McKenna could pick out the ring roads. He kept the city off the left wing as he made his turn.

Far ahead, he saw a smudge of light that would be Archangel, on a bay of the White Sea, and just over a hundred miles short of the Arctic Circle.

Beyond the city, the horizon was still bathed in vague light. There wasn't much darkness in northern latitudes at this time of year. In fact, to the residents of Sweden, Norway, and Greenland, the sun did not go up and down. It descended sideways, barely touching the horizon before beginning a slanted ascent. The MakoShark's stealthy traits were negated to some degree by the geography of the objective.

Munoz busied himself with system checks of the two pods they were carrying, to make certain that the heat of passage into the atmosphere had not damaged either the infrared and standard cameras or the film cartridges.

"How do they look?" McKenna asked.

"Green lights all the way, Snake Eyes. I'm ready if you are."

Over the northern end of the Barents Sea, McKenna started his turbojets and dropped to a thousand feet of altitude before turning westward.

Munoz brought up Pearson's map of the area on the screen, with the well sites noted by yellow dots. On the map, McKenna's north was almost exactly 270 degrees. Svalbard Island was a mass of green on the left side of the screen.

"No shippin' this side of the island," Munoz said. "Radar's tellin' me there's a dozen ships on the other side."

"Let's see them, Tiger."

On his panel screen, eleven red dots appeared. They moved slowly, and most of them cruised around the perimeter of the offshore well cluster. Two seemed to be patrolling the south edge of the ice pack.

"I don't see any aircraft, Tiger."

"Nor do I, *jefe.*"

"All right. I'm going right down the top of the string on the ice. We'll coast it at four hundred knots and a thousand feet of altitude. On the last two, numbers twenty and twenty-three, I'll put it on the deck."

"Go, babe."

McKenna climbed a few hundred feet to pass over the small island of Northeast Land, then settled back to a level flight at 1000 feet. He lined up with the first well, number twenty-four, using the map on the screen, then looked up through the windshield.

The ice appeared very rugged. Pressure ridges and chasms pocked the surface, but gave him some landmarks. The light was perhaps equivalent to a sixty-watt bulb burning in a very large room, and the surface was a jigsaw puzzle of light and dark patches.

One minute later, McKenna saw a red strobe light. No one had said the domes were identified by beacons. He'd rib Pearson about that.

The dome came up fast. It was geodesic in construction, large triangles fastened together, so that it was a series of flat planes, rather than a true globe. It was larger than he expected, maybe a couple hundred feet in diameter. That would make it twenty stories tall.

"Bingo," Munoz said. "Got it."

The next six wells passed quickly under them, McKenna counting them off, checking the map for a heading on the next one. At one point, he glanced out the left side of his canopy and thought he might have seen the running lights of a ship, some ten miles away.

After well nineteen passed under, Munoz said, "Put her down, Snake Eyes."

He bled off some speed and let the MakoShark descend to 400 feet. McKenna wanted some clearance over the domes, and he had noted that some of the pressure ridges had punched their way a couple hundred feet above the surface.

Well number twenty had floodlights blazing on the helicopter pad, and there was a small chopper sitting in the middle of the marked "X." Fortunately, there were no people working outside on the pad to watch the silent intruder whisk over them.

McKenna retarded his throttles as they passed over, to further reduce the sound of the engines at the low altitude. As soon as the well appeared in the rearview screen, he advanced the throttles again.

They got the same low, slow shots of well number twenty-two, then McKenna banked into a tight, climbing turn and headed south toward well fifteen.

At 1,500 feet, they approached one of the red dots. McKenna felt a little easier over the dark waters of the Greenland Sea. A ship or an aircraft would have to be in a very good position to spot the MakoShark against the pale sky or the ice now behind them.

The red dot got closer.

"I'm gonna get him," Munoz said.

The screen went to infrared for a moment, then to the night-vision mode, then back to the map projection.

"It's a destroyer, Snake Eyes. Wish I had a data bank aboard."

The U.S. naval commands had access to data bases that stored the unique sonar signatures of vessel propellers and could frequently identify exact ships by their sound. Occasionally, the infrared heat signatures could also be identified. The MakoSharks did have a limited data bank of radar and infrared signatures, but they were restricted to aircraft.

"Well number fifteen coming up," McKenna said. "We'll get all of them at a thousand feet, and take our close-up of number one."

The circular flight path they followed in order to photograph each well took eleven minutes to cover. Munoz snapped hundreds of photos of the wells, and he took shots of four ships. One of them was the missile cruiser.

In all, they spent seventeen minutes coasting through the area, and McKenna felt certain they had not been seen. As soon as they had their close-ups of number one, he began a steady climb to the south, gradually adding on speed.

The MakoShark cracked through the sonic barrier at 20,000 feet, 200 miles off the coast of Norway.

"You keep this heading, Snake Eyes, we could put down at Jack Andrews for a couple beers."

"Amy wants us right back. She's going to develop these herself."

"Shit. You didn't promise her, did you?"

Munoz knew that McKenna kept his promises. He just avoided making promises wherever he could.

"No, but I told Overton we'd do a quick turnaround."

"Ah, damn, *amigo*. I'm just real thirsty."

No liquor or beer of any kind was allowed aboard the space station. Overton strictly enforced that rule.

"Next time, buddy," McKenna told him.

The instrument panel screen was displaying the 200-mile radar sweep, and by the time they passed over Copenhagen at 50,000 feet, it was busy with commercial night flights between European cities. Most of those flights were at 20,000 feet or less. Some military flights were much higher, but McKenna wasn't paying much attention to them.

"Hey, Snake Eyes."

"Yeah."

"I've been watchin' New Amsterdam. A flight of two just took off from there."

"Got a heading on them."

"Goin' north."

"Suppose they have tail numbers?"

"Damn betcha."

McKenna retarded the throttles, pulled back on the hand controller, and put the MakoShark into a vertical climb. As soon as the speed drained away, he went on over onto his back, then rolled upright. He put the nose down and began searching the screen for his bogies.

"Wish to hell-and-gone we were armed," Munoz said.

Five

Col. Pyotr Volontov stood at attention in front of the general's desk. He could have been a prototype for the ideal Soviet officer. Almost six feet tall, he was slim, blond, and blue-eyed. The planes of his face had hard angles that reflected the overhead fluorescent lights. More than that, he was an intelligent man, and a thinking one. He did not often bow to impetuous and blind authority. Volontov kept his eyes fixed firmly on the photograph of the President mounted on the wall behind Sheremetevo.

Though Gen. Vitaly Sheremetevo struggled to maintain the same image as his subordinate, his age of sixty-two was catching up with him. His hair was much thinner and graying rapidly. The waist was thicker, though still successfully disguised by his uniform jackets. Less well disguised was his biting commentary for incompetence whenever he came upon it. Unlike the younger man, Sheremetevo, as deputy commander in chief of the Soviet air forces, was allowed to make whatever comments he might like to make, as well as to expect immediate reform.

Among the general's responsibilities was the PVO Strany. The START agreements had not detracted from his forces since they were so clearly defensive in nature. The PVO had over 5,000 early-warning radars, 2,500 interceptor aircraft, and 50,000 surface-to-air missiles at its disposal.

Colonel Volontov was also at Sheremetevo's disposal.

The colonel commanded the 5th Interceptor Wing, comprised of MiG-29s and located at Leningrad. Sheremetevo had followed Volontov's career with greater than normal interest. More than once, he had quietly, and unknown to the man, intervened on Volontov's behalf when the colonel had balked at ridiculous orders and come close to insubordination. Sheremetevo did not want such a promising officer shunted off into some oblivious air force job.

"You may stand at ease, Pyotr Mikhailovich."

The use of the patronymic caused just a flicker of surprise in the colonel's blue eyes. He relaxed only a trifle, locking his wrists behind his back.

"We have met but once before," Sheremetevo said. "I gave you some decoration or another."

"I remember, Comrade General. Very likely undeserved."

"On the contrary. I do not pass out medals that are undeserved." Sheremetevo himself was a Hero of the Soviet Union. He wore the honor with pride.

"Pyotr Mikhailovich," the general continued, "what is the condition of the Fifth Interceptor Wing?"

"It is excellent, General. Of my twelve aircraft, eleven are currently airworthy. The morale and capability of my pilots is not surpassed by any unit in the air force."

"Are you boasting, Colonel?"

"I am stating a fact, General Sheremetevo."

The deputy commander suspected that that was true.

"Your wing would be prepared, then, for a special exercise?"

The blue eyes enlarged by several millimeters. "In fact, Comrade General, my pilots would welcome a deviation in their routine."

"And you?"

"And myself, General. I always support a need for training, but the current schedules are . . . boring and repetitious."

"So you alter them?"

"Only in small ways, General." Volontov offered a brief smile.

"Very well. The exercise is to be called "Arctic Waste." The Fifth Interceptor Wing is temporarily assigned directly to my office. You will report only to me."

Volontov nodded his acceptance and did not betray any curiosity, but Sheremetevo thought that the commander was pleased.

"I will see that an additional two MiG-29s are made available to your wing by tomorrow morning, so that you will be at full aircraft strength, with one reserve airplane. Two reserves, if your twelfth interceptor is repaired. Additionally, two Ilyushin Il-76 tankers and two MiG-25 reconnaissance aircraft will be attached to your command."

"This begins to sound quite interesting, General Sheremetevo."

"But it will be interesting only to ourselves, Pyotr Mikhailovich. You are not to relate the details of the exercise to anyone. Is that clear?"

"Absolutely."

"Air controllers in the affected area will also be under my command, and not fully aware of the objectives. Beyond them, no one is to know the nature of the exercise. Should anyone ask you, Colonel, it is simply training in combined aircraft operations."

"As you wish, General."

Volontov's face was a bit more active now, a grim smile in place, the hard, reflective knobs of his cheekbones appearing a bit higher.

"In reality, we are doing a favor for someone."

"For someone in the Politburo, General?"

"For Admiral Hannibal Cross."

Sheremetevo saw the flicker of Volontov's eyes once again as he tried to place the name.

"But General, he is the American chairman of the Joint Chiefs of Staff!"

"Exactly."

Dr. Tracy Calvin floated underneath Mako Two, waiting while the technician opened the hatch into the passenger module. She hung onto one of the payload doors, and her face was radiant, showing no concern about the reentry flight. Her dark hair was cut short, but still drifted about her head, like an errant halo.

She wore the blue jumpsuit that would now become a souvenir of her two weeks in space, performing arcane experiments in the name of her employer, Lilly Pharmaceuticals. The jumpsuit was very well filled.

The technician backed out of the passenger module, holding an environmental suit, then helped her struggle into it. He slipped the helmet over her head and locked it into the suit collar.

When she looked back toward the hangar's control station window, McKenna waved at her. She smiled and waved back, perhaps thinking about other experiments accomplished in zero gravity.

McKenna thought he might miss her for a while. Or maybe even look her up the next time he was earth side.

The suit secured, the technician helped her slide inside the module, then followed her to make certain she was strapped in and all of the connections properly made. When he was done, the hatch closed and locked, he darted around the hangar, releasing the restraining straps from the Mako. The matte-white paint reflected the hangar lights, rather than absorbing them, like its sister. McKenna thought of the Mako as a virgin MakoShark. Pristine and sleek and naive.

Maj. Lynn Haggar and Capt. Ben Olsen, Mako Two's crew, closed their canopies. McKenna figured that sometime in the next month or two, he would take Haggar and Olsen aside and explain the MakoShark to them. They were going to be a good team. McKenna also figured he might have a little trouble convincing generals

Overton and Brackman of the wisdom of putting a female pilot in a position with combat potential. Brackman would make some comment about McKenna increasing the size of his harem, but despite his social reputation, McKenna could be very objective when professional competence was concerned. Lynn Marie Haggar was a hell of a pilot.

The payload doors closed.

First Lt. Polly Tang, the station operator tethered to the console beside McKenna, flipped a toggle to activate the speaker in the hangar. Punching a PA button, she said, "Willy, you want to clear the bay?"

The technician, Willy Dey, gave her a thumbs-up, shoved off the wing, and came zooming through the hatchway. Arresting his flight by grabbing the door frame, he tapped the red square, and the big door swung shut, rotated, and locked down. A green light above the door confirmed the seal.

"Locked and sealed, Lieutenant," the tech called out.

She still double-checked the indicators on her console, then tapped a radio button. "Mako Two, how are your seals?"

"All green, Beta Two."

Polly Tang was Brad Mitchell's chief assistant.

On the console in front of her, a small screen showed a radar readout of the immediate space around *Themis*. The revolving scan lit up a dot on every sweep.

"Mako Two, you've got a HoneyBee inbound. Six-zero-zero miles and closing at two hundred feet per minute."

"We'll dodge it, Beta."

"Ready to clear gas."

"Go."

Tang lifted a protective flap and switched a toggle. She concentrated on the readouts as the atmospheric gas in the hangar was pumped into holding tanks. *Themis* did not waste anything, especially something as precious as its atmosphere. Rather than bleeding the oxygen/nitrogen blend into space, it was pumped under pressure into reserve bladders and held until the next time the hangar was used. McKenna heard the snap of the safety dead-bolts locking the hatchway door as the atmosphere went below the level of livability.

As soon as the readout indicated almost zero pressure and atmospheric content—it never reached zero and they lost some of it—Tang raised another guard flap and inserted her key. Turning the key allowed the circuit to go active. She snapped the toggle switch.

The hangar doors were segmented into eight polyhedrons, the outside edges matching the eight-sided hangar cell. From the center, they began to slowly open outward.

Dull thumps could be heard and felt in the structure when the doors reached their full open position.

"Mako Two, you are cleared for departure."

"Bye-bye, Beta Two. See you in a couple days."

The thrusters on the nose of the Mako flared brightly as the compressed nitrogen hit the vacuum. The craft began to move backward. The thrusters flared again, and Mako Two drifted out of the hangar, Haggar and Olsen both waving.

As soon as the craft cleared the bay, Tang closed the doors, cut the lights in the hangar, and secured her console. She pulled loose the Velcro tether at her belt.

McKenna grinned at her and said, "Now that you've got some free time, Polly . . ."

Her almond eyes smiled at him. She said, "Go away, McKenna."

"Well, hell. I have to keep trying."

"And I appreciate it. I really do. But not in this life-time, huh?"

"How about the next one?"

She smiled as she pushed off the console. "As soon as I get to it, I'll think about it, okay? Right now, I've got to dock a HoneyBee. Go do whatever it is that you do."

As she sailed down the corridor, toward the rocket-docking facilities nearer the rim, McKenna snagged a grab bar and launched himself in the opposite direction. His pursuit of Polly Tang was once again in limbo, but his reputation, and hers, were still intact. They had enjoyed the repartee for nearly two years, since she came aboard. Tang had two children and was married, her husband the chief HoneyBee engineer at Wet Country.

He reached Delta Blue's hangar a minute later and found Shalbot and Sgt. Bert Embry, the ordnance specialist, already waiting for him.

"Goddamn, Colonel" Shalbot said, "this rinky-dink outfit can't even get its pilots to a meeting on time."

"Your watch must be fast," McKenna told him.

"No way." But he checked his wrist.

Embry checked the pressure and atmospheric readouts on the console, then opened the massive door. When the MakoSharks were hangared, the interior hatchways were kept closed and the control station windows were blacked out to keep the Mako crews and the contract visitors innocent of the MakoShark's characteristics.

The three of them pulled themselves through the hatchway and floated below the MakoShark. The two camera pods were still mounted on the inboard pylons, but the access doors to the pods were open, ready for the insertion of new film cartridges.

"All right, Benny. I want to move those pylons and the camera pods to the outboard hard points, then mount two weapons pylons inboard. The long pylon on the starboard and a short pylon on the port side. Same setup on Delta Yellow and Delta Green."

"Delta Red?" Shalbot asked.

"No. We'll keep the reserve ship clean for now."

"You got weapons clearance, Colonel?" Embry asked.

"We have part of it," McKenna told him. Permission to mount weapons had to come from General Brackman at Space Command, and except for a training flight when missiles were fired into the Chad desert or the Celebes Sea, the weapons approval request also followed a laborious route through the JCS and the Oval Office.

As soon as McKenna had returned from his recon flight over the ice, he had called Brackman's office.

"General Brackman is in conference."

"Ah, Milly, my love, my beautiful . . ."

"Can it, Colonel."

"Please."

"That's better. Let me see if I can break in."

Brackman came on the line a minute later. "What's up, Kevin?"

"I want to install some ordnance for these recon flights, General."

"Rationale?"

"I haven't seen the photos yet, but I got a visual on a couple ships and two Tornados. Those people are armed to the teeth."

"But they can't see you."

"We could debate that point," McKenna said. "Summertime, there's a lot of light in the area. Low on the ice, we're vulnerable to overhead aircraft."

Brackman was not afraid to make decisions, one of the reasons that McKenna respected him. "Okay, Kevin. You can mount defensive missiles. You can mount guns. Weapons release is not authorized, but I'll get on the horn to Washington and see if I can get a Presidential directive. It'll be 'fire only if fired upon,' if I get it."

"That's all I'm asking for, General."

Now, McKenna told Embry, "On the left inboard, let's install the gun pod. On the long pylon, I want one Phoenix, one Sidewinder, and two Wasps."

"Nothing like wide-ranging preparation, Colonel."

"Nothing like it, Bert."

Embry pushed off for an intercom station, to order his assistant to start moving pylons and missiles from the storage lockers, and Shalbot began to remove the access panel to the right outboard hard point. Each hard point had a number of alternative electronic hookups, depending on which pylon, and which pod was to be utilized.

McKenna had selected the longer pylon for the missiles in order to have room for the thirteen-foot-long, fifteen-inch-diameter Phoenix, as well as the nine-foot-long Sidewinder and the shorter Wasps. On the shorter pylon, they could mount the gun pod, four Wasp, three Sidewinder, or two Phoenix missiles.

It was, as far as McKenna was concerned, the minimal ordnance load. Despite the heat shielding on the modified missiles, some did not survive the temperatures of reentry. On average, they lost 12 percent of their missiles to heat-caused malfunction. So far, they had never had one of the 20-millimeter M61 rotating barrel guns fail. But McKenna had been in the air force for too many years. He knew there was a first time for everything.

"Colonel McKenna," the PA blared. "Colonel McKenna, please report to the Command Center."

"You set that up, didn't you, Colonel?" Shalbot called to him.

"Set up what, Benny?"

"Get yourself paged, just when the work is supposed to start."

"Damned right." McKenna grinned at him.

It took him four minutes to make the passage, and he found Overton, Pearson, and Sgt. Donna Amber waiting for him, gathered around the primary console below the port.

Amy Pearson had one of his reconnaissance photographs up on the main screen.

"Damn. I'm a pretty good photographer," McKenna said. "The best I know, in fact."

Amber smiled at him.

Pearson said, "The photos are okay."

"Just okay?"

"They'll do. This is the close-up of well number twenty-three. In configuration and dimension, it matches all of the others. The offshore units, of course, are on some-

94

what triangular platforms with three protruding leg mounts. The ice-based units have a similar, though smaller, subplatform, and they are also fitted with three short legs. That allows them to adjust for irregularities in the terrain."

McKenna saw that the platform was actually several feet above the ice, rather than placed directly on it. The one platform leg that was clearly visible in the picture appeared to have a spade-footed base that dug into the ice.

"We used the helicopter on well number twenty as a dimension reference," Pearson said. "It was an MBB B0105, marked for the navy, and it has thirty-two-foot rotors. The helicopter pad is seventy-five feet by seventy-five feet. They could actually get three or four choppers on it with a little juggling.

"On the ice is a twenty-by-twenty shed, which I am assuming contains equipment, storage, and perhaps a couple of tracked vehicles. Except for the leg-adjustment motors and several antennas on top of the dome, all equipment is contained within the dome. The dome has a two hundred and twenty-foot diameter."

Which was close to what McKenna had guessed. "Is that tall enough for a drilling rig, Amy?"

She nodded. "More than enough. I'd guess, however, that the dome skin is particularly thick, for insulation purposes. The antennas on top suggest VLF, UHF, VHF, and FM radio frequency capability. Additionally, the offshore platforms also have radar antennas. From the antenna design, we're estimating something similar to the *High Lark* radar used on the MiG-twenty-three. It would have an effective radius of forty-five miles."

"All of the offshore wells?"

"All of them."

"They're operating on I-Band," McKenna said. "We picked up a few of them on the threat receiver."

"As a guess," General Overton said, "they'd have to stay alert to drifting icebergs. There's a lot of those this time

95

of year. And if they protrude out of the water far enough, radar might help spot them."

"Which suggests that their fleet should include a few ocean-going tugboats," McKenna said.

Pearson agreed. "I would think so, but we haven't seen one as yet."

"Some of those big bergs would be damned hard to divert," Overton said.

"Still, three or four tugs working at the same time could effect enough deviation in course to clear a well," Pearson countered.

"Probably. The wells are all still there."

"Back to the platforms," Pearson said. "On the side of the dome opposite the helicopter pad are five storage tanks, perhaps with ten thousand gallons capacity each. On each well, tank number five vents a white, almost translucent, vapor. I'm going to run a spectrograph on it, but I suspect that the tank contains a heating apparatus of some sort.

"And that's about all that we've learned from these pictures."

Pearson tapped a few keys, and one of the infrared photos appeared on the screen.

"This is well number eight, but all of the offshore platforms have essentially the same characteristics."

There wasn't much to the picture. A hot red center expanding into lighter shades of red, then orange, then yellow, then blue.

"Given the film we used," McKenna said, "doesn't that thing look hotter than it should be?"

Amber grinned at him. "Right on, Colonel."

Pearson looked up, then said begrudgingly, "Yes. It does. I would expect the dome to be exceptionally well-insulated, to allow men to work in that environment, but we're seeing more heat loss than we should. Then, too, there's some heat loss into the sea that surprises me."

"There might be some heat generated by the pumping of oil through the casing," Overton suggested.

"Or from rotating drills, if they're still drilling," McKenna added.

"But not that much, McKenna," Pearson said.

"So you want more IR?"

"Yes. We'll use Type thirty-fifty on one camera and Type thirty-ninety on the other. Maybe I can extrapolate from the two sensitivities."

"When?"

"The sooner the better."

"Donna, you want to page the troops for me? We'll meet in the exercise compartment."

"Sure thing, Colonel."

As McKenna waited for the door to open, he heard Amber's voice on the PA. "First AS flight crews report to Compartment A-four-seven."

On board *Themis,* the flight crews were assigned to separate residential spokes, again for safety reasons. When they met as a squadron, they used the large exercise space in the hub as a briefing room.

When he floated through the hatchway into the exercise compartment, he found all but Munoz accounted for. The fitness maven, Nitro Fizz Williams, was pumping spring-loaded iron, his feet planted firmly against a wall. Di-matta was upside down, chinning himself on the upper bar of a Nautilus machine, which might have required a couple ounces of effort. Will Conover was dressed in a pair of blue shorts and a T-shirt, the scars on his arms white against otherwise tanned flesh. He had ridden an F-16 into Edwards with landing gear that collapsed on touchdown. He tore up his arms getting out of the flaming wreckage. Do-Wop Abrams had a cassette stereo pounding out Bo Diddley's "Detour."

This was the first time they had all been together in over a week. Since most of their assigned missions could be accomplished by one MakoShark, they frequently missed each other in the transit between the space station and the earth side bases.

Dimatta aimed a pouch of Coke at him, then gave it a nudge with his finger. "Here you go, Kev."

"Thanks, Cancha. Where's Tony?"

"Where else?"

"Asleep. We'll give him a couple minutes." McKenna caught the floating soft drink, pulled the flexible straw loose from the side of the pouch, and sucked on it. The Coke was cold.

When Munoz arrived a few minutes later, bright-eyed from plenty of sleep, McKenna said to Abrams, "Jack, you want to put Bo on hold?"

Abrams killed the tape.

McKenna briefed them on Pearson's concerns about the oil wells in the Greenland Sea, as well as his and Munoz's earlier flight.

Though all of the men in the room would rather be at the controls of a MakoShark, McKenna strictly enforced a Space Command regulation limiting the number of flight hours per week. A groggy or fatigued pilot or systems officer could easily destroy a MakoShark. At three-quarters of a billion dollars per copy, they weren't expendable. Delta Red was the only reserve machine, though a MakoShark coded Delta Orange was in the final stages of completion at Jack Andrews Air Force Base in Chad. It wouldn't be ready for flight trials for another month, or even two.

The Strategic Arms Reduction Treaty agreements allowed for one more craft, but appropriations had not been forthcoming from Congress. Under START, the U.S. had given up forty of a planned seventy-two B-2 Stealth bombers, but had been allowed to develop six MakoSharks. In McKenna's mind, the six aerospace fighters were the equivalent of all seventy-two B-2s.

"Any questions on where we stand so far?"

"Nope," Conover said. "Who gets the next shot?"

98

"You and I, Will, are close to max on flying time, so Frank gets the next one. I want you and Jack to hit the sack and stand by, just in case we need another run."

"I get to sack out, too?" Munoz asked.

"Your turn to play operations officer, Tiger. The paperwork awaits you."

"Shucks."

"Hot damn," Dimatta said. "And we go armed? I saw Shalbot and Embry working on Delta Blue."

"You're armed, Cancha, but only I get to pull the trigger. We clear on that?"

"Clear, Snake Eyes."

Nitro Fizz Williams, the backseater, said, "Do we finish the run at Jack Andrews?"

"I hope so," Dimatta said. "I could use a decent meal."

"Right back here," McKenna told them. "Amy wants her film."

"Well," Dimatta said, "we both want something."

The leer on Dimatta's face made halfway clear his own desires, though McKenna wasn't certain whether the pilot would rather have a shot at Pearson or at some hostile aircraft.

Malcolm Nichols spun the helm, and *Walden* heeled hard to the left. The small ice floe, protruding barely eighteen inches out of the water, but probably weighing ten tons, passed by on the starboard side.

"Jesus, Mal. That was close."

"It's okay, Jennifer. Danny saw it in time."

Danny Hemmings was up on the bow, watching for such things. He was dressed in a fur-lined parka, but Nichols could see him shivering from time to time. It might be summer above the Arctic Circle, but any breeze at all dropped the relative temperature considerably.

Nichols kept his eyes on Hemmings, halfway fearful of missing some urgent signal from his lookout.

The *Walden* was a forty-two-foot sport fisherman, an old

Hatteras with a wooden hull and thirty years of creaks, but it handled rough seas well. The seas were, in fact, relatively calm, with just a slight chop moving before a ten-mile-per-hour wind.

The boat's name and home port—Boston—were roughly stenciled on the aged white paint of her transom. The more important identification was painted in two-foot-high green letters along both sides of the hull: GREEN-PEACE.

Nichols had given up the open flying bridge the day before, when the winds became more frigid. He manned the secondary controls behind the windshield of the salon. It was warmer, but his vision was severely restricted, and Danny Hemmings and Margot Montaine, the French girl Danny had met in Cherbourg, had been taking turns on the bow.

Jennifer Pearl brought him a fresh mug of coffee.

"Thanks."

"What do you think we're going to find, Mal?"

"Damned if I know, but the captain of that Greenland fishing boat said something's fucking with the marine life. We'll just cruise by those German wells, maybe sample the water a little."

The *Walden* had been taking on supplies in Trondheim, Norway, when Nichols met the fishing boat's master in a waterfront dive. They shared a bottle of aquavit, and Nichols learned that large gams of whales were migrating out of the Greenland Sea. It was not a normal migration, the captain told him. Additionally, the fleets were finding that the fishing had become less bountiful over the last few years. The captain eagerly pointed a finger in the direction of the Germans, detailing the two times he had been turned away from the oil fields by German naval vessels.

"You think an oil spill?" Jennifer asked him.

"It's been known to happen," he said unnecessarily. "Damn sure, we'll know soon."

"If we find the wells."

No one aboard the old cruiser was a navigator. Old charts, dead-reckoning, and flipped coins were the height of the *Walden's* technology.

"We'll find them," Nichols vowed.

Maj. Wilhelm Metzenbaum commanded the *Zweit Schwadron* of the *20.S.A.G.* His pilots flew the Eurofighter, a single seat, delta-winged air defense fighter. Similar in appearance to the General Dynamics F-16 Fighting Falcon, it also had attack capabilities, able to transport ten 454-kilogram bombs in addition to two external fuel tanks. The prototype had first flown in late 1990, and Metzenbaum's squadron had been the first to be fully outfitted with the new fighter.

Metzenbaum and his wingman, *Hauptmann* Mies Vanderweghe, were currently armed in the interceptor mode, with Skyflash 90 air-to-air missiles. They had completed their circuit of the oil fields, and Metzenbaum flew alongside the tanker, waiting while Vanderweghe approached the tanker's boom. Metzenbaum had topped off first.

Metzenbaum was an eighteen-year veteran of the Luftwaffe. He had flown any aircraft the commanders had put in front of him, and he had flown it well. A short and dark man, with a thick black mop of hair, he was married and had two children, twin boys, who were about to enter the University of Frankfurt. Behind his back, the men in his squadron called him "Bear," not only because of his gruff demeanor, but because of the dense mat of dark hair that covered his chest and back.

He listened to the boom operator: "That is good, Panther Two. A little more to your left. . . ."

A voice on his tactical frequency interrupted. "Panther Leader, this is Platform Six."

The speaker from *Bahnsteig Sechs* sounded agitated.

101

Metzenbaum depressed the transmit button. "Platform Six, Panther Leader."

"Are you still in my area, Panther Leader?"

"Affirmative. Two hundred kilometers away."

"We have a small boat approaching, estimated at four kilometers distance."

"That close?"

"It must be a wooden boat, without a radar reflector in operation, Panther Leader. Radar picked it up only moments ago."

"Panther Leader to Platform Six. I will investigate. Panther Two, you will return to base."

Metzenbaum was at 7,000 meters. He eased the stick to the right, brought his left wing over, and went into a turning dive, stopping the turn when he reached a heading of 245 degrees. The speed climbed from 450 kilometers per hour to Mach 1.2. He leveled out at 1,000 meters.

Thirteen minutes later, Metzenbaum saw the red strobe light atop *Bahnsteig Sechs,* and to the south of it by a couple of kilometers, the white cruiser. A minute later, he made out the letters on the side of the boat.

Ah, damn.

Metzenbaum had no quarrel with the goals of some of the environmental groups, but some of the more fanatical groups utilized tactics that irritated him. Ramming a nuclear aircraft carrier with a small boat seemed to him both ineffective and suicidal.

Throttling back, he reduced his speed to 400 kilometers per hour and dove on the boat. On the first pass, he went by at thirty meters of altitude, the noise of his passage rocking the man standing on the bow. He grabbed for the bow rail and hung on for dear life. The boat slowed.

Metzenbaum dialed the international marine channel on his secondary Navigation/Communication radio.

He spoke in English. "Greenpeace boat, this is Major Metzenbaum of the German air force."

102

There was no response.

"Greenpeace boat . . ."

"What do you want, Major?" The voice was nasal, with just a twang of anxiety in it.

"You are cruising in restricted waters. You must turn back."

"That's damned nonsense, Major Whoever-you-are. We are in international waters, and we'll go where we want to go."

Metzenbaum circled wide to the south, climbing a few meters.

"Greenpeace boat, I inform you that you are in waters under control of the Bremerhaven Petroleum Corporation. It is dangerous to go too close to the well. You must turn back immediately."

"It's a free sea," the male voice told him.

Metzenbaum had only air-to-air missiles with him, but he was not going to hit anything, anyway, he hoped. With his rudder, he tightened his turn and lined up on the boat. Arming one of the Skyflashes, he dropped the nose of the Eurofighter until the cruiser appeared in the bottom left of the gun sight. He would not use the computer-targeting mode.

The fighter dove and closed rapidly on the boat, and Metzenbaum aimed fifty meters to the right of it, then pressed the commit button on the stick. The missile leapt from its guiding rail.

Flash of white-hot exhaust.

Plume of seawater.

Silent thump of explosion under the surface of the sea.

Another, taller plume erupted from the ocean.

"Jesus Christ! Hey, you son of a bitch! You're shooting at us!"

"You must turn back now," Metzenbaum said.

The cruiser went into a wide turn toward the south as Metzenbaum gained altitude and prepared for a long series of figure eights.

He called New Amsterdam on the squadron's frequency. "Second Squadron, Panther Leader."

"Go ahead, Panther Leader."

"Prepare to scramble Panthers Seven and Eight. They will need to relieve me in approximately forty minutes."

Metzenbaum heard the klaxon sound over the open radio circuit.

It was eight o'clock at night, still very light over the Greenland Sea.

Delta Green had been circling at 40,000 feet, taking the high-altitude infrared shots that Pearson wanted, and waiting for the two fighters and the tanker to clear the area before making the pass at 5,000 feet. The WSO had picked them up much earlier on the 200-mile scan. He had then gone passive with the radar, and just now activated it for three sweeps.

"Well, shit!" Williams said. "The guy just fired a missile into the sea."

Doing what we do to unsuspecting Super 18s, Dimatta thought. "No target?"

"None that I could see on the screen. I'll go active in a minute for another sweep."

A few minutes later, Williams told him, "The one on the deck is taking the lazy way back, Cancha. He's flying figure eights, moving toward the south at around twenty knots. The tanker and the other fighter are now two-five-zero miles south of us."

"Must be, he's got a boat down there, Nitro."

"We going to look?"

"Maybe just a quick peek."

Dimatta pulled his throttles back and eased the hand controller forward. The nose of the MakoShark angled downward, and he put it in a wide left turn, spiraling downward.

Williams changed the range of the radar to the fifty-

104

mile sweep, and the target appeared at the very edge of Dimatta's CRT.

As they reached 8,000 feet, Dimatta began to level out and line up on the target. It was dead ahead on a heading of 188 degrees. It was forty-four miles away at 2,000 feet above the sea. The HUD readout showed his own speed at 600 knots.

The screen blanked out as Williams cut off the radar.

"We want to make the pass to our left," Williams said. "That'll put dark sky above us. We go in straight, he may get a visual."

"Roger, Nitro."

Dimatta made a shallow S-turn to the left.

"I'm staying passive," Williams said, and the screen went to a direct visual. Dark seas, darkening skies.

Stealth aircraft, or no stealth aircraft, radar that actively sought targets—emitting signals—was detectable by opposing forces. The electronic countermeasures package aboard most military aircraft was capable of locating signals generated in most radar bands, from D to K. As they passed over the wells, they picked up a few chirps on the I-Band threat receiver from active radar operating from the wells. Williams squelched them out.

The threat receiver chattered.

"The German down there has a J-band," Williams said. "May be a Foxhunter radar."

"Tornado," Dimatta said.

"Or Eurofighter. They're supposed to have them, too."

"Cancha do an IR check?"

"Coming up."

Five miles away from the fighter, Williams did a quick infrared scan, picking up several heat sources. He fed them all to the computer.

"The airborne target has twin turbofans and a six-five percent chance of being a Eurofighter, Cancha. No read on the others. Behind us, we're getting a couple of the wells. The small target to the south is probably a small boat."

"He's escorting it out of the area."

"Good bet."

"How badly do we want to know details, Nitro?"

"Amy'll want to know all about it."

"Okay," Dimatta said. "I'm going to turn right onto the target. You go full mag on visual."

"Roger. Go two-six-zero. Let's take it down some."

Dimatta turned right until the HUD gave him 260 degrees. He bled off power and the MakoShark began to descend.

The cruiser had its running lights on, and Dimatta easily picked it out of the gloom that was magnified twenty-five times on the screen. Between the fore and aft lights, however, was a grayish white blob.

The HUD showed him at 3,000 feet.

"Where's that German?" Dimatta asked.

"Damned if I know. I'll put IR on the small screen . . . Okay, got him still at two thousand, six miles at bearing three-four-one."

That put him on Dimatta's right.

"Soon as we get an ID, Nitro, I'm climbing out of here to the left."

"Chicken."

The cruiser grew rapidly on the screen.

"Got it!" Williams said. "Hit it, Cancha!"

Dimatta advanced his throttles and started a climbing left turn.

"Greenpeace, was it?" Dimatta asked.

"Yeah. I've got it on tape."

Dimatta pressed the transmit button on the hand controller. "Alpha One, Delta Green."

"Delta Green, Alpha reading." It was Overton's voice.

"Alpha, we had a visual on a Greenpeace boat being run out of the target area. We suspect that it was fired on by a Eurofighter."

"Green, you have a description of the boat?"

Williams broke in. "Estimate forty feet, probably wood, white with large letters spelling Greenpeace along the hull. Current position seven-seven-degrees, nine-minutes north, four-degrees, three-minutes east."

"Roger, Delta Green. We'll see if someone from NATO or the CIA can't run them down and talk to them. Alpha out."

On the intercom, Dimatta said, "If that boat captain took a missile off the bow, he's probably running damned scared."

"And the crew," Williams said, "is busy cleaning the decks."

Milly Roget's soft voice came over the intercom. "General, you have a call on direct line two."

"Thank you, Milly." Marvin Brackman punched the button on his oversized desk set and picked up the receiver. "Brackman."

It would be Hannibal Cross or Harvey Mays. Line two was direct to the Pentagon.

It was Cross, the chairman of the Joint Chiefs. "Marv, I just got back from State."

"Were they diplomatic, Hannibal?"

"Oh, yes. And just as ineffective as usual."

"The Germans wouldn't respond?"

"They responded, but they didn't. The oil fields are a private enterprise of Bremerhaven Petroleum, and certainly, the German Department of Foreign Affairs could not interfere in the workings of a private corporation. They know none of the details. They claim."

"What about all the security the German High Command is providing?" Brackman asked.

"That's only a normal precaution extended to any German national company. We ought to apply for citizenship, Marv."

"Not damned likely, Hannibal. My grandmother on Mommy's side was Jewish."

"You hearing those rumors, too?" the chairman asked.

"Are they rumors? I talked to Appleton over at DIA a couple weeks ago. He thinks the German military is quietly culling its ranks."

"Maybe I'll invite him up here for a chat."

"Did our State people try Bremerhaven directly?" Brackman asked, to get back on track.

"Yes, but without success. The company professes to be utilizing new methods of exploration, and they're restricting knowledge of their process. They say they're afraid of industrial espionage."

"Do we have anything out of the CIA on the oil company yet?"

"Hold on, Marv. I've got a sheet here somewhere. Yeah. The corporation itself is privately held, with some thirty shareholders. There are no public records, but the Agency estimates a total investment of close to twenty-five billion U.S. dollars. They have no idea of what the debt structure looks like. All of the officers of the corporation have clear records and histories."

Brackman thought that over. "When it's that clean, and that private, with that many bucks involved, Hannibal, I tend to suspect a facade."

"The Agency does say something along the same lines. Here it is. Best estimate is that there are other investors, unnamed."

"Uh-huh. So what do we do about it, Admiral?"

"Looking for a decision, are you?"

"If you've got one handy."

"What're your *Themis* people doing now?"

Brackman checked his watch. "Should be in the middle of another reconnaissance mission."

"You find out what they learn, then get back to me. Personally, I think we ought to step up our surveillance."

"I do, too, Hannibal."

* * *

"They're not oil wells, General Brackman."

"You're certain of that, Colonel Pearson?"

"I am, sir."

"What are they?"

"That, I don't know. But the heat generation is far too high for the typical drilling or pumping platform. I ran comparisons with data from offshore wells in the North Sea and off the California coast."

On his end of the scrambled radio circuit, Brackman went silent.

In the Command Center, McKenna, Overton, and Pearson waited. T.Sgt. Donna Amber was tending the console in the communications space, monitoring the satellite system relays.

Brackman came back. "Kevin, you still there?"

From the look on her face, Amelia Pearson still didn't think that full generals should be on a first-name basis with lowly squadron commanders. It only went one way in public, however.

"Still here, General."

"I want a nightly surveillance on those wells. Continue taking infrared. Maybe we'll catch a door open, and get better readings."

Maybe, but McKenna didn't think so. "Got it, sir."

"And I want a full update on all military installations, forces, and equipment on the German mainland. Make whatever flights are required. Let's drop some sonobuoys along that underwater pipe."

McKenna did some hasty calculations. "General, I need a couple more pilots in order to stay under the maximum hours. I want to move Haggar and Olsen into the MakoSharks."

That alerted Overton, and his face reddened. "No way, Kevin."

"I don't think so, either," Brackman said.

109

Pearson had a smirk on her face. Whether she was happy that McKenna wasn't getting his way again, or unhappy that a female colleague was running into opposition, McKenna couldn't tell.

"Sir, we can't get you the coverage you want and still meet the regulations."

"To hell with the regulations," Brackman said. "You manage to ignore them, McKenna, unless you can use them in your favor. You can go ten per cent over on flying hours. I'll follow that up with a written directive."

"Still . . ."

"Besides, you're going to get some additional help from the Fifth Interceptor Wing."

McKenna struggled with the designation. It was familiar, but he couldn't place it, unless . . .

"The Soviets, General?"

"That's it. Your contact will be the wing commander, a Colonel Pyotr Volontov."

"No shit. Uh, no shit, General."

"No shit, McKenna."

Six

Pearson's alarm chirped at six A.M., and she was instantly awake. She rubbed the grittiness out of her eyes, then turned on the small lamp in her sleeping cubicle. She freed herself from the Velcro straps that pinned her against the cushioned bulkhead. Opposite her by four feet was a communications panel for intercommunications aboard the station. It included a small television screen. Some people went to sleep by watching *Casablanca* instead of by reading. In an elastic-edged fabric pouch above the panel were the books by which Amy Pearson went to sleep. Currently, she was in the middle of *The Rise and Fall of the Third Reich* and wondering why she had not read it before.

Below the communications panel was her personal locker, just about the only private area allowed her, or anyone, on board the station. Opening the twin doors, she retrieved a fresh jump suit, underwear, and her hygiene kit. She unzipped the curtain and pushed out into the corridor, then aimed herself toward the six hygiene stations. At six in the morning, only one was in use — identified by the amber light — and she let herself into a vacant stall.

Stripping out of the loose, baggy-legged sleeping garment that most of the enlisted men called a potato sack, she stuffed it into the dirty laundry hamper. Pearson used the vacuumized toilet, then gave herself a bath with a damp sponge. The only thing she really missed in her assignment on *Themis* was a long, steamy shower every morning. Floating in front of the sink, which was really a basin surrounding a vacuum nozzle, she brushed her teeth, rinsed her mouth with mouthwash, and spat into the vacuum port. None of the women on board worried about makeup. After combing out her hair, which took a while, she slipped the headband in place. She might have to have her hair cut, the next time she was earth side, she thought. She was beginning to look like something out of the '60s San Francisco. The legs, too. She used an electric razor on them. After donning bra, panties, and jumpsuit, she repacked her hygiene kit and took it back to stow in her cubicle.

Pearson was assigned to the Spoke Sixteen residential module, the one limited to military personnel. The outer end of it was the dining/recreation space, and five people were present by the time she arrived. It was a busy place, usually, with people going on shift, coming off shift, or wiling away the time between sleep and work. Pearson's days were intentionally long, and like the MakoShark pilots, she did not have a set work period.

S. Sgt. Delbert O'Hara, the chief steward, was stocking one of the three food stations mounted against the bulkhead common to the sleeping cubicles. Almost all of the station's food was preprepared earth side, brought up in refrigerated bins, and stored in the hub. As needed, it was transferred to the dining modules. O'Hara, who reported to Deputy Commander Milt Avery, but might as well not have, was responsible for the menu, and he did a credible job with what he had to work with, making frequent changes in what the machines had to offer. Over time, in fact, he had devised new recipes of his own for the specialists on earth to develop into pouchable products. O'Hara had also labeled each of the three dispensing stations—"Junk," "Back Home," and "Cuisine."

Pearson kicked off from the corridor edge and drifted up to the Cuisine station.

"Good morning, Delbert."

"Mornin', Colonel."

"What's new here?"

"Not much on the breakfast side," the sergeant said. "But try the Back Home. I just loaded a Texas Omelet that'll knock your socks off. If you had socks."

Pearson smiled at him. "You guarantee it?"

"Don't need to. Major Munoz had three of 'em this morning."

"That's a five-star rating."

"Damned tootin'."

Each of the stations had six selections, and Pearson opened the second Plexiglas door of the Back Home station, extracted a pouch labeled "Texas Morning," and shoved it into the microwave. While it was cooking, she got herself an orange juice and "Coffee, Black." The juice was already cold, and the coffee already hot.

She looked around. The porthole was showing a slice of earth, heavily clouded this morning. The large-screen TV was mercifully blank. The big mural of Tahiti appeared serene. A lieutenant from the nuclear section was playing one of the dozen electronic games lined up against the outer bulkheads. The dining rooms on *Themis* were the only places where one could actually find a table and chairs. Not that anyone actually sat in them; they strapped themselves in to maintain position while playing checkers, chess, backgammon, or cards with game pieces that were lightly magnetized, as were the tabletops. And some people liked to eat sitting down, or appearing to sit down.

Two sergeants were engaged in a mean game of chess, soft drinks floating nearby.

That left Kevin McKenna sitting alone at a table by the port.

He smiled at her.

So she clamped her breakfast pouches in one hand,

113

pushed off toward him, and caught herself as she reached the padded chair opposite him.

He actually released his restraining strap and stood up, holding onto his coffee.

"Good morning, Amy."

"Good morning." She strapped herself down, and McKenna refastened his own straps.

"You're looking radiant this morning."

"Come on, McKenna. I look the same every morning."

"I know. That's what brightens my day."

Shaking her head, she pulled the sipping tube free from the side of the orange juice pouch and took a sip.

McKenna said, "You're actually going to eat O'Hara's Tex-Mex special?"

"If Tony can handle it, I can."

"Hoo-kay, but remember the Tiger has a stomach lining made of depleted uranium alloy."

Almost all of the food served was in finger-food form. Handling silverware was too much trouble, when the peas were going to fly away, anyway. Some hot meats were served with tongs. Liquids were something of a problem, too. No gravy or sauces, unless they were imbedded in the mashed potatoes and meat.

Pearson peeled the plastic zipper open, rolled the covering down, tested the heat of the eggy roll with her forefinger, and took a bite of her Texas Omelet. She chewed twice before she got zapped.

"God . . . damn!" she blurted.

Over by the food stations, O'Hara grinned and called, "I caught one of your socks, Colonel."

"Isn't that the best damned jalapeño pepper you ever tasted?" McKenna asked.

She sucked on her juice, but had the feeling nothing would relieve the spicy coating on her tongue and the inside of her cheeks.

"It is good," she said, determined to finish it now.

By the fourth bite, her mouth was acclimated, but

114

she thought she would feel the heat until midmorning.

At least, McKenna didn't laugh at her. He asked, "What's on for today, Amy?"

"At one o'clock, I'll give the squadron a briefing."

"Covering?"

"The photos Dimatta got on the last run, for one thing. We got quite a few more naval vessels. Then, I'll background you on some of the principal players."

"Who, for instance?"

"The tail numbers you identified on the two Tornados makes them part of the First Squadron of the Twentieth Special Air Group assigned to New Amsterdam. The wing commander is a Colonel Albert Weismann, a good old boy who's been around for quite a while."

"What's the makeup of the wing?" McKenna asked, then sipped from his coffee.

"A little strange, from what the DIA has in its files. There's two squadrons of Tornados and Eurofighters—commanded by Major Gustav Zeigman and Major Wilhelm Metzenbaum, a squadron of transports, and one of helicopters."

"That is a bit weird. Lot of variety for one wing."

"Yes. It looks to me as if an entire wing is devoted to support of the well sites. Then, there's Admiral Gerhard Schmidt."

"Who's he?"

"The missile cruiser *Hamburg* turns out to be his flagship, and Schmidt's assigned as commander of the Third Naval Force. Now, Schmidt's an old hand, too, in his early sixties, and the data says he's a hell of a naval strategist and tactician. By all rights, he should be in command of a fleet."

"Which means?"

Pearson ran her tongue around the inside of her mouth, trying to erase the traces of pepper. She unlatched the sipping tube on her coffee. "Which means that something about those wells makes them important enough to require the services of top echelon commanders."

"Intriguing, Amy. You do a good job."

She nodded slightly to acknowledge the compliment. "I'm still trying to track all of the vessels attached to the Third Naval Force, but at the briefing, I'll also give you a rundown on the pilots we think are assigned to the Twentieth Special Air Group. Believe me when I say they're all hot dogs and aces."

"I always believe you, Amy."

"Do you? Why don't you like me, McKenna?"

His eyes widened, and he grinned. "Not like you? Damn, my dear, I think you've got it all backward."

"Don't call me 'dear,' please. If you had any respect for me, Colonel, you'd treat me as the professional I am."

"You want me to treat you differently than I treat Brad Mitchell or Polly Tang or Frank Dimatta? I can give you the prima-donna bit, if that's what you want, or I can be a brass asshole, or I can be me."

She just stared at him for a moment, then gathered her empty pouches for the trash vacuum. "I've got work to do."

"Put it off. We'll talk."

"Talking with you is too exasperating," she said. "And I've got to check on the civvies."

Releasing her lap belt, Pearson pushed off the chair, dumped her breakfast remnants in the receptacle, then kicked her way toward the blue hatchway door leading into Spoke Sixteen.

Traversing the spoke, she passed the four lifeboat stations, one of the reasons Spokes Sixteen, Ten, and Fourteen were off-limits to civilian personnel. Sight of the yellow hatches emblazoned with the black letters, "LIFE-BOAT," was not considered morale-maintaining for the civilians. The lifeboats were not very complex and could not survive reentry into the atmosphere. They were just simple capsules with food and air that would last thirty days. In the event of a catastrophe that consumed the entire station, each boat could sustain life for ten people while it drifted in space, waiting for a MakoShark or a Mako or, if necessary, a HoneyBee to rendezvous with it and retrieve the inhabitants.

The engineers had absolute faith in the structural soundness of the station, but just in case . . .

Keeping the civilians ignorant of the possible need for lifeboats was just another morale, as well as security, problem. Pearson thought the visitors ought to know about them, but somebody in DOD thought the clients should not have unnecessary worries.

Lt. Col. Amelia Pearson was also the security officer aboard *Themis*. Brad Mitchell was in charge of the station's environmental and structural integrity, but Pearson was responsible for containment of the less tangible, more slippery commodity of secret intelligence.

She maintained the security clearance files on all enlisted personnel and officers except for General Overton, McKenna, and herself. Those were monitored by General Thorpe at Space Command. Pearson supervised the security clearance investigations for any potential replacement of personnel aboard the station. Replacements were rare, however, since those aboard resisted rotation back to an earth side assignment, and most had extended their one-year postings to *Themis* one or more times. Outside of war, there weren't many situations in which the officer/enlisted distinctions virtually disappeared. Station personnel were selected strictly on the basis of competency in a given field.

There was a large backlog of applicants for duty on the space station, from the army, the navy, and the marines, as well as the air force. The 1st Aerospace Wing was air force-operated, but the personnel complement included all services. Maj. Brad Mitchell was a marine. Polly Tang was army. No matter where they came from, though, the military people had never given Pearson much trouble. They understood the importance of the knowledge they accumulated, and when they were earth side, they did not spread it around.

More troublesome to her brand of security were the civilian scientists on two- or three-week stints for companies that had contracted with the Department of Defense. Being scientists, they were naturally curious. Nosy, Pearson termed it. They might well defend to the death their right to protect the secrecy of an industrial process they personally developed in space, but they were less circumspect about revealing military secrets.

Pearson had devised the color scheme used on *Themis*. All interior surfaces were painted a typical, uniformly military gray. Hatchways to absolutely dangerous areas—primarily the undeveloped spokes and the air locks—were finished in red. Hatchways to spaces accessible only to particularly authorized personnel were orange and were also protected by keypad-operated locks. The nuclear reactor, communication, computer, ordnance and fuel storage areas, and the MakoShark hangars were behind orange hatches.

Areas to which a civilian might be invited, but only under escort, were identified in yellow. The Command Center, the Mako bays, and the Honeybee docking facilities qualified for yellow.

Blue was utilized for the spaces open only to military personnel, such as the military laboratories in Spokes Ten through Fourteen, and green was the predominant color used for those regions accessible to visiting civilians. Some compartments had blue/green hatchways, denoting combined usage. Various corridors in the hub had a green stripe running along the bulkhead. If an unescorted civilian didn't see green somewhere, he or she knew the territory was forbidden. Not that some of them cared one way or the other. Military people were always reminding errant civilian people of the distinction.

Of the sixteen spokes, seven were open to civilians—three of the residential modules and four of the dedicated laboratory modules, Spokes Two through Eight. The nuclear reactor power plant was located at the end of Spoke Nine. In the hub, civilians could visit the exercise room, the medical clinic, a communications space set aside for corporate contractors, the laundry, and a few other specialized spaces.

At some time during her workday, Pearson made it a point to visit various spaces in the civilian areas. She made her visits randomly, and frequently she sent M. Sgt. Val Arguento in her place. Arguento was an army communications specialist who manned one of the shifts in the Radio Shack, but who also served as the security NCO. He had had extensive experience with the Defense Intelligence Agency and with the National Security Agency.

This morning, Pearson chose Spoke Six. She followed the curving outer corridor, Corridor Two, around to it, passing a number of people emerging from the residential spokes, headed for their assigned tasks. Everyone spoke to her, and she returned the greetings with a smile.

Spoke Six had a green hatchway, and was therefore out-of-bounds to most of the military contingent. The corporate contractors often had secrets they wanted to keep to themselves. And even if they did not, the experiments taking place in the labs were often sensitive, and the scientists didn't want to be subjected to high traffic.

She tapped the green square and waited while the door unlocked and swung open. This spoke was forty feet long, and along its length, four accesses were provided, leading to small modules attached to the side of the spoke. These were hydroponic farms, where food and other flora were raised in special solutions. Artificial light was normally used, but one of the modules had a sliding shield that allowed direct sunlight to enter. It was all experimental. One of the military spokes had hydroponic farms growing wheat, rice, corn, and soybeans that were actually consumed after Sergeant O'Hara performed his magic.

119

After her Texas Omelet, Pearson thought she might revert to O'Hara's bland bean concoctions.

The laboratory on the end of the spoke was huge, eighty feet long by sixty feet in diameter. Its interior bulkheads were partially movable in order to create differently sized spaces, based on the needs of the contractor.

The contractor was responsible for providing the equipment necessary for the particular experiment, and the equipment arrived at the station by HoneyBee.

Spoke Six was currently under contract to Honeywell and to Du Pont and was therefore divided into two separate laboratories. She passed through Honeywell's space, which wasn't currently inhabited, and opened the hatch to Du Pont. Honeywell smelled of ozone, which she didn't like, and she made a mental note to mention it to Brad Mitchell.

Dr. Howard Dixon was upside down to her when she pulled herself through the hatchway. She performed a half flip.

He smiled at her. "Ah, Colonel. Welcome."

"I hope I'm not disturbing anything, Doctor."

"Not at all. I'm boiling some oxides, if you'd like to watch."

Absolutely fascinating, she thought. "I'll pass, thanks. Are you being taken care of? Is there anything we can do for you?"

"Not a thing. I'm perfectly happy."

In the immense space, he looked like a miniature, hanging onto the workbench fitted to the outer wall. But he did look happy.

The lab was a jungle of specialized instruments, consoles, and work tables to which were attached intricate lacings of tubing, vials, and bottles.

On her circuit of the lab, Pearson was careful to not touch anything. She looked primarily for things that might seem out of place, for paperwork that shouldn't be there. There wasn't much paper, of course, since most work notes and reports were kept on computer.

Computer disks leaving the station, or data and voice transfers from the client communications room, were scanned by Sergeant Arguento's computer for information that should not be included in industrial and scientific reports. The computer sought out key words and phrases in computer documents and sounded the alarm when something was amiss. Usually, when they discovered classified information being transmitted, it was unintentional on the part of the scientist. A trivial piece of scientific curiosity, a measurement of the nuclear plant output, a suspicion that *Themis* stored ordnance aboard. One nuclear physicist, who also happened to be an antinuke activist, had convinced himself that nuclear-tipped missiles were stored aboard the station. He had made a nuisance of himself searching the station's compartments for them, and had eventually been deported.

When such incidents happened, General Overton was called on for a stern lecture, and the appropriate corporate headquarters was notified. Companies like Du Pont or Honeywell or Martin-Marietta did not want to lose the privilege of experimenting in space and tended to take immediate corrective action with their employees.

Completing her inspection, she said good-bye to Dixon and passed back into Honeywell's lab. It was mostly taken up by three large, reinforced, and interconnected boxes that contained the components of a computer memory. It had been explained to her that the difference was that the memory chips were in complete vacuum. They were playing with artificial intelligence, Dr. Monte Washington had willingly explained to her.

She made a quick trip around the lab, then headed back to the spoke, reaching the hatchway just as it opened. Washington and his assistant, a bespectacled and bald man named Kensing, floated through the opening.

"Hey, Colonel Pearson," Washington said. "You're early today."

"That's because I have a full day ahead, I'm afraid, Mr. Washington."

"Ah, that's too bad. I was hoping to buy you lunch or dinner. Take in a movie."

"Maybe another time," she said, for perhaps the tenth time. Washington was persistent, though not grabby. He poked with his eyes.

She felt his eyes on her backside as she darted down the spoke.

Monte Washington might be one step worse than McKenna, she thought. At least McKenna seemed honest.

And she wondered at the question she had asked him. She didn't really think that McKenna disliked her.

Bahnsteig Eine appeared to be solid as a rock when Eisenach's helicopter settled onto the landing pad at two o'clock. The appearance was something of a deception.

The platform bases actually floated. While the platform itself stood some fifteen meters above the surface of the sea, the three legs extended downward only as far as the subsurface unit. That massive, donut-shaped structure was twenty meters below the surface, providing flotation as well as stabilization with extended, winglike stabilizers and internal, motor-driven gyros. The seabed, a crevice in this location below *Bahnsteig Eine,* was some 520 meters deep, and the platform maintained its position by means of four anchor lines.

Heavy seas were running, the troughs a meter below the white-capping tips of the waves, but the platform was steady when Eisenach, his adjutant Oberlin, and *Oberst* Albert Weismann, exited the helicopter.

Four crewmen from the platform ran out to tie the helicopter down, and the pilot descended from his cockpit to light a cigarette.

The wind was strong, forcing the three officers to grip

their service caps as they made their way across the flight deck to the dome entrance. The small door was set deeply into the wall of the dome. The walls were three meters thick, solid insulation sandwiched between aluminum skins in each of the five-meter triangular pieces that made up the dome. Next to the small door was a section of wall, four meters tall by six meters wide, which was removable so that heavy equipment could be transferred in and out of the dome.

When Oberlin closed the door behind them, they stood in a wide, high corridor leading to the back side of the structure. The deck was steel-plated in an antiskid diamond pattern. At the back of the corridor, an insulated fiberglass wall had been installed, to isolate the corridor from the drilling compartment that was located to the back of the dome.

Eisenach wrinkled his nose at the sulfur-tainted air that wafted through the corridor. A deep hum of machinery vibrated through the floor.

On his right were the living quarters, ten floors of dormitory rooms, kitchens, and recreation rooms to house the 140 men who worked on *Bahnsteig Eine*. The living spaces took up about a third of the dome.

To the left, taking up four floors, was the gigantic collection and distribution room. The heavy machinery was located in the drilling section.

Eisenach had no interest in seeing either area on this visit.

He led the way down the corridor and arrived at the elevator just as it opened.

Oberst Hans Diederman smiled widely as he emerged from the car. "Herr General Eisenach, how good it is to see you!"

Diederman was an army engineer with a widely respected mind. He was tremendously overweight, and the fat bulged his fatigue uniform. Eisenach had spoken to him repeatedly about his weight, but the engineer continued to enjoy the well-stocked pantry included in his command.

Eisenach treated the man with some deference because he was instrumental to the *VORMUND PROJEKT.* He was in charge of all twenty-four platforms, and the process had been developed by Diederman and his army subordinate engineers. Some navy and air force engineering officers, who happened to be partially knowledgeable of the project, were jealous.

Diederman did not bother with a salute, but held his callused hand out.

Eisenach shook it. The hand was hard and firm, contrary to his appearance. "Hans. How are you?"

"Wonderful! Come, come, gentlemen. Let us go up to my suite."

Diederman stepped back into the elevator, and Eisenach, Oberlin, and Weismann followed him. The engineer's bulk made the car very small.

Diederman pressed the button for Level Five, and the car rose silently. He had designed the elevator also.

When they exited on the fifth deck, the vibrations and humming of the platform were considerably reduced. The sound-deadening insulation imbedded in the walls of the control center was quite thick.

The center itself felt spacious. It was two stories tall, and the interior walls were about thirty meters long. The outside, third wall curved to the radius of the dome. In one wall was a door to the residential section. In the other straight wall were doors to several private offices.

An electronic grid map on the wall identified the immediate area, with the wells, the ice shelf, and ships in the area clearly marked. Alongside the circles signifying each well was a rectangular box displaying sets of numbers. To Diederman, and to others as well versed as he, the numbers provided pertinent and current information about each well. Temperatures, pressures, output. Eisenach had long before given up trying to interpret them.

The floor of the control center was lined with electronic consoles. There were forty consoles, with thirty-two of them currently manned.

Oberst Albert Weismann stopped by one console and peered over the shoulder of the operator. He appeared as puzzled by what was displayed on the computer screen as Eisenach had been, the first time it was explained to him.

"Now, this way, gentlemen."

Diederman led them into his office, which was spacious, and closed the glass door. The office did not have a desk. It had a computer terminal, a bank of six television screens, two sofas angled into one corner, and a huge round table with eight chairs spaced around it. The table was littered with computer printouts, diagrams, and schematics. Near one chair was a slanted control panel similar to a switchboard.

The chief engineer poured the coffee himself, drawing the strong black liquid from a large urn into ceramic cups. He passed them around as everyone took seats at the table, but did not offer cream or sugar. He placed a platter piled high with pastries in the center of the table. He swept piles of documents to one side, then plopped into the chair next to the switchboard.

"Well, then, General Eisenach. You are here for a progress report?"

Though that was not the primary purpose of his visit, Eisenach said, "Please, Hans."

Diederman pressed two buttons on his control panel and one of the TV screens came to life, showing a view from above of a drilling compartment. A swarm of men moved over the floor and along the ribs of the rig, dismantling steel beams and lowering them to the deck with an overhead crane.

"That is Platform Twenty. The well has been completed successfully, now, and we are disassembling the heavy drilling rig. It will be moved to Platform Twenty-Two."

"How long until the well-head assembly is emplaced?" Eisenach asked.

"Oh, give us another six, seven days. I will have the well on-line within ten days, General. That will give us twenty-one wells in the network."

"Very good, Hans. How about Platform Eleven?"

It had been decided by the High Command that centralizing the control and distribution on *Bahnsteig Eine* might be foolhardy. *Bahnsteig Elf,* therefore, was undergoing renovations that would allow it to perform as an alternate control station.

"Right now, I estimate another five or six weeks, General," Diederman said. He waved an expansive hand toward the control center outside his windows. "The electronics are in short supply, and we have had to wait upon the manufacturer for several weeks. The consoles, especially, are dedicated to our particular purpose."

"Would you like additional pressure brought to bear on the manufacturer?"

Diederman shook his big head. "It would not do us much good. We are still fishing for cable and pipeline on the seabed, now. It is going to take us a while to bring it to the surface and complete the junctions."

"Very well," the general said.

The second television screen came to life with a picture of another drilling compartment.

"Now, then. Platform Twenty-Three is down to three thousand meters. We broke a rotary bit and spent three days pulling pipe so we could fish for it. Right now, they're going back down in the hole with a new bit. If the geology holds up, we ought to complete in another couple of weeks. Then we'll move that rig to Twenty-Four. Hell, General, overall, we are ninety-one days ahead of schedule."

"And I, and the Fatherland, are extremely grateful for your expertise, Hans."

Diederman shrugged. "Now, perhaps you will tell me of the real purpose of your journey, General."

"Real purpose?"

The engineer grinned hugely at Weismann. "Old Albert does not come out here very often. I think he is uncomfortable at sea."

Weismann nodded. The wing commander was fifty-two years old and had been flying for thirty-four of those years. His eyes were pale and clear, and his blond hair was cropped short. At one time, his skin had also been pale and clear, but he suffered now from some epidermal rash that reddened the backs of his hands and the skin of his forehead and cheeks. He was a tall man, very lean in his tailored uniform.

"Go ahead, Colonel," Eisenach said.

"How many external cameras do you have on each well, Hans?" Weismann asked.

"There are three. Two overlook the helicopter pad, and one is located at the top of the dome. All are remote-controlled." Diederman played with his switchboard and yet another television screen revealed a view of the sea, slowly panning by. "We keep the upper camera on full rotation, watching for intruders."

"But watching the sea?"

"Of course."

"It can be aimed upward?"

"Certainly."

With several keystrokes, Diederman changed the angle of the camera. A blank, pale blue sky appeared.

"It is a boring view," Diedermann said.

"It may not be for long," the commander of the *20.S.A.G.* said.

"Oh?"

"Yesterday, one of my pilots chased off a Greenpeace ship. Near Platform Six?"

"I recall the incident. It was reported to me."

"During the encounter, the pilot believes that he saw

127

another aircraft in the area. A fleeting glimpse of an aircraft that revealed no radar or infrared signature."

Diederman looked to the general then back to Weismann. "There is such an aircraft, of course. Properly, an aerospace craft."

"Yes," Weismann said. "The American MakoShark. We have never seen it before."

"Nor have many," Eisenach said. "Hans, our concern is that the Americans may have taken an interest in your wells."

Diederman grinned. "They are mine, now? I will put them up for sale and retire a very rich man."

"It is possible," Eisenach said, ignoring the levity, "that the craft, if it was actually seen by the pilot, and if it was a MakoShark, was interested solely in the encounter with the Greenpeace ship. On the other hand, however, we do not wish to take chances."

"So, now. You wish to utilize my dome cameras? Since the MakoShark is visible to the eye?"

"Exactly," Weismann said. "Each of the dome cameras is to begin scanning the skies. I will work with your technicians to formulate a computer program to guide them—changing the scanning angle and magnification ranges. I will also set up a communications link between the monitors you must . . ."

"That costs me man-hours, Albert."

"I apologize, Hans, but it must be done. We will need three shifts of men to monitor the screens. And I will arrange a communications network between them and my wing."

"Now, General, do you really believe these aerospace craft are spying on us?" Diederman asked.

"With what we have to protect, Hans, we cannot afford to believe otherwise."

It was the first time in a long time that the entire complement of the 1st Aerospace Squadron had flown together.

The three MakoSharks backed away from their bays at six o'clock in *Themis's* evening, midnight in Bonn's. They took some time doing it, losing speed relative to the satellite, and spreading themselves sixty miles apart. McKenna wanted lots of room for error. Flying formation through blackout was not done.

It was not evening for *Themis* in real time. Her nights were erratic and short-lived, dependent upon when the orbit happened to place the earth between the station and the sun. An eclipse of the space station which might last for up to twenty minutes.

The direct sun glinted off the white plastic-clad skin of the station, making it appear much larger than it was. Up close, when approaching *Themis,* she was magnificently gigantic, seeming to loom over a minute MakoShark. In the early days, when she was just a hub and a couple of spokes, McKenna used to practice space-batics around her, zipping in close, backing off, rolling across the top of the hub to the solar array on the back side. Ease up to the Command Center's porthole and stare directly into Overton's eyes from fifteen feet away.

Overton had finally ordered a cease-and-desist on those activities, which was within his rights. He was in charge of the space station, while McKenna was responsible only for the squadron. Overton's concern had not been with McKenna's ability. Rather, he was afraid the newer pilots in the squadron, just joining it at that time, would slip and run a MakoShark right through his viewing window.

When all of the hangar doors were closed, twenty-foot high black letters were joined into the logo:

UNITED STATES OF AMERICA
SPACE STATION THEMIS
USSC-1

Every time he saw it, McKenna felt a twinge of pride. There was nothing like it anywhere, nothing to match the capability and ingenuity of Americans with a purpose.

Soyuz Fifty, the Soviet space station initiated two years before, orbited some ninety miles higher than *Themis,* but it was a limited undertaking. To date, it was comprised of five modules strung together in a straight line, and it was manned by no more than three people at the same time. The radar antenna for the most powerful radar ever developed, and housed in *Themis*'s Spoke Fifteen, was larger than the entire Soviet space station.

The Soviet Rocket Forces were having funding problems.

As Delta Blue drifted away from her mother ship, McKenna studied the new spoke. It would be Nine-B, next to the nuclear reactor, and its segments were arriving steadily by HoneyBee. So far, it was about twenty feet long, appearing spindly in comparison with the completed spokes. Four unassembled sections floated close by, secured by single ropes. The crewmen assigned to fitting the prefab pieces together had been called back inside the station for a rest break. Coincidentally timed so that they would miss seeing the departures of the MakoSharks.

The perspective changed as Delta Blue increased the gap. *Themis* became smaller against the unending backdrop of space, and with her knob-ended spokes, looked like, first, a child's Tinkertoy, than a star that had wandered in too close.

"Let's upend her," Munoz said. He had been programming the reentry data.

"Roger, Tiger." McKenna keyed the radio pad for the squadron's frequency. "Delta Blue to Delta Flight."

"Yellow, here, Snake Eyes."

"Green."

"Reverse position."

With the thrusters, he turned Delta Blue over and

waited until the confirmations came from Dimatta and Conover. He could not see either of the MakoSharks, each thirty miles off his wing tips.

"Green ready."

"Yellow's set."

"Delta Flight, program check."

Abrams, Williams, and Munos confirmed accepted reentry programs.

"Initiate sequence, Delta Flight."

McKenna watched the CRT and saw the numbers appear.

"Sixteen minutes, Snake Eyes," Munoz said. "I'm going to take a nap."

"Delta Blue, Yellow. Seventeen minutes, twelve seconds."

"Blue, Green. Fifteen minutes, twenty-two seconds."

"Not too bad, guys," McKenna told them. "See you on the other side."

The reentry passage was almost flawless. *Themis* had been over the continent of Antarctica when they started, and the three MakoSharks emerged from blackout almost directly over Turkey, the spread between them expanded to 150 miles.

By the time they had joined up on turbojets at 40,000 feet and Mach 1.8, Warsaw, Poland, was the primary landmark.

"Systems check, Tiger?"

"All internal systems are showin' number one, Snake Eyes. We lost the damned Phoenix."

"Delta Flight, systems check."

"Green reports a full complement, Snake Eyes."

"Yellow's all green."

"We burned out a Phoenix," McKenna told them, "but then it's a moot point, anyway. We'll go as planned."

"Roger, roger," Dimatta said, "Green's northbound."

Delta Green would make her run over the wells, looking especially for naval units. On the return, she would scatter sonobuoys along the estimated route of the undersea pipelines.

Conover's voice came on the air. "Delta Yellow. We're going to cruise the river."

Conover and Williams would make a wide circle to the left as far as the North Sea, then take a meandering course south down the length of the old Federal Republic of Germany, shooting low-light and infrared film of the major military concentrations. Their primary concern was New Amsterdam Air Force Base and the naval port of Bremerhaven since Pearson had identified both as home bases for the 20th Special Air Group and the 3rd Naval Force.

McKenna was taking on the old German Democratic Republic. On the first run, they would come west down the Baltic into Mecklenburg Bay, then turn south and fly all the way to the Czechoslovakian border before turning north once again. Pearson was as interested in the new or expanded industrial sites as she was in military bases. Rostok, Magdeburg, Halle, Leipzig, Zwickau, Dresden, and Berlin were the chief photographic targets.

At 500 knots, to avoid trailing a sonic boom, the round trip over land took an hour and twenty minutes. Munoz used the radar randomly, and they made momentary contact with sixteen aircraft. Two were commercial flights into Berlin and Dresden, and the rest were patrolling Luftwaffe pairs. None of the aircraft, nor any of the coastal radars, spotted them. The radar threat receiver went off regularly as they passed active radar installations, and Munoz squelched out the noise in the lower bands.

After passing over Berlin at 10,000 feet, Munoz said, "You know, *jefe,* I count four new radars along the Polish border."

"We know we're dealing with paranoid personalities, Tiger. They'd like to move the USSR to Antarctica."

"That's for damned sure. Hey, babe, we're out of targets. You want to punch it for home?"

"Let's finish it out to the Baltic. Maybe we'll spot a couple more radar installations."

"Roger. Let's . . . uh, take it to heading four-five for two minutes, then back to oh-one-oh."

McKenna turned to the new heading and watched the chronometer readout on the HUD. He also lost altitude to 7,000 feet. This stretch of Germany wasn't heavily inhabited.

A few minutes later, back on his original heading, he saw the darkness of the Baltic coming up. The scattered lights of cities along the coast identified it.

Munoz had the screens showing night-vision interpretations of the landscape. There wasn't much to be seen. A few villages along the Ucker River on their left.

Thirty miles to the Pomeranian Bay on the Baltic.

Chirp! Chirp! Chirp!

"Son of a bitch, Snake Eyes! That's a big damned J-Band transmittin'."

"Where?"

Munoz went to active radar for two sweeps.

"Headin' two-eight-one," Munoz said. "I put it on the coast five miles west of Peenemünde."

"Let's take a look."

"Let's."

McKenna eased the hand controller over and banked into the new heading.

"What's the film load, Tiger?"

"Checkin' now. I've got fifty frames of low-light, and twenty frames of infrared left. Ho-kay. The J-Band's gone off the air."

"Use up all you have," McKenna said.

He saw the installation ten miles before he reached it because it was well lit. He altered course a couple degrees to pass right over it.

At the speed they were making, McKenna only got a quick look.

"I count four large buildings and a chopper pad," he told Munoz.

"Ditto. Plus the radar antenna a quarter-mile to the east. One of the buildings, the largest, has been there for fifty years or more, Snake Eyes. We saw it, what, a year ago?"

"About that."

"I'm backin' up tape."

As they left the coast behind and McKenna started a slow, turning climb, Munoz reversed the videotape until the installation appeared on the panel screen. He froze the frame.

The old and large building had once produced heavy machinery, McKenna thought. Tractors, maybe. It was now in full operation, light spilling from hundreds of small windows. Two of the new buildings were tall and wide, kind of like hangars, but short of windows. The last building was a narrow structure, but he guessed it at over fifteen stories in height. It had an aircraft warning strobe on top. In the green-hued picture, it was difficult to tell, but McKenna thought he saw a maze of railroad tracks running into the buildings.

"Strange layout, *amigo?*"

"Could be a launch complex, Tiger."

"That's what I'm thinkin', but it's damned small."

"It only takes one launch tower for one big rocket," McKenna said.

"I think we oughta put a Wasp into it."

"Good idea, but we're not going to do it."

"I also think," Munoz said, "that we'd better tell Embry to convert our Wasps to air-to-ground."

"You're full of good ideas."

"Got lots of sleep today."

134

Seven

Col. Pyotr Volontov chose the early morning, three-thirty in Leningrad, for his first flight over the oil fields. It was also three-thirty in Murmansk, where General Sheremetevo had temporarily deployed the 5th Interceptor Wing. Even based at the relatively primitive facilities at Murmansk, 200 kilometers north of the Arctic Circle, the western side of the target area was over 1,800 kilometers away, requiring refueling from an airborne tanker en route.

On the first flight, Volontov flew cover for the unarmed MiG-25 reconnaissance aircraft, staying at 10,000 meters, 3,000 meters above the MiG-25.

Volontov's MiG-29, which NATO had codenamed Fulcrum, was a full Mach number slower than the MiG-25, which could accelerate to Mach 3.2. He considered the MiG-29 the superior attack aircraft, however. The older plane was 20,000 kilograms heavier, constructed of steel, and many models still carried vacuum tube-based electronics. In comparison, the MiG-29 was ultramodern, with Pulse-Doppler multimode radar capable of lookdown/shootdown and an infrared search and tracking sensor. His craft was armed with a 30-millimeter cannon and six AA-11 air-to-air missiles. In a head-to-head confrontation with a MiG-25, Volontov thought he would emerge the survivor as a result of his airplane's greater agility.

Maj. Anatoly Rostoken, who commanded Volontov's 2032nd Squadron, was flying the reconnaissance plane, somewhat gingerly since he had not flown the MiG-25 for a couple years.

Six hundred kilometers northwest of Murmansk, in the wavery light of a summer night, the Ilyushin tanker replenished the thirsty fighters, then climbed away to orbit and await their return. While Rostoken could now complete the homeward leg to Murmansk, the MiG-29 had only a 1,200-kilometer combat radius. If Volontov were required to use afterburners or expend fuel at a high rate in low level, high speed flight, he would need to meet the tanker once again.

After the hectic transfer of his wing to the northern base—requiring the use of six transports to transfer his ground support personnel and the wing's equipment, Volontov was happy to be almost by himself. Doing something worthwhile for a change.

The members of his two squadrons, the 2032nd and the 2033rd, were also elated at the change in routine, though somewhat mystified by the lack of detail he had provided them in briefings. General Sheremetevo, however, had ordered him to provide them with minimal information. Operation Artic Waste was simply an exercise in combined operations over the icy waters and glacial ice, with innocuous oil wells utilized as the simulated targets.

"Condor One, this is Vulture One," Rostoken radioed.

"Proceed, Vulture One."

"I have Svalbard Island on radar. Bearing three-five-four, nine-two kilometers."

"Very well, Vulture One. Go to five thousand meters and initiate mission."

Volontov reached out to switch his radar to the active mode for three full sweeps. He found the outline of the island immediately and the blip of Vulture One a half second later. Returning the radar to inactive, he nudged the stick forward and went into a shallow dive, intending to lose 3,000 meters of altitude, staying close to the MiG-25.

The HUD readout indicated a rise in his speed to 550

kilometers per hour, and he backed the throttles off to keep it from rising higher. The HUD in the MiG-29 was not as sophisticated as those in American aircraft, but it provided him with basic readings.

Rostoken was thirty kilometers ahead of him, almost to the coast of Greenland, when the radar threat alarm sang its shrill syllables.

"Condor, flight of two, bearing one-five-five, four-zero kilometers."

"Vulture, turn to zero-one-zero and climb to two-two-thousand meters," Volontov ordered.

"Confirmed."

The MiG-25 was one of the few aircraft in the world with a ceiling exceeding 24,000 meters. The American SR-71 Blackbird could do it, but it had been retired.

Feeling that the MiG-25 could protect itself with altitude, Volontov made a tight left turn and began to climb. He used the radar momentarily and found the two blips at 6,000 meters. The ground clutter from the sea was difficult to read, but he picked out a few of the wells and several ships before switching the set to passive mode.

Flying in formation like that, they would be the Tornados or Eurofighters that Sheremetevo had warned him about, rather than a commercial flight.

Volontov would have liked to buzz them, purely for the exhilaration of it, but he had been told to steer clear of patrols.

The threat receiver sounded again, and a moment later, the alarming warning appeared in red letters on the HUD—HOSTILE MISSILE LOCK-ON.

Volontov grinned to himself, tasting the rubbery tang of his face mask. The bastards thought to scare him off, locking on with an infrared-seeking missile.

Switching to the international frequency, he heard the end of a sentence in English. ". . . aircraft, identify yourself."

He did not respond.

"Unidentified aircraft, I will fire a warning shot in one minute unless you identify yourself."

To hell with General Sheremetevo, Volontov thought. He would test the resolve of these Germans.

With right stick and rudder, Volontov banked over into a dive. He activated the radar, then the armaments panel, selecting two AA-11 missiles.

He found the two aircraft quickly on the radar screen, their blips almost merged, and lined up his dive. Pushed the throttles forward.

Speed rose quickly. The airframe shuddered as he passed through the sound barrier.

Mach 1.1.

Distance to objective, twenty kilometers.

His missiles locked on to the lead aircraft. Radar-homing. The low buzz in his earphones and the HUD readout told him so.

The Germans scattered, the lead plane diving away to the left, the trailing aircraft to the right. The hostile LOCK-ON message flickered and died as the German plane lost his angle on the MiG-29.

Volontov shut down his own missiles and chuckled to himself.

The Americans would call them chickenshits.

Easing back on the stick, he pulled out of his dive at 3,000 meters above the sea, turning slightly to the right, toward a homeward course.

On the radar, the German aircraft were regrouping almost ten kilometers behind him.

"Wha-wha-wha-wha!"

The missile threat receiver sounded in his ear.

The HUD blinked at him: HOSTILE MISSILE LOCK-ON.

This one had been launched.

Slapping the stick left, Volontov rolled the plane inverted, looking up through the canopy.

Black dot circled in rosy, fiery white.

Surface-to-air, rising from a ship.

"Bastards!"

Tracking him on infrared.

He retarded his throttles, then pulled the nose on over and aimed for the missile, to get his hot exhaust out of its line of sight.

Closing fast.

Seconds away.

He opened up with his cannon, a futile gesture.

Rolled the left wing up, tugged the stick back to his crotch, shoved the throttles to military thrust.

The MiG strained as it pulled out of the dive. The G-forces drained the blood from his face.

The missile abruptly diverted its course away from him.

As Volontov regained control and began climbing, he wondered about the sincerity of the missile battery commander aboard that ship.

He was not certain that it was only a warning shot.

"Yes, General Eisenach, we launched a missile. Purely a warning. It was diverted in the last moments."

Adm. Gerhard Schmidt was in his flag plot, one deck below the bridge of the *Hamburg*. The large, thickly padded chair in which he sat was fastened to the deck, but it could swivel between the large port which gave him a view of the sea to the two-meter electronic plotting screen mounted on the interior bulkhead. The screen was now relatively quiet. The wells were indicated as yellow squares. His battle group, comprised of the *Hamburg* and two destroyers, was shown in green. The two Tornados were just leaving the screen, headed south.

Eisenach mulled that over. "First a Greenpeace ship, now an airplane."

"There were two airplanes."

"Visible on radar. American aircraft?"

"No, General. They were Soviets. Most likely a Foxbat and a Fulcrum, according to the radar and infrared signatures."

"Damn it, Gerhard! The Soviets, now?"

"They were far off their normal reconnaissance runs over the North Sea." Schmidt sat low in his chair, his elbows placed firmly on the soft armrests. He tapped a forefinger against the earlobe of his jutting left ear. "My assumption was that the Foxbat was taking pictures. This is the first time we have encountered aircraft, and we followed standing policy in challenging them, but the Fulcrum pilot was exceptionally aggressive. He attacked the Tornados."

"He fired on them?"

"No. But he was not frightened by our airborne tactics. Tactics devised by the air force, I remind you."

"So you took it upon yourself to order a launch?" Eisenach's tone carried his agitation.

"They are no longer here."

"But, Gerhard, rest assured that they will be back."

Schmidt was left listening to the carrier wave.

He shrugged to himself. He had a large number of missiles available.

Developing photographs aboard *Themis* was not a simple task. Specialized equipment had been devised which allowed the film to be placed in small compartments, a door closed, then the chemicals released into the compartment. After the prescribed amount of time, the chemicals were sucked out of the compartment. It was time-consuming, and Amy Pearson had spent most of her morning developing the hundreds of pictures—each of them marked with time and coordinates in the upper right-hand corner—brought back by the three Makosharks.

After they were developed, she passed them under a video camera, transferring the images to the more manipulative medium of computer-based imaging. Then she followed the corridors and hatchways back to the Radio Shack in the Command Center to pore over them on one of the consoles.

Donna Amber was standing the morning communications shift, succeeding Sgt. Don Curtis. As soon as Pearson appeared in the hatchway, Amber said, "Colonel, Don Curtis left me a message for you. Says you might want to review the radar tapes."

"For when, Donna?"

"Uh, let's see. Nine to nine-fifteen our time, concentrating on the Greenland region."

"Okay, bring it up, please."

The radar aboard *Themis,* with its ninety-foot-wide antenna housed in the massive fiberglass pod on Spoke Fifteen, could radiate up to fifteen million watts of energy, drawing on the nuclear reactor. At full output, it had over 400 miles of range, but that energy usage also dimmed all of the lights and slowed all of the electronic devices aboard the station. It also affected the sensitive instruments on aerospace craft within fifty miles of the satellite.

It was normally operated, from the radar operator's compartment in the hub, at low power settings, with a range of 215 miles, almost the same distance as the altitude of *Themis* above the earth. Using I-Band for lateral tracking and G-Band for altitude tracking, the radar was chiefly useful for guiding HoneyBee rockets to docking slots. A few high-flying aircraft or a few rocket launches from Vandenburg Air Force Base, Cape Canaveral, or Baikonur Cosmodrome were sometimes recorded when the Department of Defense had a particular interest. The radar's computer could scan and track simultaneously, tracking up to 120 targets at the same time. The radar was a key ingredient in the Satellite Defense Initiative system, though that program had now taken on a lower priority.

At 220 miles of scan, the ground clutter reflections, unless over relatively uninhabited areas, could be confusing. The computer filtered out much of the clutter, but with so many targets at surface level, a radar operator could get dizzy.

Because of the orbital rate of *Themis,* there was a continual movement of the tracking area above the earth. The Greenland region would have been under radar surveillance for less than twenty minutes.

Amber touched an intercom button. "Macklin, you awake?"

"Radar, Mizz Amber." The title was drawn out, reflecting Sgt. Joe Macklin's attitude toward the spat he and Donna Amber were having. Pearson had been monitoring it, alert to undue personnel problems.

"Colonel Pearson wants to see last night's tape. Start it at nine o'clock."

"Right. Coming up on channel twelve, Sergeant."

Pearson grabbed a floating tether and pulled herself close to the terminal. She tapped "one-two" into the channel selector board.

The image was manic, radar sweep and blips zipping as the tape was backed up in high-speed reverse.

It stopped, jerked forward, then ran at normal speed.

Amber watched a duplicate on her own screen.

The operator last night had extended the range as soon as he saw radar returns that looked suspicious to him. They appeared on the bottom left of the screen, slowly crossing the screen upward and to the left as *Themis* moved inexorably toward the south and the earth rotated.

An airborne blip just west of well number fifteen abruptly turned and started climbing fast. Well over Mach 2, Pearson thought. The altitude readout next to the blip showed forty, then fifty, then sixty thousand feet.

"That's got to be a Foxbat," Amber said.

"I think you're right, Donna. And he's running from something."

A second aircraft, some twenty-five miles behind the first, turned left, making almost a full circle.

Two blips, so close together they were almost melded, appeared at the bottom of the screen.

"That's what they're running from," Amber said.

"A patrol flight."

142

The images were now centered on the screen. Pearson could count all of the wells. Perhaps twelve ships in the area, though the background was snowy.

The single blip dove on the German planes.

Attack?

No. Maybe. The Germans planes parted and dove away.

Seconds later, a new target appeared, separating from one of the ships. It climbed quickly, leaning toward the single aircraft.

"Seaborne missile launch," Pearson said.

"Damn."

Then there was a flurry of darting blips, which merged, then separated. Finally, the radar return of the missile faded away as it apparently exploded harmlessly. The single aircraft, now at a much lower altitude, accelerated toward the east, climbing.

Pearson touched the intercom button.

"Radar."

"Sergeant Macklin, get me a speed and heading on each of the aircraft."

"Right away, Colonel."

As she waited, the two German planes joined up again, and the whole scenario drifted off the screen.

Macklin came back to her. "Colonel Pearson, the two in formation are at five hundred knots, heading three-five-oh. Five-two per cent probable Tornados. The aircraft in the north is nine-five percent probable MiG-25. Heading zero-nine-nine, speed Mach two point six. The other aircraft is seven-five percent probable Fulcrum, heading zero-nine-four, speed Mach one point nine."

"Give me an intersecting vector on the MiG's, Macklin."

He read off the coordinates. "That'll be in the Barents Sea, north of Sereya, Norway, Colonel."

"Thank you, Sergeant. That's all."

"Now the Soviets are involved?" Amber asked.

"Looks that way, Donna. You want to raise General Thorpe for me at Cheyenne Mountain?"

Ten minutes passed before Thorpe was located.

"Hello, Amy. Something up?"

She told him about the confrontation. "We think they were Soviet aircraft. It seems likely that they were on a reconnaissance mission."

"That would be right," Thorpe said. "Colonel Volontov's people are probably on the job."

"You don't trust our information?"

Thorpe laughed, but it was hollow. "Not that at all, Amy. You like to make decisions based on the most information available, don't you?"

"Yes," she said reluctantly.

"That's all that's taking place here. But you said there was a missile fired?"

"Yes. Surface-to-air, ship-launched."

"All right, I'll look into that. One other thing, here. The CIA interviewed the captain of that Greenpeace ship. Boat, really."

"Anything interesting?"

"Yes and no. The captain, a guy named Nichols, is a pretty ardent fellow, from the reports. And he wants to bring charges against some German major for firing a missile at him."

"He say why they were that far north?" Pearson asked.

"Chasing a rumor. We've only got secondhand hearsay on this, Amy, but apparently Nichols talked to some fishing boat captain from Greenland who said the fish were migrating out of the Greenland Sea. Nichols suspects oil spillage, and he was trying to take water samples."

"Maybe we should get the samples for him?" Pearson said. "Or for us."

"General Brackman's going to take it up with the Joint Chiefs. I think that we'll try to get a submarine in there, Amy."

"If they're shooting at airplanes, the Germans may at-

144

tempt to run a submarine off, too, General. They might get pretty upset."

"Well, yeah, that's got us a little worried."

Compartment A-47, the exercise room, did not have a screen, so the squadron members crowded into the Command Center for their briefing.

All of the available tethers were in use, and several people floated free, drifting with the air-conditioning currents. South America, verdantly bright, slithered across the porthole.

McKenna hung onto the curtain outside his office cubicle and watched as Overton raised his hand to silence the babble. Donna Amber had her head stuck through the curtained doorway to the Radio Shack.

"Ladies, gentlemen, and weapons system operators," Overton said, drawing a laugh. The general had once been a WSO. He had also ejected from a Phantom hit by a SAM-7 over Hanoi and spent a couple of hours bobbing in the South China Sea. "Our interest in the Greenland Sea in the last few days seems to have generated a lot of activity. Colonel Pearson will tell us about it."

Pearson quickly went through the details of the Greenpeace boat, the State Department's inability to elicit information from the Germans in regard to the wells, and the Soviet overflight. McKenna had been aware of all but the Red Air Force's mission.

Tony Munoz asked, "This a cooperative thing, Amy? With the Soviets?"

"All I know, Tony, is that General Sheremetevo has assigned the Fifth Interceptor Wing to gathering information. During their first flight this morning, the *Hamburg* launched a missile at Colonel Volontov, the wing commander. It was apparently meant as a warning."

Munoz spun to look at McKenna. "This is gonna get out of hand, Snake Eyes."

145

"I talked to General Brackman this morning," McKenna said. "The President has signed a contingency order for us."

"Fire if fired upon?"

"Yes, except that it has to be cleared through me. Everybody keep that in mind."

"We going to have to dodge a bunch of Soviet airplanes?" Conover asked.

Pearson responded to the question. "The 5th Interceptor Wing has been moved to Murmansk, and the unit flies Fulcrums. I understand that there are also a couple of Foxbats assigned to the wing, and there will be tankers in the area of the Barents Sea. Yes, you need to watch out for them."

Dimatta looked more than a little pained. "We're buddy-buddy, now?"

"For the time being, Frank, yes," Pearson said.

Dimatta turned to McKenna, the question still in his raised eyebrow.

"That's right, Cancha. For the time being."

The look that Pearson gave him suggested that she didn't think much of the requirement for McKenna's squadron to double-check her information with the squadron commander.

They all seemed a little disgruntled, but they settled down as Pearson went through selected pictures from the recon flight of the night before. One by one, she brought them up on the screen, pointing out features. She started with Dimatta and William's run over the oil fields.

"There's nothing new to report on the wells themselves, but there has been an interesting change in the makeup of the naval ships. We got photos of fifteen ships, including three seagoing tugs, which we hadn't seen before. New, also, is the fact that the missile cruiser *Stuttgart* has joined the fleet. Further, the naval force has been reconfigured into battle groups of three ships. Either a missile cruiser or a missile frigate accompanied by two destroyers. Some-

146

thing has changed the philosophy, but this is the kind of thing I would expect, after reading the bios on Admiral Gerhard Schmidt. The posture is a great deal more defensive.

"On the sonobuoys that Delta Green deployed, we haven't yet picked up much. A couple ships passing close to number six. Number eight picked up a submarine, the *Black Forest*, according to the screw signature, which is their newest nuclear sub. We aren't certain that every sonobuoy is located exactly on the pipeline route, but the *Black Forest* could well be patrolling the pipeline."

"You said the navy is going to send a sub in there?" Overton asked.

"Yes. I passed this information on to General Thorpe at NORAD. He is forwarding it to CINCSUBLANT."

"Good."

"All right, on to Delta Yellow's flight. Overall, we didn't find much changed in the industrial or military centers. New Amsterdam has enough parked aircraft to support the information that four wings are stationed there."

Pearson brought up a new picture, an enlarged photo of the runways at New Amsterdam. McKenna had landed there once, but it seemed like a long time ago.

With a collapsible pointer, she indicated the alert shack at the end of Runway 27. "This is the twenty-four-hour standby facility, with, as you'll notice, revetments for two aircraft. There have been alterations since our last photos of New Amsterdam, which were about three months ago. Back to the bottom right, here, about two hundred yards from the alert shack, new revetments have been built, and nine house trailers have been moved into position. Judging from the number and type of equipment deployed—Tornadoes, Eurofighters, transports, and helicopters—we believe that this is the 20th Special Air Group."

"From appearances," Nitro Fizz Williams said, "you're saying the whole damned wing is on twenty-four alert status, Amy?"

"It would appear that way, George," Pearson told him. "There were two brand new ships, a destroyer and an amphibious landing craft, in the naval section of the harbor at Bremerton. Any questions, so far?"

There were none.

"All right. Delta Blue. This was the most interesting flight, from the standpoint of changes."

A new series of pictures began to appear and disappear on the screen.

"There has been a lot of new construction in the industrial areas at Rostok, Halle, Leipzig, and Dresden. It's rapid expansion, but still, something we might have expected, given the stated intention of expanding employment and developing the eastern economy. And, yet again, some of it is disturbing. Military units on the borders appear to have a full complement of equipment, most of it appearing new. Tanks, trucks, jeeps, artillery pieces. New, though, are large truck parks, identified by the tracks leading into them. We don't know what is stored in the parks, however, because they have been hidden under camouflage netting."

Pearson pointed to a photo on the screen, dim because of the low-light film used. It looked like a big, empty field next to a gravel road. Several churned-up turn-ins from the road, crossing over culverts, provided the perspective.

"This one was taken a few miles east of Dresden. The camouflage nettings covers seven acres."

"Jesus!" Munoz said. "That's a lot of tanks."

"Some of the markings on the road are from tracked vehicles, but it's also a lot of howitzers, or fuel tankers, or ammunition storage or something else. We don't know what."

Another picture.

"Here, outside Leipzig, is a new tank farm. East Germany is expecting to sell its citizens a lot of automobiles, or it's storing a great deal of fuel. We're estimating a half-

148

billion gallons of liquid fuel stored here alone. At Rostok, there's another tank farm.

"Last, but not least, Colonel McKenna and Major Munoz shot some pictures of an expanded installation west of Peenemünde. It is clearly a launch site, but we don't know what kind of vehicle it is intended to launch."

McKenna studied the picture, much clearer than the tape he had reviewed on the return trip.

"It looks to me, Amy," he said, "as if the shell of the launch facility is designed to be moved away from the gantry on tracks."

"Exactly, Colonel."

"Which would leave an exposed gantry at least as large as any on the pads at Canaveral."

"Yes."

"Which means a vehicle designed for entry into space."

"I would agree with that."

"I wonder if it has a warhead," he mused.

Gen. Marvin Brackman was cautious on the phone, still feeling out the relationship between himself and Vitaly Sheremetevo. Adm. Hannibal Cross had passed the Sheremetevo contact on to Brackman, and they had communicated by telephone several times. The last time they had talked, they had advanced to the use of first names, but the usage was still tentative.

"Is your government going to lodge a complaint against the *Hamburg*, Vitaly?"

There was a long pause. "No, Marvin, it is not. In fact, my government does not know about the strike attempt. I am keeping that information within the PVO Strany."

"I see. Any particular reason?"

"For the moment, I wish to see if the strike was a rash move by an excitable commander. We will know more if it happens again."

"Admiral Schmidt is not particularly excitable," Brackman pointed out.

"No, he is not. But a subordinate may have been responsible."

"That is possible," Brackman said, though he felt as if something was being held back.

"And to tell you the truth, my airplane commander may have been a little rash, himself. His actions may have provoked the response he received."

Which was the way David Thorpe had interpreted the radar tape from *Themis*.

"All right, then. We'll leave it there for the time being. Did you learn anything of interest from the flight pictures, Vitaly?"

"Not very much. They are quite similar to the photographs you forwarded to me, and my analysts say the same as your analysts. There is too much heat being generated for them to be simply oil wells."

"What do you suggest as our next step, then?" Brackman asked.

"I believe we have learned all that we are to learn from infrared pictures, Marvin. I am going to attempt to interest Admiral Michy in a subsurface excursion."

Brackman considered the implications of American and Soviet submarines encountering the *Black Forest* in the Greenland Sea simultaneously.

"I have a suggestion, Vitaly. Call me back after you have talked to Admiral Michy, and I will arrange for him to communicate with Admiral Lorenzen, who is the commander in chief of submarines for our Atlantic fleet. We don't want our boats bumping noses."

"Ah, I understand. Yes, that is a good idea."

"And then, if I may ask, has your Colonel Volontov ever been to Chad?"

"I do not believe so, Marvin, and I am quite certain that he would find no interest in such a trip. But I will convince him that he will enjoy it."

"Good, Vitaly. Then, one last point. What are we going to do about that launch complex?"

"While I do not know for certain, it seems to me that the GRU will have persons in closer proximity to Peenemünde than will the CIA or the Defense Intelligence Agency."

"That is probably true," Brackman said, "though, like yourself, I couldn't say for sure."

"I will make the first inquiries, then," Sheremetevo told him.

McKenna put the MakoShark on the runway at Jack Andrews Air Force Base while it was still light out, just before seven o'clock. He taxied immediately into Hangar One and parked next to Delta Orange. The technicians working on final systems checks for the newest MakoShark abandoned their tasks to handle the after-flight inspection of Delta Blue.

They bitched about the hangar doors opening for Delta Blue's entrance, also bringing in a heat wave and a cloud of hot dry sand from the desert.

"Damn, Colonel," Tech Sergeant Prentiss said, "couldn't you have come in a little later, like in November?"

"Is it any better in November, Sarge?" McKenna asked as he descended the curving ladder Prentiss had attached to the fuselage.

"No. But it sounds cooler."

McKenna paced in a small circle. After several days in space, it always took him a while to reacquaint his leg muscles with gravity.

Munoz didn't wait for his own ladder to be placed, but stood up on the rear cockpit coaming, slipped around the raised forward canopy, and slid down McKenna's ladder.

"Thirsty, Tony?"

"I'm gonna have just one Bloody Mary and two bottles of *Dos Equis, jefe.*"

"Sounds good to me, too, but you've got to wait."

"No shit? I've been waitin' days and days."

"All in your mind, Tony. I want you to meet this guy, too."

They changed into khakis in the pilots' dressing room and waited until eight-fifteen in the control tower atop Hangar One, drinking Cokes with the air controller.

At eight-fifteen, the radar beeped.

The controller jumped up and ran for his console, pulling the headset over his head. He told McKenna, "I've got an inbound sixty miles out."

The radio speaker overhead squawked.

"Andrews Air Control."

"Andrews, this is Soviet MiG-29 eight six four seven."

"Go ahead, four seven."

"I am one hundred kilometers out, requesting permission to land."

"Preapproved, four seven. You are cleared for straight-in on Runway 18 left. Temperature one-one-three, wind four knots from two-six-two. No other traffic in the area."

"Thank you, Andrews Control. I will also require a remote parking space."

"Also preapproved, four seven. When you are on the ground, I will direct you."

McKenna and Munoz descended from the tower, pushed through the ground-level door onto the tarmac, and winced as the heat hit them.

"Hell, *compadre*, I might as well have stayed in Tucson all my life."

"Chasing *señoritas?*"

"It is my dedicated vocation."

McKenna slid behind the wheel of a golf cart painted air force blue and topped with a white, fringed sunshade.

"Does this Russian outrank me?" Munoz asked.

"By a couple grades."

"I'll ride in back."

Munoz scrambled into one of the two narrow seats on the back of the cart.

They watched as the MiG-29 came in, gear and flaps extended. Reminiscent of a twin-ruddered Eagle. It was a smooth landing and a short runout. The airplane turned around and came back toward them. Half a mile away, it turned off the strip, rolled for a hundred yards, turned 180 degrees, and braked to a stop. The whine of its engines died away, and McKenna turned the key on the electric cart and pulled away from the hangar.

"He doesn't want anyone taking a close look at that thing, does he, Snake Eyes?"

"Can't say as I blame him. We don't often park one of our top fighters on a Soviet air base. We're going to station an air cop in a pickup for him. And he demanded that he be allowed to refuel it himself."

"Paranoid SOB," Munoz said.

McKenna stopped the cart twenty yards from the Fulcrum and watched as the pilot left his helmet in the cockpit, slid out of it, and worked his way to the ground, stabbing his toes into steps behind spring-loaded doors. He closed the canopy, bent to pick up a valise he had tossed out, then approached the cart in a stiff-legged walk.

McKenna and Munoz got out and saluted. The Soviet colonel returned the salute, then shook their hands when they were offered.

"Colonel Volontov, I'm Colonel Kevin McKenna. Kevin, if you prefer. This is Tony Munoz."

Volontov had a handsome, somewhat angular face, and he smiled easily enough, but there was some rigidity in his eyes. "My superiors say we are being friendly, so, yes, let us try first names. Mine is Pyotr."

McKenna grinned at him. "Good deal, Pyotr. You want to shed that pressure suit? Before you reach boiling point?"

"I will do it here," he said and started unzipping zippers. He stripped to underwear, opened his small valise, and found a jumpsuit affair to don, then topped it with a service cap.

A blue Chevy pickup pulled up, and the air policeman driving opened his window. "Colonel McKenna, I was to report to you."

"See that aircraft, Airman? This is as close as you get to it. And no one else on this base, no matter the rank, gets any closer than you are now."

"Yes, sir."

"You have any trouble with anyone, beep me."

McKenna turned back to Volontov. "Is that satisfactory, Pyotr?"

"Quite satisfactory, Col . . . Kevin."

Munoz climbed into the back of the cart. "How about a drink, Pyotr?"

The man smiled again, his eyes a little softer. "That would be welcome."

On the ride back down the runway toward the dining hall, McKenna said, "You had a hell of a flight. Thirty-seven hundred miles."

"Yes. It required two in-flight refuelings."

"What time did you leave?"

"Late this afternoon."

McKenna grinned. Volontov wasn't going to reveal his time aloft or his speed, but McKenna figured it took him about two-and-a-half hours at around Mach 2.

The Soviet pilot openly examined the base as they left the runway and followed a ragged asphalt road. There wasn't much to be seen in the open. A HoneyBee on a flatbed was en route to a launch pad.

"You are one of the MakoShark pilots, Kevin?" Volontov asked.

"I'll have to respond 'classified,' " McKenna said.

"Of course," the pilot said. "I must admit to some envy. I have been attempting to transfer to our Rocket Forces for some years."

"Someday, you get some time off, maybe we can

154

arrange a ride in one of the Makos," McKenna offered.

"I would like that."

The dining hall was deserted, the off-duty personnel crowding the rec room. Rather than accept the available entrées from the cafeteria line, Munoz chased down a mess sergeant and had him grill three large T-bones. He introduced Volontov to Bloody Mary.

Volontov pulled the celery stalk out of his oversized glass. "What is this?"

"Don't worry, Pete. It's got vodka in it."

After a tentative, short sip, Volontov said, "And so it does."

Over dinner, they all got to know each other. McKenna briefed the Soviet wing commander on the data that Pearson had been accumulating, and Volontov provided the details of his single flight over the oil fields.

McKenna said, "Our people don't really think they're pumping oil up there, you know?"

"General Sheremetevo seems to have his doubts, also. He has said that the Germans imported twice as much oil from the *rodina*, the motherland, last year as they have in the past. I should think that Soviet oil imports would diminish with the discovery of new sources."

McKenna made a mental note of that item to pass on to Pearson. "That's a point, Pyotr."

They were working on large chunks of warm apple pie when Lynn Marie Hagger entered the dining room to pick up a mug of coffee from the cafeteria line. When she spotted them, she walked over to the table.

McKenna noted Volontov's appraisal of her slim figure, heart-shaped face, and silky dark hair. She was dressed in a flight suit. His blue eyes lightened and the corners of his mouth lifted a trifle.

Haggar spoke to McKenna as the men stood up. "Am I interrupting anything, Colonel?"

"I think we've covered it, Lynn. Would you like to join us?"

155

"I have an hour until flight time."

"Have a seat," McKenna said, then introduced her. "Colonel Pyotr Volontov, Major Lynn Haggar. Pyotr's a wing commander, Lynn."

"It is nice to meet you, Major Haggar."

"Make it Lynn, would you?"

Volontov nodded toward the pilot's wings embroidered over her left breast pocket. "You are a pilot, Lynn?"

She was sitting with her right side to Volontov, so he had not seen the left shoulder patch, a silver blue, blocky "1" on a black background, a miniature satellite and orbital line circling it. Haggar looked to McKenna for guidance in her response.

He said, "Lynn's in my squadron, Pyotr. She flies the Mako."

Volontov smiled widely, revealing good, even teeth. "I am impressed. A cosmonaut."

"When I get tired of McKenna," Munoz said, "I'm gonna be Lynn's systems officer. She needs the benefit of my experience."

McKenna noted that Munoz left the "weapons" off the "systems officer" tag. The Arizonian could be subtle when he wanted to be.

Haggar smiled at him. "Tony, your experience is primarily with hot food and spicy women. Why would I need it?"

"What more is there?"

Even Volontov laughed at that.

Haggar asked him, "Do you have many women flying in your wing, Pyotr?"

"None, I'm afraid. And none in any unit of the PVO Strany. The generals at Stavko are reluctant to place women in combat roles."

"The generals at Stavko are not alone," Haggar said to him, but she gave the dirty look to McKenna.

Eight

General Overton was in his office cubicle, the curtain open. He was entering data in his computerized daily log for *Themis*.

Pearson pushed off the hatchway of the Radio Shack, sailed across the corridor, and stopped her flight by grabbing the bar outside Overton's cubicle.

He looked up from his screen.

"Want to hear a harebrained idea, General?"

"No. But I'm going to anyway, right?"

"Right."

"Tell me."

"Everything we've got so far points in the direction of a military buildup in Germany. Fossil fuels being stored. Industrial output at peak. Equipment reserves. The wells have to be part of that, but we're stymied as to new information."

"Granted."

"In reviewing my pictures of the wells, I've noted that wells twenty-two, twenty-three, and twenty-four don't show the same heat configurations as the others. I'm assuming that they're currently drilling those three."

"I'll go with that," Overton said. "The process seems to be one of constructing a platform and dome ahead of time, then moving the drilling equipment in later. More efficient that way, I suppose."

"And they haven't built a new platform in over a year."

157

Overton pondered that. "Meaning they don't plan any more wells, after the last three are completed?"

"That's what I would guess," she said.

"That also means that, once the last three are completed, the drilling program has achieved its end."

"I'm thinking, General, that we're getting close to a deadline."

"Yes, but a deadline for what?"

"Consider Nineteen thirty-nine."

"I don't want to. You have an idea about what they are, don't you, Amy?"

"Yes. But I need to confirm it."

"Are we getting too harebrained?"

"I want to take the top off of a dome."

"Jesus Christ!" Hannibal Cross said. "You're out of your mind, Marvin."

The others on the conference call waited quietly. All of the Joint Chiefs were on the line, along with Adm. Richard Lorenzen, the commander of Atlantic Fleet submarine forces, and Marvin Brackman. On the other side of Brackman's office, David Thorpe sat in a chair and listened intently to the voices on the speaker.

Brackman finally said, "You've all seen the data. I think this is the next step."

"What did the *Ohio* get, Dick?" Cross asked.

"She sonar-mapped most of the area and took water samples," Lorenzen said. "Those platforms are anchored in depths ranging from six hundred to seventeen hundred feet. There is no oil spillage, and what's more, Hannibal, she never did pick up the sound of a pipeline. Those things make a noise, you know. Average water temperature in the area should run about forty degrees Fahrenheit, but is much higher near a well. At three hundred yards, the temperature readings were about forty-five degrees. At two hundred yards, as close as the *Ohio* approached a well, the readings showed seventy-one degrees. Rough extrapolation suggests that the temperature at the core, at the well casing, might be as high as two hundred degrees. Perhaps higher. The Soviets sent in the *Typhoon,* and she came back with similar data."

"Anyone run into the *Black Forest?*" the chief of Naval Operations asked.

"The *Ohio* left the area earlier than planned when they heard the *Forest* approaching."

The army chief of staff, a man holding engineering degrees, said, "Sounds geothermal to me, gentlemen. In an awfully dangerous place."

"Another item," Lorenzen said, "The marine life has definitely deserted the region. Sonar operators generally bitch about the number of whales fouling their readings, but they didn't pick up one whale within thirty miles of the wells. We're still analyzing water samples, but on first examination, the algae count appears to be higher, suggesting a warming of the seas. And lastly, we have recorded sonar readings of the wells. There are some big, big turbines in operation, and I think we could probably suspect turbine-generators."

"Is that enough confirmation for you, Marvin?" Cross asked.

"Colonel Pearson," Brackman said, and seeing Thorpe nodding vigorously, added his name, "and General Thorpe would like to see unprotected infrared data."

"Shit," the chairman said. "The National Security Council will come apart at the seams."

"Skip them," Brackman said. "Go right to the President and get a Presidential Finding. The CIA does it all the time for covert ops."

Cross mulled it over. "He would probably go for it, but he'll make it contingent upon another negative response to a State Department inquiry."

"Do it any way you can, Hannibal. I don't think we want to wait a hell of a lot longer. If State gets involved, insist upon a deadline for the response."

"Such as, Marvin?"

"Such as, give the Germans until ten o'clock tonight to respond."

"All right. I'll try that out. In the meantime, gentlemen, in the event that our guesswork is correct, I want everyone, meaning your immediate staff people, considering the next phase. What steps do we take?"

After he hung up, Brackman looked to his intelligence officer. "I think, David, you can contact Overton and Pearson and tell them to prepare the operation. They're to stand by until they have a final approval from me."

"Will do, Marv."

"I'm going to call Sheremetevo and tell him to keep his people out of the area tonight. When one of those domes splits open, we don't want the Soviets catching the blame. And bitch as they might, the Germans will have a hell of a time laying the responsibility at our door when they won't have radar or infrared evidence of an intruder. You're sure about the missiles?"

"Yup. Outside of a few of our people, no one has ever seen a Wasp. They don't have any identification on them, and McKenna's at Jack Andrews, now, preparing some special Wasps. There's not going to be any evidence."

"I hope not. How big is this hole going to be?"

"Just whatever Pearson needs to get a reading."

"I trust that we're that good."

"We are," Thorpe said. "That's why it's called a surgical strike."

The meeting at Templehof was a scheduled one, and Eisenach arrived on time, at three o'clock. His pilot settled the helicopter on the pad, next to a car waiting to take him to the administration building.

It was only a 160-kilometer flight from Peenemünde, but he was feeling tired. His days seemed to be getting longer, and he would just as soon be at home on the edge of the *Tiergarten*, enjoying a schnapps and putting his feet up on the windowsill.

After he was seated in the Mercedes, his adjutant, *Oberst* Maximillian Oberlin closed the sliding window between them and the driver and asked, "The progress is satisfactory, Herr General?"

"Not quite, Colonel. The engineers insist that they are on schedule, but their schedule does not correspond to anything I ever put on paper."

The driver pulled out of his parking spot and headed down the tree-lined street.

"Engineers can be wily," Oberlin said.

"Exactly. There are six vehicles fully constructed, but only the first two have all of their internal components. I am told the first is operational, but they hesitate when I ask to see all of the successful test data."

"Who hesitates, General?"

"The man who is second in charge of the project. Goldstein."

"Ah, the Jew."

"Yes. It is too bad that we need his brain."

"Though not for much longer," Oberlin said. "If the first test flight is successful, the man could be relinquished to private enterprise."

"Or elsewhere," the general said. "He has insulted me often enough."

"I can see to it," Oberlin offered.

"Please do."

"Somewhere in the North Sea?"

"That would be pleasant," Eisenach said, his mind already picturing a man stepping out of a helicopter at 2,000 feet over the sea. Not stepping out willingly, of

161

course. "Now, what surprises do the intelligence staff have for us today?"

"Mostly, they will be complaining about Schmidt's decision to launch a SAM at the Soviet airplane. They will say it draws unnecessary attention to the wells. The feeling is that reconnaissance flights do not reveal a great deal to the observers."

"Still," Eisenach said, "it is disturbing that the Soviets even mounted a reconnaissance mission over the Greenland Sea. Their normal haunts are the Barents and North Seas."

"True. And speaking of the seas, the *Black Forest* reported a possible sonar contact with a submarine in the Greenland Sea."

"Identification?"

"No. The contact was momentary."

"That is not a normal passage for either American or Soviet submarines, Maximillian."

"No, General, it is not."

"Unless it is another of their celebrated treks under the North Pole."

"Yes, that could be it. Then, too, there have been inquiries about the wells, channeled through the Ministry of Foreign Affairs."

"I see. Who inquires?"

"The Americans, the British, the Soviets, and the government of Greenland."

"All instigated at the request of the Americans, no doubt, so as to throw off suspicion on the Americans alone."

"Perhaps, General. Or perhaps it is the Soviets who are behind it."

"And that Greenpeace boat captain? Has he complained to anyone?"

"Not as yet," Oberlin said. "We thought that they might go to the United Nations and squeal like pigs, but they have been uncharacteristically quiet."

"Mmmm."

"Then, too, General, these information requests have a new requirement. They demand information about the wells prior to a deadline at twenty-two hundred hours."

"Or?"

"There is no 'or' stated, Herr General."

"But it is implied. I think, Maximillian, that it would be wise to notify Weismann. Have him maintain continual air coverage tonight."

"Very well, General. And Admiral Schmidt?"

"No. He's done enough damage so far."

In Hangar One, McKenna and Munoz watched as the two ordnance technicians installed the Wasps. There were four of the missiles to be mounted on the right-hand inboard pylon. The port pylon mounted a gun pod.

They had spent most of the day, after Volontov had taken off on his return trip to Murmansk, with 1st Lt. Mabry Evans, the ordnance specialist, preparing the missiles. The Wasp was designed with retracting fins which opened outward on launch in atmospheric conditions. In space, where the fins were useless, the gimbal-based rocket motor provided directional control. The first modifications involved replacing the fins and the motor with fixed units. Stationary fins and a stationary motor, if they were ever recovered, could not give rise to speculations about the missile being a space-based device.

TNT charges had been placed in the electronics/guidance compartment, to obliterate the black boxes upon impact. After the missile detonated, there wouldn't be an integrated circuit or silicon wafer in pieces large enough to identify.

The Wasp warheads were interchangeable, depending upon the objective—air-to-air or air-to-surface. Typically, a Wasp was prepared in the air-to-air configuration, with a warhead containing twenty-one pounds of high explosive.

Evans had asked, "What are we penetrating, Colonel?"

"That's a problem, Mabry." He showed the man a close-up photo of a dome. "They're flat, triangular panels, fifteen feet on a side. Each one is joined to the next by a four-inch-wide strip of metal. Along each edge of the strip are bolt heads, spaced one foot apart, and staggered from one edge to the other. We're pretty damned sure that behind the triangular panels is insulation, then probably an interior panel. Pearson believes the panels are aluminum, rather than fiberglass, but we don't know how thick the insulation layer is, or what it's composed of."

"Each section would be prefabricated at some factory, then brought to the site and bolted together?"

"That would be my guess," McKenna said.

"Temperatures in the area?"

"Wintertime, they get down to around eighty below wind chill," Munoz told him.

"That would be a relief, after being stationed in Chad," Evanz said. "I'm going to say that they're using a Styrofoam core, sandwiched between, and bonded to, quarter-inch aluminum sheeting, then. That would keep them light enough to handle easily during construction, and yet provide rigidity. To combat those temperatures with a minimal expenditure of heating energy, I'd think the Styrofoam would be at least a couple of feet thick."

"However," McKenna said, "according to the IO, we're less concerned here with keeping cold temperatures out than we are with hiding excessive heat within."

"Hiding it from . . ."

"Infrared measurement."

"I see. Well, hell, Colonel. I need the interior temperature."

"Unknown. But the hotshots say it could go as high as six hundred degrees."

"Fahrenheit?"

"Right."

"And we're hiding it? Damn, offhand, that could require Styrofoam walls maybe ten feet thick."

"Let's work off that assumption, then, Mabry."

"How big a hole do you want?"

"Amy-baby," Munoz said, "would like to remove three triangular sections."

"No way in hell we're going to do that. It's got to be five, if we manage a direct hit on an intersection. Triangles intersect five at a time."

"Do five," McKenna said. "Then there's another itsy-bitsy problem."

"Of course there is," Evans said. "What?"

"We strongly suspect that the domes are compartmentalized inside. Partitions, divisions, whatever. We won't get much of a reading if we open up a section over a dormitory."

"So you want three or four holes, five panels each."

"That'd be nice."

Evans calculated for a while, then said, "What I'm going to do is preset a proximity instruction in the missile computers. That will keep the missiles about twenty feet from each other on the flight in. I'll slave three of them to the first missile. You'll have to launch all four at the same time, but the pattern of impact will be spread eighty feet apart."

"Good," Munoz said.

"No way in hell you're going to actually hit an intersection of panels."

"You questioning my marksmanship?" Munoz asked.

Evans just grinned at the WSO. "We don't want to kill anyone, I suspect?"

"No, not if we can help it," McKenna said.

"I'll use fifty pounds of HE in a soft metal cone, and I'll also use a proximity fuse setting of three feet. Those hummers will go off before actually contacting the dome, but the concussion should do the job. Providing there isn't a supporting partition directly under the panels affected."

"The domes are designed to be self-supporting, from what I understand," McKenna said. "If there's a partition of some kind directly under an impact site, it wouldn't be a load-bearing wall."

"Maybe the wall crumbles, then," Evans said.

"You're overloading the warhead," Munos said. "What's that going to do to me?"

"I'm pulling the radar-seeker guidance, which will balance the weight to some extent, so you'll have to go with the visual guidance."

"At night, with only a strobe light on the dome?"

"You're the marksman," Evans said.

"Well, hell, *gringo,* if that's the way it is, that's the way it is. I'll get them in there."

"We'll still be overweight in the nose cone. You're going to lose half a Mach of speed and fifteen, twenty miles of range."

"That's okay. On visual, I want to be close in, anyway," Munoz had said.

Now the last of the revamped Wasps was jacked into place and fitted to the short pylon. Evans supervised the attachment, then walked out from under the wing and joined Munoz and McKenna.

"That's it, Colonel. As much time as we spent on them, I have to guarantee they'll work."

"Thanks, Mabry. I'll take your word."

"So what happens now?"

"Now, it's coffee time."

McKenna and Munoz walked across the wide hanger and entered the pilots' dressing room. Their pressure suits were spread out on a wooden bench, ready for donning. A fifty-five-cup coffeepot gurgled in one corner.

Munoz stretched out on a bench and went to sleep.

McKenna waited, a mug of strong coffee close by. He read the *New York Times,* a day old.

At eleven-fifteen, he called the dining hall and had them send over hot roast beef sandwiches. Munoz woke up the second he smelled hot gravy.

Chewing, Munoz asked, "What's the time, *amigo?*"

"Eleven-twenty-five."

"Ten-twenty-five in Bonn."

"That's right."

"What's holdin' them up?"

"Based purely on experience," McKenna said, "I imagine that an indecisive mind has been added to the chain of command. Oval Office, Pentagon, maybe Cheyenne Mountain. Worse, maybe one of the Congressional oversight committees got involved. There'll be debates raging."

"Figures."

At eleven-forty, the intercom buzzed, and McKenna got up from his bench to punch the button.

"Relaying radio communication to you, Colonel," the operator said.

"Go ahead."

"Kevin, Jim Overton here."

"We going, Jim?"

"Affirmative. I've just launched Delta Yellow. You can take off within the next half hour."

"Roger."

McKenna used the intercom to call operations. "Scramble my ground crew, Major. I want to be off the ground in twenty minutes."

Munoz was already zipping into his pressure suit.

Delta Blue lifted smoothly off Runway 18 twenty-one minutes later, and McKenna immediately put the craft into a climbing left turn.

167

Munoz tried to contact Conover. "Delta Yellow, Delta Blue."

"Delta Blue, this is Alpha One. Cancha hear me?" Dimatta was monitoring the operation.

"Go Alpha."

"Delta Yellow is in blackout. Give him another six minutes."

"Geez. He coulda left his answerin' machine on. Blue out."

"Okay, Tiger, let's go over."

"Roger. Ignition checklist comin' up on the small screen."

Ten miles out of Jack Andrews, at 9,000 feet above the barren desert, the rocket engines ignited. McKenna let them run at 70 percent thrust for two minutes, then shut them down at 80,000 feet of altitude and at a speed of Mach 4.

"There's the Med," Munoz said. "I met a girl in Algiers, once."

"Nice girl?"

"Out-damned-standing, *compadre*. She had one flaw, though."

"Wanted to get married?"

"You read my mind, all the time?"

They were at Mach 3.5 over southern Greece when Conover called.

"Delta Blue, Yellow."

"Go Yellow," McKenna said.

"We breezed through. I've got greens on two camera pods and a gun."

"Let's go RS-three-three."

"Gone."

McKenna tapped at his communications keyboard, entering the code which installed the thirty-third of fifty available scrambling circuits into the VHF communications channel. Only *Themis* and the operations room at

168

NORAD could monitor them on similar scrambling units.

"You there, Con Man?" McKenna asked.

"Most of me is." Conover's voice echoed a trifle, due to the scrambling.

"What's your velocity?"

"Down to nine-point-six, Snake Eyes."

"Okay, it's easier if you pick the coordinates."

"Hold one. Do-Wop?"

Abrams said, "How about six-five degrees north, two-zero degrees, seven minutes east? Seven-five thousand? We'll still be coasting."

"Tiger?" McKenna asked.

"Fine by me. You want to bet on this one, Con Man?"

"Ten bucks."

"Roger that," Munoz said, then switching to intercom, told McKenna, "Feedin' the data in. I need a headin' of zero-one-six, and I need a rocket boost of two-two seconds at six-five percent."

"You're going to waste two thousand dollars' worth of Grandma's high-test fuel pellets for ten bucks?"

"There's a principle involved here, Snake Eyes. Hurry now, 'cause I'm tryin' to keep my mind around two different trajectories."

McKenna went through the checklist swiftly, ignited the rockets, and burned solid propellent pellets for twenty-two seconds.

"Beautiful, *jefe.*"

At 0109 hours, Delta Blue reached the established coordinates, but Delta Yellow wasn't visible. McKenna flashed his running lights twice.

"Sumbitch, Blue. I see you."

McKenna looked back and upward in time to see Conover flash his own lights, several thousand feet above and a couple miles behind them.

"You owe me ten bucks, Con Man," Munoz said.

"You cheated. I can't use turbojets yet."

169

"Delta Flight, Alpha One." Pearson's voice.

"Go Alpha," McKenna said.

"Are you people planning to play games all night?"

"Just passing the time, Alpha," McKenna said. "Where we at, Tiger?"

"Moonrise in nineteen minutes, so we'd better hump it. I say we come in out of the dark side, headin' two-eight-zero, angle of attack minus four-zero, speed Mach three. On my mark, make the turn. On my second mark, take the dive. Third mark, dump the speed brakes. We want four-five-zero knots on the pass. Yellow trails by two miles."

"Con Man?" McKenna asked.

"We still on for number eight?"

"Eight it is," Munoz said. "Number fourteen is the IP."

"It's good by Yellow."

"On the pullout, Con Man," McKenna said, "make a right turn to zero-one-five. That should take us over the ice between numbers seventeen and twenty-one. Give them ten miles' distance before going to rockets."

"Roger that, Snake Eyes."

"Forty miles out," McKenna continued, "Tiger will go to hot radar and see what kind of company we have. No other radar, Do-Wop."

"Roger."

McKenna pulled his straps tighter, turned the thermostat down a notch, and brightened the HUD. He held his course dead on true north, and let the speed bleed off to Mach 3 by inching the throttle levers back.

Munoz put the rearview on the small screen, aiming the camera up slightly.

"Give me a flash, Con Man."

McKenna saw the lights on the screen.

"How's your glide?"

"I'm going to have to put my nose down pretty soon."

"Mark one!" Munoz called out.

McKenna eased the hand controller over and banked into a heading of 280 degrees. It was a wide turn. Sharp maneuvers weren't accomplished well at three times the speed of sound. The heavy atmosphere tended to cling to control surfaces.

"Two-eight-zero," he said.

Two seconds later, Conover said, "Two-eight-zero."

"Mark Two!"

McKenna nudged the hand controller forward, and when the HUD showed him minus forty degrees, eased it back to center and held it. He pulled the throttles full back and noted that the MakoShark began to lose speed steadily, though slowly.

"Arm me, Snake Eyes."

McKenna reached for the armaments panel, selected both pylons, the gun pod, the four missiles, and armed all of them.

"The birds are yours, Tiger."

"Gracias."

The altimeter readout sped through the numbers, 60,000, 55,000, 50,000.

As they passed through 45,000 feet, Conover radioed, "Yellow's got turbojets. All green. Cameras are primed."

At 30,000 feet, Munoz called, "Mark three!"

McKenna deployed the speed brakes.

"Bring the nose up to minus three-zero," Munoz said on the tactical frequency, so Conover could hear the instruction.

McKenna pulled back on the hand controller.

When they were slowed to Mach 1.5, and at 18,000 feet, Munoz went to active radar. The screen in front of McKenna lit up with returns off the sea, off wells and ships, and off two blips to the northwest.

"Countin', countin', countin'," Munoz said, then switched the radar to standby. "Three-five to target. We

171

got bogies at three-four-six, one-zero-thousand feet, and five-seven miles."

Speed Mach 1.1.

"What's the heading on the bogies?"

"Due east. They're right over the ice platforms."

"We going to intercept on zero-one-five?" McKenna asked.

"Damned close, Snake Eyes. I didn't have time to read them for speed, but they're subsonic."

"Con Man, on pullout, go to zero-two-five."

"Roger zero-two-five, Snake Eyes."

Speed 600 knots.

"I want one more time on active, *jefe*."

"Go."

The screen displayed the radar scan for two sweeps, then reverted to the night-vision image.

McKenna saw a green dome against the lighter green sea.

"Come right two degrees."

Nudge of the hand controller. The HUD showed 282 degrees.

"That's the IP . . . Mark! Hang on to that headin'. Lose the brakes, Snake Eyes."

Platform fourteen flashed under them.

McKenna brought the speed brakes in as the readout gave him 445 knots.

"We've still got five-five-zero-zero altitude, Tiger."

"Two thou should be about right."

McKenna put the nose down a little, trading altitude for maintaining his airspeed.

The throttles were still at the back detents. Infrared production from the jet engines would be negligible.

"Do-Wop, you getting an IR off me?" McKenna asked.

The MakoShark aerospace craft were equipped with infrared search and tracking sensors that had an effective range of fifty miles.

172

"Hell, Snake Eyes, you're two miles ahead of us, give or take a mile, and I can't see you on the night vision, much less the IR tracker. No output at all."

On the other side of the canopy, off to his left, McKenna could see a scattering of red strobe lights from the other wells. The running lights of three ships were ten or twelve miles away to the east.

Ahead, the aircraft warning light of well number eight was coming up fast.

He glanced at the screen. Using his helmet-aiming system, Munoz had the bomb sight high-centered on the dome in seven-power magnification.

As they approached, the WSO kept dropping the magnification.

At ten miles from target, the screen went to normal magnification. The upper-left corner lettering on the CRT flickered as the computer made its calculations, then read: TARGET: 8.17 MILES.

"Any time, Tiger."

"Give it a couple more miles, *jefe*. We're not gonna be flyin' through debris."

At six miles out, Munoz switched the screen image to the first Wasp, then launched.

Four white flares flashed in the corners of McKenna's eyes as the Wasps left the rails. Immediately, the missiles separated, following the instructions imbedded in their brains. Munoz guided with the first Wasp, and the others stuck close to it.

The green dome loomed larger on the screen.

The number one, guided, Wasp was the left one of the four fiery trails now two miles ahead of the Mako-Shark.

Shifting his head, Munoz steered the missile slightly left, toward the left upper side of the dome. The other missiles obediently shifted to the left also.

The lights on the helicopter pad flashed on.

173

McKenna watched ahead and to his left for the patrol aircraft.

"Looks to me like their radar picked up the incoming, Tiger."

"I'd think so, if they're on the ball at all," Munoz said. "Betcha they're so damned rattled, they don't know what to do about it."

"Those German pilots might know."

He glanced back at the screen just as the Wasps detonated. The screen went black, then green again as the MakoShark's own camera took over. Bright greenish-white flash as all of them went off simultaneously.

"Let's get out of Con Man's way," Munoz said.

McKenna pulled into a right bank and started to climb, his speed decreasing, but that was all right. The last sight of the dome on the screen showed him a distance to target of 3.7 miles and black gaps appearing in the dome's upper surface.

"Get me a location on the hostiles," McKenna said.

Munoz went to active radar. "Shit. Bogies are headin' in. Tornados, I think. I read 'em fourteen out and diving. Nine-five-zero-zero. Speed seven-zero-zero knots."

Munoz switched out of active mode.

Jack Abrams came on, "I've been scanning the local marine channels, Snake Eyes. There's a hell of a lot of excited German chatter."

"Okay, Do-Wop. You continue with your pass. I'm going to get behind you, then divert the Tornados."

"Delta Blue, this is Semaphore."

General Brackman's voice was very steady and very well modulated over the scrambled, satellite-relayed network.

"Go Semaphore."

"Be extremely careful. Favor to me?"

"Granted, Semaphore."

McKenna turned left, diving below and across the line of flight of Delta Yellow. He advanced his throttles until the readout gave him 700 knots. Watching the chronometer on the HUD, he estimated when Conover passed over him, then turned right again, paralleling Conover at 282 degrees, but a mile to his left.

"Let's go over, Tiger."

"Now? Are you sh . . . oh, hell yes!"

Skimming through the checklist, McKenna had rockets in ten seconds. He shoved the outboard throttles full forward and felt himself shoved back into hiz couch.

"Radar, Tiger."

"Comin' up."

On thirty-mile scan, the screen showed the Tornados eight miles away.

He applied right rudder to lead their line of flight and pulled the controller back to gain some height.

Mach 1.9.

"Under or over, *amigo.*"

"Under. They may still never see us."

"They're about four miles from Yellow. Now at five thousand." It was a guess since Munos couldn't track Conover.

Three miles.

Mach 2.4.

Two miles.

Mach 2.8.

One mile.

McKenna killed the rockets as Munoz went to night vision on the screen.

The two Tornados were displaying running lights and were a hundred yards apart, in echelon formation, almost exactly in the center of the screen.

Half mile.

More right rudder. A touch.

Mach 2.7.

McKenna edged his nose down a trifle.

The Tornado pilots were probably scanning the immediate area of well number eight for an attacker. They did not—could not—see the MakoShark coming up out of the darkness of the sea. If they had, they would have taken evasive action.

The MakoShark passed under both aircraft with less than fifty feet of separation, and it passed under in less than a half second, leaving behind a trail of violent turbulence that shocked the pilots and the weapons systems' operators who were concentrating on reaching well number eight.

With the rocket motors shut down and the turbojet throttles set at full retard, the MakoShark did not even leave a visual trail.

It left two Tornado pilots fighting catastrophe and panic. In the rearview screen, McKenna saw the lead plane leap up abruptly, then turn completely over, nosing into a spin. The wingman fought to keep his plane upright and nearly collided with his flight leader.

McKenna didn't think they would spot Delta Yellow, even by accident.

Nine

The telephone jangled shrilly in the middle of the night. Felix Eisenach detested phone calls in the middle of the night.

He rolled over and sat up, shaking his head.

The telephone rang again.

"What is it, Felix?"

"I do not know yet, Marta. Go back to sleep."

His wife was good at taking orders. She rolled over, away from him, as he picked up the receiver.

"Eisenach."

"Diederman here. We have a problem, General."

"So, tell me, Hans, what is the problem."

"The dome of Platform Eight has been blown out."

"What! How?"

"I'm at the platform now, General. I have one man dead, and five injured by falling debris. We're sending them . . ."

"What damage?"

A long pause, then Diederman responded, "There are three very large holes in the upper dome, fifty meters above the deck. That is in what we call attic space. But large pieces of debris crashed through the ceiling of the upper dormitory, and that is where the casualties . . ."

"The equipment, Hans? Is it still operating?"

"Yes, of course. Structural and engineering damage is minimal."

"The cause?"

"Obviously an attack from outside sources, General. Nothing else would explain the kind of damage I see. The dome imploded."

"The Soviets?"

"I have no idea, General Eisenach. No one saw the intruders. No radar contacts, no visual sightings."

"You have talked to Weismann?"

"Two of his aircraft were in the area. They saw nothing, but they complained of running through heavy turbulence."

"It is the Americans, then. It was their stealth aircraft." Diederman did not respond.

"This will require investigation."

"You will tell the High Command?" Diederman asked.

"I will leave here shortly. I want you to prepare a full report."

"Of course, General. Perhaps you would visit the hospital at Bremerhaven and speak to the injured men."

"Yes, perhaps. Later."

It was eleven o'clock at night, *Themis* time, before Amy Pearson and Donna Amber got the film packs from Delta Yellow.

It was one in the morning by the time the two of them had developed the film and run the video comparisons with similar wells in California, Italy, Mexico, Japan, and New Zealand. They worked on the computer terminals in the Radio Shack, and McKenna, Munoz, Conover, and Abrams hung around in the Command Center, poking their heads into the Shack every few minutes to check on progress.

"What do you think, Donna?" Pearson asked.

There were two images on the monitor, the screen split to show the infrared image of well number eight situated next to an infrared image of a well located near the Sierra Nevadas and operated by the California Power Company.

"Well, Colonel, the sites are different. The California well is located on land and doesn't have the same spread of heat in the soil as the German well has in the water. Ignoring the outer edges, though, and concentrating on the core, they look just about the same."

McKenna floated through the hatchway, took one look at the screen, and said, "You were right, Amy. Geothermal tap."

"Damned right, McKenna." Even though it rankled a little, she felt as if a compliment were in order and added, "You did a good job."

"Not all my doing. Tony pulled the trigger. And while I think about it, I'd like to have you send Mabry Evans one or two of those pictures, so he gets some feedback on how his ordnance worked."

"All right, I'll do that."

Donna Amber said, "I don't get it, at all. If we've got geothermal wells in California, why can't the Germans have them?"

"On the legal side, you're probably right, Donna," McKenna said.

"The purposes will be the same," Pearson said. "It's an energy source. Tap into superheated steam and boiling water, and use it to run turbines coupled to generators, transforming the steam energy into electrical energy. Typically, there's a primary well, extracting the steam and boiling water. It's run through the turbines, then the cooled water is injected back into the earth's crust through a secondary well. The spectrograph shows some steam containing earth elements. Sulphur, primarily. Lots of condensation. There's no excessive salt content, so it's fresh water, rather than seawater."

"The California wells exhaust a lot of steam," Amber pointed out.

Pearson pointed to the storage tanks mounted to the back side of the dome. "I suspect that is what these tanks are for, a series of traps used to reduce the quantity of by-

179

product steam. It disguises the true nature of the well."

"There's still some vapor emitted from the fifth tank," McKenna said.

"Yes. And then again, perhaps they've developed a method to extract yet more energy from equipment placed in those external tanks," Pearson said. "That would give them a primary source and several secondary sources, plus hiding the vapor output."

"It's a hell of an undertaking. As I recall most of those wells have to go down twenty-some miles," McKenna said. "Plus doing it offshore. Some geologist discovered the right location."

"Maybe they found some undersea geysers?" Amber said.

"I doubt it, in that area," Pearson told her. "But obviously, like Kevin says, the Germans have a geologist who guessed right. And Donna, a geyser is useful if it's hot enough, but a geyser produces both steam and water. Steam alone is better, and that's called a fumarole. Down in the earth's crust are fractures which collect the steam and trap it in place. The objective of drilling a well is to hit one of those fractures."

"If they're just energy taps," Amber asked, "why hide them at all?"

"Two reasons," Pearson said.

"We'd better put in a call to Cheyenne Mountain," McKenna told her.

She checked her watch. "It's eleven-thirty there."

"Hell, Amy, I'll make the call. It's the best time of all to get a general out of bed," McKenna said. "It gives you a chance to see them operating at their best."

Gen. Marvin Brackman called Hannibal Cross at his home in Arlington Heights.

"You know what the hell time it is, Marvin?"

"I know, Hannibal. But you'll want to hear this. I've got

180

a set of pictures, and they're being transferred to your office by data link."

"You've confirmed that the wells are geothermal taps, then?"

"We think so, yes. Pearson says she's ninety-nine percent sure."

"Generating electricity?" Cross asked.

"Almost certainly."

"That fits in with some information the CIA has developed. Quite a bit of German industry has been converted to electrical usage. New plants are driven by it. Older plants have been switched to coal from fuel oil. What do you suppose the electrical output is, Marvin?"

"We'll have to get some of the academics busy on it, Hannibal, but for the moment, Thorpe and Pearson have an estimate. One complex of several geothermal wells in California generates three-quarters of a million kilowatts. That's enough to run a small city. That's also slightly better than the output of Hoover Dam."

"You're shitting me."

"Not in the least. Pearson and Thorpe argue that, given German ingenuity and engineering and strong thermal sources, each platform could develop five hundred thousand kilowatts at minimum. That's twelve million kilowatts for twenty-four platforms. Equal to two Coulee Dams. And that's the minimum, Hannibal. Thorpe thinks it might run to fourteen or fifteen million on the top end of the estimate range."

"That's a hell of a lot of power, Marvin."

"And it gets cheaper every day they're in operation. In no time at all, the Germans will not be dependent on imported energy."

The chairman of the Joint Chiefs grunted, as if he were finally climbing out of bed. "Worse than that, in a conflict situation, they've got a strong source of energy that allows them to divert petroleum fuels to military usage. They may, in fact, already be doing that."

"You've seen the tank farms."

"What would be the next step, Marvin?"

"If it were me, preparing for war on a long-range plan? I'd start hardening the storage sites. Bury the tank farms. For all I know, some of the fuel storage is already underground. I'd probably have presited some kind of platform defenses. SAM and AA units that could be quickly shipped out to the platforms and set up on those oversized chopper pads. It's a rationale for the large pads. To stave off the superpowers, I'd have some long-range hardware in reserve."

"Peenemünde?"

"Maybe. We have anything back on that, Hannibal? I haven't heard from Sheremetevo."

"Nothing from the CIA or DIA, yet. I'll put some matches under a few butts. I did see a CIA report that said travel to Germany was becoming more difficult. Stricter controls on issuing visas."

"The countdown may have started, Hannibal, and all we're doing is accelerating it."

"We'll know when we see what the response is to the attack on the well. If Bonn doesn't scream like a stuck pig, I'm going to worry."

"They won't have any evidence, no place to point a finger, and that may keep them quiet."

"Perhaps. Okay, any other implications?"

"Yes, a major one. One of the reasons for disguising the wells is to hide the development of a tremendous new power source. But there's another reason, too. If the court of world opinion knew about the risks of geothermal taps at sea, the Germans would never have gotten the first well drilled."

"Tell me about the risks, Marvin."

"First, there's simple accident. A number of years ago, one of the California geothermal wells blew a wellhead. It's difficult to control unknown pressures from five miles down. They had steam, boiling water, red-hot mud spewing all over the landscape. Quite a few personal injuries."

"We still drill," Cross said.

"Sure, because the risks of drilling on land are acceptable. A blowout mostly goes straight up and dissipates. I don't know about seaborne platforms, Hannibal. Pearson says those wells have anywhere from six hundred to seventeen hundred feet of probably unsupported well casing. Get a major storm in the area, lose an anchor on a platform, break a casing."

"And?"

"And turn loose an uncontrolled spigot of steam into the Arctic. Up to six hundred and fifty degrees Fahrenheit," Brackman said.

"Damn. That high?"

"That high. I don't know what one broken wellhead would do to the ecology, but it wouldn't help it."

"And we shot missiles at the son of a bitch?"

"Shot high, Hannibal. But that's the other risk. Attacking those wells could unleash a catastrophe. Can you imagine twenty or twenty-four uncapped wells pouring hot gases and water into the Arctic?"

"Meltdown?"

"My contact at the University of Colorado, who is also grumbling about being awakened at night, says yes. Within a year, we'd see rising water levels on all Northern European coasts. Half asleep, he still estimated a couple of feet of increased water level, and probably more. That might put some ports out of commission. It would disrupt the North Sea oil fields. The low-lying countries—Holland, the Netherlands—would have long refugee lines. Not to mention the damage to underwater life, both fish and plant life. There'd be environmentalists crawling over the steps of every capitol in the world."

Hannibal Cross was silent for a long moment, then said, "Marvin, I'm going to roust out a few of the heavy brass and a few of the heavier civilians. You get McKenna hot trying to locate a few of the weak spots. If

183

we can't attack the wells, we've got to find somewhere else where the system is vulnerable."

"That might work for us, Hannibal, but what about Mother Nature? If we just leave the wells alone, sure as hell, someday there's going to be an earthquake, a tidal wave, a Force Ten gale that will take out those wells and upset a lot of balances."

Oberst Albert Weismann and *Direktor-Assistent* Daniel Goldstein climbed down from the scaffolding gingerly. Weismann did not like heights, unless he was in a cockpit, and the top of the scaffolding was eight meters above the concrete floor. His fingers trembled slightly until he reached the floor.

The banks of bright fluorescent lights overhead gave his face an ashen pallor. It made the rosy rash of his skin more noticeable, but Weismann did not think that Goldstein noticed his discomforture.

When his feet were once again firmly planted on cement, Weismann looked back up at the rocket for several minutes to regain his composure. The rocket was long and sleek, finished in a matte gray, the diameter growing by phases from the tip of the nose to the base. Stubby wings protruded from the first and second stages. The German flag was imprinted on each of the three stages and the nose cone. The rocket was reclining on its side, half encased in a steel-wheeled cradle that mated to the pair of railroad tracks leading under the massive doors on the end of the building.

There were four cradles in this building, two each side by side, and four more in the adjoining building. Six of the cradles were occupied by the thirty-meter-long rockets, but only this one had been certified by the scientists as ready for launch.

Possibly certified.

Every time he had toured the complex, Weismann had

been confronted with, ". . . just one more little problem. A simple glitch, Herr Colonel."

In the control thrusters or control surfaces. In the hydraulic system. In the fuel pumping system, in the inertial navigation system, in the computer backup software linkage, or in . . . the list went on forever. There were many complex systems, thousands of places open to potential failure, he had been told more than once.

It was difficult to believe Goldstein when he said, "It is absolutely functional, Colonel. A tribute to those who have designed it and worked upon it."

"It is more a tribute to the Russians, and perhaps, the German who acquired the blueprints from the Baikonur Cosmodrome, would you not say, Herr Director-Assistant?"

Goldstein gave him a pained look. "There was much to be improved upon over the Soviet design."

"Is that true? The Russian rocket has been operational for three years, Herr Goldstein. This one has yet to perform a maiden voyage."

"The Russians have experience and a capable work force, Colonel."

"Another excuse?"

Weismann was at least twenty-five centimeters taller than the scientist. He looked down on a shaggy mop of gray hair that made him feel much cleaner with his own close-cropped blond hair. The scientist's face sagged at the jowls, making Weismann feel less than his fifty-two years.

Weismann was in uniform. He was always in uniform because he was proud of it. The Jew wore baggy brown slacks covered with a dirty gray lab smock. There was never a display of pride.

"The warhead, Goldstein?"

"Is operational, also. It is not, of course, a nuclear warhead. We have five Multiple Individually Retargetted Vehicles stored in the bunker a half kilometer from here. The MIRVs are composed of eight separate twenty-mega-

185

ton nuclear warheads. Ghost One is armed only with high explosive, for the test flight."

Gespenst I was almost a year behind its scheduled test flight. The High Command had been frustrated in its desire to publicize a successful intercontinental/space orbital vehicle capable of delivering Germans into space or destruction to the other side of the world. Like his superiors in Bonn and Berlin, Weismann also wanted to put Moscow and Washington and London and Paris on notice, notice that those capital cities fell under the shadow of yet another nuclear threat. Notice that their interference in German national matters was subject to extreme reaction.

The *Gespenst* program had been considered essential to the German reemergence as a power to be reckoned with, and Albert Weismann was very gratified that the program had been placed under his command, an adjunct to the *20 S.A.G.* The constant delays had naturally brought pressure upon himself, but now, now he was nearly ready.

"How long, Goldstein, until we are ready for a test flight?"

"Herr Colonel, it only requires some four hours to transport the rocket to the launch pad, to raise it in place, and to fuel it. In a crisis, the countdown could be shortened, perhaps, to an hour."

"How long?"

"There is the matter of the nose-cone mating, of course, Herr Colonel."

"The no . . . what now?"

"For the test flight, we have had to fabricate a nose cone not designed for the Ghost. At the moment, it does not mate properly with the third stage. A matter only of days, Herr Colonel."

Maximillian Oberlin was correct. This Jew was more a bottleneck than an asset. It was quite possible the man was sabotaging the project in subtle ways. Oberlin had wanted to get rid of him immediately and let *Direktor* Schumacher assume the tasks of final preparation. Weismann had had to explain that Schumacher was not a scientist, merely the son of a banker who was a major underwriter of the *VORMUND PROJEKT.* The son was in dire need of a respectable job title.

"And of course, Colonel Weismann, we have yet to complete the debugging of the flight software."

Weismann's shoulders slumped. *Mein Gott!*

The intrusion of the Russians. The destruction of the dome on *Bahnsteig Acht.* The platforms seemed suddenly vulnerable, and the supreme weapon was not available to protect them.

"As of this moment, Goldstein, the Ghost Project is on sixteen-hour shifts. If I do not see sufficient progress within the next few days, we will increase that to twenty hours."

"That seems unduly harsh, Herr Colonel."

Weismann drilled the stubby scientist with his eyes. "Not as harsh as it could be."

Spinning on his heel, he marched to the office built into the corner of the building, ignored the secretary who looked up to him, and picked up her telephone. He dialed the number of the *Zwanzigste Speziell Aeronautisch Gruppe* operations office.

When the officer on duty answered, he said, "Get me Major Zeigman."

A five-minute, intolerable wait.

"Zeigman."

"Major, your squadron has tonight's patrols?"

"That is correct, Colonel."

"From midnight on, I want four aircraft on each patrol. Do not group them. One pair at two thousand meters, one pair deployed at ten thousand meters above the first pair. The higher aircraft are to separate by five kilometers. Reverse the direction of the patrol circuit."

"Understood, Colonel. Are we to anticipate hostile aircraft?"

"Expect the American stealth planes."

* * *

The *Themis* Command Center felt deserted. Everyone except McKenna and Sergeant Arguento, who was manning the Radio Shack, had gone to their dining compartments for dinner.

The intercom buzzed.

McKenna pulled himself close to the main console and pressed the keypad. "Command."

"Radar, Command. I've got Mako Two one-five-zero out, closing at one-seven-five feet per second."

"Copy that, Radar."

Mako Three was docked aboard *Themis,* and Mako One was at Peterson Air Force Base.

McKenna punched the general public address system. "Lieutenant Polly Tang. Lieutenant Tang to hangar bays for docking."

On the Tactical 1 frequency, the primary frequency used by the MakoSharks, Dimatta said, "I've got her here, Colonel, pushing me out. You want me to hold?"

McKenna thought about it, but only for two seconds. The orbit of *Themis* had been calculated into this mission. "No, Cancha. Proceed as planned."

On the intercom to the hangars, he said, "Lieutenant Tang, Command. Mako Two inbound."

"Roger, Command. I've got it."

He switched to Tac-3, the chief frequency utilized by the Makos. "Mako Two, Alpha One."

"Go ahead, Alpha."

"What's your manifest, Mako?"

"In order of importance, Alpha?" Lynn Haggar asked.

"Why not?"

"Foodstuffs, solid fuel pellets, circuit boards for Honeywell, chemicals, Colonel Avery."

"Hey, damn," the deputy commander of *Themis* said. "I'm gone for a week, and get shoved to the bottom of the list?"

Haggar laughed.

"Mako, reduce velocity to one-six-zero FPS."

"Complying, Alpha."

McKenna searched the monitor selector board and found the key for the camera mounted on the exterior of the pod of Spoke Fifteen. He tapped it, and the screen gave him an exterior view of the hangar side of the hub. He moved the image to a secondary screen and brought up the radar image on the main screen.

On the visual monitor, one set of hangar doors were open, and Delta Green slowly emerged from her bay. As he watched, another set of doors opened as Polly Tang had an assistant prepare for Mako Two's arrival.

Tac-1. "Delta Green, you've got a Mako inbound."

"We'll keep our eyes wide open, Alpha. You think this is wise?"

"Had to happen some time, Cancha."

"Command, Radar. Mako Two six-five miles out."

"Copy, Radar."

Tac-3. "Mako Two, stay alert for an outbound vehicle."

"Roger, Alpha. We've got it on radar."

McKenna found the remote camera adjustment stick, keyed if for the right camera, and aimed the Spoke Fifteen camera outward, following Delta Green.

Dimatta was turning the MakoShark stern-forward, when the Mako drifted past him. The MakoShark was already becoming invisible against the blackness of space. The white Mako was a complete study in contrast.

Haggar hit her transmit button, "That's it, Kevin!"

"Let's maintain radio protocol," McKenna said into his microphone.

"Roger that, Alpha," Haggar said.

Twenty-five minutes later, just after Delta Green ignited her rockets for the reentry sequence, Lynn Haggar and Ben Olsen, her WSO, shot into the Command Center. Both of them were still in pressure suits, and McKenna figured she was making about fifteen miles an hour when she grabbed onto Val Arguento to halt her flight.

Arguento, at the doorway to the Radio Shack, grinned at her.

"Requesting permission to enter the Command Center," she said.

"Come on in," McKenna told them.

"My God, Kevin, it's beautiful!"

Olsen had a grin that threatened to eclipse the room. "She was armed, Colonel. I saw pylons with two Sidewinders and four unknowns."

"You got a peek, huh?"

"You let us," Haggar said.

"Oh, no! If Brackman or Overton should ever ask you, it was purely by accident."

Haggar's face sobered. "Ah. I see."

"Step at a time, okay?"

"All right, Kevin. I appreciate it."

"Now, I want you both to grab a bite to eat, then go to Ben's cubicle. I'm going to accidentally leave Tac-1 open on Ben's intercom circuit. I want you to listen in. Sergeant Arguento."

"Yes, sir."

"Could you print out a copy of Map GS-1014 and accidentally drop it?" That map pinpointed the wells.

"Damn right, sir." Arguento turned back into the Radio Shack.

"And no one talks to anyone about these accidents," McKenna ordered.

He got three affirmative responses.

They were right on the deck, five hundred feet above the coast north of Bremerhaven, holding 500 knots.

The screen displayed a flickering green land-and-seascape. Zipping beneath them.

"I'm not seeing shit, Cancha."

"Still four or five miles, Nitro Fizz."

They were looking for the first mainland pumping station on the Germany end of the supposed pipeline. The aerial photos of the past several years all displayed a rather innocuous group of five large buildings and three five-foot-diameter pipes emerging from the sea.

"Camera set for side view," Williams said.

"Roger."

Instead of the traditional view from above, they were coming in low and to the seaward side of the complex, taking photographs from the side. Amy Pearson wanted side-view elevations.

On the highway below and inland, a dozen sets of headlights cut the night. Out to sea on his left, Dimatta saw several ships, but couldn't tell whether they were German naval vessels or not.

McKenna had forbidden the use of radar. No alerting the ground installations.

"Got it, Cancha. Give me two points right."

Dimatta tapped the hand controller.

The right side of the screen showed the group of tall buildings sitting at the top of a short cliff.

"Snap, snap, snap!" Williams said, "I got twenty each of low-light and IR."

Twenty-six miles later, they got photos of the second pumping station, located on the headland near Coxhaven, then Dimatta applied left rudder and started a climb. He took the MakoShark to 12,000 feet of altitude, but stayed subsonic on turbojets.

A leisurely ride.

"We set on the sequence, Nitro?"

"Cut straight across the offshore wells on a heading of three-zero-five. We're looking for anything associated with the wells, but not directly attached to a platform. Cables, pipelines. We want close-ups of well number one. Then, on the ice, headed east, we're also looking for exposed pipelines and cables."

"You and I may eventually get along," Dimatta said.

"Not if you keep eating pasta and Hollandaise and that Greek stuff."

"Hey, you're going to start me dreaming about it, and we got an hour to target."

"Think about broads."

"I'll think about taking them out to dinner."

"Radar, Command."

"Radar here."

"We over the horizon, yet?"

"Over, and target area coming up, General."

Overton switched the screen display to the repeat image from the radar. McKenna, Pearson, Milt Avery, and Arguento all moved closer for a better view. Donna Amber was in the Radio Shack, monitoring the satellite relays for voice communications. No one wanted to lose contact with Delta Green.

"Command, Radar. I'm going to extend the range to two-two-zero."

There was some clutter over the Arctic Ice Pack. The dark screen flickered with snow.

"Radar, Command. Back it off a little."

The radar operator shortened the range, and much of the false radar return disappeared.

They waited twelve minutes until the edge of the ice, and the ice platforms appeared. The orbit was a bit two far to the west, and platforms twenty-two and twenty-four, on the east end, did not display on the screen. Svalbard Island wasn't present, either.

Delta Green was not displayed, of course.

McKenna moved to a microphone. "Delta Green, Alpha One."

"Go Alpha."

"Squawk me once."

"Roger."

As the radar sweep passed the lower-left corner of the

screen, a bright blip appeared as Dimatta flipped on the IFF, then flashed out.

"I've got you," McKenna said. "Just making your turn to the east?"

"Roger, Alpha. We're coming up on well number twenty-three."

McKenna found himself counting silently, trying to keep pace with Dimatta while looking at a nearly blank screen. Blank as far as friendlies were concerned.

Three minutes.

"Command, Radar. I've got bogies."

Two of the Tornados were at 2,000 meters, headed west over the ice. Mac Zeigman had reversed the normal course, and was covering the ice platforms before turning south to the offshore wells.

As was his preference, Zeigman was flying alone in *Tiger Führer*, having left his weapons system officer depressed and alone on the tarmac at New Amsterdam.

Zeigman and his wingman were at 10,000 meters. He could not see his wingman, some four kilometers to his right in the dark. Below, he had occasional glimpses of *Tiger Drei* and *Tiger Vier* when their silhouettes passed over white stretches of ice.

To keep his adrenaline level stable, Zeigman tried to think of this patrol as the typically boring routine of the past months. Still, something in *Oberst* Weismann's tone had suggested that it might not be.

Despite himself, the adrenaline level was fluctuating. He felt keyed up.

Ready to unleash his tension on someone.

Or something.

"Tiger Leader, this is Platform Eighteen."

"I hear you, Platform Eighteen."

"We may have seen something on the dome camera."

"What is that, Eighteen."

"Unknown, Tiger Leader. A flash of darkness."

The ground crews were also tense, Zeigman thought, but then again. . . .

"All Tigers, Tiger Leader. Alert, now."

He did not listen to the rash of affirmatives on the radio, but banked slightly to the right, to give himself a better view of the ice.

There. His two Tornados.

And there, two kilometers ahead of them, a shadow racing.

He could not make out the shape. It was a darkness fleeing along the ground.

"Tiger Three. Unidentified aircraft dead ahead of you, two kilometers. Come to the left four degrees."

"Affirmative, Leader."

"Tiger Two, let us engage."

"Leader," said Two, "I do not see it."

"Join on me, Two."

Zeigman rolled on over until he was inverted, then pulled the nose down. By the time he reached the proper altitude, the unidentified airplane would be east of him, and he would come down on it from its rear.

He flashed his wing lights once for the benefit of *Tiger Zwei*.

He had not taken his eyes off the phantom, and he cursed to himself when he saw his two low-level fighters pass right over it.

"Tigers Three and Four, reverse course. You have missed him."

Only briefly did Zeigman think about trying to contact the unidentified airplane on an international frequency. If he did communicate with it, the pilot might give in quickly.

And ruin a perfectly good shot.

His speed climbed to Mach 1.

Altitude 2,500 meters. Pulling out of the vertical dive.

The shadow taking form.

Delta wing. Long, long fuselage.

It was alerted. Started a right, climbing turn.

Without thinking about it, his fingers had run automatically through the sequence of arming two of his Sky Flash missiles.

He switched his radar to active.

Nothing. Only the aircraft of his own flight.

He tried the IR seeker.

A bare flicker.

The missiles would not track on radar-homing or infrared.

He flicked the switch that selected guidance from the hand controller.

The aircraft—it had to be a MakoShark—almost centered in the gun sight.

Launch.

Flash of rocket fire.

Trails arcing toward the climbing delta shape.

Concentrating hard with the hand controller. Up, now, and to the right.

Homing in.

The four bogies had appeared abruptly from the right side of the screen, almost over well number twenty-one.

Pearson gasped, "Damn it!"

McKenna studied the screen readouts, checking altitudes, then thumbed the microphone. "Cancha, you've got bogies almost directly ahead. There's a pair at six-two-hundred and another two spread out at three-zero-thousand. I don't think they've spotted you."

"Roger, Snake Eyes. Can we go radar?"

"Hold off. I don't want them homing one in on you."

Waiting.

No blip for Delta Green.

The two low-level targets changed course slightly.

The high-level fighters started to dive.

"Okay, Cancha. They've got you. Hold course twenty

seconds, then go to one-one-zero and start climbing. Seven-zero percent throttles."

Waiting.

The tension in the Command Center was palpable.

The blip of one German fighter was losing altitude fast, now moving back to the east.

"Command, Radar. Two missiles launched."

"Scramble, Cancha!"

"We see 'em, Snake Eyes. No sweat. Can I punch this bastard out?"

McKenna sighed and looked at Overton. The general kept his face passive. Pearson's eyes were wide.

"You've been fired upon, Delta Green. Fire at will."

"Hot damn!" Dimatta said over the intercom.

"Give me two Wasps, Cancha," Williams said.

Dimatta's arm reached out for the armaments panel even as his helmet was levered full back against the collar of the flight suit so he could look upward. The two missiles coming at them were black pupils surrounded by harsh white eyes.

He glanced at the armaments panel, hit pylon two and missiles one and two.

Looked back at the missiles.

Now.

Slammed the throttles full forward.

The MakoShark accelerated abruptly.

The missiles flashed by behind them, headed for the ice. He didn't watch for impact.

Roll hard right, pull the hand controller back.

On its side, the MakoShark looped back toward the first two fighters. The one that had fired its missiles at them slashed the night above, trying to pull out of its dive and regain altitude.

The enemy had to be up high, looking down, to spot them, unless they went to active radar.

"I need radar, Cancha."

"Take it."

The radar image flickered onto the screen.

The MakoShark radar could scan for new targets while simultaneously tracking and holding up to twelve targets. As Dimatta pulled out of his sideways loop, rolling upright, he saw the orange sight scooting across the screen, guided by Williams's helmet.

"Lock on one," Williams said. "He's at three thousand. Next one's higher."

Dimatta pulled the hand controller and the nose went up.

"Lock on two."

"Go, Nitro."

"Committed . . . launched."

The tracks of the two missiles appeared on the screen, spreading out, homing on the active radars of the two fighters.

The fighters went into evasive action as their threat receivers detected the Wasps.

"They're Tornados," Williams said.

"Were," Dimatta corrected him.

The radar screen indicated the other two were in a tight circle at five thousand feet. One of them started to dive toward them. More tentatively, the second one followed his leader.

Dimatta continued into a right turn, headed north.

On his left, a bright splash of white against the semi-dark sky partially killed his night vision.

"That's one," Williams said.

Another splash of light.

"And two."

The threat receiver sounded in his earphones.

"Incoming locked on," Williams said.

Dimatta hit the Tac-1 frequency. "Snake Eyes?"

"That's enough, Cancha," McKenna said. "Lesson taught."

197

"Kill the radar, Nitro."

"Done."

Again, he rolled onto his right side and pulled the nose into a tight loop. The hostile missile, having lost its radar target, missed them by half a mile.

At Mach 1.8, they passed over the last well a few seconds later.

"That last picture's going to be blurry, Cancha."

"Way it goes, sometimes."

Dimatta wasn't going to review this mission in his mind for a while, not until they returned to *Themis*, but his blood felt as if it were singing in his veins.

He wasn't even hungry.

And behind him, he thought that two German Tornadoes were frantically searching a barren landscape for him.

And finding only fragments of Tornadoes.

Ten

The *Hochkommandieren* was composed of the commanders-in-chief of the army, the navy, and the air force. Along with innumerable advisors, staffers, and flunkies. The overflowing headquarters building and three annexes were located in Bonn, close to the civilian government to which the High Command reported.

The three men who headed Germany's military establishment took themselves and their charter very seriously, and they took the civilian government somewhat less seriously. Chancellors and legislators, they reasoned, could not possibly understand the fine nuances of strategy, tactics, overt and covert operation, and proud tradition.

Gen. Felix Eisenach understood the subtle distinctions that existed between the civilian and the military leaderships. The civilians wanted a strong, world-respected posture for Germany without paying too much for it, and they set that policy for the High Command, leaving the strategy for achieving it to men who had fought as youngsters in, and been soundly defeated by, World War II.

With the sting of memory still aching in their minds and with the annual debate and underfunding of military appropriations by liberal thinkers in the *Bundestag,* the marshals, generals, and admirals had been pressured to look elsewhere for funding to meet their charter.

They found the necessary support in a loose confederation of bankers, entrepreneurs, and financial manipulators of like mind. The confederation operated under the *VOR-MUND PROJEKT.* Where the shortsighted tinkers and tailors who made up the *Bundestag* failed to provide, the GUARDIAN PROJECT supplemented. The bankers, naturally, sought more than military and national stature. The were looking for long-range profits and were already beginning to see them in increased employment, an expanding industry, and a growing economy. The revenues from the sale of new energy flowing from the Greenland Sea was already meeting the debt obligations of capital investment and would show a sliver of profit in this fiscal year.

Both the visible government in Bonn and the invisible underwriters of the GUARDIAN PROJECT were willing listeners to reports of advancement. Setbacks, extended timetables, and minor failures were not received as well.

Thus, when Eisenach left the High Command headquarters, after listening to the two marshals and single admiral, he understood his instructions. There would be no advertising of the losses on the Arctic Ice the night before. Such a revelation would generate spirited and vivid debate in the federal parliament, and quite possibly, investigations into the Bremerhaven Petroleum Corporation, the makeup of its board of directors, and the role the military played in economic development.

More undesirable, from the High Command's point of view, was a public discussion of the tremendous amount of energy production and energy reserves that had been developed over the past three years. Wars were won or lost, based upon the availability of energy. Ships stayed in port and aircraft on the ground when there were no fuels available. Armies, with their insatiable need for ammunition, stores, and support services, became immobile when the fuel tanks of trucks, jeeps, and tanks went dry. Any airing of the rationales for the High Command's objective of hoarding energy supplies and sources was to be avoided at all costs.

As Eisenach and Oberlin descended the steps of the headquarters building, *Oberst* Albert Weismann joined them. He had been waiting in the corridors outside the staff rooms, in the event that he might be called upon to explain how his two Tornadoes had been shot down.

When Eisenach saw him, he stopped in the middle of the long, wide flight of marble steps and waited. The street ahead of him bustled with pedestrians and automobiles, most of them good Germans on their separate ways home, to work, or to lunch. Not one of them, he was certain, realized how hard their country was working for them.

"General?" Weismann asked.

"The mood was not playful, Colonel."

"That is understandable."

"Steps must be taken."

"I agree," Weismann said.

"The presited defense units are to be moved to the platforms," Eisenach said. "You will arrange with Admiral Schmidt for their transport and use your heavy helicopters to emplace them."

"At once, General."

"Then, remember that our public relations with the High Command, the government, and"—Eisenach swept his hand palm up toward the street—"the people are most important, Albert. They all must understand our increased stature and our equivalence with any power in the world. We need to have the Ghost Project operational."

"I have already taken steps toward that end," Weismann said, glancing at Oberlin.

Oberlin nodded slightly.

"It would be helpful, too," the general said, "if I had better news to deliver the next time I enter this building. I want to be able to say that American intruders have been shot down."

"Or Soviet?"

"Or Soviet. Neither country will, I think, raise public

objections, if that should happen. It would only open the doors to scrutiny of their, or at least, the Americans', actions in destroying our aircraft."

Oberlin and Weismann both nodded their agreement.

"Small confrontations go unnoticed in those barren spaces," Oberlin said.

"That is true," Eisenach said. "In the particular area of operations, there are very few witnesses to such incidents. We can demonstrate our resolve to either the Americans or the Soviets quietly and simply. Bring me the ears of a pilot, Albert."

"I will, General."

"Goddamn it, McKenna! Dimatta could have boosted his ass out of there. He didn't have to shoot back, for Christ's sake! I know his damned profile. He's quick on the trigger."

"All of that is probably true, General Brackman. But to keep the facts straight, Frank didn't make the decision. He asked permission, and I gave it. Don't blame Frank, and don't blame it on the heat of battle."

McKenna was tucked into his office cubicle, where he had slept the balance of the night. He had been thinking about the joys of a turnaround flight to, even, Borneo, where he could get a hot shower when Brackman had called. The general had just read the debriefing report.

"You discuss that decision with Overton?"

"No. Jim's responsible for *Themis*. The squadron is my baby. I'll take the heat."

"Give me a rationale," Brackman said. "One that will pass muster when I send it to Washington."

"Dimatta was fired upon."

"Come on, Kevin! You're talking to me, remember?"

"All right, Marv. Arrogance."

"What the hell are you talking about?"

"The whole setup aches with an overtone of arrogance.

I don't know what's going on in the civilian government, but the old guard military acts as if the last forty years haven't meant a damned thing. The buildup of arms and armies is taking place blatantly, as if the world isn't watching. The commanders tromp over anything in their path. The Greenland Sea wells defy any common sense in regard to the environment. Punch a missile into the sea near an old wooden boat? No big goddamned deal. Frank didn't hear, and I didn't hear, either, any warning from the Tornado pilot, Marv. He came in shooting, as if he owned the Artic. I wanted him, and his bosses, to know that he doesn't own it."

Brackman pondered for a while. "Okay, Kevin. I buy it. Sending the message, I mean. I don't know whether or not Harvey Mays and Hannibal Cross will buy it."

"You know what makes it a credible message, Marv?"

"I have an idea."

"It's almost four o'clock in Bonn. Have the White House or the State Department received any irate ambassadors?"

"No. And we didn't get any as a result of the attack on the well."

"How much do you want to bet that Bonn doesn't even know what's taken place, or is taking place?" McKenna asked. "Anybody want to pin the chancellor down?"

"No bets. You suggesting we inform Bonn that their military is out of hand?"

"I'm not suggesting a damned thing. The policy people in the White House, at Foggy Bottom, and on the Hill are going to screw it all up, anyway. And somehow, I don't think the German chancellor would take kindly to interference in his administration, no matter the reasons or the facts."

"All good points, Kevin. Okay, put that aside for now. What did you get me?"

"Pearson is still wrapping up her analysis, but from

what I saw, we're not going to find many weak points in the transmission lines. The only exposed points are where the pipes—they look like pipelines—come out of the sea on the mainland. That may be subterfuge. Dummy pipelines. There are three of them at each of the pumping stations. From the side-view pictures, each of the pumping stations is built on top of a cliff, some one hundred yards back from the shoreline. My gut feeling, Marv, is that the pumping stations are also dummies. I think that each platform has its own turbine generators, and the electric output goes right into undersea cables, is collected at one or two central points, perhaps also on the sea bottom, and then transferred to the mainland, coming ashore underground. I believe that the distribution centers are located in hardened, subterranean excavations under the pumping stations. Further distribution within the country is also below ground."

"Shit. No place where we could cut the flow of electrical energy?"

"Not if you go by my guts," McKenna said.

"I keep asking this. What's next?"

"Let me talk to Amy and Jim and get back to you."

"I'll call Washington and see if you and I still have jobs."

"We had an airborne warning and command craft in the area, and we did see one side of the confrontation, Marvin." Vitaly Sheremetevo did not tell Brackman of his jealousy concerning the MakoShark aerospace craft. Watching the radar tapes, seeing four darting blips chasing nothing at all, then watching nothing at all shoot down two high-technology German fighters, had been an exercise in frustration.

Even for an observer.

An observer who had found himself unexpectedly rooting for an American.

Heresy.

"It is disconcerting, isn't it, Vitaly? I saw our own tapes."

"The important thing," Sheremetevo said, "is that we have achieved a new phase."

"Direct hostilities, Yes."

"And with no concurrent admission or announcement from Bonn."

"It gets 'curiouser and curiouser.' That's a quote, Vitaly."

"From whom?"

"I'll send you a copy of the book."

"What do your Joint Chiefs of Staff have to say about this?"

"They're discussing it with the SecDef. Secretary of Defense. I imagine that he'll then discuss it with the President and the National Security Advisor. It may be weeks before I hear from them again." Brackman's laugh did not sound very amused.

"On this side, Marvin, I have had to confer with a small defense committee of the Politburo. As you say, discussions are under way."

"In the meantime, Vitaly, I'm finalizing the objective I would like to see."

"Which is?"

"I want to take those wells out of commission. For two reasons. I want to reduce the threat of war, and I want to eliminate the threat to the environment."

"I can agree with that," Sheremetevo said. "Yes, I will support the position. How do we do that?"

"That's the hell of it. I'm not certain how we go about it. There's got to be a weak link somewhere."

"The transmission cables would be my preference."

"That's my preference, too, Vitaly. We just can't find the damned things."

Amy Pearson worked at her desk in her office. On two

of the screens, she had called up copies of telexes that had been forwarded to *Themis*.

The first one was half amazing, less in its contents than in its correspondents.

CLASSIFICATION TOP SECRET
Decode: 06/17/0841

TO: DIR, CIA
FROM: CHMN, KGB
SUBJ: PEENEMUNDE FACILITY
1) AGREE FACILITY IS LAUNCH COMPLEX.
2) SOURCES INDICATE PRESENCE OF
GERMAN NATIONAL EXPERTS IN PHYSICS,
AERONAUTICS, ENGINEERING,
COMPUTING. PERSONNEL COMPLEMENT
APPROXIMATELY SIXTY PROFESSIONAL
STAFF THREE HUNDRED SUPPORT
STAFF.
3) LOCAL POPULACE BELIEVES FACILITY
EXPERIMENTAL LABORATORY.
4) AGENT INTERVIEWED TWO SITE
WORKERS—COOK, ALLOYS TECHNICIAN,
OBTAINED FREEHAND DRAWING SIMILAR
TO USSR SRF-32 MULTIPURPOSE LAUNCH
VEHICLE. (PARTIAL SPECIFICATIONS MAY
BE PROVIDED UPON EXECUTIVE
REQUEST.)
5) AGENT OBSERVED COL. ALBERT N.
WEISMANN, CMDR, 20TH SPECIAL AIR
GROUP AT SITE.

Pearson thought that communications between the chairman of the *Komitet Gosudarstvennoy Bezopasnosti* and the director of the Central Intelligence Agency were extremely rare. The original of this message might go for big bucks at a Sotheby auction fifty years from now.

On content, she was highly interested in the apparent

connection of Weismann with the launch complex. That put the 20th Special Air Group, already identified with the geothermal wells, into some kind of relationship with a rocket launch facility.

Reading between the lines of item four, she thought that the KGB suspected that the German rocket was a copy of one of their own. There was very likely an in-depth search for spies taking place at the Baikonur Cosmodrome in Tyuratam. A "multipurpose launch vehicle" didn't tell her much. Intercontinental Ballistics Missile? Space entry vehicle? Or both?

She turned to her keyboard at the third screen and quickly typed a request memo to Gen. David Thorpe, copy to General Overton, asking for a follow-up on item four, a listing of specifications for the Soviet Rocket Forces SRF-32, over the President's signature. She felt that knowing the capability of the SRF-32 was suddenly important.

On screen two was a copy of an extract from another telex, directed to the CIA's European division in the Intelligence Directorate from an unknown agent or asset in the field. The agent apparently kept a vigil over the High Command's headquarters in Bonn and one of his entries for the current morning read:

1116 HOURS:
GEN. FELIX EISENACH, COL. MAXIMILLIAN
OBERLIN, COL. ALBERT WEISMANN
DEPART HC HDQTRS TOGETHER.
NOTE: EISENACH CURRENT ASSIGN
AS SPCL ASST TO MARSHAL HOCH. OBERLIN
AIDE TO EISENACH. WEISMANN
CMDER 20TH SAG.

Thorpe, or someone assigned to the task in the CIA, had extracted the entry and forwarded it, she was certain, because of the reference to Albert Weismann.

The man was showing up everywhere. At New Amsterdam, at Peenemünde, and now with importance enough to be present at the High Command's headquarters in Bonn.

She reached forward and tapped an intercom button, "Communications, IO."

"Sergeant Arguento, Colonel."

"Would you set up a link with the CIA's database right away, please."

"Two minutes, Colonel."

Anyone who reached flag rank in the German military rated a complete file, and after a quick scan, Pearson found Eisenach's. She dumped the file to the station's mainframe memory, then took her time going through it, deleting innocuous and duplicated data, and coming up with a brief word-picture of the man.

She didn't like the picture.

Old-line military aristocracy. Pampered, complete education. Lots of family money. Long-term marriage. Career on hold for a long time, until Germany reunified.

And in the background of the snapshot, the items that agents and researchers had uncovered over the years. As a legislative liaison, the general had been known as an inveterate manipulator. It was suspected that he held blackmail files on a number of influential people. He had had twelve extended extramarital affairs, and all twelve of the women had, at one time or another, been severely beaten. One of the women had vanished a few months after Eisenach had learned that she was Jewish.

That was a recurrent theme. On the professional side, in every position he had ever held, or every office over which he had authority, the researchers suspected that he had weeded out every Jew or minority and fired or reassigned them.

Pearson didn't like the man, and she had only just met him on paper.

She composed messages for CIA and DIA, asking for

details of Eisenach's assignment as an assistant to Marshal Hoch, then as an afterthought, requested additional personal data for Oberlin and Weismann.

Then she transmitted copies of her file to Overton's and McKenna's offices, where they would be queued in the correspondence file behind the rest of their daily messages.

She figured McKenna would never get to his.

Mac Zeigman had a photocopy of a picture taken by a *New York Times* photographer. It had been shot through the windshield of a car east of Peterson Air Force Base in Colorado and showed the barely discernible shape of what the reporter purported to be a MakoShark taking off from the base.

The reporter had been right.

"That is it," Zeigman said.

He handed the photocopy back across the desk to his commanding officer.

Weismann took it, dropped it on the blotter, and then leaned back in his wooden swivel chair. The chair squeaked. The backs of his hands were reddened with his skin rash and from scratching them. Zeigman wondered if the man had ever seen a doctor about his problem.

"I will have the picture enhanced and blown up to pass out to the air crews," the commander said.

Zeigman looked through the windows at the runway. Two Eurofighters took off in formation, turbojets whining, the dark kerosene vapors trailing wispily behind them.

They were in the command quarters of the *Zwanzigste Speziell Aeronautisch Gruppe,* in what had originally been the standby facility for aircrews on 24-hour alert. Weismann liked having his headquarters this close to the runways, even if the scream of jet engines continually interrupted conversations. In the outer office, Zeigman could hear operations officers speaking on telephones and radios.

"Well, Mac, you're one of the few who can say that you've seen it."

"Truly a privilege, Colonel," Zeigman said, the sarcasm heavy.

"And you say that you could not get either a radar or infrared lock?"

"Neither. I had to guide the missiles by hand. Then the bastard accelerated so quickly, I lost him."

"Perhaps, Mac, if you had had your weapons officer with you, the result would have been different. Altogether different."

Zeigman kept his silence. He was being chastised, and worse, he knew it was warranted. Had he attended to the flying, and had he had his weapons officer along to guide the missiles, the Luftwaffe might well have a downed MakoShark to examine. He had already lambasted himself. To be that close, and then to miss!

"When he went to active radar, chasing Tiger Three and Tiger Four, I did get a positive lock-on," Zeigman said. "But then I lost it when the radar was switched to passive."

Weismann leaned forward and planted his elbows on top of the old wooden desk. The chair squeaked again. He placed his fingertips together and studied them.

"It is going to require a change in tactics, Mac. We must put more faith in the weapons system operators."

"Yes."

"The Eurofighters will not stand a chance alone against them. Nor will the Tornados unless we concoct new methods."

"Perhaps not," Zeigman reluctantly agreed.

"Let us get Metzenbaum in here and devise a method of using the Eurofighters and the Tornados in combination. What would you think of that?"

Zeigman thought about it, about using the single-seat fighters as bait, and he liked it.

Mako Three, piloted by Maj. Kenneth Autry, was on space duty, retrieving dead or malfunctioning satellites and transporting them to *Themis* for repair and retrofit.

That program alone had enhanced the stature of the space station. Abandoning communication and reconnaissance satellites in space, then replacing them by boosting new satellites into orbit atop Titan rockets or in the bay of the Space Shuttle was extremely expensive. NASA and the Space Command estimated that the savings accrued from reconditioning existing satellites amounted to over four billion dollars in the current fiscal year.

McKenna was killing time until Headquarters, USAF Space Command responded to Pearson's latest hot flash. He, Polly Tang, and T. Sgt. Benny Shalbot were in the module of Spoke twelve, which had several bays similar to the hangar cells of the hub, watching Ken Autry and two men on Extra-Vehicular Activity, EVA, through the bay window and the open hangar doors.

Autry had maneuvered the Mako to within fifty feet of the open hangar and parked it. The craft was on its side, in relation to McKenna, its opened payload doors facing him. Extending from the payload bay were four slender grappling devices, and they were lovingly clamped to the primary housing of a Teal Ruby satellite. The Teal Ruby could not be pulled into the Mako's cargo bay, or for that matter, into the module's repair bay, because its combination solar collector panels and antennas extended forty feet on each side of the satellite body.

The two crewmen were dressed in white environmental suits with all-purpose packs strapped to their backs. The packs contained the life-support system and the thrusters used for mobility outside the station. Both men were tethered by long life lines.

"Mako Three," said one of the crewmen over the open radio, "You can release now."

"Roger."

The grappling hooks released their grip and withdrew into the bay.

"You're clear, Mako. Do it slow, now."

Three thrusters, on nose and wing tips, fired, and the Mako drifted away, then began to maneuver for docking in another hangar. The payload bay doors closed.

The crewmen moved in on the Teal Ruby and started dismantling the solar wings so that the three components could be brought inside for repair.

"Damned slow buggers, ain't they?" Shalbot said, tapping his electronics diagnostic box. "I shoulda been done with this job by now, and back in my bunk."

"We can't all move at your speed, Benny." McKenna said, taking Polly's hand in his own and giving it a squeeze.

"Don't I know it?" Shalbot said.

"What are you doing?" Tang asked him.

"Moving at my own speed," McKenna said.

"Too fast for me," she told him, gently withdrawing her hand. "I've got to go put Mako Three to bed."

"Where did I go wrong?"

"I'll think about it, then tell you," she said.

McKenna went with her, jetting across the large open space of the interior half of the module. Affixed to its bulkheads were workbenches mounting the latest technology in electronic diagnostics and repair. Oscilloscopes, computers, monitors, digital measuring devices. McKenna was glad he didn't have to understand them and amazed that Benny Shalbot knew the functions of each one.

They went down the spoke together and passed through the hatchway into Corridor 2, the main path around the perimeter of the hub.

"Bye-bye, Polly," he said as she pushed gracefully off a bulkhead and sailed into Corridor 1B, which crossed the hub behind the hangars.

"Good-bye, Colonel. Don't be depressed."

"I am, dear, I am."

McKenna crossed to Spoke thirteen and opened its orange door by tapping his code into the keypad. Locking the hatch behind him, he traversed the spoke quickly and unlocked the module door with the same code.

Spoke thirteen was used entirely for fuel storage. It was divided into subcompartments containing JP-7 jet fuel and solid fuel pellets. An intricate maze of piping accepted incoming fuel from HoneyBee rockets or, lately, from the solid fuel manufacturing plant in Spoke eleven, and transferred both types down the spoke to the various hangars. The safety precautions were as complete as they could be. Fire extinguisher nozzles protruded from all bulkheads. In the event of a leak or fire, automatic valves closed off the lines into the hub. If a fire was not containable, the entire spoke and module could be detached from the space station with exploding bolts and pushed off into space by heavy-duty thrusters attached to the outer housing.

The PA system coughed, then said, "HoneyBee inbound. Major Mitchell, could you cover?"

He didn't hear Brad Mitchell's response.

McKenna made his rounds, checking the tags on each fuel compartment. The fuel technicians and Brad Mitchell made regular inspections, dating, timing, and signing off on the tags. McKenna did the same, jotting the time, the date, and his initials as he checked each set of pressure and temperature indicators. He looked for leaks at all valve and fitting junctures.

When he left, he made sure each of the hatchways was fully secured.

He followed the perimeter corridor on around the hub, stopped and talked to Sergeant Embry for a moment, and directed Dr. Monte Washington back toward his own territory. Washington tended to explore.

"You see anything green around here, Doctor?"

The head swiveled. "Sorry, Colonel. Got lost."

"Don't get lost anymore. There's lots of green, earth side."

Washington sneered at him, reached for a grab bar, and shoved off ahead of him. McKenna didn't think the computer specialist liked him. And didn't care.

He reached the Command Center to find Milt Avery manning the main console. The primary screen held a view of the hanger side of the hub, and a radar repeat was shown on Screen 2. There were six more screens, each showing some section of the space station. Screen 8 was an exterior view, the camera trained on the growing Spoke 9B. Three figures in EVA suits were lining up a curved piece of the spoke.

Avery had been in the astronaut corps before his assignment as deputy commander of the station. He had taken the space shuttles through nine successful missions. A short and quiet man, Avery was not easily perturbed. McKenna thought he would be a good man in a crisis.

"Hi, Milt."

The colonel turned his head to look at him. "Hello, Kevin. Have you been checking on that Teal Ruby?"

"All but in the bay, Milt. And I made a pass through fuel storage. Looks fine."

"Good," Avery tapped a line into the computerized log he was working on. "Overton and Pearson said for you to meet them in Sixteen's dining hall."

"Damn. I just passed there. Oh, by the way, I chased Washington out of Corridor Two, near Fourteen."

"One more infraction, and I'm going to ask Jim to boot him out."

"I could drop him off on my next flight," McKenna offered. "Say somewhere over Poland."

"Sounds good to me."

McKenna went back to Spoke Sixteen, passing through the four safety hatches. He got a bag of coffee and heated a roast beef sandwich from the Back Home machine, then carted them over to the table where Pearson and Overton had strapped themselves down.

There was no one else in the compartment, and

McKenna figured the general had shooed them out.

Pearson was studying a mural fixed to one bulkhead. A soft view of Tahiti. There were lots of murals and pictures in the residential spokes.

"I believe that's about three miles south of Papeete, Amy. We could pop down there for a couple days."

"You including me?" Overton asked.

"Well, actually, Jim, I wasn't."

"He's not including me, either," Pearson said. She sat up against the lap belt and crossed her arms on the table. She had to hold the table edge with her fingers to keep her arms down.

McKenna forced his sandwich partway out of the pouch and took a bite of it.

"Amy and I," Overton said, "had a long talk with Brackman and Thorpe and a couple of experts they found somewhere. The consensus is that the wells, platforms, and ancillary structures are now off-limits. Judging by the infrared and low-light photos of well number eight, the dome is divided internally into three sections, probably living quarters, administrative area, and wellhead section. The dome walls, by the way, are ten feet thick, Styrofoam sandwiched between aluminum sheeting. The well area appears to be completely open under the dome, and the experts say they can interpret the photos to show the wellhead and several turbine generators. Don't ask me how, Kevin, because the low-light shots were blurry as hell down within the dome. They're looking at the heat structures. Anyway, on number eight, the wellhead itself is estimated at three hundred and fifteen degrees of temperature. That's the metal. Temperatures within the well itself are estimated at six hundred and twelve degree Fahrenheit."

"Don't touch it, in other words?" McKenna said.

"Not with your hand, not with a Wasp. If the wellhead is damaged, or even if the platform's anchor lines are severed and the platform drifts, snapping off the well casing,

215

all hell will literally break loose. Superheated water and steam spilling into the Greenland Sea will either kill or drive off the marine life. If all of those wells were to let go, the results could be catastrophic."

McKenna had already stored a few mental pictures of Amsterdam, Stockholm, and Copenhagen under water.

"Does Brackman still think we need to find the undersea cables? The last reconnaissance run should have killed that idea."

"Oh, he thinks we can find them, all right. Amy had the idea."

McKenna looked to her and grinned. "You always do."

"We're going to do some electromagnetic mapping," she said, holding his gaze with her own.

He almost made a snappy comment about her use of "we," then fortuitously did not. She was, after all, part of the team, and McKenna didn't want to exclude her.

"Sounds like a damned good idea," he said.

And got a smile in return for a change.

ground will drive forces toward the Greenland Sea, or
Jan mayne and the Greenland Sea will either fall or
drive off the maritime IOC. If all or their bases were in

Eleven

"We set to go, David?"

Thorpe was in his chair overlooking the operations center, and Brackman went in and stood beside him, looking at the big plotting board on the far wall, through the windows of the crow's nest. Almost all of the targets currently being tracked were displayed in blue and red.

"Getting there, Marv. The First Aero put down at Merlin twenty-five minutes ago. We should get word soon on the equipment."

Brackman checked the lower right-hand corner of the plotting board. The island of Borneo had three yellow dots on it.

He tracked back across the map and found Murmansk. There was one green dot superimposed on the city.

"What are the Soviets sending?" he asked.

"Sheremetevo's operations officer is supposed to call me in the next half hour, Marv, but the early word was eight Fulcrums and an AWACS."

"This is the first time we've ever shown the Reds in green, isn't it?" the commander said.

"Grates a little, doesn't it?"

Mildenhall Royal Air Force Base on the east side of England had a lavender dot. That would be the Boeing E-3 Sentry. Brackman had decided that he wanted an AWACS of his own aloft to watch over the action. Now that missiles had been exchanged, he was going to maintain much closer scrutiny. *Themis* could not be relied upon for a constant overhead surveillance because of her orbit, and there was no reason, just yet, to call the Jet Propulsion Laboratory in Pasadena and have a KH-11 moved into an overhead orbit. Besides, that might entail getting the National Security Agency involved and briefed, and the more agencies with an interest, the more difficult it was to reach decisions.

"Where are you spotting the Sentry, David?"

"At forty thousand feet over Greenland's east coast, if that's all right with you, Marv. It'll give us the coverage we want, but keep her out of the fray, if one develops."

"Overflight permission?"

"We've got it."

"Okay, yeah, that's good. McKenna give you any idea on the timetable?"

"He said a couple hours or a couple weeks," Thorpe told him. "It all depends on Benny Shalbot."

Col. Pyotr Volontov sat in his borrowed, jury-rigged office half a kilometer from the main runway at Murmansk. He thought the chair was a castoff from the Great War. The iron casters squealed, and the left arm was loose.

He rubbed his cheeks with the fingers of his right hand, deciding he should shave before takeoff time. The face mask tended to grate and rub his face raw when he had a stubble of whiskers.

Volontov had just talked on the telephone with Martina, the dark-haired, fair-skinned woman to whom he was betrothed. The engagement seemed to have become more permanent than marriage, now approaching two years of endurance. Neither Martina Davidoff, who was a medical doctor specializing in obstetrics in Moscow, and whose father happened to be an admiral in the Red Banner Northern Fleet, nor Volontov had yet felt inclined to take that last step.

There was comfort in their relationship. Each had an

escort for the more important social events, and neither had to devise excuses for an unmarried state to parents or friends. On long weekends at Admiral Davidoff's *dacha* outside Moscow, they had each other.

Several times, they had set a wedding date, but acceptable delays had intervened. Volontov was sent on temporary duty to Afghanistan or Egypt or Iraq. Martina had a closely watched experiment of one kind or another under way. Her research absorbed her time like a sponge, and Volontov had his airplanes and the responsibility of his wing command.

The telephone rang, startling him out of his review.

"Colonel Volontov."

"Colonel, this is Major Petrov."

"Yes, Micha, what is it?"

"We have a message from General Sheremetevo's office. Permission is granted for the use of eight MiG-29s, two tankers, and one Airborne Early-Warning craft."

"Very well, Micha. We will utilize seven aircraft from the 2032nd. I will fly as lead of the first flight. Tell Major Rostoken that he will lead the second flight and that he is to select the pilots. We will brief at . . . what time did General Sheremetevo give?"

"None, Comrade Colonel. We are waiting on a United States Air Force sergeant."

Benny Shalbot had bitched for most of the reentry flight from *Themis* to Merlin Air Force Base. He didn't like his seat in the passenger module, couldn't see a damned thing, didn't like the environmental suit, didn't like leaving his responsibilities aboard the space station in the hands of his junior, and most of all, he didn't like Borneo.

It was too isolated.

There were none of the right kind of women around. Shalbot did not define his kind of woman.

What there was at Merlin Air Force Base, however,

were the electromagnetic measuring electronics necessary for Pearson's mapping project. They were not designed for use with the MakoShark, however, and Benny Shalbot also became necessary to Pearson's project.

Once on the ground, though, Shalbot ran around Hangar One three times to recondition his leg muscles to gravity, rounded up a large bunch of technicians, confiscated most of the tools and electronic black boxes in sight, and disappeared into the hangar with the three MakoSharks.

Complaining all the while. He wasn't happy with the magnetometers they would have to use. "Shoddy, sumbitchin' low-tech shit."

McKenna and his five squadron members ate lunch in the dining hall.

McKenna took a long shower.

Munoz and Abrams went down to the beach to swim with the sharks.

Nitro Fizz Williams took a short jaunt into the jungle, looking for fruit right off the tree, and arguing with the monkeys. He collected a lot of exotic flowers, and he saw a leopard. He decided to return to the base early.

The squadron got together again in the evening for dinner, and McKenna sent boxed meals over to the hangar for the technicians. After dinner, they spent an hour going over the mission.

McKenna and the others found a dormitory bunk room, turned the air conditioning on high, and crawled under the sheets after taking half-hour showers. McKenna tried to invent a shower that would work in space.

At five-thirty in the morning, the intercom buzzed, and McKenna rolled out of his top bunk, hit the floor on his feet, and pressed the button.

"This had better be good."

"I got you set up, Colonel."

"We'll be there in ten minutes, Benny."

Munoz was bright-eyed and ready to go and the others

220

complained bitterly and almost meaningfully when McKenna roused them. They dressed and crossed the dark grounds, still hot and humid, to the hangar.

Unlocking and slipping through the judas door, McKenna saw the three MakoSharks lined up, noses out, ready to go. Each had two pylons mounted, one gun pod, and four Wasps. Underneath them, the crewmen that Shalbot had bossed were flaked out, slumped against crates and tractors, spread out on the floor. Coke and Pepsi cans, lunch boxes, and candy wrappers were scattered around on the floor and on castered toolboxes. The normal aroma of JP-7 fuel was augmented with the acrid odor of sweat.

Shalbot, grimy and stained and baggy-eyed, grinned at him. "The sumbitch works, Colonel."

"Guaranteed, Benny?"

"Fuckin'-A."

"How'd you do it?" Munoz asked.

"Wanted to put 'em in a pylon pod, but we couldn't route the cables. Ain't enough room without screwing up the pylon mounts. So what we did, we made ourselves some bird cages outta plastic tubing and suspended the magnetometers inside the cage. The cage fits into the payload bay, hooks right onto the module-securing hardware. Then we ran the cables through the avionics bay and into the rear compartment. The control setup looks like shit, but it works okay."

"Sounds good, Benny," McKenna said.

"Yeah, well, I got to get the WSOs up on Delta Blue and explain how to make this stuff work.

While Shalbot conducted his tutoring session, the weapons systems officers standing on the wing around the open cockpit, McKenna went to a phone on the hangar wall, called the duty officer, and dictated a message to him for the base commander. All of the technicians who had worked for Shalbot on the retrofit were to get three-day passes and a free round-trip flight to Singapore.

Then he composed a message for Volontov in Murmansk, using the codes he and the Russian had agreed upon when they met in Chad.

"This goes to Murmansk, Colonel?" the duty officer said. "In the USSR?"

"That's right, Lieutenant."

"I, uh, I wonder if, uh, maybe I should wake the base commander?"

"Not necessary, Lieutenant. If that message isn't on its way in five minutes, I'll have the chairman of the Joint Chiefs give you a call to confirm it."

"Yessir. Right away, sir."

When Shalbot was through with his teaching session, he and the backseaters slipped down the ladder from Delta Blue's rear cockpit. The technicians began to groan and moan, then crawled to their feet.

McKenna thanked them for their work and said, "You all get the rest of the day to sleep, then you're off to Singapore for a couple days."

"All right! . . . way to go . . . damn sure!"

"Not me," Shalbot said.

McKenna looked at him.

Shalbot poked a thumb over his shoulder at the MakoShark behind him. "Those boxes won't take the ride outta the atmosphere, Colonel. Ain't designed for it. You're going to have to recover at Chad. If you get me a ride on a Lear, I'll meet you there and pull the tape cartridges. We'll leave the magnetometers at Chad."

"Damn, that sounds sensitive. How well are they going to stand up under normal flight, Benny?"

"They weren't designed for use on attack planes, Colonel. I don't want you pulling more than three G's."

McKenna looked to Munoz. "What's that do to our flight schedule, Tiger?"

"No more than three G's? Hang on."

Munoz scrambled up the ladder and into his cockpit to

use the computer. Four minutes later, he stood up and leaned out of the cockpit.

"We can still do it tonight, if we hustle out of here, Kev. We're gonna lose sixteen minutes, acceleratin' that slowly. But we can still hit the objective before dawn. We're gonna come out the other end nice and bright, though. It might be a little dicey."

"Okay, we'll do it, anyway," McKenna decided. "Suit up, guys. Benny, you're an ace."

Shalbot looked at the stained concrete. "Just get me a Learjet, Colonel. I always wanted my own Lear."

McKenna went back to the phone on the wall and called the duty officer again to send a second message to Pyotr Vorontov. He also issued orders to wake up two pilots for Shalbot's Learjet.

The three MakoSharks were off the ground at six-forty in the morning, Borneo time.

Three hours and twelve minutes later, on the northern side of the equator, over seven thousand miles from Merlin Air Force Base, they descended from 100,000 feet.

It was two-fifty-six in the morning, and the sun was already rising in the northern latitudes, though still low on the horizon.

Crossing the Austrian border, McKenna pressed the stud for the Tac-1 frequency, already set in a scrambling mode. "Delta Flight, break."

"Yellow gone."

"Green doing it."

On either side of him, Dimatta and Conover began to pull away. The three MakoSharks would make the single run northward flying parallel, but with forty miles between each of the craft. Shalbot had said that would give the mapping coverage a slight overlap.

"Alpha One, Delta Blue."

"Go ahead, Blue." Overton was on the microphone.

"Six minutes to IP, on schedule."

"Copy, Blue."

223

"Semaphore, Delta Blue," McKenna said.

"Delta Blue, this is Semaphore," General Thorpe said.

"Semaphore, did you get my message about the need for a Hot Country recovery?"

"Roger. The boss wants to know when we started having tech sergeants running the air force."

"Yeah, well, I don't have any promotion allocations for my squadron," McKenna said, "but I want him to be a master sergeant by the time we get back. Can master sergeants run the air force?"

"They already do," Thorpe told him. "I'll process your oral recommendation, and we'll see if we can't find an allocation somewhere."

Munoz broke in, "You've got my recommendation, too. How about silver oak leaves? Got any of those laying around somewhere?"

"Can it, Tiger. I appreciate that, Semaphore. How we doing for Cottonseed?"

"Cottonseed's four minutes from station. He's standing by on this frequency," Thorpe said. "Condor and Vulture are in alert status."

"Roger, that. Are we a go?"

"Go, Delta Blue."

McKenna checked the HUD. Mach 1.4. Altitude 42,000. Green LED's everywhere.

On his right, the low sun was threatening, a pink nipple on the horizon. At lower altitude, though, it would be dark enough for the first part of the flight.

The plan was to make a curving pass northward, starting over the German mainland, swinging around the jut of Norway over the North Sea, continuing over the Norwegian Sea, and then into the Greenland Sea. Pearson was hoping to trace the electromagnetic anomalies out of Germany to the offshore platforms.

They had to do it at 600 knots. Right at 690 miles per hour. Slower was better, faster might jumble the readings, since, according to Shalbot, the tape recording mechanism was equivalent to, "the one Moses used."

The distance was 1,900 miles. It would take two and three-quarters hours, and they would hit the platforms in strong early morning light.

McKenna pressed the Tac-2 button, preset for the frequency he and Volontov had agreed upon. It was not a scrambled frequency.

"Condor One, Delta Blue."

"Delta Blue, this is Condor One. Proceed."

"Condor, we'll be on our IP in two minutes. You might want to start engines in about forty minutes."

"Copy forty minutes. Condor out."

Back to Tac-1. "Cottonseed, Delta Blue."

"Go ahead, Delta Blue."

"What do you see me flying into?"

"Blue, we no longer have coverage of your area, but an hour ago, two Eurofighters and two Tornados took off from New Amsterdam, headed north. Mildenhall RAF reports two Tornados flying the French border. You've got eleven scheduled commercial flights in the area of operations. I can read them off for you, if you like."

"We've got the commercial aircraft input already," McKenna said. "What about in your area?"

"We're showing three formations currently. The flight makeup appears to consist of two Tornados and two Eurofighters, Blue. We have a flight approaching the ice, a flight on the southbound leg, and two tankers are aloft at three-zero-thousand, south of Svalbard. Then, we're expecting the flight from New Amsterdam."

"Thank you, Cottonseed. Delta Blue out."

On the intercom, Munoz said, "They're beefin' up the beef, *amigo*."

"Looks that way, Tiger."

"IP!"

McKenna set the elapsed time counter on his chronometer to zero, then eased the hand controller forward. By the time they passed over Bremerhaven, the MakoShark

225

was steady at 600 knots and 3,000 feet of altitude. Dimatta and Conover each checked in with the same readings.

Munoz cussed Shalbot's jury-rigged controls, lashed to the left side of his cockpit, but seemed to think the magnetometer was operating.

Bremerhaven was dark, the streets identified by long rows of street lights. A few early risers were up, pushing headlight beams along the shaded streets. The naval base was well lit, a destroyer and a freighter putting out to sea side by side. New Amsterdam Air Force Base launched a multiengined jet transport of some kind that took off to the east.

No one seemed to notice them.

"Let's make the turn, Snake Eyes."

McKenna used a lot of space to make a left turn to a heading of 345 degrees.

"Green turning."

"Yellow turned."

"Copy," McKenna told them.

Twenty minutes later, they all turned back to dead north. If the expectations were correct, Delta Blue was approximately over the eastern cable.

"I wish to hell I could get a concurrent readin' on this thing," Munoz said. "I don't like not knowin' what we're gettin'. If anything."

"Trust to God and Benny Shalbot, Tiger."

Twenty minutes after that, Munoz said, "Arctic Circle, *jefe.*"

"Roger."

He called Cottonseed and got an update on the German patrol planes.

McKenna went to Tac-2. "Condor One, Delta Blue."

"Proceed, Delta Blue."

"What's your situation, Condor?"

"On station, the last two aircraft are almost finished refueling."

226

The Fulcrums were circling at 30,000 feet over the Barents Sea, fifty miles out of range of radar aboard either the offshore platforms or the tankers replenishing the German aircraft.

"Condor, you have two flights of mixed Tornados and Eurofighters. Flight One is currently refueling south of Svalbard. Flight Two is on the western edge of the ice pack. I'd appreciate your help."

"Delta Blue, Condor. We will depart these coordinates now."

It was getting light out, the dawn a milky gray spreading over a darker gray sea. To the east a few miles was some cloud cover, but it wasn't doing Delta Blue any good. It might mask Delta Green for a while.

Unable to change his speed, heading, or altitude, McKenna felt a little exposed.

"One o'clock high," Munoz said.

McKenna looked up. There were four aircraft in a loose formation.

"They're southbound and down," Munoz quoted. "Those assholes are thinking about sausage and eggs, not us."

"I don't think so, either," McKenna agreed.

He estimated that the Germans were flying at 30,000 feet. Having successfully completed their patrol of the platforms, they were not looking for intruders in the middle of the Norwegian Sea.

Ten minutes later, the German planes were out of sight to the south.

But he saw a ship coming up on the horizon.

Zeigman circled to the east of the tanker, waiting for his last two planes to be fueled.

He was watching the sea. It was bland and mesmerizing, shades of gray. Most of his days and nights were that way. The northern regions always gave a feeling of overcast, even when the sun was shining. As he came around,

Svalbard Island appeared in his windscreen, also bland. It was fifteen kilometers away.

Idly, he automatically swept the instrument panel with his eyes. He glanced at the radar scope.

What!

He counted the blips, then pressed the transmit button. "Tiger Flight, break off refueling and join on me. Panther Leader, do you hear me?"

Wilhelm Metzenbaum, *Panther Führer,* came back to him immediately. "Panther Leader, Tiger."

"Go to military power, Panther Flight, and join on me. I have eight targets, possibly Soviet aircraft, at one-six-zero-zero-zero altitude, three-five kilometers, my bearing zero-three-eight."

As his wingman and second element closed in on him, Zeigman advanced his throttles and began to climb.

"You are an asshole," he told his weapons system operator over the intercom.

"Major?" squeaked *Hauptmanm* Fritz Gehring.

"You should have seen the Russians earlier."

"I am sorry, Major."

"Do not be sorry. Keep your eyes open. We will arm all systems now."

Within minutes, Wilhelm Metzenbaum's flight sidled in next to them.

"Tiger Leader, our new tactics will not work against MiGs."

"Agreed, Panther. Take the Eurofighters and go to three-five-zero-zero-zero meters. We will make the first strike, and you the second."

"One strike is all we have in us, Tiger Leader. Our fuel supply is limited."

"One pass is all you will need," Zeigman promised, "if that."

He worked his shoulder muscles and stretched his fingers. He felt good, all charged up.

MiGs.

He had never attacked MiGs before.

Gerhard Schmidt listened to the radio exchanges of the German pilots, sitting in his upholstered chair in his flag plot aboard the *Hamburg.*

Provide them with a warning, Tiger Leader. Shoo them away.

He heard nothing.

Schmidt looked at his aide, Werner Niels. The man looked slightly sickly.

"Lieutenant," he said to his plotter, "have we a radar contact with those aircraft?"

The *leutnant* spoke into his headphone, listened, then tapped his keyboard. Eight green rectangles appeared on the plotting board. They were east of Svalbard Island, heading east-north-east.

"I am sorry, Herr Admiral, the radar can reach only Tiger and Panther flights. The Soviet airplanes are beyond our range."

Schmidt detested seeing only half the battle. His mind was good at imagining the things he could not see, one of the reasons he was an excellent tactician. His brain kept track of unseen destroyers, frigates, and submarines with only minimal input as to course, heading, and speed. He anticipated the intentions of ship commanders with frequent success. Airplanes, and their arrogant operators, were much more difficult.

He studied the plotting board. One by one, the green rectangles blinked out as they chased the Soviet aircraft out of radar range.

Just below the ice cap on the plotting board was his own ship, the *Hamburg,* and her escorts. The second battle group, centered on the *Stuttgart,* was also out of his radar range, but plotted by hand. It was forty miles off the northern coast of Norway. The third battle group was near Iceland, practicing maneuvers. The fourth group patrolled the southwestern edge of the offshore platforms.

Two of the tugboats were fending off an ice floe at *Bahn-steig Zwei,* and the other was standing by near *Bahnsteig Vierzehn.* A fuel tender was approaching the fourth battle group.

He looked out the big window at the coming day. The visibility was good for about a kilometer.

He turned back and studied the plotting board.

"What do you think, Werner?"

His aide broke off a trance between himself and the board. "I think, Admiral, that all of our air cover has fled to the east. There is not one airplane in the sky over the ice or the offshore platforms."

"My observation, also."

Schmidt thought about it for one more minute, then keyed the intercom button set into the arm of his chair.

"Sir?" Kapitän Froelich said.

"Captain, I want you to sound General Quarters. Alert the second and fourth battle groups to do the same. Also alert any of the platforms that have been armed. All anti-aircraft and missile batteries are freed. They may fire at any aircraft they see."

"But, Admiral! Our fighters . . ."

"Are off on a wild-goose chase, Captain. Do as you are told."

The klaxon sounded immediately.

Delta Blue passed almost directly over the ship.

"It's a fuel tanker, Snake Eyes. Unarmed."

"Think they saw us?"

"Damned sure of it. Couple of those guys nearly fell overboard, gawking."

"Okay, then. The alarm's been sounded. You can play with your radar set."

"Finally."

McKenna saw the first of the platforms coming up. The dome had a bare, dull gleam of morning reflecting off of it. It was light enough now to see that the sea had a rough look to it. The waves were capping at about four feet, he guessed. White spume sprayed from the crests.

He hit Tac-1. "Delta Flight, arm missiles and guns, but maintain your courses. They're on to us, but completing the map is the priority. Do-Wop, you still monitoring the Soviet channel?"

"Roger that, Snake Eyes. They've got themselves a skirmish going. From their AWACS guys, who are recapping in English for me, I make it seven missiles fired on both sides, no hits. The Sovs are starting to break it off, and two of the Germans have skedaddled. The tankers are headed east, so maybe they're short of go-juice.

"Okay, Do-Wop, keep me posted if anything gets out of hand. Cottonseed, you there?"

"Go, Delta Blue."

"Any readings?"

"Nothing airborne. You feel like squawking me?"

McKenna hit the IFF switch, counted to three, then killed it.

"Got you, Delta Blue. Four miles to the first platform. That's number nine. Then you'll see number one off your right wing, then number seven off your left. Then you'll see the *Hamburg*, dead on."

"What's she doing, Cottonseed?"

"She and her two destroyers are now turning south. I'm going to call it one-seven-seven degrees. They've probably gotten a report from that fuel tanker."

"Thank you, Cottonseed. Blue out."

The radar screen showed three targets, wells nine, thirteen, and five.

"Going back to visual, Snake Eyes."

The screen went to gray. Gray sea. Gray day.

McKenna checked the HUD. Airspeed 600 knots, altitude 3,000 feet. Boring routine, gray day.

"Hey, *hombre!* That sucker's armed."

231

McKenna looked down at the magnified image. On the helicopter pad near the dome, two antiaircraft guns had been mounted. On the far side of the pad were two SAM installations, the missile mounts sporting three cylinders each. Midway between them was a small house trailer topped with a radar antenna.

"Kill the radar," he said.

"Already done."

"Alert the others."

Munoz called Dimatta and Conover and passed on the information.

"Delta Blue, Semaphore."

"Go Semaphore."

"Do we read armed platforms?"

"Two AA batteries and two SAMs on nine."

The platform was coming up quickly.

"Abort the mission."

"That'll piss Amy-baby," Munoz said, fortunately on the intercom.

"Delta Yellow, Delta Green, abort," McKenna said. "Semaphore, I'm going to take it on through. My course is right up the middle, and if we don't get it now, we may not get it at all."

Brackman's voice: "Delta Blue, you had an order."

"Hey, Semaphore, if it gets hairy, we'll boost out."

A couple seconds of carrier wave.

"Very well, Delta Blue. Use your judgment."

Airspeed 600, altitude 3,000.

"We've got to do some critical thinkin' about our ordnance loads, *jefe*. All we got is air-to-air."

McKenna reached out and armed all four of the Wasps and the gun. "Do the best you can, Tiger. Scare hell out of them, anyway."

At one mile, the AA guns opened up.

Puffs of flak began to pop around them.

McKenna held course, speed, and altitude.

"Amy better kiss you for this, *amigo*."

"Precisely."

One of the SAM emplacements started to rotate, the missiles tilting over toward them.

Nothing happened.

"They can't figure out where the hell we are on radar," Munoz said.

He launched one Wasp, waited a count of three, then launched a second.

McKenna saw the rocket trail as the first one homed in on the SAM radar trailer. Munoz guided the second by hand toward the closest AA gun.

Germans scattered like ants in a Raid storm. McKenna saw two men go over the side of the platform into the sea. He thought it would be pretty damned cold.

Whump-whump.

The Wasps detonated, one after the other.

Whoosh.

Delta Blue flashed over the platform.

"Scratch one AA, one SAM radar," Munoz said. "Hell, they never even got a missile off."

Seconds later, they went by platform number five and found it unarmed.

Platform one was armed, but they passed it six miles to the west, and the dome was between them and the well's defensive armament.

Platform seven wasn't armed, either, but it had the *Hamburg* for company.

"I think we have all the electromagnetic readings we want to have," McKenna said.

"I'm sure that's true, *compadre*."

"Shall we go home?"

"Chad, Chad, Snake Eyes. Beer and a Bloody Mary."

"Right you are."

The cruiser fired its first missile as McKenna went into a left turn, streaking over platform seven.

"Incoming," Munoz said. The volume of his voice didn't even raise.

McKenna tightened his turn, rolling his right wing vertical.

"The G's, Snake Eyes! The G's!"

"Oh, shit! I forgot."

Pushing the hand controller forward, McKenna relieved the gravitational forces. He didn't want to lose anything recorded by Shalbot's sensitive equipment and have to rehash this flight.

The right wing was still up, the MakoShark in knife-edge flight.

The rearview screen showed the SAM homing on the flicker of heat it was getting from one of the engines.

"That one's a heat-seeker. Another one launched," Munoz said.

"Chaff."

Munoz released a flurry of aluminized confetti intended to confuse the missile's guidance system.

"Flare."

The WSO punched out two magnesium flares. The brightly burning flares might draw off a heat-seeking missile.

McKenna touched the right rudder, turning right — climbing, and hiding his exhaust from the missile. He shoved the throttles full forward, watching the gravitational force readout.

When it reached 1.9, he backed off the throttles.

The SAM exploded just behind them.

"Jesus, that was close!" Cottonseed said. "You've got another coming, Blue!"

McKenna rolled upright, still climbing, passing through 9,000 feet. The airspeed indicator held at Mach .9.

The SAM was a deadly black eye in the rearview screen.

"Blow off a Wasp, Tiger."

Instantly, the Wasp launched from its rail, then dove downward under Munoz's guidance.

The SAM liked the hot exhaust of the Wasp better than

234

the neglible one of the MakoShark. It curved away from them, disappearing from the rearview screen.

"Delta Blue, Semaphore. You all right?"

"A-one. Just taking care of the IO's interests, Semaphore."

At ten o'clock in the morning, Felix Eisenach appeared in Marshal Hoch's office, as ordered.

Eisenach was accompanied by *Oberst* Maximillian Oberlin and *Oberst* Albert Weismann. All of them were in immaculate uniform, but the sleeplessness of an early morning was in their eyes.

Marshal Hoch had abandoned the discipline of military weight training fifteen years before. Eisenach judged him to be close to 135 kilograms, all of it hanging from a very short frame. His jaws bulged, and his eyes were recessed behind plump cheeks and overhanging eyebrows.

Despite the appearance, he was still a marshal, and he was still very intelligent.

His face was flushed with his indignation.

He stood behind his desk and said, "There are two things, Felix."

"Yes, Herr Marshal?"

"This." Hoch held out a sheet of paper, and Eiseenach stepped forward to take it. Oberlin and Weismann remained near the door.

Eisenach read through it quickly. Another request from the American State Department, this time addressed to the High Command, demanding explanations for the activities in the Greenland Sea.

"I would direct them to the Bremerhaven Petroleum Corporation, Marshal Hoch."

"Yes. And the next communiqué will be more fiercely worded."

"So be it," Eisnach said. "By then, we shall have Ghost

235

operational and flight-tested. Then, you will see a change in the American tone."

Hoch glared hard at him from those deep-set eyes. "Perhaps."

Eisenach waited in silence, not eager to hear of the second item.

The marshall turned his head on his bull neck to look at *Oberst* Weismann. "You have an explanation for this morning's fiasco, Colonel?

Weismann's red face became redder. "I have no excuses that are acceptable, Herr Marshal. I was at Peenemünde when the attacks came. My squadron leaders took it upon themselves to engage the Soviets."

"Leaving the platforms without air cover."

"Yes, Herr Marshal."

"And not even, as a byproduct, managing to shoot down a single Soviet aircraft."

"Yes, Herr Marshal. The MiG pilots were very good, and the plan well executed. As soon as our planes were drawn away from the platforms, the MiG's turned and ran. Nine missiles were fired, six from our aircraft, but the distances were too great for accuracy."

Hoch turned back to Eisenach. "Admiral Schmidt seems to have been the only one prepared to meet an enemy, General. Must we always rely on the navy?"

"No, Herr Marshall, not again."

Twelve

"Depth charge missiles? Depth charge missiles!" Sergeant Bert Embry was a trifle outraged. "No way, Colonel."

McKenna spoke into the open mike, "What do you think, Mabry?"

Lt. Mabry Evans at Jack Andrews Air Force Base said, "It's an interesting problem, Colonel."

Evans was looking at a photocopy of the same map that McKenna, Embry, and Pearson were scanning in the Command Center. Pearson had taken the electromagnetic mapping tapes and printed them on clear plastic. The map was fuzzy and highly irregular. The instruments had picked up anything that generated or carried electricity. The earth itself was a source in many places, creating false returns. High voltage sources were best defined, but factories and automobiles on the mainland had produced spots. The city, with its concentration of televisions, stereos, radios, washers, dryers, computers, and the like, was a dim, sloppy blur. At sea, especially along the coast in the shipping lanes, large ships could be pinpointed. In the north, the wells themselves stood out clearly, reinforcing the turbine-generator theory.

The transmission lines had been less clearly defined than Pearson had hoped, perhaps because of the depth of the seabed for much of the distance, or perhaps, as Evans had suggested, because the cable itself was mildly armored and insulated. Still, there had been enough of a pattern to

237

define two transmission lines extending from the supposed pumping stations on the mainland up through the North, Norwegian, and Greenland seas to the wells. Among the wells themselves, it was difficult to exactly note the cables, but the electromagnetic patterns from all wells seemed to converge on wells number one and eleven for the most part.

Pearson had drawn in inked lines, following the centers of two parallel patterns, dotting the lines when the patterns were not totally revealed, then overlaid the clear plastic on a map of the region. The consensus was that the Germans had laid two cables a mile apart. Both probably carried electrical energy, but one of them backed up the other in case of a breakdown or other interference. That theory was supported by the two receiving stations on the mainland.

Evans said, "I don't suppose we could take a shot at the two places where the cable comes ashore? I'm pretty sure they're buried pretty deep, below the dummy pipelines, but that would have the best chance for success."

"No, Mabry. I won't even ask Brackman about that. The mainland is going to be off-limits. In fact, I suspect that anything south of the Arctic Circle will be off-limits. We don't want any of our sorties witnessed by passersby."

"Who passes by?" Sergeant Embry asked.

"A Greenpeace boat, for one."

"How about where the cables leave the platforms?" Embry asked. "I know that takes twenty-four shots, instead of two, but we could maybe slice a cable directly under the platform."

"Forget it, Sergeant," Pearson said. "We don't know the configuration of extraction and injection well casing in relation to the cables. We won't take a chance on hitting the well casing, the anchor lines, or some other stabilization lines that I suspect are attached to the casing and cable."

"There's a spot," McKenna said, "at seventy-five degrees, four minutes north and two degrees, seven minutes east where the western cable appears brightest. Amy has the depth shown as three hundred and twenty feet."

"Undersea mountain," she said.

"Would a Phoenix or Sidewinder penetrate to that depth?" McKenna asked.

"Uh-huh," Embry said.

"No, Colonel," Evans agreed with the NCO. "We could maybe devise a warhead with a depth fuse, and even come up with a Rube Goldberg electromagnetic homing device, but the guidance is going to come apart on us as soon as it hits the sea. This is purely a guess, but I don't think any of the ordnance in our inventory is going to go much deeper than fifty feet before it goes haywire."

"Damn it," McKenna said.

"But, if you could pull a few strings, Colonel, maybe we could turn the MakoShark into a torpedo plane."

Embry nodded.

Pearson asked, "You think so, Mabry?"

"It's worth a try, Colonel Pearson. I need to get hold of a half-dozen Mark 46s. That's a heavy mother, almost six hundred pounds, but it's solid-fuel propelled, and it's aircraft adaptable."

"Why don't we just send navy planes?" Embry asked.

"Because this is still a funny, covert war," Pearson said. "None of the parties are admitting publicly that anything is going on. We'll continue to use the stealth craft."

McKenna called Brackman, but got Thorpe, who said he would check on the torpedoes.

When Thorpe called back, he said, "The *Kennedy* is off Cyprus. She's loading and launching a C-2 Greyhound within the hour. You get your torpedoes and a naval crew to help you mount them. I want a complete attack plan before you go with this, Kevin."

"I'll put Colonel Pearson right on it," he said, then passed the information to Evans.

"We go from Jack Andrews, right?" Evans asked. "I

239

mean, those torpedoes are never going into space, much less reenter the atmosphere."

"We go from Chad. Damn it, I was just there."

After he signed off the radio, Pearson said, "How come I get all the paperwork?"

"Because I have to sleep," McKenna said. "Then pop off to Chad for a shower."

Her eyes got a little dreamy. "Someday, somebody's going to figure out a shower for this place."

"Ah, the one I had last night. This morning, actually. Suds lathered all over, smooth, slippery, warm spray. . . ."

"Stop it!"

"You should have been there, Amy." He grinned.

She shook her head in resignation, and McKenna almost regretted teasing her.

Almost, but not quite.

He did regret patting her on the fanny a couple years before.

Donna Amber sailed out of the Radio Shack. "I've got some orders directed to the commander, First Aerospace."

McKenna took the sheet from her. "Maybe I'm being transferred?"

"We can hope," Pearson said.

"No," Donna Amber said, "this is for one of my kind, enlisted."

McKenna scanned the sheet and found:

PROMOTED TO MASTER SERGEANT E-7

Benjamin J. Shalbot, AF17667903, TSgt E-6, 1st AS, SPACOM.

McKenna said, "Donna, would you get on the PA and ask General Overton, Colonel Avery, and Sergeant Shalbot to come to the Command Center."

"Right away, Colonel."

The ceremony was brief, and McKenna slapped the

stripes he had picked up at the Jack Andrews base exchange against Shalbot's arms. They stuck to the fabric of the jumpsuit with double-sided tape.

Shalbot said, "Shucks."

McKenna said, "Okay, Master Sergeant, you need to get ready for a ride to Hot Country."

"Ah, sh . . . ah, hell, Colonel. Again?"

"I can get someone else."

"Not on your life."

Wilhelm Metzenbaum, the "Bear," was edgy.

He and Zeigler had been thoroughly reamed by Weismann for abandoning coverage of the wells to pursue an obvious diversion by Soviet MiGs.

Obvious, after the fact. Weismann, Eisenach, and Hoch had not been on the scene, but they knew what was obvious.

Metzenbaum was not a complainer, but he was getting fed up with the crap surrounding the oil wells. Something definitely was not right. He had told Olga about it yesterday. She said he should retire. He said he had two years to go. She said he had the twins to think about it. Where would they be without a father?

Where indeed?

Metzenbaum leaned his head low and to the left to sight the rearview mirror. The Tornado was there, above him and to the right by a hundred meters. Higher yet, at 6,000 meters was the other pair, also one of his Eurofighters and one of Zeigman's Tornadoes. The four of them had taken off from New Amsterdam an hour before.

He was not happy with the new pairings. Weismann and Zeigman had assumed that the American MakoSharks would attack a Eurofighter first since its pilot would have his hands full flying the plane in evasive maneuvers, much less attempting to guide his missiles by hand. That gave the Tornado, with its weapons system officer, an advantage. The Tornado would spring to the rescue.

Of course.

He was bait, a minnow, a worm on the end of the line.

Below on the dark sea, a freighter cruised, its wake prickling with phosphorescence. Under its deck lights, he saw a heavy, twin-rotored helicopter lashed to its afterdeck. More antiaircraft and missile batteries for the platforms. Seven of the platforms had now been armed, but judging by the performance of the gun and SAM crews at *Bahnsteig Neun,* it was a wasted effort. A total waste of men, equipment, and *deutsche marks.*

Deutschland über alles. The spirit was in the air, the aroma rich and heavy on the military bases. He knew what people like Eisenach and Weismann were thinking, and it sickened him. As soon as his two years were up, he would retire from the Luftwaffe and purchase a small shop to run near his cottage. He would take weekends off and visit the boys in Frankfurt.

Metzenbaum scanned the HUD, then the panel. The radarscope displayed the three other aircraft and the freighter. His was the only active radar.

Fish. He was a fish.

Waiting for a bigger fish to come along.

Metzenbaum did not think much of his chances against a super aircraft that he could not see nor shoot at.

Yet again, he scanned the skies above. They were overcast at 4,000 meters, 3,000 meters above him. He had elected to fly low, using the lighter hue of the clouds as a movie screen. Behind him, *Tiger Sieben's* silhouette was clearly visible against it.

As was the dart that zipped quickly past, several kilometers to the east.

He never took his eyes off it. The slim shape disappeared when it crossed caverns in the clouds, reappeared against foamy bases.

It was moving faster than his flight, which had been holding 550 knots. Metzenbaum clicked his radar off, advanced his throttle, and began to climb. Turning slightly to the right he began to close on the dart.

"Tiger Seven, stay with me. No radar." He blinked his wing lights once for his wingman's benefit. "Panther Two, go to zero-zero-eight, and begin losing altitude. There is a MakoShark below the cloud cover at two-five-zero-zero meters and descending."

Still there. He kept himself from staring directly at it, looking instead slightly ahead of it, and holding the silhouette in his peripheral vision.

Closer.

A thousand meters away, it took on the delta shape. Sleek. So black against the cloud base.

Metzenbaum armed all four of his Sky Flashes, aimed them with his gun sight, and launched.

"Incoming," Munoz said matter-of-factly. "Four hot ones, Snake Eyes. Seven hundred yards."

"Hell, he's right on our tail," McKenna said. "Going over."

"Hit it! Now, please."

The rocket motors had been on standby since Delta Blue had passed below 30,000 feet. McKenna shoved the throttles in and sank back into his lounge seat as the MakoShark leaped forward. He hauled back on the hand controller, and the nose pulled up. Seconds later, they entered the clouds. Droplets of moisture hit the windscreen and trailed backward over the canopy.

In the rearview screen, he saw the four missiles swoop upward after him, now locked onto the rocket exhaust.

He killed the rockets, pulled the nose on over, and was headed south, inverted.

Rolled upright.

The four missiles kept climbing straight up, looking for the heat trail they had lost.

The screen gave up the night vision view as Munoz went to radar.

"Bogies dead ahead, Snake Eyes. Two of 'em, eight thousand feet, two miles and closing fast."

Delta Blue had no missiles.

Two of the hard points held four torpedoes, and the other two mounted a gun pod and a camera pod.

"Two more below us. Under the clouds. All of 'em will be lookin' for our radar."

McKenna armed the gun, held his head upright, and at the right side of the cockpit, raised a protective flap, and pushed the switch that interfaced the helmet with the MakoShark's computer controls. The secondary trigger was mounted in the front of the armrest, so he would not have to grip the hand controller.

An orange gun sight appeared on his visor.

Moving his head slowly downward, the sight dropped to the bottom of the windscreen, and the MakoShark immediately followed, lowering her nose, slanting down toward 8,000 feet.

Forefinger on the trigger.

"Come right a hair," Munoz ordered.

McKenna moved the sight to the right.

The MakoShark followed.

"You should have it any second, *jefe*."

There.

A thousand feet above the cloud tops, now coming up, looking for him.

Two missiles blossomed from under its wings.

Munoz killed the radar almost as soon as the threat receiver went off. The CRT flashed HOSTILE LOCK-ON, then lost it.

Outlined nicely against the clouds.

Eurofighter, by its rudders.

The two missiles missed them by a couple hundred yards.

The pilot might not have him visually, looking up at a dark sky.

Straight-in.

Five hundred knots on the HUD.

Lead it.

He dropped the gun sight in front of the German's line of flight.

The MakoShark dipped almost imperceptively.

And pressed the trigger.

Hot green tracers arcing out from the pod.

Dancing on the sky and clouds.

Traipsing toward the fighter.

The German saw them, whipped a wing over and tried to dive away.

The twenty millimeter shells stitched across his canopy, then the left wing.

The wing shredded and peeled away.

Red-yellow flames licking.

Delta Blue flashed over its victim as McKenna raised his head.

Active radar again.

"The other one's hightailin' it. Take her down!"

McKenna canted his head, then pulled it back, and the MakoShark rolled inverted, then dove into the clouds.

"Keep comin', keep comin' . . . upright. Left turn hard."

McKenna rolled upright, turned to the left.

"Right there! Come back right."

To the right.

"See him?"

"Not yet, Tiger."

"Well, shit! I see him."

"You have radar."

"Oh, right. This one's the son of a bitch that fired on us first."

At 5,000 feet, McKenna scanned the lower side of the cloud bank with his eyes, not moving the helmet.

There he was. Another Eurofighter.

He was in a tight circle, coming back to where his threat receiver had shown him an active radar.

McKenna was about to say something when Munoz shut it down again.

But the Eurofighter pilot had seen him.

He was diving hard.

They lined up on each other, McKenna seeing a front-view silhouette against the cloud layer. The German had to be working mostly on instinct.

No missiles fired. He may have only had the four.

Three thousand feet, McKenna judged.

"Brave bastard," Munoz said.

The German opened up with his guns. Red tracers whistling above the canopy.

McKenna pressed his trigger and pulled his head back a little.

The first shells—about thirty of them—went right through the Eurofighter's engine intake. The turbojet exploded and spewed debris in flaming arcs.

McKenna jerked his head back, pulling the MakoShark into a tight loop, but still felt the pings as they flew through some of the debris that filled the air.

When he straightened his head, the rearview screen showed him a ball of flame plunging toward the sea.

"You had it, Tiger. Brave guy."

"Tornado comin' up under us. Two launched." The radar had flashed on, then off again.

McKenna rolled hard to the left.

Jammed the rocket throttles forward.

The sky behind them lit up as the rockets fired.

The HUD went quickly to 600 knots, 700, switched to Mach numbers. 1.1. 1.5.

He pulled the throttles back.

"Lost the missiles, lost the Tornado. He's tryin' to figure out what happened."

A minute later, Munoz flashed the radar again. "He's goin' west, still looking for us. The other Tornado is joinin' up with him."

"Let's go back to the map, Tiger."

McKenna switched off the helmet interface. It worked well enough, but was hard on the neck muscles.

The map appeared on the screen, and the GPS navigation satellites pinpointed Delta Blue's position on the map. The coordinates of the target—a spot in the ocean—appeared at the top right of the screen.

During the skirmish, they had drifted a hundred miles west and north. McKenna turned until the target was due north on the screen.

"What'd you think, Snake Eyes?"

"About what?"

"About how she handled with a ton of torpedoes hangin' on the wings."

"Not bad, Tiger. A little sluggish, maybe."

What he was really thinking about was the courage of the man in the Eurofighter. He thought he might have liked knowing the guy, then decided against that. He didn't want to know anything about either of them.

Forget the years of training, the Red Flag exercises over the Nevada desert.

It wasn't the same. There was no training for this.

McKenna had killed his first two men.

He wasn't happy about it.

"Eleven miles to target, *amigo*. Let's put it on the deck."

"The torpedoes went right in on target, Marv, and two of our sonobuoys recorded four explosions. I don't think we got the transmission cable, though. There's been no excitement at either end of the cable. No ships racing out to run down a break."

247

Brackman listened to Overton's report, then said, "How's McKenna?"

"Fine. They're on the ground at Jack Andrews. There's a couple hours of work, repairing some dents they picked up from the debris."

"Beyond that, Jim?"

"The man himself? You know Kevin. He's not giving much away. Still, I think he'll be fine. Munoz, too."

"Dimatta didn't show any aftereffects with his first encounter, did he?" Brackman asked.

"No, not obviously. But then his profile is different from McKenna's. Frank did have a couple talks on the sly with Doc Harvey, and that may have helped him."

"Watch him close, Jim. Keep him out of the Ma-koShark for a couple days."

"And when he says 'no?' "

"You outrank him."

"You ever known that to make a difference with McKenna?" Overton asked.

"No. Not much of one, anyway."

Thirteen

"You should talk to the widow," Weismann said.

"Do not tell me what I should, or should not, do," Eisenach said into the telephone.

"I have reviewed the radar tapes from the Tornado. Major Metzenbaum gave his life for Germany, willingly and with valor, General Eisenach. He was of the very best."

"His wife is a Jew, is she not?"

There was a long pause on Weismann's end of the telephone. "I do not know."

"You should pay closer attention to the dossiers of your men, Colonel."

"Pardon me, Herr General, but that does not negate his actions last night."

"You are having a change of heart, Albert."

"Not at all."

"Then recommend him for a medal. I will honor it."

"Thank you."

Eisenach leaned back in his chair and drummed his fingertips on the top of his desk. Through the window, he saw a soldier mowing the lawn, and farther away, a transport taking off. The daily routine at Templehof had not changed. It was as if the battles taking place in the north had no effect whatsoever on the rest of Germany. But they did. They affected every true German's right to his own destiny. And Felix Eisenach was privileged to assist in shaping that destiny.

He was not about to allow his vision to be blurred or obliterated.

"How many MakoSharks do the Americans have, Albert?"

"It is not known, Herr General. The treaty allows them six, but I believe that one or two have not been funded by their Congress."

"So, we are being harassed by, perhaps, only four of these stealth airplanes?"

"It seems to be enough, Herr General. Spotting them is a fluke."

"Then we need more eyes looking. I will see that you receive another eight pilots and Tornados from the Sixteenth Air Wing. Integrate them into your coverage."

"Very well, General. And I am going to reduce the daytime flights to one aircraft every three hours. The stealth planes fly by night."

Eisenach considered the move, then said, "I agree. And Peenemünde?"

"The scientists are fabricating a new collar for mating the nose cone to the third-stage body."

"The software?"

"All but finished, I am told."

"They may then begin programming the test flight?"

"I should think so," Weismann said.

"The target for the test will be the American space station."

"Herr General?"

"Perhaps we can deflate their resolve to interfere in German national interests, Albert. Along with removing that damnable aircraft carrier."

The sun shone brightly today, for a change. The sea was smooth, much bluer than was normal. Off the starboard flank, the coast of Greenland was barely visible on the horizon. Ahead, as they turned to the east, the top of the dome of *Bahnsteig Zehn* was just peeking above the sea.

The two destroyer escorts trailed on either side, three kilometers off the stern, matching the turn. Their wakes appeared very white.

Gerhard Schmidt lowered his binoculars and returned to the bridge from the wing.

The brilliance of the day and the brisk, chilled salt air had given him hope, clarified his thinking.

Kapitän Rolf Froelich stood up from his chair, holding a steaming mug. "Coffee, Admiral?"

"Please, Captain."

A steward appeared a few minutes later with a ceramic mug on a silver tray, and Schmidt accepted the mug. The hot liquid warmed him.

"Rolf, let us go to the CIC."

The two men descended one deck and entered the Combat Information Center. Computer and radar consoles lined the bulkheads, and a large electronic plotting table occupied the center of the space. The duty officer was a young, smooth-faced *leutnant*.

Schmidt leaned on the edge of the table with one hand and studied the plot. The third battle group, recalled from their maneuvers off Iceland, was closing in to starboard. The second battle group had achieved its station, south of Svalbard Island and a few kilometers east of *Bahnsteig Sechs*. The fourth group, led by the *Stuttgart*, was still steaming off Norway.

The fifth battle group, given to him this morning on loan from the 1st Fleet, and composed of a new destroyer, an elderly destroyer escort, and a helicopter carrier, was only 250 kilometers into the North Sea, outbound from Bremerhaven.

"Tell me once again, Rolf, of the *Black Forest's* report."

"Simply, Admiral Schmidt, that they tracked four torpedoes early this morning. Mark 46s, they believe. At first, they thought that the *Black Forest* was under attack, but the torpedoes ran wild for several minutes and finally detonated on the seabed."

"And the coordinates, again?"

251

The *Kapitän* signaled a plotter, and a yellow circle appeared on the plotting table.

"Depth?"

"Ninety-seven meters, sir," the plotter said.

"They're trying for the ca . . . the pipeline, Captain Froelich." Occasionally, Schmidt forgot that most of the navy still thought they were oil wells.

Froelich leaned over to study the plot. "Outside of the approaches to the mainland, that would be where the pipeline is located in the shallowest waters. This is perplexing, Admiral. Why would the Americans want to sever the pipeline when the platforms are so exposed? Even the attack on Platform Nine was confined to the defensive batteries."

At some point, the *Hochkommandieren* must include all of its commanders in the secret, Schmidt thought. He said, "All I am told, Rolf, is that the Americans and the Soviets appear to have entered a conspiracy to deprive Germany of new energy sources. The rationale, apparently, is to keep us subservient to the superpowers."

That was the ordered, prevalent subterfuge, and Gerhard Schmidt did not think much of it.

Schmidt stood up. "All right, then. Signal the third battle group to turn north and take up station off Platform Ten. That will protect the southwest flank of the oil field. The second group has the southeast flank already. I want the *Stuttgart* under way on a course of three-four-five degrees as soon as possible. By late night, she and her group should be in position two kilometers east of those coordinates."

The *leutnant* was writing quickly on a notepad.

"Then, signal the fifth battle group to make flank speed northward along the track of the pipeline. They will not achieve the objective yet tonight, but they might be able to protect the approaches, if the aircraft continue coming from the south.

"Captain Froelich, we will make flank speed toward that spot in the ocean." Schmidt stuck out a finger and pointed at the yellow circle. "We want to be two kilometers south-east of it."

"You think they will make another attempt, Admiral?"

"I am sure of it."

"Very well, sir." Froelich stepped to an intercom mounted on the bulkhead and passed the orders to the bridge. Within minutes, Schmidt felt the vibrations in the deck as the *Hamburg* increased revolutions.

It was a good feeling, this preparation for action, after so many months of ennui.

"Then, Captain, we want flare shells. If we do not have enough, radio Bremerhaven and have them flown out to all ships. We want every gun firing flares with every third shot.

"We are going to light up the bloody night."

The HUD readouts were right on. Airspeed 400 knots. Altitude 1,200 feet. The screen displayed the night-vision image of flat landscape.

The orange bombsight bounced around the screen.

"You want to arm me, Con Man?"

Conover dialed "BOMB LOAD" on the selector, raised the protective flap, and thumbed the toggle switch upward.

"You're armed, Do-Wop."

"IP."

"Noted."

"Bay doors."

Conover flicked the flap out of the way and clicked the switch. The green LED illuminated.

"Doors clear."

The complex slowly appeared in the top edge of the cathode ray terminal.

Conover glanced at the HUD, then to his left and upward. The Aeroflot passenger airliner was still heading west at 25,000 feet.

Back to the screen. The launch tower was now centered. The bombsight dropped below it, a thousand yards in real space.

The "LOCK-ON" signal appeared in orange letters in the upper-right corner.

"Committed," Abrams said.

Five seconds later, the small parachute blossomed in the rearview screen.

"Left three degrees."

Conover eased the controller over.

"LOCK-ON," on the screen again.

"Committed."

As soon as he saw the parachute flutter open, Conover retracted the payload bay doors, then tapped the throttles forward.

They were over water, climbing. The Pomeranian Bay had a few ships in it, dots of red and green running lights.

"I don't think we alerted anyone important," Abrams said. "I'm still showing that big damned J-Band operating, but he didn't get us."

"If he yelps, we'll see if a torpedo works against a radar," Conover said.

Going to Tac-1, he said, "Alpha One, Delta Yellow."

"Go, Delta Yellow." Pearson's nice low tones on the other end.

"LP-12s are deployed. You now have ears in Peenemünde, Alpha Two."

"Thank you, Yellow. Proceed with Phase Two."

"On the way. Yellow out."

"If McKenna doesn't make a move on her soon," Abrams said on the intercom, "I'm going to ask her to marry me."

"You're already married."

"Yeah, but my wife only rarely gets to see me in action. By now, Amy knows what I'm really like."

"Yeah. A junior officer."

Conover advanced his throttles to 80 percent power and achieved Mach 1.9 at 30,000 feet before easing them back

254

to a cruise setting. Some people in Denmark probably heard the sonic boom, but Conover didn't think they'd call the cops.

The lights of Copenhagen were spread below like a twinkling quilt. He thought it strange that he couldn't spot a red light district among so many white lights.

"Let's keep her steady on three-five-oh, Con Man."

"Got it."

Conover turned it over to the autopilot and settled back in his seat, working his arms to relieve some of the tension created by low-flying bomb runs.

Abrams played with his computer, lining up satellite relay stations, until he had KXKL out of Denver. It specialized in golden oldies, and was one of Abrams's favorite stations.

Jody Reynolds, "Endless Sleep," filled Conover's headphones.

"Jesus, Do-Wop, can't you find something a bit more upbeat?"

"Hey, it's a good song. Anyway, it'll be over in a minute."

When he was growing up, Conover hadn't paid much attention to music. He always had something better to do. But after a couple years with Abrams, he had learned to like most of the old stuff. He didn't have much choice.

They listened to Buddy Holly, Elvis, the Temptations, Diana Ross, Guy Mitchell, and the muted thunder of the turbojets. No clouds tonight, and the stars were brilliant. The sea was so dark, it melted into the horizon. Occasionally, phosphorescent flashes could be seen. A group of three ships, turning out some knots. They had to be German navy, he decided, in formation as they were.

At two-twenty in the morning, Conover retarded throttles and began a slow descent.

"Delta Yellow, Hot Country." McKenna still sounded pissed. The word floating around the base was that he'd been grounded, but no one on the continent of Africa was going to mention that out loud.

"Got you, Hot."

"Con Man, see if you can't make your drop at wave-top and three-five-zero knots. We may have been too high and too fast and screwed up the guidance on impact."

"Copy that, Snake Eyes. We do it at wave-top and three-five-oh."

"Luck. Hot Country out."

Fifty miles from the target, Conover armed everything. They were carrying two Mark 46 torpedoes on the outer pylons, a gun pod on the port inner pylon, and four Wasps on the starboard inboard pylon. Two of the Wasps were warheaded for air-to-air and two for air-to-surface.

Abrams brought up the map on the screens and interfaced the Global Positioning Satellites. Delta Yellow was centered on the screen, and the target coordinates were dead ahead.

"Con Man?"

"Yo."

"Something doesn't feel right. Can I go active a couple sweeps?"

Conover felt a little itchy himself. The Germans had jumped all over McKenna the night before, but they had had the clouds working for them. He couldn't see anything around him, but that didn't mean much. Aircraft and, possibly, naval ships might be running dark.

Distance to target: twenty-five miles.

"Con Man?"

"Yeah?"

"You heard the question?"

"I'm thinking about it. Yeah, okay, two sweeps, but wait until we're five miles from target. If we see something, I still want to get the fish dropped before we scoot."

"Roger."

The distance to target continued to shrink as Conover slowed the MakoShark to 350 knots and descended to twenty feet over the water. The fuel load was down a third. Low-level flight on turbojets in the Mach numbers consumed the JP-7 quickly.

At five miles, Abrams switched on.

The sweep didn't make two complete revolutions before all hell broke loose.

Thump, thump, thump!

Magnesium flares erupted all around them, bursting at close to 3,000 feet, then drifting downward in their parachutes.

"Jesus Christ!" Abrams shouted. "There must be a hundred of them."

Four miles. Conover felt like his portrait was being taken. There were hot lights everywhere.

"Steady on, Do-Wop. We're going to dump the fish first thing."

"Got it. Take her down a tad."

Puffs of flak started to explode off their flanks. Conover took a quick scan through the windscreen. He could see the muzzle flashes of big guns and antiaircraft guns.

"I count six ships, Do-Wop. They're even using the heavy stuff."

"SAMs coming soon, then. Three miles."

A detonation above them threatened to drive the MakoShark into the sea. Conover fought the turbulence and pulled up a few feet higher.

"Two miles."

"LOCK-ON," hit the screen.

"One mile. Committed. Do whatever you want to do, Con Man."

Conover shoved the throttles full forward as soon as the MakoShark jumped, losing the weight of the torpedoes.

At a hundred feet of altitude, he banked left.

Wham!

The airframe shook with the impact.

He was forced back into level flight.

"Took a piece of wing tip, I think," Abrams said.

"Shit. Call Alpha."

"Alpha, Delta Yellow."

"Go Yellow."

"We've got some structural damage, extent

257

unknown . . . Jesus! Seven SAMs, Con Man. . . ."

Amy Pearson gripped the microphone stand to keep from floating away.

The screen on the console was blank. She felt deprived of necessary knowledge. They should have put the AWACS plane in the air.

"Yellow, Alpha. Repeat."

"Wing tip damage maybe, Alpha. We've got SAMS. I'm going to be busy."

"Copy, Yellow. Keep Tac-1 open."

"Roger."

She heard grunts from either Conover or Abrams.

"Left, left, left . . . hard . . . now climb . . . chaff! . . . dodged it! . . . up, babe, up . . . punch a flare . . . shit!"

Then there was carrier wave.

Pearson hit the intercom. "Donna, did we lose the relay?"

"No, Colonel. We lost the transmitter."

"Alpha Two to Hot Country."

"Hot Country, go Alpha."

"Is Snake Eyes there?"

"Yeah, just a . . . no. I don't know where he's gone."

God. Every time he was needed.

"Send somebody to get him," she ordered.

On Tac-2, the Jack Andrews air controller said, "Delta Blue, I don't have authority for your takeoff."

McKenna retracted the landing gear.

"Let's go over, Tiger."

"Already? You want to get us some altitude first, Snake Eyes?"

"We'll get it fast enough."

"Sure, but take it easy. We got those torps hangin' out there, and they're not all that streamlined."

Delta Blue was armed in the same way as Delta Yellow had been.

"Delta Blue, this is Jack Andrews Control. Come back to me."

"Jack Andrews, Semaphore." General Brackman's voice was unmistakable.

"Go ahead, Semaphore."

"All restrictions are lifted. Delta Blue is now authorized for flight."

"Roger, Semaphore, Jack Andrews Control out."

"Delta Blue, Semaphore."

McKenna depressed the stud. "Go ahead, Semaphore."

"I want a plan, right now."

"Search and rescue," McKenna said.

"Approved. No search and destroy."

McKenna thought about the Mark 46s on the pylons, how good it would feel to see one of them plow into the hull of a cruiser.

"Yes, sir. No destroy."

Over the Mediterranean, Munoz scanned the sea with radar, then jettisoned the torpedoes. They went through the checklist, then ignited the rockets for a five-minute burst.

Delta Blue covered most of the distance at Mach 4.5 at 60,000 feet.

Periodically, Munoz tried the tactical channels, "Delta Yellow, Delta Blue."

Nothing.

"Delta Blue, Alpha One." General Overton's voice.

"Delta Blue."

"Let's assume he's still aloft."

"Let's," McKenna said.

"The IO figures he'd try to make Hot Country, and she's calculated a possible flight path."

Pearson came on the air and gave the beginning and ending coordinates to Munoz.

"How do you figure that, Alpha?" With a quick mental picture, McKenna could tell the flight path was too far to the west.

"Because Con Man is left-handed," Pearson said.

259

"Gotcha," Munoz said. "He'd pull out to the west."

McKenna rolled into a left bank.

"I'm figuring structural damage that'll keep him below sonic speeds," Munoz said on the intercom. "Do-Wop reported a wing tip, but he's obviously lost his antennas."

The radio antennas were imbedded in the skin of the right wing. It was not a hopeful sign.

"Say six hundred knots at best," the WSO said, "and figuring our speed and the time we left, we want to start looking hard over Sweden."

"Suppose he can give us an IFF?" McKenna asked.

"That antenna is in the left wing, *amigo*. There's a chance."

"Go active."

Waiting.

McKenna was accustomed to waiting after so many years in the military, but the practice didn't make it any easier. Thinking about Conover and Abrams down in icy water didn't help, either.

"You worried, *jefe?*"

"Yeah, Tony, I am."

"So am I. Somebody was waiting for him."

"Yes. Somebody figured it out. There were only ships involved, so it must have been that admiral."

"Schmidt?"

"Right. Amy was right about him."

"Let's hope Amy-baby's right about Con Man, too," Munoz said.

She was.

Munoz found the IFF south of Stockholm.

"Hot shit! Got 'em, Snake Eyes."

"You sure?"

"Positive. He's shut it down now, so he's only squawkin' every once in a while. Three-two miles. Go to three-three-eight."

McKenna turned to the new heading, backing off on the throttles.

A few minutes later, Munoz said, "We're going to overshoot him. Bring it back to seven hundred knots, and make a wide three-sixty."

McKenna went into a shallow bank to the right.

"There he is again! Take her down to two-two-thousand."

As he put the nose over, McKenna checked the eastern horizon on his left. The sun was peeping, spreading opaque light at altitude. By the time they reached the Mediterranean, they'd be in full daylight. And if Delta Three couldn't handle much more altitude, they would be in danger of being spotted by Greek or Italian aircraft.

To hell with it. If they were seen, they were seen. Conover's IFF went off the screen again, but Munoz had his position, speed, and track in the computer.

They came up behind Delta Yellow almost silently. Abrams obviously wasn't running active radar.

McKenna closed in at 620 knots, easing up close to the right wing. He was within a hundred feet before he could see clearly. The right wing tip skin was shredded, as were a couple of the spars under it. The right rudder was gone.

He slowed, pulled back on the controller, and rose to a position above and behind the damaged MakoShark. Looking down on it, he saw that a fifteen-foot-wide slice of skin had peeled away from the upper wing, taking the radio antennas with it. The ribs, spars, and fuel tanks were fully exposed.

"Goddamn," Munoz said. "I don't know how he's making the speed he is."

"Has to, to maintain lift, I expect. This is going to be one high-speed landing."

McKenna touched the throttles, and Delta Blue advanced on her sister ship. He banked slightly outward to give Conover some room, then flashed his wing tip lights.

Delta Yellow jiggled a little at the shock of seeing them. Abrams turned on the cockpit lights so McKenna and Munoz could see that they were all right.

They waved, and Munoz switched on his own cockpit light and waved back.

With a flashlight, Abrams Morse-coded their damage estimate, which included a malfunctioning navigation computer. The backup wasn't working, either.

The fuel supply was adequate for recovery in Chad. Conover wanted his aerospace craft repaired immediately, top goddamned priority. He had an appointment in the Greenland Sea.

McKenna depressed the Tac-2 button. "Alpha One, Delta Blue."

"Go ahead, Delta Blue."

"We've got them."

"Son of a bitch!" Overton said.

"That's pretty mild," McKenna said, "compared to what I'm reading in Morse code."

Fourteen

Kapitän Ernst Blofeld accepted his mug of coffee, then sat on the single sofa in the admiral's quarters, next to Werner Niels, the admiral's aide. It was a spartan room without even a picture of the admiral's family present, but Schmidt suspected it was spacious and homey to a submarine commander. He thought that men who were amenable to life under the sea had to be somewhat crazy, but he respected their courage.

The steward backed out of the compartment and pulled the door shut behind him.

Schmidt was in his swivel chair at his desk, the top of which was exceptionally neat, and he turned toward the submarine commander. "Well, Captain?"

"There has been no damage to the cables, Herr Admiral. We traversed the area three times, utilizing remote video cameras, and found everything intact."

"Were they even close?"

"It is difficult to tell, but we located several possible points of impact. None were closer than twenty meters. The torpedo guidance mechanism must target on electromagnetic generation sources, but the cables are well armored, and the presence of other sources in the region, such as the ships, must confuse the torpedoes."

Schmidt nodded his understanding. "What else, Captain Blofeld?"

"We have discovered three sonobuoys in the last couple of days, and we have destroyed them."

263

"So. They are listening to us?"

"Yes. Generally along the line of the cables. They were American sonobuoys."

"I do not doubt it. Undersea traffic?"

Blofeld sipped his coffee. "The *Ohio* was snooping around the fringes of the platforms two days ago. Yesterday, the signature of the Soviet submarine *Typhoon* was heard to the east of Svalbard by the *Bohemian*. They run when we approach, Admiral. They are not even interested in games of tag."

The *Bohemian* was the second of the submarines assigned to the *Dritte Marinekraft*.

"But for how long will they run, Ernst? We are, I think, testing the patience of people in high places in Washington and Moscow."

Werner Niels said, "General Eisenach and the High Command seem to think they will eventually go away."

"Among the three of us," Schmidt said, "General Eisenach and the High Command are fools. They rely on the introduction of their magical Ghost missile to establish instant military and political parity. It will not happen. I think it is up to us to defend the GUARDIAN PROJECT."

"The *Stuttgart* claims a MakoShark kill," Niels said. "Perhaps we will prevail simply by attrition? The Americans have only four or five of the machines."

Blofeld looked at Niels, then the admiral, and proceeded cautiously. "The commander of the *Stuttgart* may be mistaken. We detected no aircraft crash on sonar, and we could find no debris."

Schmidt had been skeptical, himself. He had been on the bridge during the battle, had seen the MakoShark for only moments at the time it dropped its torpedoes, and had marveled at its slippery image and acceleration. "You are very likely correct, Ernst. The stealth craft have proven to be close to invincible. However, we also have some invincibility. I believe that, short of using tactical nuclear devices, which they will not do, the Americans will be unable to breach the cables. We are going to leave the fifth battle group to patrol this region."

Niels got up, retrieved the insulated pot the steward had left behind, and poured more coffee for everyone.

"And I believe that the Americans and Soviets know, or think they know, the true nature of the wells. They will not attack them for fear of creating a fury they cannot quell. Tell me, Ernst, if you were seeking a way to destroy the system, how would you go about it?"

"Without attacking the wells, and knowing that I could not reach the undersea cables, Admiral?"

"Exactly."

"I would infiltrate frogmen under Platforms One and Eleven and attach limpet mines to the cables collected there. All twenty-four cables from the platforms congregate at Platform One and, I think, Platform Eleven, as the alternate distribution center, now has nine cables in place."

"You think that way because you are a submariner, Ernst."

"Of course, Admiral."

"But I happen to agree with you. Niels, we want a message to the Twentieth Special Air Group, requesting that sonobuoys be sown around the perimeter of the offshore wells and along the ice. We will listen for intruders, as well as position our battle groups around the platforms."

"As you wish, Admiral," Niels said, jotting the note on his pad.

"And, Ernst, I think that the *Black Forest* and the *Bohemian* will give up their patrols of the cables. You will concentrate your efforts around the wells."

Delta Blue slipped into her bay, then came to a stop with a *whoosh!* of the forward thrusters. As the hangar doors folded shut behind him, McKenna and Munoz began shutting the operational systems down.

Polly Tang waved at them from the window overlooking

the bay. McKenna waved back, then contacted Beta One and dumped the maintenance files.

"Got it," Mitchell said.

"And, Brad, I want full service on Blue immediately. What's the status on Green?"

"Lube and oil coming right up, Kevin. Green arrived two hours ago. All systems checked out, and she's being refueled right now."

"Good. Great."

"Tell me, please," Mitchell said, "what Con Man did to my bird."

Among maintenance people, ground crews, and pilots, there was an unresolved dispute over ownership of an aircraft or, in this case, an aerospace craft. It didn't matter that the taxpayer had put up the cash or that the air force held the title.

"When I left Hot Country, Brad, they were still running checks. So far, the primary navigation computer has to be replaced — it took a chunk of shrapnel, four solid fuel containers are cracked, two wing ribs and one wing tip spar need to be replaced, she needs a new right rudder and two thruster nozzles, and we've got to replace two hundred square feet of wing skin that disappeared. He burned up a couple tires getting it on the ground at two-eight knots."

"Oh, hell, that's only a couple days' work."

"That's what Benny Shalbot said. He stayed behind to do the electronics rehabilitation. On the rest of it, they're flying in some people and materials from Martin Marietta and Rockwell."

"Yeah, okay. Anyway, I'm glad everyone's all right. They are, aren't they?"

"A-one, Brad."

Sometimes, in their anxiety over the craft, the maintenance people forgot about the pilot people.

Tang gave them a green light as soon as the atmosphere in the bay had reached the correct content and pressure levels, and McKenna and Munoz opened their canopies, unbuckled their straps, and released their communications cables and environmental hoses. McKenna unfastened his helmet, slipped it off, and stuck it under his arm. The hatch opened and several technicians darted into the bay.

"Me for bed," Munoz told him.

"Not just yet, Tony. I've got a job for you."

"Unmerciful bastard, aren't you?"

"Got a reputation to uphold."

McKenna pushed hard off the MakoShark toward the hatchway, grabbed the frame as he passed through, and deflected his flight toward Polly Tang.

"Catch me, love!"

She looked up from the console and stuck out a stiffened left arm. Her palm caught McKenna in the chest and arrested his flight.

"Thanks. I needed that."

"Any time," she told him, then went back to securing the console controls.

"What Makos are aboard, Polly?"

"Just number two."

"You know her schedule, offhand?"

"Due to return to Peterson tomorrow afternoon. Sixteen hundred hours, I think."

Pressing the PA button on the communications system, McKenna checked his watch and said, "Your attention, please. There will be a briefing for all pilots and system officers at eleven hundred hours in Compartment A-forty-seven."

He repeated the message one more time, then he and Munoz went down the corridor to the pilot's dressing room, took sponge baths, changed into jumpsuits, and stored their flight gear in their lockers.

By the time they reached the exercise room, Dimatta, Williams, Haggar, and Olsen were already there. Dr. Monte Washington was working out on a Nautilus machine.

"Dr. Washington, I'm afraid we need some privacy for about ten minutes."

267

"Hey, damn it! I got as much right to be here as you do. With the money my company is . . ."

"Dr. Washington, I want you to go to your quarters and pack your belongings. You'll be leaving on the next flight earth side. That will be with Major Haggar at oh-eight hundred in the morning."

Washington's mouth dropped open. "McKenna, you got no right to talk . . ."

"Check it out with the station commander, Washington. Now, get out."

Washington extricated himself from the machine, put on a sullen pout, and left the compartment. Munoz closed the door behind him.

McKenna looked at his pilots, all of whom were waiting expectantly on him. "Check rides," he said.

Dimatta said, "Damn, Snake Eyes. I haven't had a check ride in six months."

"It's the other way around this time, Frank. I want you to take Lynn and Ben over to your bay and give them a close-up look at Delta Green. They need a full rundown on the weapons, radar, and threat systems, plus any other system they don't have on a Mako. Then, as soon as Delta Blue is serviced, you're all going out."

Haggar's eyes were about the size of twenty-millimeter shells.

"Frank, you'll take Ben as your backseater. Lynn, you and Tony will fly Delta Blue. I'm fond of it, so don't break it, please. George, I want you to monitor both flights, and throw some problems at them—a systems failure, maybe, and a couple of missile runs."

"Target?" Williams asked.

"Use a gun pod and a couple of training Wasps on each craft. Make Neptune or Pluto the target."

Williams nodded.

Dimatta looked to Haggar. "Boom-Boom, I think."

"Don't you dare," she said. "There was a stripper in Atlanta named Boom-Boom."

"That's who I was thinking of," Dimatta said.

"Chauvinist!"

"Country Girl, I think," Munoz said, "and Ben's obviously the Swede."

Olsen grinned, his Nordic face showing his pleasure.

Dimatta scowled for a minute, thinking, then agreed, "Yeah, Tiger, that'll do it."

McKenna was happy to see the two of them accepted into the stealth half of his squadron. Attaching the nicknames was the first step.

"This will be a space-only familiarization flight of two hours," he said, "and you'll stay within a thousand miles of *Themis*. Questions?"

Munoz said, "See, Lynn? Just like I told that Russian colonel. I knew I'd be gettin' you."

Dimatta grinned at McKenna, "Do I need to ask about authorization?"

McKenna grinned back. "No."

Lynn Haggar started to say something, perhaps appreciative, but McKenna gave her a small negative shake of the head, then left the exercise room. He went back up Corridor 1-B and turned into the maintenance office. Mitchell, a fuel technician named Lennon, and Bert Embry were there, and McKenna spent a few minutes reviewing the current stores of fuel and ordnance with them. He ordered more Wasps and JP-7.

"Right away?" Mitchell asked. "That's going to throw off the HoneyBee schedule."

"Right away, Brad. I don't want to come up short if we need something."

Mitchell turned to his computer and called up a listing. "We've got a hot contract with Lockheed, and their equipment is slated for the next seven HoneyBee launches."

"So kick them back three or four."

"They'll raise hell in Washington."

"Tell them to call Brackman."

"You mean I get to throw some weight around? That'll be a first."

McKenna was stifling yawns by the time he reached the

Command Center. He had been up and about for too many hours straight, in violation of Space Command's policy. Overton and Pearson were waiting for him. He thought he detected a little fire in Pearson's green eyes. Her auburn hair floated out from her head like dark fire.

"Where have you been?" Pearson asked. "We've been waiting."

"Miss me, dear?"

"Not so much that I'd notice."

"Now, children," Overton said. The front of his blue jumpsuit was stained with grease and oil.

"What have you been doing, Jim?"

Overton brushed the stain on his chest with his fingertips. "Ventilation motor failure in Eight."

The general wasn't above getting his hands dirty, one of the reasons McKenna liked him.

He brought them up to date on the condition of Conover, Abrams, and Delta Yellow. "And I ordered more ordnance shipped up from Merlin. Lockheed may complain a little, Jim."

"Did you also request some more torpedoes from the navy?" Pearson asked.

"No. It's time to abandon that scenario. We're not having any success, and last night proves that your Admiral Schmidt lives up to your billing of him, Amy. He knows damned well where to wait for us. I'm not taking chances with my people where the probability of success is so low."

Pearson looked a little crestfallen, but McKenna was certain she would not argue with him, not after Conover's close call.

Polly Tang's voice came over the intercom and interrupted them. "Command, Hangar. Preparing Delta Green for launch."

McKenna reached out a hand and pulled himself over to the console. "Hangar, Command. Proceed."

"What's that, Kevin?" Overton asked.

"We're doing check rides with Dimatta and Munoz."

"With, or for?" Overton wasn't stupid.

"With." McKenna sighed. "I'm having Haggar and Olsen get a feel for the MakoSharks."

"Shit! Kevin, you know the position on that."

"I had a close call with Conover and Abrams, Jim. I want backup. As soon as we get them oriented, I'm going to give them Delta Red to practice in."

"Why not Autry and Chamberlain?"

"They're nowhere near as ready as Haggar and Olsen, that's why. Damn it, I'm the squadron commander."

"You may have to put Conover and Abrams in Delta Red," the general said.

"Their buggy is going to be fine," he insisted.

"I'm going to have to talk to Brackman."

"Please do."

Overton stared him down for a minute, then let it go. McKenna was assured that the station commander would be having a very long conversation with General Brackman, and that Brackman would be tracking him down soon thereafter.

Pearson watched them carefully, but McKenna thought that his decision about Haggar had taken some of the fire out of her eyes. There was a mellow quality present when she looked at him. The green had paled a bit.

Finally, she broke the silence with a question. "I assume you have a new strategy?"

"We may have to call in the navy. We use Volontov's MiGs and the MakoSharks to create a diversion, then slip a couple subs under the platforms."

"To run blindly into an anchor cable or well casing?"

"I admit that it's going to take a little thought. I'll need some help."

"What do you need?" she asked.

"I need to sleep for a few hours. You want to help me with that?"

That got the fire back in her eyes.

Gen. Marvin Brackman was in Washington. He had been called to testify before the Senate Appropriations

Committee in regard to Space Command appropriations for the next fiscal year. He didn't bother mentioning the practical applications of the MakoShark and *Themis* currently under way, and no one on the panel brought up the matter, either.

So far, only the *Village Voice* and a deep page in the *New York Times* had mentioned the complaint of Malcolm Nichols, captain of the Greenpeace boat *Walden*. And Nichols had not mentioned potential oil spillage, only that a German air force pilot had fired a missile at him. That charge had been denied by the German Foreign Ministry, further increasing Nichols's rage. He was trying to find a German lawyer to sue the Luftwaffe.

After his testimony, Brackman had been driven to the Pentagon in an air force staff car to have lunch with Harvey Mays and Hannibal Cross. They ate late and alone in the flag dining room, all of them opting for the day's promoted special of veal.

"My aide says you did a nice job with the committee, Marvin."

"You never know how well you did until the appropriations are announced, Hannibal. The feedback in Washington is damned slow."

"The feedback," Mays said, "would be a lot snappier if any of those senators knew about what we're doing in the Greenland Sea."

"True. I don't know why it's still under wraps."

"I think we can thank the Germans for that," Cross said. "At this point, I don't believe there's any question but that they don't want the world to know about those geothermal taps, or the environmental hazard they pose."

"Or the military buildup," Mays said.

"That worries me," Brackman said. "What I'd really like to do is hit a few of those equipment parks and fuel dumps with some thousand-pounders. We could at least set back their plans a few years."

"That would have every congressman and reporter in town involved in the brouhaha in nothing flat," Cross said. "No, we can get away with what we're doing in the north because the Germans aren't going to complain. That's the President's opinion. He believes we can stave off German ambition by shutting down those wells."

"The hell of it is," Brackman said, "we're not having any success. When I talked to McKenna early this morning, before he went back to *Themis*, he was ready to give up on the cables. Of course, he'd damned nearly lost a Ma-koShark and two crewmen."

"He's too close to his squadron members," Mays said. "As a commander, he should have a little more distance."

"Maybe, but it's a unique squadron, Harv. It has to be run differently."

"Getting back to the immediate problem," the chairman said, "does McKenna have something in mind?"

"Nothing solid yet. He may want to involve the navy, but he's supposed to get back to me later today."

"Not that I mistrust the navy, Admiral," Mays said to Cross, "but I'm leery of doing very much underneath those platforms."

Cross harumphed.

Brackman said, "One thing McKenna did point out, that we should have done some time ago. We ought to set up a couple naval task forces, maybe one out of England with the Brits involved, and one out of the Soviet Union. They should be outfitted with submersibles, salvage ships, the right kinds of equipment, and all of the experts we can find."

"In case a well blows out, Marv?" Mays asked.

"Or in case they all blow out. If the Germans let us, we're going to have to make an attempt to cap them."

Cross chewed his veal with vigor, then said, "Christ! We're going to have to put McKenna in a staff job and make him a general."

"He'll resist all the way, Hannibal."

"I know, and that's good. But damn it, we should have been covering that base."

"You'll look into it?"

"Yes. It'll take telephone calls from the President, I suppose, but we'll put something together. And we'll do it damned quickly. I'll have the CNO find out where his specialized ships are located, and figure out how soon he can get them into the area."

"Not too close, just yet," Brackman said.

"We may need some troops," the air force chief of staff said, "to secure the platforms if we make a move on them."

The JCS chairman's face sagged. "This may escalate way beyond what we want, gentlemen."

It was nearly ten o'clock at night before Brackman called him back. Sheremetevo was at home, a spacious, nine-room apartment that was far too large for his needs since the children — young adults — had moved out. He had been widowed for three years, and he still felt the loss. The empty rooms seemed to echo.

The general sipped his second brandy and stood at the living room window, looking down on the lights of Moscow. From his eighth-floor vantage point, he could see the dark bend of the Moskva River where it passed under the Borodino Bridge. The foliage was thick this time of year. In the distance were the flood-lighted mosques and spires of the Kremlin, shining like new gold in the night.

The telephone rang, and he crossed to the end table to pick it up, settling back onto the flowered sofa.

"Vitaly, I'm sorry to be so late getting back to you, but it's been something of a hectic day."

"It is all right, Marvin."

"Let me bring you up to speed." Sheremetevo listened while Brackman detailed the trap that Schmidt had set for the MakoShark, the damage to the craft, and the failure to sever the cable.

Brackman also told him of the plan, to come through the U.S. President, to prepare a crisis task force.

"That is an excellent idea, Marvin. I shall support it with the Politburo on my end."

"Great. It may require a few of your *Spetznatz* troops, to secure platforms if we have to make a frontal assault in order to cap the wells."

That was dismaying. "That may be difficult. It will involve the army and the entire Politburo. Is the United States also prepared to commit troops?"

"I don't know, yet, Vitaly. We're going to propose the Rapid Deployment Force."

"This may be the start of another Great War," Sheremetevo said.

"I don't like it, either. Now, you called me. Have you got something new?"

"Yes. Disturbing developments."

"Uh-oh. Should I be sitting down?"

"Well, Marvin, I am sitting down."

"Let me have it."

"This morning, I met with a major of the GRU who had just returned from reconnaissance mission to Peenemünde. The Germans not only have constructed a copy of our rocket, it is all but finished. The major thinks that it will be operational within the week."

"Damn. From the specs I read, it's intercontinental."

"It can also be utilized as a space vehicle."

"What about a warhead, Vitaly?"

"Using the American joke, Marvin, I just told you the good news. The bad news is that the Germans have acquired nuclear warheads."

"Oh, shit! What kind?"

"Multiple Individually Retargeted. I do not know the size or how many warheads each, but according to the major, there are five MIRVs in a deep bunker near Peenemünde."

"That puts a new spin on the ball," Brackman said.

Sheremetevo almost missed the analogy. "Yes."

"We're not going to attack the mainland."

"Nor are we, Marvin."

"But we're going to have to do something dramatic."

"And quite soon," the commander of the PVO Strany agreed.

Frank Dimatta was disappointed at the decision to cancel the torpedo runs. Since his downing of the two Germans over the ice, and especially since Conover and Abrams were zapped, he had been looking forward to his chance at the cable. And maybe another Tornado or two.

Instead, Pearson and McKenna stuck him with a milk run over the wells at 60,000 feet, taking update pictures. One pass to the east, and one to the west.

"That's it, Cancha. Let's go home."

"What do you think, Nitro, of taking a practice run against the *Hamburg?* Scare shit out of that admiral."

"I like it, but sure as hell, I'd want to pop a Wasp at him. Then, too, McKenna would have us scraping grease off the hangar floors at Nellis."

"Might be worth it."

"Might be, but let's hang loose. The boss will come up with something soon."

"And you can bet the brass at Cheyenne Mountain will turn him down."

"Maybe, and maybe not," Williams said. "Come around to one-seven-one, and let's get her up to Mach five. Josie says we have a window in sixteen minutes."

"Will Josie let us stop off in Paris? I'm hungry."

"Josie says, 'later.'"

Amy Pearson and Donna Amber developed the photos and transferred them to video. Arguento showed up in the photo lab in the hub as they were finishing.

"Nice timing, Val," Amber said.

"You don't get to be a master sergeant in the air force, Donna, without knowing how to avoid work. Hey, Colonel, I've got a problem."

"Wonderful," Pearson said.

"The Washington guy?"

"The President or Monte?"

"Dr. Monte. Overton confined him to Spoke Three and the communications compartment until we get a chance to transport him. Well, my monitoring computer sounded off, and when I checked his message traffic, I found some schematics of our radar computers and a complete personnel listing for the station."

"Damn it. Any of it get out?"

"No. When I saw him log on to the system, I put him on five-minute delay."

"Okay, good. You can tell him he's now confined to quarters. My order. I'll take it up with the general, if I need to, but Washington's leaving the station later this afternoon, anyway."

Arguento had been watching the screen as Amber double-checked the video. He said, "They're getting ready for a siege, aren't they?"

"What do you mean, Val?" Pearson asked.

"AA and SAM on all but three of the platforms now. And a fifth group of ships."

Pearson had missed that. "Where do you see the ships?"

"Back up three or four frames, Donna. There."

Pearson squinted her eyes, poring over the photo. It was a large-scale shot, taking in all of the wells. Besides several individual ships—the tugboats and supply tenders, she counted four groups of three ships each, almost at each corner of the offshore wells. The northern groups were splitting the distance between the offshore platforms and those on the ice. She did not see the . . . yes, she did. Clear at the bottom of the photograph. Another three ships standing guard over the area where they had attempted to bomb the cable.

"You've got good eyes, Val."

"That, and timing."

"How do you read this?"

"I think some German is getting worried about us."

"I hope he's got something to worry about," she said.

"Oh, he does," Amber said. "If I thought the Germans were better than us, I'd have joined the Luftwaffe."

McKenna didn't awaken until almost two in the afternoon. *Themis* time.

After several days of one- and two-hour snatches of sleep, he felt fully refreshed.

Ready to go.

And he had a plan.

Still strapped against the padded wall of his sleeping cubicle, he reached for the communications panel and tapped in the number for the Command Center.

Colonel Avery answered the call.

"Is Amy around there, Milt?"

"No. She was up most of the night and early morning and said she was going to take a nap."

"I'll run into her somewhere," he said and unstrapped himself.

Unzipping his curtain, McKenna pushed out into the corridor, crossing it, and stopped next to the one labeled, "Pearson."

He tapped on the wall.

Then he tapped again.

"Go away."

"I need to talk to you, Amy."

She unzipped the curtain part-way and stuck her head out, only inches from his face. She didn't have the headband on, and her heavy red hair was tangled and weightless. Her eyes were sleepy, her head tilted back as she peered beneath half-lowered lids.

McKenna lacked willpower in some areas, and he couldn't resist. He kissed her.

A short, light kiss on the lips.

Pearson almost responded, her lips soft and warm. She nodded sleepily once, then her eyes opened wide in realization.

278

Before she could get into a protest mode, McKenna said, "I've got it."

"Got what?"

"The answer."

"The answer to what?"

"It's time to stop playing cat and mouse. That's what Eisenach wants, because he can stonewall and get the time he needs."

"The time for what?"

"To strengthen his defensive position and get that rocket off the ground."

"What in the hell are you talking about?" she asked.

"We're going to load up everything we've got, and take out those wells."

Alarmed, she said, "We can't do that! There's too much risk, Kevin."

"Just watch us," he said, while noting her use of his name.

Fifteen

"The Americans used it in Vietnam," Mac Zeigman said. "They called it *Wild Weasel.*"

With the loss of Metzenbaum, Zeigman was now the operations officer of the *Zwanzigste Speziell Aeronautisch Gruppe.* He was a hungover operations officer, after a late night of carousing in Bremerhaven. It had been his first free night in weeks, and he had used it well, if not too wisely.

Memory of some woman yelling at him. Had to be slapped around a little.

He had a raging headache that made tracking the conversation difficult.

"Yes, but they used the tactic offensively over Hanoi," *Oberst* Weismann countered. "The decoys were used to draw SAM fire, then the attack aircraft fired on the SAM radars. The MakoSharks are not targeting SAM radars, and we would not be using it offensively."

"The principle will work here, also, Herr Colonel. I have discussed it with the planning staff."

"Review every incident for me, Major. Tell me what were the targets."

"Other than photographic reconnaissance?" Zeigman said. "Platform Eight's dome was destroyed. Platform Nine was attacked, as was the pipeline."

"And we have lost four aircrews," the wing commander said. "Two Eurofighters and two Tornadoes. The result of engagements initiated by ourselves. Now, again, the purpose of the overflights?"

Zeigman thought about it, then said, "I cannot explain Platform Eight. The rest of the flights over the wells were intended to gather information. On the night of the Soviet diversion, the air cover was drawn off so that the Americans could once again photograph."

"And Platform Nine?"

"Only the defensive batteries were hit."

"Then?"

"Their attention was diverted to the pipeline. That was the first real offensive operation, utilizing torpedoes."

"Which tells you?"

Again, Mac Zeigman pondered, silently urging his head to clear. "They learned what they wanted to learn about the wells, then decided to cut off the oil flow by disrupting the pipeline. They are not going to attack the wells."

"Yes," Weismann said, idly scratching the back of his hand. "That is what I think. Additionally, Admiral Schmidt also believes the next efforts will be directed at the wells, though under them."

Zeigman was not certain he would make a good operations officer. He was a pilot, and a damned good one. In the air, he made instantaneous decisions that had made him a survivor. On the ground, hashing and rehashing the intentions of American or Soviet commanders, he became quickly bored and muddled.

He was born a killer, not a plotter of when or where or who should be killed.

"I am going to tell you something that perhaps will explain, not only the interest of the Americans and the Soviets, but also their reluctance to approach the wells." Weismann rubbed his forehead. Soon he would have no skin left, Zeigman thought.

He waited.

"This is highly classified information, Major."

He nodded.

"The wells are not what they seem, not oil wells. They are geothermal taps."

Zeigman shrugged his shoulders elaborately. A well was a well.

The commander explained the tremendous amount of energy to be drawn from the platforms when they were all completed. Over sixteen million kilowatts of electrical power.

Zeigman did not much care.

Weismann explained the dangers, what might happen to the ice and to the water levels if the wells were damaged.

So?

"So, like Admiral Schmidt, I am certain the wells themselves will not be attacked. The Americans are not foolhardy. They will continue to make their attempts on the cables."

"Under the platforms?"

"Perhaps."

"That means submarines, Herr Colonel. The interceptors will be useless."

"Not necessarily. My thought, Major, is that the Americans, or the Soviets, or both, will attempt to penetrate the underwater screen placed by the Third Naval Force. I also think it likely they will, as they have done, create a diversion for Schmidt's ships with aircraft."

Zeigman winced as a lance of pain caromed around his brain. "I could agree with that."

"Therefore, we will modify your modified *Wild Weasel* tactic. Think of it, Mac! Schmidt's naval ships become the decoys. The invaders will try to divert the ships, and Schmidt's guns will throw up flares. And . . ."

"And it will be a duck shoot," the new operations officer said. Finally, here was something that excited him and diminished his headache.

"Exactly! Now, we must analyze the MakoShark's behavior. The time of night it has appeared, the normal approach routes, what we know of its armament, its speed and maneuverability. If we deploy most of our squadrons, we can overcome it with numbers."

It sounded like a good idea to Zeigman.

Goldstein was lying to him, and the pseudodirector of the *GESPENST PROJEKT,* the banker's son, knew absolutely nothing. The Jew had the banker's son tied up in a web of misinformation.

Eisenach knew this, and it enraged him.

The constantly delayed project would be delayed again and again, and he had no recourse but to develop quickly a new strategy which would force the Americans and the Soviets to remain behind their borders.

After arriving at Templehof from Peenemünde by helicopter, Eisenach transferred to a Piaggio PD-808 executive jet for the flight to Svalbard Island. He sent Oberlin back to headquarters to watch over the daily tasks while he was gone.

By one-thirty, the jet had landed on Svalbard Island at the airfield which was leased from the Norwegians, and Eisenach had made his preparations by way of the jet's sophisticated communications systems. The plastic explosive, detonators, and radios had been ordered.

If there was a drawback to the location of the wells, it was to be found in their distance from mainland Germany. Marshal Hoch and Eisenach had both tried to persuade the geologists to drill farther to the south, but to no avail. They must go to where the geology permitted the taps, not the other way around. The expense had been enormous, millions of *deutsche marks,* for the undersea cables. And helicopters could not reach the platforms from the mainland. Always, there was the transfer of aircraft en route.

Eisenach descended from the airplane into heavy drizzle and mud coating the concrete. He buttoned his uniform topcoat as he splashed his way to the helicopter. It was a navy helicopter, and the two pilots got out of the cockpit to salute him and help him into the back seat. He tossed his briefcase and the overnight valise that he kept in the Piaggio onto the floor next to him.

The pilot climbed back into his seat and said, "The flight will be very rough, Herr General. The weather is not cooperating with us."

"A little rain shower?"

"The front has yet to come through. It is worse to the east of us."

Eisenach smiled grimly. "We will just have to do our best, then."

Shaking his head negatively, the pilot turned back to his controls, donned his headset, and started the two Allison turboshaft engines. The general put on his own earphones to help drown the noise of the engines, then buckled his seat belt. As they lifted off, Eisenach saw his executive jet pilots chocking the wheels and tying the aircraft down. They had complained of the stopovers at Svalbard, having to spend their days in the tiny operations hut. He estimated that the visibility was almost a mile.

Within ten minutes of flight, it was down to a quarter-mile. The rain was much heavier, sluicing over the Plexiglas bubble of the helicopter in thick streaks. They were flying low, less than a hundred feet above the ocean, and Eisenach could see ice trying to form on the water. It looked like gray sludge floating on the surface of the sea, damping the waves. The salt content was high enough to keep it from totally freezing at −4 degrees Centigrade— the water temperature reported by the pilot, but the thought of going down in it was chilling, also. A man would not live for long, perhaps five minutes.

The BO-105 bounced radically, short up and down strokes that kept Eisenach from concentrating on anything but where the water was and what the pilots were doing. He could tell that the pilot was fighting the controls, and several times, thought about returning to Svalbard.

His heart was beating faster than usual.

Bahnsteig Acht went by on the right, identified by the pilot over the headset, and Eisenach used binoculars to examine it. Though it was difficult to see much from the erratically moving helicopter, he thought that the repairs to the dome had been completed.

It had been a difficult few days for the men on the platform, exposed to the weather while replacement panels were installed.

"Platform Eleven will come up on our right, Herr General," the pilot said.

He never saw it. The visibility had drawn down so tightly that even the roiling surface of the water disappeared from time to time.

When they reached *Bahnsteig Eine,* the wind was blowing fiercely. In midday, it was dark enough to require landing lights on both the pad and the helicopter. The radio operator on the platform reported gusts to forty kilometers per hour, and ten men in parkas emerged from the dome to steady the helicopter as the pilot fought it to a landing. The rain was almost horizontal on the platform, and as the turbines died, he could hear it slapping the windshield like gunshots.

Eisenach was immensely relieved to be on something solid again, but hoped that his relief was not evident in his face. He pushed open his door, slid out of the helicopter, and leaned into the wind, holding his hat with his gloved left hand. The raindrops pelted his face like sand. He left his luggage for someone else to bring.

Oberst Hans Diederman was waiting just inside the doorway for him. His fatigue uniform appeared tighter on him. His demeanor was just as bubbly as ever. "Herr General Eisenach! How good to see you!"

The same greeting as ever, also. Eisenach firmly doubted the man's sincerity.

"Good afternoon, Hans."

"This is not a day to be flying, General."

"It was not too difficult," Eisenach insisted as he stripped off his dripping topcoat.

It was warm inside the dome. Despite the insulation between the living spaces and the wellhead, it often became overly heated. The Russians would love it, Eisenach thought. They had a fanatic devotion to overheated buildings.

"I want to see the wellhead, Hans."

"Right this way."

They walked down the wide corridor to the fiberglass wall, and Diederman opened a thick door, then stepped over a raised coaming. Eisenach followed.

This third of the dome was not subpartitioned in any way. There were lights at deck level, but the upper reaches of the dome were almost black. It seemed a great deal of wasted space, and indeed, the domes were larger than necessary for living and operating needs, but the high empty spaces were necessary to accommodate the drilling rigs. Though the rig was no longer in place here, it was anticipated that it would have to be reinstalled occasionally in order to clean the injection well. On his left was another door, leading to the control room, and a triple-paned glass window which allowed the operators to view the wellhead and turbine generators.

There were three turbines, and the high-pitched whine of them threatened the eardrums. Eisenach knew the schematics well. Two of the turbines were driven off of the steam and hot water rising from the well, the third was driven by the residue of steam still available from the first two. Exhaust vapors then went through the succession of tanks attached to the back side of the dome, one of which contained a small turbine generator that produced more than enough electricity for the platform's own operations.

Huge condensors collected the spent steam and vapor, reduced it to water, and sent it to the massive pump that injected the water back into the earth.

Walking the deck was an adventure in itself. Piping of a dozen diameters, the largest a meter across, created a maze. They were painted white and yellow and red. One had to step over, duck under, and slip around the conduits in order to cross the decking.

A light gray haze seemed to float in the space, and the walls dripped constantly with moisture.

It was hot, over a hundred degrees. Heating the domes had never been a problem. Rather, after this, the first platform, had been constructed and the drilling completed, they had had to install air conditioning. Maintaining the sensitive electronics at steady temperatures had been a necessity.

Diederman handed him a pair of cushioned ear protectors, and once he had them in place, the scream of the turbine generators was bearable. The engineer led the way through the pipe maze. large yellow signs were attached to most of the pipes. Steam. Hot water. Valves were everywhere, most of them remote-controlled, serving no discernible purpose, but required for safety, if steam pressures became too high to contain and had to be vented, and for diversion so that one or all of the turbines could be shut down for servicing.

Thickly insulated cables, strung on ceramic insulators, emerged from the generators, were routed above the piping, and directed into the space beneath Diederman's control center. There, the electricity was filtered, transformed, and channeled in ways that Eisenach did not understand. He knew only that the electricity drawn from the other operating platforms was collected there, then distributed into one of the two undersea cables. The undersea cables, he had been told, carried 220,000 volts.

Diederman drew him to a stop outside a guardrail that circled the wellhead. The railing protected a space that was four meters in diameter. The well cap, of some cast alloy, was head-height above the deck and was almost two meters in diameter. Several large pipes emerged horizontally from it, leading toward the turbines. The well casing, a meter in diameter, rose through an oversized hole in the decking. Exterior air was allowed to flow in around the casing, helping to cool it. Still, the casing and wellhead were tinged a yellowish-brown from the heat.

Diederman leaned toward him and yelled. Eisenach had

to pull his ear protector away from his ear to hear. "Three hundred and eighty degrees Fahrenheit! Now, we could boil your tea instantly."

Eisenach nodded, shifted the ear protector back in place, and peered down through the gap between the well casing and the deck. He could see the wave tops five meters below. Depressed wave tops, coated with the icy sludge.

The perspiration was running down his face, and his armpits were damp. He wiped his face, tapped Diederman on the shoulder, and they threaded their way back through the maze to the corridor and the elevator.

He had missed lunch, but Diederman was happy to have a second lunch, and the director ordered thick ham-and-rye sandwiches and coffee delivered to his office.

They sat at the big table, Diederman's console close to his hand.

"So, now, Herr General," Diederman said, talking with a stuffed mouth, "you have come triumphantly through a summer storm, only to look at a wellhead?"

"Yes, Hans, I have."

"To what purpose?"

"To make alterations to the platforms. A fail-safe mechanism, as it were."

Diederman frowned.

"Below the deck, a meter above the sea surface, we are going to attach plastic explosive to the well casings. I imagine that it will probably have to be insulated from the casing in some manner."

Diederman's eyes flew wide open, a feat of some magnitude with all of the fat around them.

"We will also place explosives on each of the anchor cables."

"This is fail-safe, Herr General? Pardon me, but it is asinine!"

"It is fail-safe in that it will deter further attacks by the Americans."

"You are to publicize this foolish act, now?"

288

"A leak or two through the intelligence networks should accomplish what I want, Hans."

"You want to endanger all of the men aboard these platforms, do you?" Diederman's face was beet red with his anger.

"Not at all. The explosives will be remotely triggered from here only, and will require a key which you will carry. It is an engineering problem for you. We want the anchor lines to break first, then the casing to detonate. The platforms will float freely away."

"You are very certain that this can be accomplished, Herr General."

"Of course. I have already ordered the plastic explosive and the radio equipment. Admiral Schmidt's frogmen will assist you."

If he did not count food, engineering problems were Diederman's joy. The anger faded from his face as he said, "You have forgotten the injection wells. They will also have to be severed, and . . ."

Amy Pearson was in her office cubicle, performing a routine visual check of the station. It was not an assigned task—Brad Mitchell had that duty, but it had become a habit for her. She liked to know what was going on around her.

With her fingers tapping out camera numbers on the keyboard, she watched the screen as it jolted from one view to the next. Interior shots of corridors, spokes, modules, priority compartments like the nuclear reactor or the HoneyBee receiving docks. The exterior shots came from six cameras mounted on the spokes. She hesitated when the exterior view of the hangars came up on Spoke Fifteen's camera. Delta Blue was departing, slowly sliding away from the station.

She wasn't certain that she was totally in favor of McKenna's mission. He had had to spend nearly an hour with her, finally convincing her—almost convincing her—of the soundness of his logic.

She had finally signed off on the plan, as had General Overton, but her signature included the statement, "with reservations."

McKenna was so damned stubborn.

But he kisses pretty well.

She brushed away that thought quickly and asked Donna Amber on the intercom to connect her with the National Security Agency at Fort George G. Meade, Maryland.

The giant facility tapped in on almost all of the television, telephonic, and radio communications in the world. The sonobuoys and listening posts that the MakoSharks had scattered from Europe to South America were monitored by the Agency.

When Amber had the connection made, Pearson asked for the German section.

"MacDonald."

"I thought you might be on duty, Walt. This is Amy Pearson."

"Hello there, honey. You up in the cold blue sky?"

"I think we're just about directly over Tokyo."

"Boy, I tell you. If my heart were up to it, I'd take you up on your invitation to visit."

She had never met MacDonald in person, and she didn't know whether he truly had a heart condition or just weak nerves.

"You're missing the best view ever."

"Don't I know it. What's up?"

"I wanted to see if you've had any action on some of our listening posts." She read him the list of code numbers she had compiled.

MacDonald was the section chief, and he yelled for one of his subordinates to go check the machines. With voice communications, the NSA had computers similar to Val Arguento's to scan for key words in the millions of dialogues. With sonobuoys not covered by the navy, the continuous output was recorded on tape machines. The listening posts were more sophisticated, collecting sounds for half an hour at a time and then compressing them digitally into a sixty-second blurts radioed to a satellite.

On the NSA's end, the messages were decompressed into real time, then saved on tape.

She and MacDonald chatted for several minutes, then he said, "Here we go, Amy. On your sixteen sonobuoys in the Norwegian and Greenland seas, only four are still operational. We have the *Bohemian* passing through seventy-five degrees north, but that was three hours ago. Farther south, on buoy three, we picked up the screws of a fishing boat.

"The Elbe River LP's at Kothen show a marked increase in the frequency of traffic, Amy."

"Which way, Mac?"

"Northward. Sounds like heavy tugboats, so there's probably long strings of barges."

It could be increased industrial goods, but she suspected that military material was being moved.

"How about Peenemünde?" she asked.

"No dramatic changes," MacDonald told her. "Automobile traffic. Once in a while, we hear machine tools."

"Okay, thanks, Mac. Look, if you hear anything out of the norm at Peenemünde, give me a call, will you?"

"Sure. In fact, I'll program what we have into the computer as a base pattern, so we can get an automatic alert if there's anything strange that comes up."

"I appreciate it."

"Come and see me some time."

After she signed off with MacDonald, Pearson spent half an hour thinking about McKenna's proposal. Thinking about what could go wrong.

Resetting her tether straps to give her a little more freedom, Pearson switched on her computer and keyed in her access code to the main database. She called up the photographs taken of well number eight, selected the clearest low-light shot, and then transferred it into her graphics program. That program let her manipulate the image, and she duplicated it, side by side, then rotated one so that she had a top and side view of the dome and platform. The side view looked a little squashed, so she elongated it until the dome appeared round again.

The top view displayed the openings created by Mabry Evan's warheads. Through the holes, she could discern three distinct partitions, dividing the diameter into three almost equal sections, so she erased the remaining portion of the top of the dome, then drew in the partitions. The section containing the wellhead and turbine equipment, which were blurred in this photo, was at the back of the platform, opposite the helicopter pad.

She wished she could erase the ceilings of interior spaces and see what was below them, but had to guess that they were housing and operational spaces. Probably five or six floors of them.

Erasing the dome face in the side view, she sketched in approximate floor levels. The dome's diameter was constant from the deck of the platform up to midheight, then it began to curve in toward the middle. For the upper hundred feet, any floor installed would be smaller in area than the floor below it. Still, it would be possible to fit in as many as fifteen floors with adequate head room and floors thick enough to carry ventilation, power, and plumbing.

She went back to her top view. Peering closely at the photograph, it seemed to her that there was a fair amount of distance between the top of the dome and the first apparent ceiling on the inside. As a guess, she would say at least fifty feet. She went back to the side view and erased several top floors.

What seemed logical to her is that the dome on every platform was similar. They were, after all, mass-produced as preformed parts. The well itself would be at the back of each platform. There was something else she knew.

What was it?

On the electromagnetic maps.

She called up the maps on a second screen and studied them closely.

Wells one and eleven gave off more electromagnetic pulses than did the other wells. For the most part, the pattern indicated that the power cables from most of the platforms converged upon both one and eleven.

Primary and secondary collection and distribution centers. Well number one would be the primary, since it was drilled first.

She looked at her manipulated drawings and thought that maybe McKenna was right.

Again.

Damn him, anyway.

"Sorry to drag you all this way, Colonel, but with something of this magnitude, I like to see the face of the man with the proposition," Adm. Hannibal Cross said.

"I don't mind the trip, if you don't mind the hour, Admiral," McKenna said.

It was after eleven. McKenna and Munoz had put down at Peterson Air Force Base, Munoz headed for a cab and the city lights, and McKenna and General Brackman had commandeered an F-111 swing-wing bomber for the flight to Washington. Brackman flew, claiming that he rarely got the chance to get behind the controls anymore. It was the primary reason to avoid becoming a general, McKenna had thought. It was funny how that exalted goal of his—to get that star—had evaporated so easily. The house he had grown up in, with a World War II vet father, had instilled him with a sense of duty and responsibility, and somewhere along the line, he had come to the conclusion that his duty was best served right where he was at.

"Around here, Colonel, there aren't any early or late hours. It's always late."

"Yes, sir."

"Sit."

They were in the chairman's sumptuous office, which overlooked the Potomac and the River Drive entrance to the Pentagon, and they all moved to a small round conference table in one corner. Cups had been set out, and a tray containing a Thermos pot of coffee, sugar, and cream rested in the middle of the table. There were yellow pads and pencils for everyone. A copy of McKenna's two-page telex was in front of every padded chair.

Everyone included the chairman of the Joint Chiefs of Staff; General Mays of the air force; General Brackman; Adm. Carl Woldeman, the chief of Naval Operations; and Gen. Budge McAdams, the army chief of staff.

McKenna counted seventeen stars on five left shoulders and decided he was in company where he didn't belong. Or did not want to belong. They all had experiences similar to his own, but they had adapted to the ultracomplex politics that flowed around the head of the military and the head of the government. McKenna had little faith in politics.

"Before we get into your proposal, Colonel McKenna, we've got one little item to take care of," Cross said.

"Yes, sir, I suppose that we do." McKenna knew what was coming.

"I'm referring to Major Lynn Haggar."

He kept his silence.

"It is not the policy of the Department of Defense to put our female members in situations where they might be subjected to hostile fire. That's the policy, Colonel, and you've subverted it."

"No, sir, I have not."

"You'd better explain that," Harvey Nays said.

"Major Haggar is simply learning to fly the MakoShark. She's capable and extremely competent. There is no intention of placing her in a combat situation. The MakoShark primarily flies reconnaissance missions, for which she is qualified. More qualified, gentlemen, than most of her peers. The number of people who are certified to fly either a Mako or a MakoShark is extremely limited. I take only the best pilots, and they are rare."

"But with the situation we have in Germany . . ."

"If it came to that, I'd fly on her wing," McKenna said. He turned to look at McAdams. "We had women flying combat during the excursion to Panama. They did well."

"That was inadvertent," Budge McAdams said.

"If Major Haggar encounters combat, it will be inadvertent," McKenna said.

"You don't have anyone more prepared . . ."

"No, sir, I do not."

"Inadvertent?" Nays asked.

"Yes, sir."

Brackman said, "General Overton says she's already flown the MakoShark."

"And did quite well, General."

Mays looked at Brackman, who shrugged, then at Cross and nodded.

Cross Said, "Keep her out of dangerous situations, Colonel. She is not to be scheduled for any flight over Germany or German interests. We're not altering policy, but we're allowing you to develop her as a recon pilot."

"Thank you, Admiral."

He tapped the telex. "Now then, what you're proposing is definitely a dangerous situation, isn't it? And you've set it for three days from now. Why is that?"

"For the most part, it's preparation time. I've got to get Delta Yellow checked out and airborne. I know that Admiral Woldeman is already accumulating a task force of specialized ships off the coast of England, but he will need a few more days. General Brackman said that the British are participating, and that the Soviet Union may do so. If you approve my operation, General McAdams will have to alert the Rapid Deployment Force and get them to England.

"From a more global point of view, which I admit is not my bailiwick, I understand that the Germans may have ICBM capability within the week. That would alter our position drastically, I think, and perhaps prevent our ever doing anything about the geothermal wells. I'm in favor of taking care of the problem now, before the Germans can stop us, and before there's an accident.

"Therefore, I believe we need a 'go' or a 'no go' yet tonight."

Hannibal Cross shook his head dejectedly. "We'd have to, at minimum, get the President out of bed."

"The hours are long in this town, Admiral."

Cross studied him. "Yes. I believe I mentioned that. What do you want to call this thing, Colonel?"

The flag ranks would want to discuss the details yet, and probably suggest a few thousand changes that McKenna might resist, but he had the feeling that everyone in that office had already made up his mind.

It would be a matter of convincing the White House and any other agencies the President felt should be involved.

"For the media, when they see the troops on the move, Admiral? I'd say it's a training exercise, perhaps a joint exercise with the British and Soviets. Call it Operation Whale-Saver. That might get the environmentalists on our side for a change."

Sixteen

Kapitän Rolf Froelich was nervous and trying not to show it, Schmidt thought, but then every man in Schmidt's small fleet was nervous.

Three successive nights of maintaining battle stations, with no sight of the enemy, did terrible things to both morale and the state of readiness. Sleeplessness, inaction, boredom. It could lead to mistakes.

For all Schmidt knew, the American MakoSharks had been romping unseen through the offshore wells each night, shooting their pictures. The probe by submarines that he had convinced himself to expect had not occurred. Neither the *Black Forest* nor the *Bohemian* had had sonar contacts to report. The fifty sonobuoys deployed around the field only picked up the screw signatures of slowly cruising German naval vessels.

Maybe it was the spell of bad weather that was holding them off.

For the past three days, it had been overcast, the sun and its warmth blotted out. Frequent rain squalls passed through the region, drenching everything, including gun crews shivering throughout seemingly long nights. The weather was another morale-breaker.

Froelich waited until Schmidt finished brooding, staring out the window of his flag plot. When he turned back to the *Hamburg*'s commanding officer, he had not come up with any answers.

He did have an observation. "The weather is lifting, Rolf."

"A little, Admiral. The meteorologist says that we will continue to be overcast, but that the rain should let up. None is forecast, anyway."

"A small favor. Well, shall we get on with it?"

Froelich moved to the electronic plot on the bulkhead, and the *leutnant* operating it sat up at his console.

Not many of the symbols on the map had changed in the last days. The wells did not move, though they might if Eisenach's stupid "fail-safe" plan were activated. The ships of the *Dritte Marinekraft*'s first four battle groups were now holding their stations. The fifth battle group was 200 kilometers away, approaching the wells. Schmidt had relieved them of their duty over the cable.

The picture displayed on the map was fairly complete. The basic information was fed to the admiral's plot from the Combat Information Center, which obtained its information from the radar sightings of all ships in the fleet, as well as the Luftwaffe aircraft flying cover.

Extending a collapsible pointer, Froelich aimed it at a group of red blips northwest of North Cape, Norway. "The Soviet ships out of Archangel continue to move at cruise speed. The group has been joined by three stragglers."

"It is how large, now?"

"Fourteen vessels, headed by the rocket cruiser *Kirov.* There are several *Kotlin Sam* class destroyers and two troop carriers. The balance appear to be service and supply ships."

"And the other group?"

The pointer slipped across the screen to a spot 300 kilometers due east of Daneborg, Greenland.

"The American and British task force still contains seventeen ships, Admiral. They have not moved farther north in the last eight hours, but appear to be on track to meet the Soviet group."

"Operation Whale, they are calling it?"

298

"It was advertised as such in the newspapers. A joint naval exercise."

"But no more details since that announcement?"

"No, Herr Admiral."

"I do not like the presence of the two salvage ships in the Anglo force," Gerhard Schmidt said. "Nor do I like seeing the *Tarawa* . . ."

The *Tarawa* was an amphibious assault ship, with a capability of landing 1,800 soldiers by helicopter and landing craft. The reconnaissance flights had detected no large contingents of troops aboard the ship, but they could easily be kept below decks.

"Tell me, Rolf. What is your estimate for the minimum amount of time it would take either of those task forces to reach us?"

"The slowest of the ships can make eighteen knots, Admiral. It would take about fifteen hours for the British-American force, nineteen hours for the Soviet group."

They were much closer than Schmidt liked. He also did not care to be outnumbered almost two-to-one, even if some of the ships were merely noncombatants.

"The aircraft?" he asked.

The pointer flew over the map. "Colonel Weismann has just two aircraft up at the moment, here and here. He continues to insist upon using his strength at night. One of the Eurofighters detected an airborne warning craft here, over the eastern coast of Greenland. It is probably supporting the British-American task force. Both task forces have helicopters up, ranging in front of them. Anti-submarine warfare craft, probably."

"If we stopped the fifth battle group right where they are, the Americans and Soviets would intercept them sometime tomorrow," Schmidt said.

"Do you want to do that, Admiral?"

"No. I want them here, so that we have three battle groups on the southern side of the well field. All right, Rolf, thank you."

As soon as the *Kapitän* left, Schmidt said, "Lieutenant,

locate General Eisenach for me. I believe he is still on Platform One."

Five minutes passed before the telephone at his side buzzed. He picked up the receiver.

"Felix," Schmidt said, "I want to bring you up to date on those task forces."

It took him two minutes.

And as he had in their last two conversations, Eisenach brushed them off, like he would a fly. "You worry too much, Gerhard. It is simply a show of force. The Americans could not breach our security with their airplanes, so now they will march across our front door with their ships. I am not frightened. Are you frightened?"

"Yes, Felix, I am. Amphibious assault ships scare me. Salvage ships scare me."

"Why?" the general asked. "It is only a pitiful armada, assembled with vessels that were close by at the time they needed them."

He partially agreed with the general. If Gerhard Schmidt wanted to put together a show of force, he would do it with seven or eight warships, not seventeen ships that included unarmed vessels.

"Nonetheless, Felix, I believe you should talk to the High Command. I want permission to unleash my guns, and my submarines, against hostile vessels if I need to do so."

"Then you have it, Gerhard."

Schmidt wondered when Eisenach had obtained that kind of authority, the authority to start a war.

"I want it in writing."

"Then you shall have it in writing. You will not need it, however."

"I hope you are right," he said.

"I know I am right. This afternoon, this evening at the latest, Ghost I is to be placed on its launch pad."

Eisenach sounded almost gleeful.

With as many setbacks as the *Gespenst* program had suffered, and with as many aircraft as the *20.S.A.G.* had

300

lost, Gerhard Schmidt thought that it was up to him to prepare for battle.

The GUARDIAN PROJECT commander's frame of mind, Schmidt thought, was not conducive to such planning, so he must take it upon himself.

"Now, Lieutenant, find Colonel Albert Weismann for me."

Daniel Goldstein was standing outside the doorway to his own office.

Weismann told him, "Shut the door, Goldstein."

The Jew reached inside and pulled the door shut.

Weismann uncovered the mouthpiece of the telephone. "All right, Admiral. Yes, I am aware of the ships."

"Are you also aware of the makeup of each flotilla?"

"Yes. Cruisers, destroyers, salvage ships."

"Do you know what that means?"

"General Eisenach says a show of force."

"And do you believe that?"

Weismann did not. "I think they're standing by in case of an accident. A blowout."

"Caused by?" Schmidt asked.

"An error in judgment or aiming. I think the Americans may try to torpedo the cables under the wells."

"Do you, now? I had not thought of that, Colonel. I am preparing for an infiltration of the offshore platforms by submarine and frogmen."

That was a surprise to Weismann. "The defense planning group has not mentioned the possibility."

"They wouldn't. They're all air force."

Weismann knew of the admiral's disenchantment with the air force. Worse, having lost four aircraft, and having had Zeigman and Metzenbaum abandon coverage to chase decoy Soviets, his disenchantment had some foundation.

"Perhaps, Admiral, they will do both."

"We should prepare for the eventuality, Weismann."

"When, do you think?"

"If it were me planning operations for the other side, I would pick tonight. The weather is projected to be better than it has been for several days, though there will still be a high overcast."

"I will alert my squadrons."

"Tell them not to go running after specters, will you?"

Weismann depressed the telephone bar, then dialed New Amsterdam. As normal, it took a while to run down Zeigman, but he was discovered asleep in his quarters.

"Colonel?" with a yawn.

"Mac, what do you have planned for tonight?"

"Give me a minute to wake up. Let me see. We're running two Eurofighters directly over the wells. They, as well as the ships, are an inducement to attack. I have scheduled six Tornadoes for the overhead coverage. The first aircraft go at eleven o'clock. There will be two changes of the guard."

"We are going to send them all," Weismann said.

"Are you crazy? Herr Colonel."

"I think not. We will keep four tankers aloft through the night, replacing them as needed. You may keep your two low-flying decoys, but all of the rest, including the aircraft on loan from the Sixteenth Fighter Wing are to be deployed over the wells."

"Throughout the night?"

"Yes."

"That's twenty-four planes, Colonel."

"I can count, Major. We want four of them armed with the Saab Rb05 air-to-surface missiles."

"You are expecting a major offensive, Colonel?"

"The signs point toward it, Mac. Do not unduly alarm the squadrons, however. They will be suspicious, as it is, due to the number of planes."

"All right. Why the A-to-S?"

"There are British, American, and Soviet surface ships gathering. We may need to dissuade them."

"Yes. I saw them on last night's patrol. Will you be flying?"

Weismann wished it were possible. "I am stuck here for the night. Good hunting, Mac."

He hung up the telephone, scratched the side of his neck, and got up to open the door.

Goldstein waited stoically in the hallway, leaning against the wall.

"Let us see what you have accomplished, *Herr Direktor-Assistent.*"

They walked down the corridor together and emerged from the office complex in the back of the building onto the assembly floor. The second rocket in line was being fitted with one of the MIRV warheads. The technicians handled it as if it were hot, but Weismann knew that, until it was armed, it was quite safe. Not even a fire or explosion would detonate the nuclear charges. They were not finally armed until a barometric device assured that the warhead had reached at least 3,000 meters of altitude.

Gespenst I had its new collar installed, and Weismann stopped below and looked up at it. The collar was of bare metal and shiny next to the gray paint, but he was not looking for appearance, only for function.

The test warhead, loaded with 300 kilograms of high explosive, was suspended in the air from an overhead crane. He backed away and watched as the nose cone was lowered, then fitted back into place by six technicians. The men appeared exhausted, their lab coats grimy, their faces matching the coats.

"See, Herr Colonel? A perfect fit."

"How long, Goldstein?" It was already getting dark outside.

"Perhaps a couple hours to secure it and complete the wiring. Then we will roll it out and mount it on the pad. If the weather holds, we will have our first launch at eight o'clock in the morning." Goldstein tried to sound excited, but failed.

"We will have our first launch yet tonight, Goldstein."

"But, Colonel! The men need rest!"

"They can rest tomorrow. The software?"

"Is ready," Goldstein professed. "But, Colonel Weismann, it is unthinkable to actually target the American space station. We can change the program quickly."

"Goldstein, you do not know the meaning of 'quickly.'" Weismann looked at his watch. "In half an hour, six air force specialists in ballistics and computers will be here to examine the software."

The look of anguish that passed over Goldman's face confirmed his suspicions.

"Right now, Goldman, General Eisenach wants to see you at his headquarters in Berlin."

"Now? I am a mess. I must wash and change clothes."

"It is all right. You will be coming right back."

Weismann signaled to the two helicopter pilots.

He wondered if Goldstein would be surprised to find Maximillian Oberlin waiting at the helicopter for him.

Probably not.

McKenna was talking to Polly Tang at the hangar operations console when Pearson came sailing along the corridor.

He reached out a hand, she grabbed it, and he pulled her to a stop.

She seemed a little breathless. Her headband was slightly askew, and her face seemed subdued.

When she realized he was still holding her left hand, she used her right hand to extricate it from his grasp.

Polly Tang grinned.

"What's up, Amy?"

"There's a bit of a flap in Washington, D.C."

"Oh?"

"Dr. Monte Washington went right to the press as soon as his company fired him. Told them that *Themis* was a battlestar, armed to the teeth."

"It make the papers or TV yet?" McKenna asked.

"No. But there's a mob of reporters that is all over the White House and the Pentagon, trying to get confirmations."

She was worried, McKenna thought.

"You talked to Brackman?" he asked.

"Yes, along with Jim."

"How long does he think Admiral Cross can hold them off?"

"A day. Two at the most."

"That's all the time we need. Cross can give them the whole story after tonight. I won't mind being called in front of a Senate hearing panel after those wells are closed down."

McKenna looked through the window. Munoz was supervising the installation of the final Wasp. The MakoShark appeared particularly lethal with all four pylons mounting missiles. Additionally, two retractable mounts had been installed in the payload bays, each armed with four Wasps. In total, there were twenty-four missiles loaded, half of them warheaded for air-to-surface and half for air-to-air. The three MakoSharks would depart with seventy-two missiles, and McKenna hoped to have at least sixty of them survive the blackout.

He was already in his environmental suit. It was augmented for this trip with thigh pouches containing emergency equipment, including an emergency locator beacon. A battery pack that could power the heating elements in the environmental suit was strapped to his side. If one of the MakoSharks went down in an icy sea, the heated environmental suit might keep a pilot and a WSO alive for around twenty-five minutes, enough time for the search-and-rescue planes that had been moved into Daneborg to reach them. The uninflated Mae West felt bulky around his neck. All of it made him feel clumsy, even in a weightless environment.

"What's this?" Pearson asked, reaching out to pluck at the harness webbing he wore.

"You mean the parachute?"

"Yes. You guys never wear parachutes."

"Too damned uncomfortable, Amy. We have to take the cushions out of the lounge seats."

"So, why now?"

"Makes us feel better," he said, not ready to get into involved explanations. "You all set?"

"Yes. The KH-11 is sending good pictures, but it's mostly clouds."

A KH-11 spy satellite had been moved into geostationary orbit over the Greenland Sea two days before. It had infrared and night sensors.

"What's the cloud status?" he asked.

"Fairly solid between eight thousand and fifteen thousand feet. There are a few holes beginning to show, but not near the platforms. For anything under fifteen thousand, we'll be relying on Cottonseed's radar."

McKenna checked his watch, which he had reset to German time. Ten o'clock. He looked back up the corridor and saw Conover and Dimatta hanging onto the consoles outside their hangars. Dimatta was talking to Lynn Haggar, who was handling the hangar controls for his launch. Ben Olsen was working with Conover. McKenna gave them a thumbs-up.

"Time to go."

"Be careful," she said, still looking worried.

"Tony's keeping an eye on me."

Tang blew him a kiss, and McKenna smiled at her, then pushed off the console, grabbed the hatchway, and pulled himself into the hangar.

Benny Shalbot helped him strap in.

"How's the new stripe, Benny?"

He didn't wear the insignia on his jumpsuit, of course. No one did.

"Shit," he said. "They're starting to call me 'Sarge' now. I feel like a lifer."

He was a lifer.

"Just respect talking, Benny."

"Sure, Colonel. But, anyway, the pay's better."

Once his straps were tight and all of the umbilicals connected, Shalbot shoved off.

Tang used her PA system. "Clear the bay, please."

306

"You ready, Tiger?"

"I've been ready for two days, Snake Eyes. Got to a point, there, where I was havin' trouble fallin' asleep."

Seven minutes later, the doors opened, McKenna fired the thrusters, and the MakoShark drifted backward.

Tang and Pearson waved at them.

All of the MakoSharks reversed ends and the WSOs finished programming the computers.

Delta Blue had a nine-minute wait for a window.

"Not bad," Munoz said.

McKenna ran radio checks, testing his transmission and reception with Alpha One, Semaphore, Cottonseed, Condor One, and Robin Hood One, the lead craft of the four airplane rescue squadron, all C-130 Hercules planes.

"Delta Yellow," he called on the Tac-1 frequency. "How's she holding up?"

"Better than new," Conover told him. "I haven't seen this much green since the last time I was in Borneo."

"One minute, Snake Eyes," Munoz said.

Automatically, his eyes went to the CRT and the TIME TO RETRO FIRE. Munoz was right, as usual.

"Keep the shiny side up," Overton said.

"Tell me, which side's the shiny one, Alpha?" Munoz radioed back.

"The one without missile exhaust burns. Don't bring any missiles back, huh?"

"Roger that . . . four, three, two, one," Munoz said.

McKenna double-checked his straps as the computer took over the rocket throttles. As the levers advanced silently, he was shoved back into the couch. The vibration in the floor felt familiar and good.

Themis disappeared from the rearview screen, and McKenna hated to see her go.

The rocket burn was longer than normal, going for two minutes and forty-two seconds.

The computer turned Delta Blue nose forward at Mach 19.6 and adjusted her for the forty-degree nose up angle.

The sun was hot and bright, trying to defeat the bronze

tinting of the canopies. The earth was a wonderful blue under their position. South Pacific. McKenna picked out Tahiti and thought about the mural in Sixteen's dining compartment. Put Pearson in the front of the mural.

At ninety miles of altitude, McKenna felt the grip of the atmosphere slowing the craft.

"We have coolant flow, Snake Eyes."

The two blue lights on the HUD confirmed it.

The windscreen went to red-orange, and the stars disappeared.

He notched up the air conditioning by two clicks as the heat picked up.

As they came out of the blackout, the windscreen losing a yellow hue, Munoz called *Themis*, "Alpha One, Delta Blue at two-three-five thousand, Mach twelve-point-four."

"Copy that, Blue."

Conover and Dimatta checked in a few minutes later, and McKenna set up rendezvous coordinates over the northeast coast of France.

Then he radioed Murmansk on Tac-2.

"Condor One, Delta Blue."

Volontov had been waiting by a microphone. He responded immediately. "Proceed, Delta Blue."

"You've got twenty minutes, Condor."

"We must wait that long?"

Volontov sent the message for the tankers to take off right away, then called General Sheremetevo. While he waited for the general, he looked around his operations room. It was crowded with pilots checking the weather and talking to each other, simultaneously eager and anxious. When he caught the eyes of his two squadron leaders, he pointed a forefinger upward. They nodded and began moving through the mob, tapping their pilots on the shoulders.

Like Volontov, the general had also been waiting, though perhaps more patiently. He was at Stavka where he could keep an eye on the action relayed through the airborne warning and control aircraft, which had already been aloft for several hours.

"I have just talked to McKenna, General. They are in position, indicating that they have final approval."

"As do we, Pyotr Mikhailovich. You may take off at any time you wish."

"It will be a few minutes," Volontov said.

"You are aware that the Germans have twenty-four aircraft up?"

"Yes, Comrade General. The space station relayed that information as soon as the fighters left Germany. There are also four tanker aircraft. I suspect they intend to stay the night."

"Do you think that they are forewarned, that there has been an information leak, Pyotr?"

"I don't know, General. Probably. It looks as if they expect us."

"Would you do anything differently, suspecting that that is the case?" Sheremetevo asked.

"No, General. My pilots are ready."

"I wish you luck, then."

Volontov hung up the telephone and stepped outside the operations building. The MiG-29s were lined up in two rows, the twelve aircraft of his own 2032nd and 2033rd squadrons, plus eight more provided by the 11th Fighter Wing. He had organized them as three squadrons. He would lead the 2033rd as Condor Flight, providing overhead coverage, and Maj. Anatoly Rostoken would take the Vulture Flight, the 2032nd, as the lead elements, the point of the spear. Maj. Arkady Michovoi would command the eight planes of the Tern Flight. Unlike the first two squadrons, which were armed with AA-11 missiles, Michovoi's was armed with the new AS-X-10 air-to-surface missiles. It had a range of only seven kilometers, but was extremely accurate, guided by a semiactive laser.

For two days, they had been practicing McKenna's recommended tactics with the AS-X-10. The Tern Flight aircraft would have to be very low, very close, and very precise.

The wind off the Barents Sea was brisk, chilling his face. In the darkness, he could see scraps of paper blowing across the runways. Portable lights moved around the aircraft, as did the ground crews in their yellow parkas. Tractors with empty missile trailers pulled away, and the start carts were spotted between every other plane. Pilots were climbing into their cockpits.

Volontov walked across the tarmac to his own MiG, shrugged out of his parka, and was helped into his parachute harness by his crew chief. He pulled his helmet on, then climbed the ladder and swung his legs into the cockpit.

He powered up the instrument panel and the inertial navigation computer before strapping in. It always took several minutes for the gyros to come up to speed.

His crew chief, on the ladder beside him, checked the connections, then said, "I want my airplane back whole, Colonel."

"I want you to have it that way." Volontov smiled.

The tower gave them permission to start engines, and ten aircraft started right away. Minutes later, after the start carts were connected, the last ten were under power. The noise of forty 8,300-kilogram thrust Tumansky turbofans revving up was earsplitting.

Volontov closed his canopy after the crew chief pulled the ladder away. The cockpit was cold and he turned up the heater all the way.

After making certain that his first tactical frequency was set at the proper frequency for contact with his wing and that the second frequency was adjusted to the one agreed with McKenna, Volontov called the tower.

"Murmansk, Condor One requesting taxi and takeoff clearance for a flight of twenty."

"Condor One, you are cleared for Runway Ten right, takeoff in pairs. Wind is eleven knots, gusting to twenty, direction one-seven-zero. Temperature is two degrees."

That was Centigrade, just above freezing. The water would be much colder. Volontov was wearing two sweaters and a pair of long underwear under his pressure suit, but they would not do much for him if he was forced down in the sea.

Releasing the brakes and turning on his wing lights and anticollision strobe, he pulled out of line for several meters, then turned right. His wingman followed, taking up a position off Volontov's right wing.

The rest of the wing fell into line as the commander's MiG passed the front row. A half kilometer later, he turned left onto the runway and braked to a stop. No other aircraft was scheduled, but he had checked the skies anyway.

Gurychenko, his wingman, took up a position to his right, and Volontov blinked his lights. Advancing his throttles, then releasing the brakes, Volontov allowed the MiG to roll. Gurychenko stayed right alongside.

He pushed the throttles outboard and shoved them into afterburner.

The MiG leaped like a ballet dancer. Halfway down the stage, she rose into the air, and he retraced the landing gear and flaps.

When he achieved 600 knots and 2,000 meters, Volontov shut down the afterburners. He continued to climb, waiting for the others to group around him.

There was very little talk on the radio. Everyone had his own thoughts to tend to, and the flight strategy had been ingrained after several briefings.

When the wing was complete, Volontov advanced his speed to Mach 1.5. They climbed quickly through low and scattered cloud cover and emerged into a starlit night. The clouds were like rolling plains below. Billowy steppes.

Three hundred kilometers out of Murmansk, Volontov spoke on the first tactical frequency. "This is Condor One. Code Neva. I say again, Code Neva."

Condor Flight continued to climb, seeking the 15,000 meters they would maintain, while Vulture Flight leveled off at 6,000 meters and accelerated to Mach 1.7. When they were twenty kilometers ahead of the main group, they would return to Mach 1.5.

Tern Flight stayed at 6,000 meters. At the first sign of radar contact, they would dive to a hundred meters off the water and attempt to avoid the radar. After a few minutes passed, Volontov checked the positions by switching his radar to active.

Every one was in place.

He was proud of them.

His heading was shown as 000 degrees on the HUD, the reading taken from the gyroscopic compass. Magnetic compasses were less than reliable in the far north. The downward pull of magnetic north tended to depress the needles and make them jump from side to side.

Each of the flights met two tankers and topped off their fuel.

When the computer informed him that he had achieved 80 degrees north latitude, he checked his watch. 1112 hours, German time. They were two minutes ahead of schedule.

There would be ice shelf down there, but the clouds, which had been closing in, blocked a view of it.

On the second tactical frequency, Volontov said, "Delta Blue, Condor One."

"Go Condor, you've got Blue."

"Code Silver Lake."

"Copy Silver Lake. Code Ural."

"I receive Code Ural. Good luck, Delta Blue."

"Same to you, fella."

On the first tactical frequency, Volontov told his wing, "Code Volga."

The entire flight turned to the west, Condor and Tern Flights waiting one and a half minutes, in order to stay directly behind Vulture flight.

Half an hour later, Rostoken reported the first radar probes.

* * *

312

Felix Eisenach was enjoying a late-night brandy with Hans Diederman in the engineer's quarters on the fourth level when the duty officer called.

Diederman hung up the telephone and grabbed his jacket from the back of the sofa.

"There has been a radar contact, Herr General. Unidentified aircraft."

Eisenach retrieved his own uniform jacket and slipped into it as he followed Diederman out of the small apartment and down the corridor to the operations room.

The dome did not have a military-type plotting screen, but one of the consoles was displaying the radar picture relayed by one of the Tornadoes over the ice platforms.

The console operator was a little excited. "I count . . . eh . . . count twenty aircraft, Lieutenant. Now, wait. Eight of them have disappeared into the clutter of ground return. They are flying very low."

The duty officer looked up to Eisenach.

The general was extremely disappointed. He had been certain that attacks by aircraft were a thing of the past. Either the secret service's leaking of the information about the fail-safe explosive devices had been ignored, or had not reached the proper ears. He should have used the newspapers, as the Americans had with the task force information.

"How many interceptors do we have up?" he asked.

The *leutnant* spoke to the operator. "Let us see our own radar."

The screen flickered then displayed the area covered by the radar antenna on the dome. The Soviet—they had to be Soviet from that direction—aircraft were out of range.

With his finger, the operator checked off blips. "Twenty-four, Herr General."

Twenty-four? That was all of the aircraft assigned to Weismann. Had the *oberst* known something that Eisenach had not known? The man had trouble communicating.

Nevertheless, Eisenach was happy to see all of the aircraft.

"Some of them are joining to meet the Soviets," the *leutnant* said. "See here? Ten of them."

"That is good," Eisenach said, relieved that Weismann had apparently instilled some discipline in his pilots.

The telephone rang, and the duty officer picked it up, listened, then handed the phone to Eisenach. "It is Admiral Schmidt."

Eisenach took the handset. "Yes, Gerhard?"

"Did you know that twenty Soviet airplanes are coming at us, Felix?"

"Yes. I am watching on the screen."

"And did you also know that the Soviet and British-American task forces have been turned northward and are making flank speed?"

"It could be expected," Eisenach said. "As I mentioned to you."

Inside, his stomach felt like jelly.

"I must have missed that mention," Schmidt said. "I am going to sound General Quarters, and I am freeing my guns and missiles."

"Of course," Felix Eisenach said. "That is what you must do."

Seventeen

The AEW&C plane was an Ilyushin II-76 using the call sign Sable. The air controller had a baritone, unflappable voice. He sounded so rock-solid that Volontov agreed with NATO. They called the airborne early warning and control aircraft version of the II-76 *Mainstay*.

"Condor, Vulture, this is Sable"

"Proceed, Sable," Pyotr Volontov said.

"You have ten targets on intercept course, velocity Mach 1.2. We interpret them as four Eurofighters at seven thousand meters and six Tornadoes at twelve thousand meters. They have you spotted, so you may as well go to active radar."

Volontov activated the radar set. The sweep lit up so many blips that it took him several seconds to sort them out.

He depressed the transmit button, "Sable, Condor. The Eurofighters appear to be a probe."

"Agreed, Condor."

"Vulture Flight, scatter," Volontov ordered. "Condor, Vulture, Tern, arm all."

Volontov raised the protective cover and armed his guns and missiles. He selected two AA-11 missiles from the inboard left and right pylons.

On the radar screen, he saw Rostoken's flight of six break up as preplanned. Three fighters spread out and began to climb toward the four Eurofighters. The other three hung back for a second, then went to afterburners and started to climb toward the Tornadoes.

The distance to initial contact was fifty kilometers. One of the Eurofighter pilots was nervous. He released two missiles, probably Sky Flashes, far too early. The small blips dashed across the screen and died an early and ineffective death.

Tern and Condor Flights maintained their steady advance at Mach 1.5.

At forty kilometers, just inside the Sky Flash effective range, the Eurofighters fired eight missiles at the lead MiGs. Volontov thought that the Germans were too obviously trying to draw an attack by all of his craft.

The three lead MiGs returned fire with six missiles, then took evasive action, their blips disappearing in a cloud of chaff and flares.

The Eurofighters came on.

The Tornadoes at 12,000 meters held course and altitude. They were thirty kilometers behind the Eurofighters.

Volontov looked up through the windscreen. A second later, a white flash in the distance. Then another.

Sable reported. "Vulture Four is hit. One Eurofighter hit."

Another transmission with lots of static. ". . . Vulture Five . . . turbo . . . jets . . . woun . . . down . . . eject."

"Sable to Mother Hen." The air controller read off the coordinates of the downed MiG to the rescue craft.

He would bail out over the ice, but Volontov was doubtful of the man's chances. Georgi Andrenko. Twenty-six years old, a joker in the barracks. Married for less than one year. Volontov's resolve built up inside him, along with a boiling hatred.

"Vulture One to Two and Three. Dive now!"

On the screen, the three Vultures who had begun to climb toward the Tornadoes suddenly altered course and dove toward the Eurofighters.

316

The three remaining Eurofighters, their formation already disrupted by evasive tactics, began to dive as all of Vulture Flight converged on them.

That committed the Tornadoes. All six began a quick descent. Volontov watched until they passed through 8,000 meters.

"Condor. Tern Flight go to Mach two. Condors Three, Four, Five, and Six, Engage."

Volontov dearly wanted to go with them. But he and Gurychenko would remain the cover for Tern Flight and go in for the cleanup. Tern Flight had to be protected.

He advanced his throttles and watched the HUD readout rise to Mach 2.

The screen began to fill with missile firings. All order disintegrated. Sable chanted instructions as the air controller tracked each airplane.

His earphones filled with a cacophony of Russian voices. "Vulture Seven, go left! . . . Got him! . . . Six, two missiles on you . . . hard, now, hard, now dive . . ."

Mac Zeigman flew alongside the drogue and watched as his lighted fueling probe entered the cone.

"Here she comes, Tiger Leader," the Pelican One fuel controller told him.

He trimmed his controls as the weight of the fuel was taken aboard the Tornado. He was not paying a lot of attention to the fueling process, a dangerous lack of concentration.

He was listening to the voices intoning the battle to the northeast. Longing to be there. Knowing he could do it better than anyone else.

"Major . . ." his WSO said.

He looked at the fuel readout. "All right, Pelican. That does it."

"Right, Tiger Leader. Next!"

Easing the throttle back, he pulled out of the drogue, then switched off the light and retracted the fuel probe.

He put the nose down and slid under the tanker, allowing the next plane to close in.

He checked his radar scan. Panther flight's air battle was out of range. Four of Panther flight's Tornadoes still circled north of him, over the center of the ice platforms.

Four of his own squadron's aircraft were to the west, circling, waiting, while the two Eurofighters were below the clouds, near the center of the offshore platforms. He had three other Tornadoes with him southeast of the field. Svalbard Island was invisible below the cloud cover. The stars were clear against a black sky. Two hours to moonrise.

He checked the chronometer. Soon, he would have to release the second and third elements of his own squadron for refueling, also.

He called the element in the north. "Panther Nine, Tiger Leader. What is your fuel state?"

"One-three-zero-zero kilograms, Tiger Leader."

"Wait ten minutes, then join Pelican Three."

"Affirmative, Tiger Leader."

Zeigman eased in left rudder and left stick and went into a shallow left turn as his wingman slipped in alongside him.

His eyes roamed the dark valleys and mountains of the clouds.

To the south.

The MakoSharks would come from there.

And very soon.

They had done it before.

The Soviets would not draw him off, again. He put the dog fight out of his mind and focused on the south.

Tiger Drei and *Tiger Vier*, finished with their refueling, joined up off his left wing, in a four-finger formation.

The HUD gave him the speed and altitude. Five hundred knots and 10,000 meters, conserving fuel.

Seeing nothing.

He scanned the radar screen. They were moving south

318

of the fields now. Schmidt's three battle groups showed up clearly, on stations ten kilometers south of the first platforms. The four airborne fuel tankers were spaced to the west, also at 10,000 meters.

Would the naval ships draw the MakoSharks when they came? Or would the stealth aircraft elude them after the nearly fatal encounter of several days before?

Would the MakoSharks attempt to torpedo the cables below the wells, as Weismann assumed they would?

They should have an airborne control craft up. He could not decipher the action being reported on Panther flight's radio frequency, but it sounded as if there were fewer voices.

He could not see the MakoSharks.

"Tigers Two, Three, Four, we will take a peek under the cloud cover."

Zeigman eased the stick forward, and the Tornado glided downward. The thick blanket of clouds rose toward him, then wrapped wispy trails around him.

Pearson, Avery, Overton, Arguento, and Amber held onto tethers and handgrips and watched the main console screen. The view of the Persian Gulf through the port was being totally ignored.

The KH-11's night-vision, real-time image was being computer-enhanced, but there was little to be seen. German planes circled above the clouds. Four of them had just disappeared as they went below the cloud cover.

To the northeast, the conflict with the Soviets had also disappeared as the aircraft descended below 15,000 feet.

The speakers were silent. The Delta flight was maintaining an unnecessary radio silence on Tac-1, as far as Pearson was concerned. She wanted to know what was going on. McKenna and Volontov were not communicating on Tac-2. Arguento had located the Soviet tactical channel on a radio, but the dialogues were disjointed, in Russian, and as Val Arguento said, "probably scrambled."

Arguento had also located the probable German air and naval frequencies, but they were also scrambled.

One of the secondary screens displayed the radar repeat from the AWACS airplane, Cottonseed. Numerous targets were shown on the scan, each identified with a code and an altitude. The codes clarified the blip as, for example, German and Panther — "G/Pntr."

Overton touched the intercom button for the radar room. "Radar, Command."

"Radar, sir."

"Let's go to the plot program."

"Coming up, General."

Arguento tapped the keyboard, cleared the screen, and set it up for the plot mode. A few seconds later, a stylized map of the area appeared, along with a few dozen white squares. The computer was accepting both radar and KH-11 data, merging them, and displaying the total input, without the barrier of cloud formations.

Arguento played with the keyboard, changing the wells to yellow, the Soviet planes to red, the German ships to blue, and the German planes to orange. The American and Soviet AWACS and search-and-rescue craft remained white. Finally, he overlaid the grid that the Delta flight was using on their maps to mark coordinates.

There were no MakoSharks.

The dogfight in the northeast appeared frantic, the blips so close together that they merged and the ident tags left the screen. One flight of eight, at low altitude and inserted by the computer from the order of battle, rather than from visual or radar contact, had pulled away from the melee and were headed west.

"There were ten Germans and twenty Soviet planes in that bunch," Overton said. "The eight must be the ground attack squadron, but I only count thirteen left."

"Nine planes down," Amber said.

Pearson wondered what this looked like on NORAD's

larger screen. Brackman and Thorpe were maintaining their silence, but they must be on the edge of their chairs.

She pulled herself close to the microphone. After a heated debate with McKenna and Overton, she had been designated the operations officer for this mission. McKenna had unexpectedly taken her side.

"Delta Blue, Alpha Two."

"Go ahead."

"Squawk me once, if you can."

Delta Blue's IFF signal appeared briefly on the screen.

"I read them sixty miles out," Arguento said.

"Thanks, Blue. That helps," from Cottonseed.

The MakoSharks were not yet using radar, so their interpretation of events came over the radio channel from Cottonseed or Alpha.

Pearson pressed the transmit button, "Delta Blue, the current situation is as follows: four Tornadoes at R-twelve, six-nine, seven thousand, heading one-nine-zero; two Eurofighters. . . ." She read off the rest of the coordinates, imagining Munoz, Abrams, and Williams feeding the data to their own computers.

"Delta Blue," she said, "if they can't refuel, it'll be a shorter night."

"Alpha Two," Munoz asked, "what were those tanker coordinates again?"

McKenna hated wearing gloves when he was flying, but he pulled his on and pressed the wrist fittings into the groove of the environmental suit.

He scanned the HUD. They were holding 60,000 feet and Mach 1.2.

Dimatta came on the air. "I get the two on the west, Snake Eyes. The jerks are bunched up."

"I've got the east-bounder," Conover said.

"Leaves us the closest one," McKenna said. "Tiger?"

"Arm 'em all, Snake Eyes, and let's go huntin'."

321

McKenna raised the flap, selected all pylons, and armed all missiles. The eight in the payload bay would remain in reserve because he didn't want to slow down enough to open the bay doors.

"All yours, Tiger."

"Gracias."

They were keeping Tac-1 open so that each of the Mako-Sharks knew what the others were doing. He heard Conover and Dimatta arming their weapons.

He couldn't see them, but knew that Dimatta was six miles to his right and Conover was six miles to his left.

"Let's do it, Deltas."

Easing back on the throttles, McKenna tapped the hand controller forward and the nose tilted down. Minus twenty-five degrees. On the bottom right of the HUD, fifteen small green lights displayed the live missiles on the pylons. They had lost one during the blackout period and had jettisoned it over the Norwegian Sea.

"Delta Blue, Condor," came in on Tac-2.

"Go."

"Tern Flight is making its turn on the wells."

The Fulcrums making the ground attack had to come from the north, rather than the east, in order to approach the platforms on the ice from the correct angle.

"Copy, Condor. What's your status?"

"We have shot down six German aircraft. I have lost three. We are chasing the remaining four hostiles."

McKenna noted the pronoun distinctions in Volontov's statement. Volontov was part of his wing when it came to optimistic reports. His losses were personal. McKenna felt the same way, and his esteem for Volontov took another giant step upward.

"Good show, Condor. We're jumping off, now."

Thirty miles from the coordinates provided by Pearson, McKenna said, "Deltas, go active."

The screen, which had been showing green fluffy clouds, jumped to the radar display in the fifty-mile range mode. The orange targeting flower appeared.

"Hot damn, *jefe!* There he is."

The orange circle, guided by Munoz's helmet, squirted to the upper right of the screen and found the tanker. Off to the right and left, McKenna saw the other targets.

LOCK-ON!

"Heat-seeker. Committed. And gone," Munoz said.

The Wasp whisked away, and one of the green missile lights on the HUD blinked out.

The Wasp II's speed was about 1,700 miles per hour, but it took longer to cover thirty miles.

Slightly over one minute.

The tanker, which was apparently outfitted with threat warning equipment, began to dive.

Too late.

There were two explosions, a blindingly white one as the Wasp went up one of the two port turbojet exhausts, then a bright yellow-orange detonation as hot splinters of the destroyed engine sliced into the gigantic fuel tanks and ignited the vapors of partially emptied tanks.

"Scratch one tanker," McKenna said.

"And two," from Conover.

Two heartbeats.

"Three . . . and now four," Nitro Fizz Williams reported. "Let's go get us some wells," McKenna said.

He dove into the clouds.

Mac Zeigman had immediately jammed his throttle into afterburner, pulled into a loop, then rolled upright to reverse his course as soon as his WSO announced the active radars.

"They are diving quickly, Major. All of the tankers have been destroyed."

"Give me a damned heading," Zeigman demanded.

"I am working . . . they are at seven hundred knots, three-five-oh degrees, our bearing zero-one-eight."

"Intercept?"

The HUD readout showed his speed up to Mach 1. The Tornado shivered. His three element members had reversed course, also, but their slower reactions left them almost a kilometer behind him.

"Intercept course is zero-zero-four."

He banked the craft slightly to the left.

"Tigers Two, Three, Four, join on me. Quickly now! Arm all weapons."

"Tiger Leader, Panther Nine."

"Tiger Leader," Zeigman acknowledged.

"We have eight hostiles on the look-down radar at one thousand meters altitude. They are spreading out and initiating attacks on the wells."

"Stop them."

"But there are two hostiles approaching from ten thousand meters, also. And our fuel state is eight-five-zero kilograms. We must refuel."

"There is no more fuel, Panther Nine. You might as well attack. Now!"

Albert Weismann and Maximillian Oberlin were in the computer center at Peenemünde, watching over the shoulders of the experts brought down from Tempelhof as they verified the computer programs.

"Here it is!" a *hauptmann* shouted.

"What?" Weismann demanded.

"A simple loop instruction inserted into the guidance program. The rocket would have gone mad."

"Can you correct it?"

"Easily, Herr Colonel."

His fingers flew over the keyboard, and the cursor on the screen exchanged new letters for old in the incomprehensible line of instructions.

"There. It is done."

"Excellent, Captain. Now, if you would please load it into the rocket computers."

He and Oberlin exchanged smiles. Oberlin had been positively cheerful since returning from his helicopter flight. He had told Weismann, "The old man did not think he could walk on air. He cried. Unfortunately, I think he had a heart attack as soon as he went out the door. I had wanted him to think about it all the way down."

"Yes. Very unfortunate," Weismann had agreed. "One day quite soon, however, you and I will see many more walking on air."

They were almost to the doorway of the computer center when an *unteroffizier* slid to a stop outside the glass door. He pushed it open.

"Colonel Weismann! There is an emergency call for you."

Weismann walked over to a computer console, picked up the phone, and punched the blinking button.

"Weismann."

It was the operations officer at New Amsterdam. "Herr Colonel, there is pandemonium at the wells!"

"Let us not have it here. What is happening?"

"We are being attacked!"

"We?"

"The wells, Herr Colonel. Twenty Soviet aircraft. The American stealth planes also. We have lost nine fighters and four tanker aircraft."

Weismann shook his head. The tankers. Unarmed aircraft. The Americans and Soviets were diabolical.

"What is Schmidt doing?" he demanded.

"I do not know. The attackers are just now reaching the oil field."

Zeigman's defenses had not held up. Still, there were fifteen fighters left, apparently.

Though probably not enough.

"Keep me posted, Major." He slapped the telephone down.

"It is bad, Albert?"

"Not good at all, Max," he said, then turned to the noncommissioned officer. "Corporal, you go find that banker's son. We are launching immediately."

As soon as the Tornadoes dove on the Tern Flight MiGs, Volontov advanced his throttles to military power and put his nose down.

He reset the radar range to thirty kilometers, to make the blips more distinct.

Below, the ice gave off a dim luminescence. Ahead, the platforms had extinguished their red warning lights.

The well the Americans had labeled number seventeen was twenty kilometers away. The Tern Flight was nine kilometers away, pulling well apart from each other as they lined up on their assigned targets.

Two more kilometers and they could begin targeting with the lasers, locking a laser dot onto a dome in precisely the right spot, high and away from the wellhead. The computer would hold the dot in place, and the missiles would home on it. The objectives, as McKenna had related them, was to demonstrate that Soviet and American fighters did not fear attacking the wells, to disrupt the operations, and to create panic and a loss of morale among the platform personnel. It would make the landings by American, British, and Soviet troops go very smoothly.

The four Tornadoes seemed hesitant, unable to choose among so many targets.

"Condor Two, you will shoot down the westernmost airplanes."

"Of course, Condor One."

It was too easy. His radar could track up to eight aircraft at once.

Volontov used the miniature stick guiding the target flower on the screen to encircle the lead aircraft, clicked the button to lock on to it, then circled

326

the second Tornado and locked on to that one also.

The beep in his headphones of the missile heads confirmed that the missiles had secured their targets, the Tornadoes' active radars, and would not let go.

He depressed the commit button on the stick.

The computer thought about for a halfsecond, decided the time was right, and launched two AA-11 missiles.

They dove into the night, trailing hot white fire.

Munoz extended the range of the radar as they came out of the clouds.

"We've got four comin' from the southwest, *jefe.* Another four convergin' from the west. Hey, Do-Wop! You see 'em over there?"

"Got them, Tiger."

Nitro Fizz Williams said, "There's three more headed this way from the northeast, but I see MiGs hot on their tails. I don't think they're going to make it . . . nope. Boom! One down."

McKenna scanned the screen, evaluating positions.

"We can beat the interception before the first pass, Deltas. Go over to rockets for two seconds on my mark. That'll boost us out of the interception course, but we'll have to use speed brakes before we reach the ships."

"Roger that, Snake Eyes," Dimatta said.

"Wilco, since I'm playing navy," Conover acknowledged.

"Mark !"

Delta Blue accelerated from 700 knots to Mach 1.5 in six seconds.

McKenna shut down the rocket motors and checked the radar screen. The Germans had been left far behind.

"Cottonseed to Delta Blue."

"Come on."

"You've got the lead time. Info item: ASW choppers from the task forces are dropping ashcans on submarines. Watch out for those choppers on your way back."

"Got it, Cottonseed."

McKenna focused his attention on his battle group of ships, the one located on the south-center of the platforms. They were coming up rapidly.

Each of the MakoSharks was taking on one battle group before their attacks on the wells.

Mckenna dumped his speed brakes, fighting to get down to 700 knots, to improve the accuracy.

"Range forty miles, Snake Eyes. I want the payload bay, save our wing-mounted stuff."

As the speed came down, McKenna opened the payload bay doors, extended the first rack of missiles, and armed all four of them.

"There you go, Tiger."

"Good. It's all ASM."

Twenty miles.

The three ships ahead of him were already firing flares. Either the Tornadoes behind him had raised the alarm or the ships were tracking the radar.

The orange circle darted about the screen under Munoz's control, picking out each of the ships and locking missile heads onto the targets.

"I'm usin' two Wasps off the outboard pylons also, *amigo*."

The Wasps weren't large enough to cause extreme damage to anything as big as a destroyer or cruiser unless the depleted uranium, armor-piercing warhead penetrated the steel plates at water level. McKenna was hoping to cause enough damage on deck, or maybe fires, to create some panic.

"Any time, Tiger."

Munoz launched the six missiles just as the ship in the center, the cruiser, launched four SAMs at them.

"Shut her down, Tiger."

The radar went passive, disappearing from the ship's tracking system.

He put the nose down and headed for the water, leveling off at a thousand feet. He retracted the forward missile rack and lowered the aft rack, arming the missiles.

"We got two strikes, Snake Eyes," Dimatta called. "Lookin' good."

Delta Green was a few miles closer to her targets.

"Goddamn!" Munoz said, watching the night-vision screen. "Love those Wasps. Right on track, right on target."

Ten miles.

Flares erupting everywhere.

On the screen, the greenish-white trails of all six Wasps winked out almost simultaneously, followed by six green eruptions.

"Six hits!" Munoz said.

Glancing through the windscreen, McKenna saw the blossoms dying out as flames began to spread.

The four SAMs shot by, three thousand feet above them.

"Give them a couple more, Tiger."

"Roger, codger."

Two more Wasps leaped from their rails on the aft bay rack and began to home on the cruiser.

The frequency of flare firing diminished.

Five miles.

The *Hamburg* was clearly defined in the light of her own flares. McKenna saw both missiles slam into the bridge and detonate.

Blue-yellow-green-red-orange flame everywhere.

The antiaircraft guns opened up, but the concentration of fire was erratic and almost purposeless.

McKenna nudged the hand controller and banked to the left, passing the ships in a three-mile arc. As he rolled upright, he looked to his left. All three ships had fires of some degree raging.

The firing from the ships died away.

"Come right three degrees," Munoz ordered.

"Right three. How about you, Cancha?"

"We're through the heavy stuff, Snake Eyes. Lining up on number six."

"Josie says we got them licked," Williams added.

"Con Man?"

"Fuckers got my right aileron."

"You canceling?"

"Hell, no. We're flying this mother."

"You sure it's all right?"

"Damned sure. Bastards! That's twice now."

The dome of well number nine was completely dark, the platform invisible against the darkness of the sea.

Munoz went over to infrared tracking on the screen, and the heat emitted by the dome appeared as a dim red ball on the screen.

They couldn't get a distance on the infrared, but they had a direction.

"We want the right side on this one, Snake Eyes."

"Got it, Tiger."

McKenna hoped that Pearson's drawings of the dome interiors were accurate. He wanted to blow a few big holes in the dome on the side away from the wellhead and let the weather in. Create chaos and discomfort among the platform personnel. Give the task forces time to move in with their *Spetznaz* and Rapid Deployment Force troops and secure the wells.

"One in the dome and one on the pad," McKenna said.

"Roger."

The dim red ball got larger and larger.

"Launching," Munoz said.

The missiles sailed away, guided by Munoz's helmet.

The platform defenses never opened up.

They never saw anything to fire at.

There were two detonations, and then Delta Blue passed over the platform.

In the rearview screen, McKenna saw bright lights, interior lights shining through a jagged-edged hole in the night.

"Number five's next, then number one," Munoz said.

"Give me a heading."

"Three-four-five."

"Coming around."

"Hey, *compadre?*"

"Yeah."

"I'd better do a quick check on those four Tornadoes behind us."

"I'm watching them, Delta Blue," Cottonseed said. "They're circling around now, wondering where the hell you've gone. Ah! Now they have an idea. I suspect they see light on platform number nine. And six. And ten. And three. We've got five hits on the ice, so far. Some of those Fulcrums are turning for another pass."

"How about the four hostiles chasing Delta Yellow?"

"Just now turning north. If I knew where Yellow was, I'd give him a distance."

Conover said, "Check my IFF."

"Okay, babe, got you. Hell, they're twenty miles behind you, headed in the wrong direction. The MiGs over east splashed a couple more. Both Eurofighters."

Platform number five was holed without return fire, but they ran into an active defense of well number one. The defensive batteries couldn't see them, however, and AA fire and SAM launches were being directed blindly, hoping to hit something.

Munoz put three missiles into number one, one through the dome, and two into the SAM radar trailers.

"Next target eleven," Munoz said.

"Con Man?" McKenna asked.

"Ten, twelve, fifteen down. Two and seven coming up."

"Cancha?"

"Six, three, and four are ventilated."

There were fires on several of the platforms. The seascape was becoming defined with bonfires low on the water.

"I'm out of ASMs, Snake Eyes. Got six air-to-airs, though."

"Use them up," McKenna said.

They put two of them into platform eleven, then McKenna went into a hard right turn and headed south again. Because of its location between nine and six, platform number thirteen had been skipped on the first pass.

It was time to correct the omission.

Three minutes later, Munoz said, "I need radar to pinpoint it, Snake Eyes."

"Go radar."

A moment after the radar image hit the screen, Munoz yelled, "Jesus Christ!"

McKenna's eyes jerked down to the screen.

Tornado diving, closing fast.

Wha-wha-wha!

The threat receiver sounded overly loud to him.

Check the screen.

Six missiles fired.

"Son of a bitch is right on our ass," Munoz said.

McKenna rolled right, then left, shoving the throttles in. He was too low for much maneuvering.

"Hard left, Snake Eyes."

Whip the hand controller over.

"Rockets! Now, now, now!"

McKenna slapped the throttles.

But not before two Sky Flash missiles slammed into the starboard engine nacelle. The right wing erupted in a ball of flame.

Eighteen

"Got that son of a bitch!" Mac Zeigman exuded.

"I did it! I did it!" his backseater wailed.

Zeigman had the stick full back, pulling out of the steep dive. His face sagged under the oxygen mask with the additional gravity generated by the hard maneuver. As the Tornado came level, then vertical, he straightened the stick and worked in some aileron.

Straight up on afterburners, rolling.

Celebrating.

Blood pounding in his ears.

Threat receiver screaming.

Where?

And the tail came off.

The whole aft end of the Tornado detonated and shredded. The rudders went slushy under his feet.

Zeigman's eyes went to the rearview mirror and saw the WSOs face.

Could not see it.

The man's visor was filled with blood. His head had exploded.

And the nose came down, the aircraft tumbling, still going upward.

Reaching the apex, slowing, then picking up speed again as it started down toward the cold, dark sea.

Still tumbling wildly.

Automatically, frantically, he worked the rudders, trying to stop the tumbling.

That did not work.

Reached between his legs and grabbed the red ejection handle.

That did not work, either.

Watched the cold, dark sea.

After downing the two Tornadoes over the ice, Volontov had continued south, climbing back to 2,000 meters, watching the radar screen, asking Sable to point out hostiles. Lieutenant Gurychenko stayed right with him, some degree of excitement in his voice after having made his own first two kills.

Sable had pointed out the four Tornadoes directly to the south, and Volontov had been scanning the skies, aware of the small fires burning on a dozen platforms, trying for a visual contact. On the radar screen, they were sixteen kilometers away.

He had seen the yellow-orange ball of the explosion low against the sea, appearing where no aircraft was to be seen by the eye or by his radar. As soon as it hit the sea, there was a second, terrific detonation. The self-destruct package, protecting vital secrets.

He knew it was a MakoShark, and he wondered who the pilot was.

The blip on his screen was not moving in any linear direction, but the altitude readout showed him to be climbing rapidly. Volontov locked on, committed, and released two AS-11s.

The Tornado blew up nine kilometers in front of him, and he banked left, looking for more.

"I have another, Condor One," Gurychenko reported.

The radar was becoming clearer, with fewer blips on the screen.

The two low-flying Eurofighters were almost out of radar range, headed south.

Two more Tornadoes that had been part of this flight were streaking southward, running from the MiGs.

He continued his circle, coming back toward where the MakoShark had exploded. He looked for parachutes, but did not see them. If they had ejected successfully at that low an altitude, they would already be in the water.

East and west, the wells burned. Several ships were on fire.

"Condor One, Condor Two. The fuel state."

Pyortr Volontov refocused his eyes on his own HUD. A blinking amber light told him he was several minutes away from critically low fuel. Too frequent use of the afterburners at low altitudes.

He came out of his turn headed eastward, beginning a slow climb.

"Sable, Condor One."

"Proceed, Condor One."

"Send a tanker our way, please. Fuel state is close to critical."

"He is on the way, Condor."

"Status report?" Volontov asked.

"Tern Flight has lost one aircraft to a SAM from one of the platforms. Vulture Flight has three down—one pilot recovered from the ice, and Condor Flight is missing two. Germans shot down, one-six interceptors, four tankers."

"Thank you, Sable." Volontov switched to his second tactical frequency. "Delta Blue, Condor One."

"Condor One, this is Delta Yellow. I can't raise Blue."

"I believe he is down north of platform one-three by several kilometers. I am, however, very low on fuel."

"I'm on my way, Condor. Thanks."

Gurychenko pulled in on his wing as they climbed through 7,000 meters.

Volontov felt depleted, completely let down. He thought about the numbing, unexplainable letters he would have to write. He wondered if Colonel McKenna had a wife to whom he should write. He was happy that no one would write a letter to Martina.

And he thought that perhaps their engagement had lasted long enough.

Wilbur Conover rolled right, turning onto the heading Abrams gave him. It took a while. He figured he had about 30 percent control on the lateral axis. He wouldn't be doing any victory rolls.

He wouldn't be using rockets, either, and he took the rocket motors off standby.

"Squawk me, please, Yellow and Green," Cottonseed said.

He hit the IFF for one second.

"Thank you. Yellow, you're closest."

"Roger, Cottonseed. I've got the hammer down. I heard the mayday."

McKenna had said, "Delta Blue, mayday. Ejecting." Calmly. Not a tremor in his voice.

"We do have an ELB signal," Cottonseed said. "Robin Hood Two is closest and reports ETA in six minutes. Robin Hood Three is trying to locate a Soviet pilot on the ice."

"Copy that, Cottonseed. Hostile aircraft status?"

"Two Tornadoes and two Eurofighters southbound. Mildenhall reports tankers leaving New Amsterdam. You have four Tornadoes on your right, Yellow. They're circling."

"Damn," Abrams said. "I've still got seven air-to-air."

"We're not in shape for much horseplay, Do-Wop."

"Yeah, I know. Okay! I've got the Emergency Locator Beacon. Come right . . . hold it."

"Can you reach him on voice yet?"

"Not yet, Con Man. Those damned radios only have a mile of range. Another minute or two."

Conover asked on the open channel, "Robin Hood Two, where are you?"

"Delta Yellow, we're on the two-six-five radial of the ELB. Four minutes."

Conover hoped the damned environmental suit heaters worked. Whenever he tried the ailerons, he hoped even more that the heaters worked.

The fires below were dying away, both on the platforms and the ships. He couldn't tell, but thought that none of the wells had blown out. He wondered what condition the platform workers would be in by the time the task forces reached them. He figured that the ships were about twelve or thirteen hours away.

"Snake Eyes, you read me?" Abrams called on the emergency channel.

"Got you, Do-Wop. Fortunately, I can't see you."

"Tiger?"

"I'm here, damn it! And it's gettin' cold. You wanna tell someone to put a foot in it?"

"ETA in three. Either of you injured?"

"Pride," McKenna said.

"I'm gonna have to get out of this suit and see if anything important's frostbit," Munoz said.

"Hang loose," Abrams said.

"Ain't nothin' hangin' loose, brother. All scrunched up tight."

Adm. Gerhard Schmidt was commanding the *Hamburg* from the shambles of the CIC. The bridge of the cruiser was gone, along with *Kapitän* Rolf Froelich, the second mate, and the helmsman.

All of the windows had been blown out of his flag plot, one deck below the bridge.

The *leutnant* who did his plotting for him was sitting at a console, manning a microphone and taking damage reports. His head was wrapped with a bloody white T-shirt.

"Herr Admiral, the flooding has been contained in Compartment Four."

"Good, Lieutenant. We'll keep her afloat yet. The steerage party?"

"They are in the compartment. Ten minutes, they say."

The magnificent cruiser was going to have to be steered by hand from the rudder compartment. The work party was rigging block and tackle.

"What of the other ships?" Schmidt asked.

"The destroyer *Erlich* is listing badly. The captain says it may have to be abandoned. The *Mannheim* is standing by and beginning to take crewmen off the destroyer. All others report fires under control. The northern battle groups are undamaged."

And one day, Schmidt promised himself, he would find out why. He suspected they had not fired one gun or one missile battery, even against the radar-visible MiG fighters.

"Tell them they are to begin evacuating the platforms. As soon as they have collected survivors, they are to return to Bremerhaven."

"Very well, Admiral. Captain Blofeld, sir."

Schmidt crossed to the table and took the headset from the *leutnant*.

"Blofeld?"

"Yes, Admiral. I am sub-surface, with my antenna raised. We escaped a heavy barrage of depth charges. The *Bohemian*, is standing by, also, five kilometers from the Soviet task force, though she is slightly damaged. I have the Americans and British in sight."

"Secure all weapons, Captain, submerge, and wait

338

for the task forces to pass over. Then return to port."

"Admiral?" Blofeld's voice contained his amazement.

"As you were ordered," Schmidt said.

He knew when to give up the field. There was always, always another day.

Delta Yellow was in a wide circle above them. Conover had turned on his running lights to reassure them, and it *was* reassuring.

When a wave raised him high enough, McKenna could see a few fires to the north. He could not see any stars. The white and orange parachute floated on the surface forty feet away. The first thing he had done when his feet hit the water was to get rid of the parachute, unhooking the shrouds from the harness before his hands became too stiff. He didn't want to be entangled in it.

He couldn't see Munoz.

The two of them figured they had landed a quarter-mile apart, a fair distance considering they had ejected at about a thousand feet of altitude, but they weren't going to waste energy swimming toward each other.

The Mae West kept him floating on his back.

The heater seemed to be working.

Or at least struggling.

McKenna sensed that his body temperature was steadily going down. His joints seemed to move slowly. The gloves were tight, not allowing much of the suit's heated air into them, and his hands were numb.

The flesh of his face felt numb, also, though he couldn't touch it. The helmet visor was splattered with salt water, giving him a wavery vision of his immediate vicinity.

Nothing worth looking at, anyway.

Except Delta Yellow's lights.

They had been in the water twelve minutes.

"Con Man?"

"Yeah, Snake Eyes?"

"How's that aileron?"

"What aileron?"

"Don't give me any shit."

"I've got about thirty percent, Snake Eyes."

"Fuel status?"

"Low, but okay."

"I want you to move out for Hot Country."

"Cancha will be here in a couple minutes, then I'm gone."

"Do-Wop?" Munoz asked.

"Hey, Tiger?"

"What're you listenin' to?"

They got to hear half of Jimmy Rodgers' "Honeycomb," before another voice broke in.

"Delta Blue? Robin Hood on the line."

"Go, Robin."

"I want a balloon right away."

"You've got one up," McKenna said.

"Just one?"

"At the moment."

"Hey, shit!" Munoz said.

McKenna had not told Munoz that he had not deployed his own balloon yet. He had pulled it out of his leg pouch, but held it deflated against his chest.

"You first, *amigo*," McKenna said. "Put a light on it."

"*Jefe* . . ."

"Now, damn it!"

McKenna saw the halogen flashlight beam that Munoz aimed up at the balloon. The bright orange balloon was off to his right and stood out against the dark sky. He couldn't see the steel cable that descended from it to connect with Munoz's parachute harness.

The running lights of the C-130 appeared low on the

340

water, followed shortly by the roar of its four turbo-props. It was flying as slow as it could and still remain airborne.

Coming on.

Closer.

It passed overhead, the trailing loop snagged the balloon and cable, and Munoz was gone.

In almost a flash.

On the radio, Munoz yelled, "Goddamn!"

And dropped his flashlight.

McKenna lifted the balloon away from his chest with his left hand and found the plastic handle with his right. He couldn't bend his fingers very well, but he got the handle between his forefinger and third finger and jerked.

The helium cartridge popped and the balloon began to fill.

He let it go and it rose slowly, then more rapidly, trailing the wire cable behind it. When it reached the fifty-foot length of the cable, it jerked him slightly, held him a bit more upright in the water.

Delta Yellow was headed south, and her running lights went out.

"Bye-bye, Snake Eyes."

"Take care, Con Man."

"Cancha get the big guy outta the water, Robin Hood?" Dimatta said.

"Hey!" Robin Hood said, "Next pass. We only do one at a time, but we never miss."

The Hercules had flown several miles to the east while they winched Munoz aboard. Now, McKenna saw it make a tight circle and come back toward him.

He unclipped his flashlight from the harness and fumbled with the slide switch. It finally came on, nearly blinding him. Gripping it tightly, he aimed it up toward the balloon.

341

Nice orange orb.

Waiting.

Building wail of the turboprops.

Stiffen the back, tense the muscles.

Involuntarily.

He didn't actually see the loop catch his cable.

WHAM!

He was out of the water, almost horizontal in the air, seawater spraying off of him.

He still had the flashlight, surprised at that.

The Hercules began to climb.

He felt the cable vibrating as the winch started.

McKenna heard the cannon long before he heard the turbojet engines.

A shadow passed between him and the clouds.

He was on his back, looking up, when he saw the silhouette.

Tornado.

The son of a bitch was going to shoot down a rescue aircraft.

The shadow disappeared.

The winch picked up speed, drawing him in faster.

Pushing his head back until the helmet collar would not allow further movement, he looked back and up. The cargo bay of the C-130 appeared invitingly warm, red-lit, gaping. A crewman in a flight suit and parka, trailing a safety line, stood out on the lowered cargo ramp, guiding the cables.

The balloon passed by the man, and the winching stopped while the balloon was detached.

Fifty feet to go.

And here came the Tornado again.

McKenna felt numb and helpless. If he'd had a gun, he'd have emptied it at the bastard. He saw the winking of its cannons when it was still a mile away.

Then the orange blossom as it exploded.

Then the blinking wing lights of Delta Green as it crossed the Tornado's path, jinking high to avoid the debris.

He was floating on the air current, and the turbulence increased as he was reeled into the C-130's prop wash.

He felt his shoulder being grabbed, fingers reaching in to grip his harness.

And then he was aboard, the crewman grinning at him. Still hanging from the cable that passed through an overhead pulley, his feet couldn't quite reach the ramp.

The winch backed off, his feet touched down. His toes weren't feeling anything.

The seawater was still dripping from his environmental suit.

The crewman helped him walk back on the ramp and into the cargo bay. McKenna popped his visor loose, breathed the real air, and absorbed the din of the engines.

Both felt good to him. He stripped off his gloves and detached his helmet.

Worked his fingers. They began to sting as feeling came back.

Munoz was sitting in one of the lowered hammock seats on the right side of the bay, drinking from a big Styrofoam cup of coffee.

A medic slapped a hot cup into his hands, and McKenna nodded his thanks.

"Hey, *compadre*," Munoz yelled above the engines. He was grinning insanely.

McKenna leaned over him and spoke loudly into his ear. "You owe the USAF for a flashlight. But we'll collect it from your pay."

"Probably costs the same as a MakoShark," Tony the Tiger said.

McKenna grinned back at him, turned around, and gave a thumbs-up to the crewmen and medical staff who were standing and lounging around the huge interior.

Against the forward bulkhead, he saw where some of the transport's crew had stacked parachutes and M-16 assault rifles.

Nineteen

"Cottonseed, Robin Hood Three."

Go ahead, Three."

"We just lifted off the ice. Got us a Soviet pilot with a nasty chest wound."

"Three, come on back to Daneborg."

"Roger that, Cottonseed. Robin Hood Three out."

Silence.

Then: "Cottonseed, Robin Hood Two."

"I read you, Two."

"Delta Blue One and Two are aboard and whole. They're walking around, and Two wants a taco."

"Copy, Two. Bring it home."

"Well, hang on for a minute, Cottonseed. Delta Blue One's got some kind of idea."

Pearson was so relieved, her hands trembled. She gripped her left hand in her right to hide it. Overton was grinning broadly, perhaps masking his own concern. Milt Avery did a somersault in the middle of the compartment, something she didn't often see from a full colonel.

Val Arguento and Donna Amber gave each other a high five, the contact of their palms sending each of them in opposite directions across the Command Center.

The telephone buzzed, and when she lifted it from the console, Pearson heard only a squeal. Amber pushed off a bulkhead, sailing into the Radio Shack to check on the satellite relays.

345

When the relay was reestablished, she heard, "Is Colonel Pearson around there somewhere?"

"This is Colonel Pearson."

"Hey, honey. Walt MacDonald in NSA's German section."

"Hello, Walt. Is something the matter?"

"Well, I don't know. My monitoring computer yelped on one of your LPs, and I just got through checking the tape."

"Which one?"

"Peenemünde. Sounds to me like railroad cars moving on steel rails. Hell of a racket. Big diesel engines moving stuff around."

"How long ago?"

"According to the tape it started about half an hour ago, and they're still clanking around."

"Thanks, Walt. I'll get back to you."

Pearson replaced the phone in its holder, and pulled herself up to the microphone. Overton and Avery were staring at her.

"Semaphore, Alpha Two. Are you still monitoring?"

"This is Semaphore," General Brackman said.

"The LP at Peenemünde suggests heavy equipment moving. We need to check on it, and fast."

A long pause. Brackman said, "Delta Yellow is close to that route."

"Delta Yellow to Semaphore," Conover said, "I'm copying you."

"What's your condition, Yellow?" the general asked.

"Subpar, but I can make six-five-oh knots. I've got to stay subsonic."

"How far are you from Peenemünde?"

"Hold one. Do-Wop?"

"I make it one-zero-five-zero miles," Abrams said.

"About an hour and a half, if I squeeze a couple more knots out of her," Conover said.

346

"We'll live with two hours, if we have to," Brackman told him. "Don't push it. But see what you can see."

"Roger that, Semaphore. Delta Yellow out."

Pearson had thought that the battle was over, but now she wondered if it wasn't just beginning.

After splashing the Tornado that attacked the Hercules, Dimatta had rolled out to the west, looking for the last three in that flight.

He felt good about that one, better than he had felt after downing the first two over the ice. This one had been a son of a bitch.

Where were the others?

Abrams had them on radar.

"Making like jackrabbits, Cancha. Headed southwest. Maybe they're going to defect to England."

"What speed are they making, Do-Wop?"

"Slow. Five-zero-zero knots at twelve thousand feet. Bet they're low on fuel, conserving."

Dimatta checked his own fuel load. Soon, he would have to turn for Jack Andrews, or he'd be boosting on rockets and coasting.

"I just lost one of them from the screen, Cancha. Probably flamed out. You want to chase the other two?"

"I'm about flamed out, myself, Do-Wop. Let the sea have them, if they don't make it."

Scanning his HUD, he noted the lack of green lights in the bottom right corner. "Hell, Do-Wop, we couldn't do anything about them, anyway."

"Damn. I'm checking. Nope, no missile control, Cancha. We must have taken debris somewhere. Maybe the electronics bay."

"Anything else showing bad?"

"No, that's it. But we sure want a full checkup on the ground before we go home."

Dimatta circled back toward the Hercules, and was surprised to find it moving northward.

"Where's that sucker going?" he asked Abrams.

Before the WSO could respond, Tac-1 brought up McKenna's voice. "Cancha, you there?"

"Damn near right beside you, Snake Eyes. What's up?"

"How's your fuel?"

"Got plenty of pellets. Maybe an hour of JP-7."

"Ride herd on platform number one for a little while, will you? We're going to make a visit."

"Roger," Dimatta said, wondering what the hell was going on.

Abrams spoke up on the intercom, "What the hell's going on?"

Semaphore asked the same question. "Delta Blue, what the hell's going on?"

McKenna laid the headset aside without responding and waddled back to the ramp. Munoz was waiting for him, standing next to the cargomaster.

"Never, ever, ever thought I'd be a Green Beret, *amigo.*"

"Me, either, Tony."

They were both still in their environmental suits, but had discarded the helmets and gloves. The parachute harness was snug, and they had located webbing belts on which to hang their extra magazines, flashlights, K-Bar combat knives, and M-16s. They each had two fragmentation grenades.

The cargomaster patted them roughly on the shoulders, then pointed to the port bulkhead, where a red light had changed to amber.

McKenna moved carefully out to the edge of the ramp and crouched. The wind screamed around him.

348

The light changed to green.

He stepped off, Munoz right beside him.

He thought Munoz had yelled something, maybe, "Geronimo!" but couldn't tell in the combined noise of the engines and the prop wash.

He tumbled once, then pulled the rip cord.

They were jumping from 1,500 feet, and there wasn't much margin for error. After an enforced jump from a thousand feet, though, it seemed as if he had plenty of time.

The parachute casing released with a loud pop, and the drogue chute streamed the fabric out above him. When the canopy blossomed, the sudden deceleration jerked him upright, then swung him from side to side.

"Hey, Kev! Twice in one night. We'll have to start a club."

Munoz was to his left, slightly above him.

"You start the club, Tony," he yelled back. "I'll be the treasurer."

The sea was dark around them, more terrifying now that he had been in it once tonight. His toes ached, but that was a good sign. To the northeast, he saw a fire which was probably on number eleven. The lights of some ship were closing in on it.

Slightly below and ahead of him was the dome and pad of platform number one.

There was a helicopter on the pad, but no one near it. The AA and SAM batteries appeared deserted.

Almost the whole top of the dome on the near side was gone, and the hole was defined by the interior lights shining through it.

He tugged on the left shroud, spilling air, and changing his direction.

He wouldn't mind falling short, landing on the pad, but he didn't want to overshoot and go in the water again.

349

Cold wind hitting him on the left. His face felt red from the cold.

Still too high and too far right. The wind was drifting him. He pulled on the shrouds again.

Unclipped the M-16 from its D-ring on the web belt. Looked up.

Munoz was dumping air. They were closing toward each other.

The canopies bumped.

Dome coming up fast.

One more tug.

The edges of the hole were jagged, sharp aluminum shards pointing at him.

Over the hole, and Munoz's canopy was fighting his own for space.

The light was coming from the well section and from two bulbs he could see in the top floor of what must be a residential area. There were a couple beds showing through the wreckage where the dome had collapsed on the inner ceiling, also tearing large holes in the ceiling.

A body in one of the beds, the back of its head dull brown-bloody red.

The canopies bumped again as the two of them dropped through the hole.

It was a lot farther from the dome roof to the interior ceiling than he had expected.

He hit hard on ceiling panels, and his legs went right through the soft gypsum board. His hips stopped him, and he hit the quick release buckle on the harness with the palm of his hand as the canopy collapsed around him.

Setting the M-16 aside, McKenna leaned back on his right hand and tried to get his legs free. The gypsum buckled under his hand, but he got his right leg free, rolled over on to a joist, and pulled his left leg out of the hole.

Scrambling, he rose and stepped out of the harness, bent to retrieve the rifle. Peering down through the hole, he didn't see anyone moving around.

Munoz was already free of his chute and waiting for him, standing on the juncture of two walls.

The noise was tremendous. He hadn't expected that much noise.

Munoz gestured down into the well section of the dome with the muzzle of his rifle.

McKenna, stepping on ceiling joists and avoiding large chunks of dome panels, crossed to his WSO and looked down. They were about a hundred feet above the floor. There weren't as many floors inside the dome as Pearson had expected. Down on the deck were three gigantic turbine generators, as well as enough pipe to plumb several houses. Steam vapor, smelling highly sulphurous, gorged out of the section.

The attack hadn't shut down the generators.

"What now, *jefe?*" Munoz yelled.

"Down."

He crossed to a large hole. Joists were broken here, and large pieces of aluminum had crashed through the ceiling, burying the room. Massive hunks of styrofoam were everywhere, like boulders strewn on a hillside. The room below was dark, though light spilled into it from somewhere else.

They slid down the face of the debris and found themselves standing in water. The ceiling was at least ten feet above. Big, spacious rooms to detract from the claustrophobia of the dome interior.

McKenna saw an open door into a lighted hallway and sidled toward it while slipping the safety on the M-16. He put his back to the wall, then peered around the doorway.

No one there.

The hallway was awash in water, also, and he saw the

reason for it twenty feet away. One of the rooms had caught fire after the missile attack. Blackened walls in the hallwày and the charred remains of mattresses. A limp firehose snaked down the corridor.

The racket of the generators was noticeably decreased. At the end of the hallway was a steel door with a sign on it. Written in German, the message was one that he couldn't interpret much beyond the one word of *VERBOTEN*.

Also on the door was a large "5."

Well, that helped a little.

General Felix Eisenach was totally humiliated.

The *VORMUND PROJEKT* was in ruins.

Almost.

The Control Center was in pandemonium. People dashing about aimlessly, telephones ringing, alarms buzzing. Some of the soldiers had been issued weapons. Frightened console operators remained at their posts only by the sheer intimidation of the giant Diederman.

Oberst Diederman strode back and forth along the rows of consoles, watching the ever-changing flow of information coming in. Stunned almost beyond speech, Eisenach sagged against the first console, where he had watched the eradication of Germany's premier aircraft wing.

Diederman walked past him. "No blowouts. A leak on Platform Fifteen. We continue to generate power."

Precision. The attackers had precision. Eisenach wished he controlled such precision.

Two consoles down, an operator held up his hand. Diederman whirled toward him. "Sergeant?"

"Platform Eight, Herr Colonel. A ship approaches, saying Admiral Schmidt has ordered evacuation."

"Are they in danger?" Diederman asked.

The *feldwebel* spoke into his microphone, listened, reported: "There is no danger, Herr Colonel. The fires are out, there is damage to the dome above the engineering spaces. They have five wounded and the interior temperatures are dropping."

"They are to remain at their duties," Diederman ordered. "We must not shut down production."

Diederman went to another console and attempted to reach Schmidt. After a few moments, he did, and Eisenach listened with detachment to the argument.

The general had almost lost track of events. Three domes only were undamaged. The Soviets and American ships approached steadily.

Spinning toward the *leutnant* still standing by him, Eisenach said, "Get me Peenemünde."

"At once, Herr General."

It took four minutes to run down Weismann.

"Yes, General Eisenach."

"Your squadrons are destroyed."

"I know this. I have been hearing from New Amsterdam." Weismann's voice carried dispair.

"The Ghost. Launch it now."

"Soon," Weismann said. "The tower shroud has been moved back, and it is erected on the pad. The fueling is under way."

"Immediately!"

"It will go nowhere without fuel and computer programs, General."

"Speed it up!"

"The ballistics people have computed the space station orbit and the interception path. It will be soon."

"Speed it up, I said!"

"As you wish, Herr General."

Weismann hung up on him.

"Herr General," the *leutnant* said, "Marshal Hoch wishes to speak to you."

"Say that I will get back to him. Can you not tell that I am busy?"

Shrugging, the *leutnant* spoke into his phone.

Eisenach had not moved from the spot where he had been standing for forty minutes. Now he took a step, found his legs almost dead.

"Diederman."

The big man came back toward him. "Yes, General?"

"The radio control?"

"No need for that, General. Everything continues to operate smoothly. The engineering sections hum." Diederman tried to smile, but the dark eyes sunken into his face did not join in.

"The foreign ships approach. In hours, they will assault the platforms."

Alarm appeared on the *leutnant*'s face.

"Nonsense. This is German property.

"I want it now."

The smile went away. "It is right beside you."

Eisenach looked down to where the engineer pointed. A small black box affixed to the top of the console. One green light, one unlit light, and a key slot.

"Give me the key."

Diederman dug into his pants pocket and came up with a small key on a ring with a brass tag. It was unmarked. "The delay is one hour?"

"It is as you ordered, General."

Eisnach inserted the key, twisted it, then pulled it out. Slowly, he bent the key tang back and forth until it snapped.

"I suggest you call Schmidt back, Hans. He has an hour to get the men off the platforms."

Diederman shook his head in dismayed resignation, Eisenach thought.

354

Eisenach also thought that people were going to remember his name. He had done his best for the fatherland.

"Now, Lieutenant, find my pilots and tell them to prepare the helicopter."

Diederman was staring at an *unteroffizier* at a far console.

The man was sitting with his hands in his lap and his chin resting on his chest.

"Corporal, what the hell are you doing?" Diederman shouted.

The head jerked up, whipped around.

"Colonel?"

"What is going on?"

"Colonel, I think the dome camera saw parachutes."

"Back up the damned tape! Call the security squad!"

Eisenach knew then that he had done the right thing.

Cottonseed was reporting ships closing on the platforms. German ships from the north.

Dimatta stayed in his wide circle over the platform, wondering what McKenna and Munoz were doing.

"Fifty minutes' fuel, Cancha."

"When it gets to ten minutes, Nitro, we'll keep that for reserve, and boost on rockets."

"Snake Eyes and Tiger?"

"The Herc is still here."

He kicked in the autopilot. Going around in circles was boring him.

"Delta Green, Semaphore."

"Go, Semaphore."

"What's Snake Eyes doing?" Brackman asked.

Dimatta had only met the commanding general once, but he'd never forget the voice.

On the intercom, he asked Williams, "What's the boss doing?"

"Beats the hell out of me. Maybe looking for . . . how about self-destruct devices?"

"Good, Nitro. I like it," Dimatta said and went back to Tac-1. "Semaphore, Snake Eyes is checking for self-destruct explosives. We don't want the Germans doing what we tried not to do."

"Copy that, Delta Green. Semaphore out."

"Jesus, Cancha! What if I was right?"

"Hell, I don't know. Be like Kevin to think of it, though."

"Yeah," the WSO said, "but you know what else? These platforms are spread over a few hundred square miles. Only one way they're going to set off explosives."

"By radio." Dimatta looked out the left side of his canopy at the dome. At the undamaged top of it, the radar antenna continued to rotate. A mini-forest of UHF, VHF, and other antennas was sprinkled around it.

"What have we got left, Nitro?"

"Air-to-air, but they're not working, remember."

"Let's go with landing gear."

"Mow 'em down. Gotcha."

Dimatta disengaged the autopilot and brought the MakoShark into a tight left turn, lining up on the dome.

"I'm ready," Williams said.

Dimatta lowered the landing gear, feeling the increase in drag tug lightly at the hand controller.

The screen displayed the dome on the night-vision lens.

He retarded his throttles on the approach.

"Down a tad, Cancha."

The antennas came up fast, and he leveled out, using the light spillage from the left side of the dome as his landing strip.

The right gear slammed into the antenna group.

356

Sparks and metal flying.

As they flashed across the top of the dome, Williams reported, "Communications blackout."

McKenna and Munoz went to the floor when they heard the racket from above, the sound of tearing metal.

It died away, they looked at each other, shrugged, and stood up.

The steel *Verboten* door was locked and would not budge. McKenna turned to his right, found another steel door, and pushed it open to find a stairway.

"This way, Tony."

Munoz closed the door quietly behind him, and the two of them went sideways down the steel staircase, keeping their backs to the wall and the M-16s at port arms.

It was a series of halfflights, with landings at every halfstory. Below, McKenna could hear voices speaking in German.

On the fourth floor, he opened the stairwell door and looked out on a corridor that matched the one above. There was no apparent fire damage here, but water dripped from the ceiling.

No bodies, alive or dead.

He stepped into the hallway and tried the door at his right, which did not have a forbidding sign or a lock. Opening it an inch he peered into yet another corridor. This one was wide, about thirty feet across. It didn't match the interior plan Pearson had drawn. He'd have to let her know she wasn't infallible.

Or maybe he wouldn't say anything about it to her. Damn, he was getting conservative.

The hallway was wide and long, from the well section to the outer curve of the dome. There were three Ping-Pong tables and a few electronic games situated around.

On the other wall he saw an elevator door and another door with the black letters *Verboten*. That seemed to be the place he wanted to be.

If not for the ten men milling about in the recreation space. They were armed with assault rifles and carried steel helmets.

The door across the way opened and an officer stuck his head out. Yelled.

The men snapped to attention, then donned helmets.

McKenna shut the door.

"Kev?"

"I think somebody wants to meet us." He unclipped a grenade and pulled the pin.

"You don't want to meet a new friend?"

"Not these." He twisted the door handle, hauled the heavy door back, and rolled the grenade in.

Slammed the door.

Hit the floor with Munoz right beside him.

Heard yelling.

Dull boom.

The door blew out, slammed him in the shoulder.

Munoz yelped.

Smoke and dust and debris in the air.

McKenna pushed the door off of himself and struggled to his feet.

The Germans had been flung all over the room. Blood and flesh splattered the Ping-Pong tables and walls. Some of them were groaning, and some were screaming, and some were deathly silent.

The lieutenant in the other doorway was on his back, his hands clutched to his face.

Munoz hadn't moved.

Keeping an eye on the opposite door, McKenna dropped to his knee.

"Tony?"

He moved his head groggily.

There was a long gash in his forehead, blood rushing freely from it.

"Hey, Tony?"

"Yeah. Yeah. I'm all right."

"You sure?"

"Hell of a headache. I'm okay, *jefe.*"

Munoz rolled over and pushed himself up onto his hands and knees. The blood dripped from his head onto the carpeted floor of the hallway.

McKenna dug into his right thigh pocket and came up with the first aid kit.

Munoz took it from him, settled onto his buttocks on the floor, and leaned back against the wall. He found his M-16 and rested it across his legs.

"Go, *amigo.*"

With a quick glance around the corridor, McKenna dashed across it and slammed into the wall next to the doorway. The wall was smeared with blood and riddled with shrapnel. The lieutenant moaned.

He inched his head around and looked inside.

Rows of electronic consoles.

A whole herd of people, down behind the consoles, peering over them.

A huge man in a uniform shirt, but with no insignia, leaned against the back of a chair, his arms crossed, staring at the doorway.

And a general. In full uniform. His face was almost black with his fury.

He didn't see any guns in there, so he pushed off the wall and stepped through the doorway, careful to avoid the lieutenant. Kept the M-16 trained lazily in the direction of the senior officer.

The general stared at him.

McKenna got close enough to see the name tag on his breast pocket.

Eisenach.

What do you know? This was the guy Pearson tried to find out more about, but whose assignment as a special assistant to Marshal Hoch had been ultrasecret.

He walked sideways and looked down the next row of consoles. Fearful faces looked back at him. He didn't see any weapons.

"General, you tell a couple of these people to tend to the wounded in the hallway."

The general didn't move.

The big man barked an order in German, and five men leaped off their knees and ran to the doorway.

McKenna checked the door and saw Munoz standing beside it. He had a bandage plastered to his forehead, but it was already orange.

"Tony?"

"I'm still here. Got it covered on this end."

McKenna turned back to the German general. "The way I have it, Eisenach, you're in charge of all this shit."

Still not responding.

McKenna nodded at the big guy. "Who are you?"

"Colonel Hans Diederman. You are?"

"Colonel McKenna. U.S. Air Force. Well-wisher."

"I am sure," Diederman said.

No humor there. "What do you do in this room?"

Diederman looked at the general, then back to McKenna. "Monitor operations of the wells. Peaceful wells, Colonel McKenna."

"They are very dangerous wells," McKenna countered. "You have no controls in here?"

"None. And now, we have no monitoring. The antennas are gone."

McKenna tilted his head to scan several of the screens. They were all blank.

"You have no radio communications?"

"None at all," Diederman said.

The general's face finally mobilized, changing from

360

fury to something else. Fear? It looked as if he might have a heart attack.

"You and your people have overestimated the dangers, I am afraid," Diederman said.

"What happens in a Force Ten gale?"

"Nothing. I designed these platforms myself."

Egomaniac?

Eisenach looked down at the first console, then quickly away.

McKenna released the stock with his left hand and pointed downward at the floor. "What's down there?"

"The Switching Center."

"Collects and distributes the electricity?"

"Exactly. You have destroyed an enterprise designed solely to help mankind, Colonel McKenna."

"Jesus, Diederman. How long has it been since you've been on the mainland?"

The man frowned. "Several weeks ago."

"But you're usually here?"

"I am."

"Then you don't know that the juice you're generating is replacing other energy consumption so that Eisenach and his buddies can store up fuel for war? Along with all the new tanks and ships and planes?"

Diederman swung his big head toward General Eisenach and stared.

"You will never prevail."

"I'll be damned. You can talk, General."

"I know things you do not know."

This son of a bitch was a walking zombie. Staring right through McKenna.

"You probably do. Like what?"

One hand lifted slightly and turned palm up. Not much of a gesture.

"This? This? Only a mild setback. The Aryan nation is destined to lead, to control, to people this world."

One of those.

McKenna shifted the muzzle of the assault rifle toward the general. He now thought that Eisenach was more dangerous than Diederman.

"And even now," Eisenach said, "you have won nothing. You will have, in fact, created an environmental calamity. It is your own doing."

"What the hell are you talking about?"

Eisenach smiled at him.

Diederman pointed to a black box on the first console. A red light was blinking on the face of it.

"The general thought it would be an excellent idea to wire each of the wells with explosives. That box activates the system."

Eisenach smiled. "It cannot be stopped. The wells will all erupt within fifty minutes."

"However," Diederman said, "I did not think it was such a good idea. The explosives are in place, but they are not wired."

Eisenach spun around toward the big man, his mouth agape, a snarl emitting from it. He pawed his uniform jacket, scratching, digging.

And came up with a Walther automatic.

Diederman moved fast for his size. He went down sideways, kicking a castered chair at Eisenach.

The technicians scattered, diving under desks and chairs.

The chair caught Eisenach in the knees as he fired his first shot. The report rang in the confined space, but the slug went into a wall.

The general toppled over the chair, then fell trying to get off it. He rolled onto the floor and raised the pistol at McKenna.

McKenna shot him in the forehead, slamming his head into the floor, snapping his eyes wide open.

A very small hole, barely trickling blood.

"Good shot, *amigo*."

McKenna wasn't so sure. Maybe hatred for this kind of bastard got in the way of justice.

The long, slow, rambling, errant wheels of justice. Diederman struggled to his feet.

"Colonel," McKenna said, backing toward the doorway, "I think you'd better get your people back to the mainland."

The large German didn't say anything. He just looked at the body of the dead Nazi.

McKenna and Munoz ran back across the corridor and down the stairs. Several men rushing up the stairs, to see what all the noise was about, changed their minds, and ran back down ahead of them.

By the time they reached the first floor and stepped out into another wide and long corridor, there were only a half-dozen men to be seen. And they quickly disappeared through a doorway on the left.

It was a hushed atmosphere, despite the muted whine of the turbine generators on the other side of the corridor's end wall.

"How you doing, Tony?"

"Aspirin'll take care of it."

"None in the kit?"

"Sure. I took six."

McKenna rushed across the corridor to another *Verboten* door and found it locked. He backed away and fired four shots into the lock.

The 5.56-millimeter slugs disintegrated the lock and the door swung open.

There were six men inside the three-story-high room, and they all cowered against the back wall. Thick cables traversed the space, fifteen feet and more off the floor. Metal-clad boxes lined the room and ran in rows down its center. All of them bore markings in German and control panels—dials, gauges, digital readouts, levers, buttons.

"If it says 'on,' Tony, we want it off."

"Damn betcha, *compadre*."

The six men didn't move as McKenna and Munoz went down the rows, throwing switches.

McKenna envisioned various parts of Germany going dark. The mainland engineers, with no warning that the Greenland generators were going off-line, would be scrambling to find new sources of energy with which to restore power. The fact that it was night might help them out a little, but tomorrow, those factories and industries that had converted from fuel oil and coal to electricity might well be shut down.

One of the men against the back wall began to babble in excited German.

"What's he sayin', Kev?"

"Damned if I know. I'd cover a bet, though, that shutting the output down will throw an overload on the turbine generators on all of the wells. Might even burn them out."

"Too damned bad," Munoz said. "What about the alternate route, though? On eleven?"

"Their communications are down. The people on eleven might not find out until it's all over."

The lights in the Switching Room blinked, came back, blinked again, then went out. A few seconds later, they came back on, but very dim.

"Emergency generator," Munoz said.

As soon as they'd reversed as many switches and levers as they could find, McKenna gestured with his rifle and herded the Germans out of the room.

Then he and Munoz burned up two magazines apiece of 5.56 ammo. The racket was deafening, and when they were done, the control panels were a shambles.

They slipped into the corridor to find twenty men

gathered around, backing away as they changed magazines.

"Hey!" McKenna yelled.

The mob stopped moving.

McKenna crossed the corridor, picked out two men, and relieved them of their parkas. He tossed one to Munoz and they slipped into them, then pulled the hoods over their heads.

Munoz led the way to the door and outside onto the helicopter pad.

The rotors were already turning, the faces of the two pilots lit by red instrument panel lights.

"Leave the rifles," McKenna said, dropping his onto the deck.

Munoz dropped his own, and they marched across the pad toward the chopper, looking, McKenna hoped, like departing German bigwigs.

The pad was littered with pieces from the dome. One of the SAM radar trailers lay on its side, shattered. The other one was gone entirely, probably blown into the sea.

The wind coming across the pad was chilled, but not too strong.

They performed the obligatory ducking from rotors that were high overhead, but it helped to conceal their faces.

Munoz parted from him, headed toward the other side of the chopper. When he reached the helicopter, a small MBB converted to command use, McKenna ignored the passenger compartment, reached for the pilot's door, and jerked it open. He leaned in toward a startled pilot, flicked open the quick release harness buckle, then hauled him out of the cockpit.

"Sorry," he said. "This one's taken."

The man spluttered his indignation in German while McKenna scrambled inside and pulled on a headset.

Munoz had similar success and similar indignation on the other side. When he plopped into the copilot's seat, he asked, "How long's it been since you've flown rotary, Snake Eyes?"

"Fourteen, fifteen years."

"That's comfortin'."

"Like riding a bicycle," McKenna said, running the throttles up. When the tachometers showed high, but not yet in the red, he pulled collective.

And nearly went back into the dome, overcorrecting for the wind, skittering across the pad, dragging the skids, before he got it stabilized and airborne.

The wind was strong enough to not disregard little mistakes.

"Oops," Munoz said.

McKenna got a feel for the stick, put the nose down, and raced off the platform toward the east. "Just find us a radio channel, huh?"

Munoz had to use the unscrambled frequency for Tac-2.

"Snake Eyes, that you in the chopper?"

"Roger, Delta Green."

"You fly like shit."

"That's because he thinks it's a bicycle," Munoz said.

"Cancha, I want you to put down at Daneborg. Think you can get it on the ground there?"

"Tight, Snake Eyes, but we'll do it. I'm going to radio ahead for fuel."

"Good. Take off. Robin Hood, you there?"

"Got 'im."

"You still have some of our flight gear. And I don't know if we're going to figure out this German equipment. You want to lead us to Daneborg?"

"I always wanted a Pathfinder code name."

* * *

Conover had been relieved to hear McKenna's voice on the air.

Abrams had told him on the intercom, "Told you so."

"Go to hell."

When the coast came up, Conover lost altitude to 2,000 feet, and they passed silently over Peenemünde.

"Okay, you can get us back some altitude, Con Man."

"What'd you see?"

Conover had not watched the night-vision screen. His focus was on the HUD. He was starting to get a few red lights on electrical and hydraulic systems.

"Not good," Abrams told him, then went to Tac-1. "Alpha Two, Delta Yellow."

"Go ahead, Yellow," Pearson said.

"The rocket's on the pad, Alpha. Tanker trucks around, vapors like they're transferring hydrogen and oxygen. Lots of lights and lots of people scurrying around. Very active. They're going to launch that hummer soon."

"Thank you, Yellow. Alpha out."

Conover didn't like the sound of it. He wondered what the target was, and given what had just taken place in the Greenland Sea, was almost as certain that he didn't want to know.

Twenty

General Brackman felt as drained as if he had been flying the combat mission himself.

Despite the fact that it was all over except for the mop-up, he and Thorpe remained in the crow's nest overlooking the Command Center. Milly had replenished the coffee and the Danish. Delta Yellow was approaching Greece. Delta Green had taken off from Daneborg. On the big plotting board, the Soviet and British-American task forces continued to close in. They would be there by midmorning to begin the monumental task of plugging the wells.

Brackman did not understand the technology, but someone had said that the wells were to be pumped full of concrete for several hundred feet below the seabed and the well casing above the seabed broken off. The Germans would be allowed to tow their platforms out of the Greenland Sea and to remove them from the ice.

Just details. The small things had to be cleaned up. He would have to testify before Congress, of course, and justify the loss of a three-quarter-billion-dollar aerospace vehicle.

The politicians would bring pressure on the German government. Already, the CIA was reporting exceptional activity at the High Command's headquarters in Bonn. Middle of the night changes in leadership?

And one pressing detail.

"What about this rocket at Peenemünde, David?"

Thorpe sighed and looked over at him. "I don't know, Marv. The launch could have been scheduled for months. Even years. The only thing that bothers me, beyond knowing about those MIRVs, is the fact that Weismann has been seen around there so much."

"Maybe Sheremetevo will have something when he calls."

Brackman had spoken to the Soviet general half an hour before, after Delta Yellow's report.

Finally, a telephone buzzed, and after a duty officer signaled him, Brackman got up to cross the room and take the receiver.

"Brackman."

"Marvin, this is Vitaly."

"Your people find out anything?"

"The rocket is warheaded only with high explosive, Marvin, but the target is your space station."

"Goddamn. You're certain?"

"The information was obtained in Berlin, from Eisenach's headquarters. The German ballistics and rocketry experts have been working on the programming for some time."

"Thank you, Vitaly."

Brackman hung up the phone. He looked at the map. All of the 1st Aerospace Squadron was earth side, beat up, and exhausted.

Themis was defenseless.

A few hundred pounds of HE detonated in the hub would completely destroy her, scatter the spokes, upset the orbits of the individuals units. There would be expensive pieces of space station reentering the atmosphere for years.

The people. His people. He could get them into the lifeboats in time.

Some of the spokes could be released and perhaps saved. The fuel module. The nuclear reactor was also quickly detachable.

Brackman checked the map.

369

The intelligence officer was watching him, concern evident in his face.

"David, could we see the satellite deployment?"

Thorpe gave the order and purple circles appeared on the map. The ID tags next to them identified the satellite type, orbit, and coverage.

"That Rhyolite over Poland, David, in geostationary orbit. Can it pick up Peenemünde?"

"Maybe the edge of it, Marv. We can give it a look-see."

"Do that. We need to know when that rocket launches."

Weismann and Oberlin had been in the control bunker for the past hour, sitting in an observation room above the launch and flight controllers. Both of them were talking on telephones.

The commander of the *20.S.A.G.* had attempted several times to reach Eisenach, but there were no communications between the platforms and the mainland. He had finally reached Schmidt.

The admiral sounded entirely defeated. "Your elite wing no longer exists, Weismann. They performed poorly."

As he listened to Schmidt's long list of criticisms, the rage built within him, and he finally slammed the telephone down.

Oberlin looked at him, holding his hand over the mouthpiece of his phone. "There are brownouts and blackouts all over Germany, Albert. The platforms are off-line."

Weismann barely heard him. "That fucking Schmidt!"

"What?"

"He won't defend the wells against the invading task forces."

"That is treason," Oberlin said. "I will shoot him myself."

"He says there's nothing left to defend."

Oberlin's shoulders sagged. "Then, it is all over, Albert. There will be investigations, charges, court-martials."

Weismann looked at the video monitor. The last truck, one of those containing hydrogen, was driving away from the launch pad. *Gespenst I* stood proudly in her gantry, wreathed in the vapors of condensing oxygen. Most of the launch personnel had already withdrawn. She was brightly lighted from floodlights on the ground and on the gantry shroud which had been rolled a quarter of a kilometer away.

He saw the digital clocks mounted on the far wall of the bunker. It was 0114 hours. The second clock gave the time to launch: 01.21.43.

The flight time to impact was one hour and six minutes.

"No, Max. We have one more chapter to write."

"The minute that rocket launches," Brackman told her on the secure microwave telephone link, "the NORAD and JPL people will begin determining its track. If it looks as if it will come anywhere near *Themis*, you are to abandon the station. That is an order, Colonel Pearson."

"Yes sir."

"There are no qualifications. No ifs, ands, or buts. You pass that on to Overton immediately."

"Yes, General."

As soon as she hung up, Pearson touched the PA button.

"General Overton, Colonel Avery to the Command Center."

She repeated the announcement, then switched to Tac-1. "Delta Green, Alpha Two."

"Green here," Dimatta said.

Pearson relayed the warning from Brackman.

McKenna's voice responded. "Alpha, you have a projected launch time?"

"No. Snake Eyes? Where are you?"

"They're in my payload bay," Dimatta said.

"But there's no passenger module!"

"Like monkeys, hangin' onto the missile racks," Munoz said. "Plugged into oxy and commo, sittin' on the third parachute issued to me tonight. Still, it's almost better'n the place I grew up."

NORAD was listening.

Brackman spoke, "Delta Green, Semaphore. What's your craft status?"

"Up and sailing, Semaphore," Dimatta replied. "We're just coming up on Norway at three-eight-thousand. About twenty-eight-hundred out of Hot Country."

"Weapons status?"

"There, we've got a problem, Semaphore. I've got six air-to-airs that I'd like to drop in on Peenemünde with, but we can't fire them. We think we've got a chunk of shrapnel in the electronics bay."

"Alpha Two," McKenna said, "here's what you do. Get Embry and Shalbot and have them arm Delta Red with eight air-to-air Wasps and eight Wasps configured for space firing. That's going to take about forty-five minutes. Put Haggar and Olsen on alert. In fact, have them watch the arming and have Embry brief them on the missiles."

Overton and Avery arrived in the Command Center as McKenna finished, and in time to hear Brackman interrupt. "That's not an option, Snake Eyes."

"That's the only option I see at the minute, General." McKenna's voice had some heat in it.

"Shit." Pause. "Comply with that, Alpha, but they're not to launch until I give the word."

"Roger, Semaphore." Brackman would be calling the Pentagon now, she thought.

"Then," McKenna said, "we'll try to work out a backup option. I need to have someone get in touch with Mabry Evans and have him arm Delta Orange the same way."

"Delta Orange is not yet flight certified," Semaphore said.

"Beta One, you listening to this?" McKenna asked.

"Right here, Snake Eyes," Brad Mitchell said.

"Run it down for me."

"Beta Two's pulling the data up now. Okay, Delta Orange. All flight systems have checked out, including communications, navigation, and computer systems. None of it has been flight tested. We don't yet have weapons guidance linkage systems completed. The rocket motors have not been tested. At all."

"Would you fly it?" McKenna asked.

"Hell, no. Well, maybe. This is the fifth one we've done, Snake Eyes. We've gained experience, and we've had few glitches."

"Hell, *compadres*, I don't need guidance systems. I've got a steady hand," Munoz asserted.

"Fuel it up and arm it," McKenna said. "Cancha's going to put this thing in overdrive, and we'll be touching down in an hour."

No one said anything. Overton shook his head.

Pearson thought about all of the things that could go wrong. Especially with untested systems.

After a long silence, Semaphore finally said, "Consider it done, Snake Eyes."

"One more thing," McKenna said, "Delta Orange is now Delta Blue."

When the payload bay doors opened, McKenna and Munoz climbed down from the missile racks and dropped to the tarmac. It was hot as hell, dry heat attacking McKenna's face as soon as he had the helmet off. The heat felt good after the freezing temperatures at high altitude. The battery pack for his suit heater was fully depleted. His right knee hurt, probably the aftermath of one of the jumps tonight, and his back was stiff from sitting on the bay doors.

Ducking out from under the MakoShark, McKenna walked forward along the right side of the fuselage and looked up until he found the hole. Not very big, maybe six inches in diameter, it was located right in the center of the electronics compartment.

They weren't going to turn Delta Green around and send it out again.

Dimatta came around the nose and joined him.

"Shit," he said.

"Sorry about that, Frank."

"I can take Delta Orange."

"Not anymore," McKenna said. "She's Delta Blue now."

The newest MakoShark had been shoved to the front of the hangar, and fifteen people surrounded it, finalizing its preflight checks. The banks of overhead fluorescent were bright after a couple hours in the payload bay.

Munoz said, "I'm gonna find a head, then climb in."

"Lead the way, Tony."

When they came back from the men's room, they climbed the ladders, slid over the coaming, and settled into their new cockpits. Everything smelled pristine, with just a taste of electronic burn-in and JP-7 fuel.

"Delta Blue, Delta Red."

McKenna pulled his helmet in place and plugged in. "Go ahead, Country Girl."

"I'm two minutes from blackout. Do I stay space side or go in?"

Since giving the approval for Delta Red's launch, Semaphore had stayed out of it. It was McKenna's squadron.

McKenna checked the chronometer: 0218 hours.

"Tiger?"

"Last reports say it's still sittin' on the pad," Munoz said.

"Bring it in, Country Girl. It'll be easier if you can catch it on the ground. Swede, if it's still down by the time you get there, put a couple into the third stage. If it's airborne, and you can reach it, use heat seekers."

"Roger, Snake Eyes," Olsen said.

"Delta Red going black."

On the intercom, Munoz said, "Risky, isn't it? Maybe

we should have her hang around close to *Themis?* Wait until the rocket gets there?"

"I thought about it, Tony. But the brass haven't let me give them enough practice time. If it's on the move, it's going to be tough to hit. I'd rather give them a sitting target."

"Gotcha, *amigo.*"

Munoz put the flight checklist up on the rearview screen, and McKenna ran through it while Munoz double-checked all of his new electronics.

The tractor towed them outside, and he fired the turbojets. They had been broken in on the test stands, and they ignited right away. The tach readouts on the HUD were right on the money for idle.

"Jack Andrews Control. Clear skies all around, Delta Blue. No other aircraft, no clouds, no wind. Typically Chad."

"Thanks, Control. We're off."

He released the brakes, and the MakoShark began to roll. After a short sprint down the taxiway, McKenna turned into the center of the runway. He locked the brakes and ran the engines up.

Good readings all the way. He brightened the HUD, turned down the air conditioning, checked the frequency settings on the radios.

"Tiger?"

"I'm as green as I'm gonna be this trip, *jefe*. So far, so good."

Tac-1 sounded off. "Alpha One, Delta Red."

"Go Red," Overton said.

"On path at two-three-eight thousand, Mach twelve-point-nine."

"Copy."

"Rocket status?"

"Still on the ground, Red," Overton told her.

"We're commencing flight plan for Peenemünde. Delta Red out."

"Punch it, Snake Eyes," Munoz said.

"Punched."

He released the brakes and slapped the throttles forward. The MakoShark leaped forward for her maiden flight. Eagerly, he thought.

All of the control surfaces felt too smooth, too unaccustomed to his touch. There were supposed to be sensitivities that he was missing, a grainy feel to the throttle handles, a pebbled surface for the hand controller.

"Rotate," Munoz said.

He eased the controller back and felt the MakoShark depart the ground. The wheels quit rumbling, and he retracted the gear, then pulled in the flaps.

"Off at oh-two-three-two hours, Snake Eyes."

The hand controller was too soft, responses had a hairsbreadth of delay. As the MakoShark climbed, McKenna tapped the keyboard, trying new settings for the hand controller. They were at 30,000 feet and Mach 2.2 by the time it felt right.

"Okay, *jefe*. Got us a course for Germany."

"Delta Red, Delta Blue, Alpha Two. We have launch! I repeat, the rocket has launched."

"Shit!" McKenna said. "Let's go over, Tiger."

"First time for everythin'. Checklist comin' up. Let's do this one carefully, Snake Eyes."

As they went through the procedure of checking pressures and loads and preparing the rocket motors, McKenna called Haggar.

"Delta Red, Delta Blue."

"Go ahead, Blue."

"How's your intercept?"

"Be . . . Swede's checking now. Hold one."

The rocket motors ignited, and McKenna pulled the controller back, taking the MakoShark vertical.

"Sweet, sweet music," Munoz said.

Thrust coming up, eighty, ninety, a hundred percent.

"Kill the jets, Snake Eyes."

376

He shut them down going through 50,000 feet.

"Delta Blue, we're going to miss an intercept by two hundred miles. The rocket is on a southeast track, but we're short."

McKenna could hear the disappointment in her voice, and knew it was as much the result of her inability to protect *Themis* as it was the missed chance of proving herself.

"Country Girl, you remember the pictures of Peenemünde?"

"Roger, Snake Eyes."

"Munitions bunker to the east, with the nukes?"

"Right."

"The two big assembly buildings?"

"Right."

"Avoid the bunker, but dump your load into the buildings. They've got four or five more of those rockets that they shouldn't have."

"Roger that, Delta Blue."

McKenna waited for Brackman to intervene concerning an attack on the mainland, and when he didn't, said, "Semaphore?"

"This is Semaphore, Delta Blue."

"Will you confirm that order?"

"Confirm what? We must have missed it."

Brackman never missed anything.

"Alpha One, did you hear an order?" Brackman asked.

"Negative," Overton responded. "You want to repeat, Delta Blue?"

"Oh, let's skip it," McKenna said, knowing it was his skin that would fry if anyone raised hell.

"By the way, Delta Blue," Brackman said, "we need an IFF on you for the satellites."

McKenna turned on the IFF and all of his running lights.

Four minutes later, two minutes after he had shut down his rocket motors, Thorpe called, "Delta Blue?"

"Go Semaphore."

"We have tracks. *Themis* is now over Antarctica. The rocket will achieve an orbit of one-nine-zero miles at seventeen-sixteen hours, Eastern Standard. We're assuming a booster burn that will aim it for an orbit of two-two-zero miles, but it will be pursuing the station, coming up from behind at closure rate of around three hundred miles per hour. Impact estimated for seventeen-forty-one hours."

"I'm getting this down and input," Munoz said.

"We show you at two-three-zero-thousand feet, Mach one-four. You will need another rocket burn for six-point-four-five minutes, and you will need to alter course to the following coordinates."

Munoz keyed the celestial coordinates in to the computer as Thorpe read them off and immediately tapped the commit button.

The readout on the CRT read: ACCEPTED.

Then: EXECUTING.

The MakoShark's nose leaned toward the northern horizon.

It was the first time they had exited the atmosphere toward the north. Most launches of rockets attempted a southeastern trajectory, using the earth's spin to their advantage.

"Executing new course, Semaphore. What will that do for us?"

"You will be approaching *Themis* head-on, at a combined closure velocity of four-one-thousand miles per hour."

"Will we be in time?"

Brackman's hesitation was ominous. "No, Delta Blue. You're going to be about one minute short. We're working on the problem."

More ominous was Brackman's order to Overton. "Prepare your lifeboats, Alpha One. Civilian contract personnel are to be loaded first. At seventeen-twenty hours, we will want you to disengage the reactor and fuel module spokes."

At 0242 hours, German time, Haggar called. "Alpha One, Delta Red."

"Go Red."

"Departing Peenemünde for Hot Country. We're reporting heavy damage to two buildings and an apparent launch control bunker at Peenemünde. The launch gantry is severely damaged. There are fires raging out of control in both buildings, and six storage tanks, probably hydrogen and oxygen, have exploded."

"Copy, Delta Red."

"I hope she fried the people who launched this bastard," Munoz said on the intercom.

"Nice going, Country Girl, Swede," McKenna said. "Welcome to the team."

Pearson was feeding the mainframe computer with every bit of data she could find, but only three symbols appeared on the Command Center's main console screen. Over a graphic arc depicting part of the station's orbit line was placed a large white circle.

That was *Themis*. Her home.

Don't threaten my home, you bastards.

Down to the right, a red circle had steadily been gaining on them, rising into their orbit.

Up to the left was Delta Blue, also below the orbit, but soon to be on it.

On the screen, Delta Blue looked to be the same distance from *Themis* as was the red circle.

But there was a difference.

A fraction in time.

Fifty-two seconds.

NORAD and the JPL had not come up with an answer.

Any increase in Delta Blue's speed would boost her into another orbit.

At 1727 hours, after the radar compartment reported the warhead on its scope, Overton said, "Milt, blow the explosive bolts on Spokes Nine and Thirteen, then order everyone into lifeboats."

Pearson looked at the screen again. The rocket was some thirty miles below the orbital path of the space station and seventy miles behind them. The closure rate was about three hundred miles an hour.

Closing five miles every minute.

Fourteen minutes to go.

Quickly, she fingered the keyboard, ordering the computer to overlay the projected trajectory of the rocket.

The line appeared on the screen, intersecting with the station's orbit ahead of where the station was currently shown.

"General," she said. "Can we hold off?"

"Amy. We're under orders."

"I need the reactor."

"For what."

"To power the radar. We want to shut down all unnecessary systems, and give everything we've got to the radar."

A pale Donna Amber was hanging onto the Radio Shack doorway. Her face brightened immediately. "I read you, Colonel. I'll start calling everyone and tell them to close down anything still drawing power."

Overton looked at the secondary screen showing personnel gathering in the spokes near the lifeboat stations. He said, "It's a hell of a risk, Amy."

"Are we going to just stand aside and watch while some asshole blows away all we've worked for?"

"I'll call Brackman."

Brackman made Overton poll the crew and civilian clients over the intercom. The vote was unanimous. Even the civilians bought in.

By 1734 hours, all station personnel were aboard the lifeboats, but the boats had not been released from the spokes. The station was in darkness except for the Command Center where Pearson and Overton waited. Donna Amber had had to be ordered to leave the Radio Shack.

The radar operator had been the first to volunteer to remain at his post, which was located in the hub and probably most vulnerable if the warhead impacted.

"Seventeen-thirty-five hours, Colonel," the radar operator reported. "Antenna's directed at the target."

Six minutes away.

"Take it to the max," she ordered.

The Command Center's lights and video screens dimmed as the operator poured fifteen million watts of energy into the antenna. Though the antenna was directed away from the station, Pearson felt the power. Any person in line with that radiation would have been incinerated. She felt the static electricity charging along her arms and legs, sparkling in her hair.

She grabbed Jim Overton's arm and hung on tightly.

Neither of them had anything to say.

"Damn, *amigo,* that sucker's coming up fast!"

"You're the one with the steady hand," McKenna reminded him.

"I didn't expect to meet it at forty-fuckin'-thousand miles an hour."

The direct vision screen displayed *Themis* at full magnitude. A dot that had grown quickly into a blob.

Below her, the sun glinted off a pinhead. German warhead.

McKenna had already armed all eight of his space-configured Wasps. They were only going to have one chance, and they were going to fire them off at one-tenth-second intervals. The computer had accepted the fire command, but with no linkage in the guidance systems, Munoz had to determine when, and in which direction, he was going to fire the first one.

Orange targeting circle on the screen, slithering around.

Themis became an orange.

"Guessing six hundred miles," Munoz said, dropping the magnification.

Themis contracted, then became an orange, again.

Then a cantaloupe.

The screen flashed to radar output.

"Two-one-six miles, *jefe*."

A watermelon.

"Hot damn!" Munoz yelled. "Amy-baby blew it off course. Screwed up its innards."

The powerful radar emissions had interfered in the warhead's electronic brain, setting off thruster bursts.

A half second.

The station accelerated at them.

"It's still gonna hit!" Munoz yelled.

"But later, later!" Pearson called. "Off-course by one-point-two minutes."

Themis went past them so fast, nearly a half mile away, that her image barely registered on McKenna's brain.

And time was gone.

The tiny warhead sailed into the orange circle.

Munoz squeezed his trigger.

The Wasps launched.

The warhead blew up in a white spark that appeared tiny against the blackness of the universe.

And then the spark was gone, far behind them.

"Hell of a lot of effort, for all of the fireworks we got," Munoz complained.

Twenty-one

The western sky was tinted orange and red and violet, and the air had chilled nicely.

Above the southwestern horizon, not blotted out by the yellow lights around the swimming pool, a bright white star flickered.

"That's *Themis*, lookin' good," Munoz said.

McKenna didn't answer, but he thought so, too. He took another sip of his *Dos Equis*.

He turned his head to look at the dark bulk of Buttermilk Mountain. That looked good to him, also.

"You see the six o'clock news, Kev?"

"Didn't bother."

"They got six of the wells concreted in."

"Good."

"They found Weismann's body in the launch control bunker. Lynn did it up right."

"That she did."

"The Germans are callin' for new elections. Want the military overhauled."

"That's good, too, Tony."

"Jesus, *jefe*. Wish you wouldn't talk so damned much."

"My mind's elsewhere," McKenna said, which was true.

"That case, and seein' it's dark, *amigo*, it's time for me to be gettin' on."

"See you later, Tony."

Munoz put his bottle on the table, pushed out of the chaise longue, and walked around the pool. He stopped to

383

talk to the blonde, fidgeted around for a bit, then sat down beside her. When the waiter appeared, he placed an order for something or other.

"You didn't get your hair cut today, McKenna," Pearson said. Her voice floated in the semidarkness, coming from the chaise on the other side of him.

"You didn't, either. But I don't mind."

They sat silently for ten minutes, McKenna very aware of her presence.

Finally, McKenna said, "Well, I think I'm going to take another hot shower."

"Me, too," she said, getting up to take his hand.